DATE DUE

The
LAST HELLION

The
LAST HELLION

Loretta
Chase

Five Star
Unity, Maine

Five Star Romance
Published in conjunction with Avon Books,
a unit of the Hearst Corporation.

Cover photographs © Alan J. La Vallee

August 1999
Standard Print Hardcover Edition.

Five Star Standard Print Romance Series.

The text of this Large Print edition is unabridged.

Set in 11 pt. Plantin by Rick Gundberg.

Printed in the United States on permanent paper.

Library of Congress Cataloging in Publication Data

Chase, Loretta Lynda, 1949–
    The last hellion / Loretta Chase.
        p.   cm.
    ISBN 0-7862-1989-0 (lg. print : hc : alk. paper)
    I. Title.
PS3553.H3347L37 1999
    813´.54—dc21
                                                          99-26433

The
LAST HELLION

Prologue

Longlands, Northamptonshire
September 1826

The Duke of Ainswood's family name was Mallory. Genealogy scholars agreed that the family originated in Normandy and was one of several by that name to settle in England in the twelfth century.

According to etymologists, the name meant unhappy or unlucky. In the Duke of Ainswood's family history, however, the name meant Trouble, with a capital "T." Some of the duke's forebears had lived long, and some had lived short, but all had lived hard because that was their nature. They were hellions, born that way, notorious for it.

But times had changed, and the family had finally begun to change and quiet with the times. The fourth duke, a wicked old rip who'd died a decade earlier, had been the last of his generation. Those he'd left behind were a new breed of Mallory, more civilized, even virtuous.

Except for the only son of the fourth duke's youngest brother.

Vere Aylwin Mallory was the last Mallory hellion. At well over six feet, he was the tallest of them all and, some said, the handsomest as well as the wildest. He had his father's thick chestnut hair, and in his eyes—the darker green of earlier generations—glinted centuries of wickedness and the same invitation to sin that had undone generations of women. At

7

nearly two and thirty years old, he'd done more than his share of sinning.

At present, he was making his way through the wood of the great Longlands estate, the country home of the Duke of Ainswood. Vere's destination was the Hare and Pigeon public house in the nearby village.

In a mocking baritone, he was singing the words of the Anglican funeral service to the tune of a bawdy ballad.

He had heard the burial service so often in the last decade that he had it by heart, from the opening "I am the resurrection and the life" to the final "Amen."

"Forasmuch as it hath pleased Almighty God of his great mercy to take unto himself the soul of our dear brother . . ."

At "brother," his voice broke. He paused, his broad shoulders stiffening against the tremor that shook his big frame. Bracing an arm against a tree trunk, he gritted his teeth and shut his eyes tight and willed the wracking grief to subside.

He'd done enough grieving in the last decade, Vere told himself, and he'd shed enough tears in the seven days since his first cousin Charlie, the fifth Duke of Ainswood, had breathed his last.

He lay in the mausoleum at present, with the others Almighty God had "pleased to take" in the last ten years. The endless succession of funerals had commenced with that of the fourth duke, who had been like a father to Vere, his own parents having died when he was nine. Since then, death had claimed Charlie's brothers along with their sons and wives, several girls, and Charlie's wife and eldest son.

This latest funeral, despite years of practice, had been the hardest to bear, for Charlie was not only dearest to Vere of all his Mallory cousins, but one of the three men in the world Vere looked upon as brothers.

The other two were Roger Barnes, the Viscount Wardell,

and Sebastian Ballister, the fourth Marquess of Dain. The latter, a dark giant more commonly known as Lord Beelzebub, was universally regarded as a hideous stain upon the Ballister family escutcheon. He and Wardell had been Vere's partners in crime since Eton. But Wardell had been killed in a drunken brawl in a stable yard six years ago, and Dain, who had departed for the Continent some months later, seemed to be settled in Paris permanently.

There was no one left who mattered. Of the main branch of the Mallorys, only one male remained besides Vere: nine-year-old Robin, Charlie's youngest, now sixth Duke of Ainswood.

Charlie had left two daughters as well—if one cared to count females, which Vere didn't—and in his will named Vere, as nearest male kin, the children's guardian. Not that this guardian need have anything to do with them. While family loyalty might dictate tolerance of the Mallorys' last hellion—much as tradition dictated the naming of guardians —no one, not even Charlie, could be so blindly loyal as to believe Vere suited to the task of bringing up three innocent children. One of Charlie's married sisters would do it.

The guardian position, in other words, was purely nominal, which was just as well, for Vere hadn't spared his wards a thought since he'd arrived a week earlier—in time to watch Charlie depart for the hereafter.

It was all, horribly, exactly as his uncle had predicted ten years earlier, when Vere sat by his deathbed.

"I saw it when they were gathered about me," his uncle had told him. "Saw them parading in and out. Unlucky ones. 'He cometh up, and is cut down, like a flower.' Two of my brothers were cut down long before you were born. Then your sire. And today I saw them, my sons: Charles, Henry, William. Or was it a dying man's fancy? 'He fleeth as it were a shadow.' I saw them, shadows all. What will ye do then, lad?"

At the time, Vere had thought the old man's wits had failed. He knew better now.

Shadows all.

"Got that right, by Lucifer," he muttered as he pushed away from the tree. "A bloody prophet you turned out to be, Uncle."

He took up the service where he'd left off, singing the solemn words more lustily as he walked, and occasionally directing a defiant grin heavenward.

Those who knew him best, could they but observe him at this moment, would understand he was goading the Almighty as he'd so often goaded his fellow mortals. Vere Mallory was looking for trouble, as usual, and this time he was trying to pick a fight with Jehovah Himself.

It didn't work. The troublemaker neared the end of the service without Providence offering so much as a thunderclap of disapproval. Vere was about to launch into the Collect when he heard twigs snapping behind him and leaves rustling amid the hurried patter of footsteps. He turned . . . and saw the ghost.

It wasn't truly a ghost, of course, but near enough. It was Robin, so painfully like his father—fair and slight, with the same sea-green eyes—that Vere couldn't bear to look at him, and had managed not to for this last week.

The boy was running toward him, though, so there was no avoiding him. There was no ignoring, either, the sharp tug of grief—and yes, rage as well, to Vere's shame, because he could not help resenting that the child lived and the father was gone.

Jaw set, Vere stared at the boy. It was not a welcoming look, and it made Robin stop short a few paces away. Then the boy's face reddened, and his eyes flashed, and he hurtled at Vere head foremost, butting his surprised guardian in the stomach.

Though Vere's abdomen was about as soft as an andiron—like the rest of him—the lad not only kept butting, but added punching. Oblivious to their vast disparity in age, size, and weight, the young duke pounded away at his cousin, a maddened David trying to fell Goliath.

None of the civilized new breed of Mallorys would have known what to make of this unprovoked, desperate, and seemingly deranged attack. But Vere was not civilized. He understood, couldn't help it.

He stood and let Robin rain ineffectual blows upon him, much as Robin's grandfather, the fourth duke, had stood once, many years earlier, while an enraged, newly orphaned Vere pounded away. He hadn't known what else to do except cry, which at the time was for some reason absolutely out of the question.

As Vere had done, Robin kept on, fighting an unmoving pillar of adult male until he wore himself out and sank, exhausted, to the ground.

Vere tried to remember his rage and resentment of moments before. He tried to wish the child to the devil, tried not to care, but it didn't work.

This was Charlie's boy, and a desperate boy he must be, to slip past the family and servants' vigilant guard and brave a dark wood, alone, to find his dissolute cousin.

Vere wasn't sure what the child was desperate for. It was clear enough, though, that Robin expected Vere to provide it, whatever it was.

He waited until Robin's panting subsided to more normal respiration, then hauled the boy to his feet. "You shouldn't come within a mile of me, you know," Vere said. "I'm a bad influence. Ask anyone. Ask your aunts."

"They cry," Robin said, looking at his scuffed boots. "They cry too much. And they talk too soft."

"Yes, it's horrid," Vere agreed. He bent and brushed off the boy's coat. The child looked up at him . . . with Charlie's eyes. But younger and too trusting. Vere's own eyes stung. He straightened, cleared his throat, and said, "I was thinking of leaving them to it. I thought I'd go to . . . Brighton." He paused, and told himself he was mad even to contemplate it. But the boy had come to him, and the boy's father had never once failed Vere. Except in dying. "Would you like to come with me?"

"To Brighton?"

"That's what I said."

The too-young, too-trusting eyes began to glow. "Where the Pavilion is, you mean?"

The immense architectural phantasmagoria known as the Royal Pavilion was the analogously immense King George IV's idea of a seaside cottage.

"It was, the last time I looked," Vere answered. He started walking, back toward the house.

His ward promptly followed, running to keep up with his elder's long strides. "Is it as fanciful as it looks in the pictures, Cousin Vere? Is it truly like a palace in *The Arabian Nights*?"

"I was thinking of starting out first thing tomorrow morning," Vere said. "The sooner we leave, the sooner you can judge for yourself."

If it had been up to Robin, they would have started out that very minute. If it had been up to his aunts and their husbands, Vere would have set out alone. But it wasn't up to anyone else, as he told them a short while later. As the child's legal guardian, he didn't need anybody's permission to take Robin to Brighton—or Bombay, for that matter.

It was Robin himself who silenced their objections, however. The sound of thumps drew the family out of the drawing room in time to see the young duke lugging his portmanteau down Longlands' great staircase and through the cavernous hall to the vestibule.

"There, you see?" Vere turned to Dorothea, Charlie's youngest sister, who'd protested longest and hardest. "He can't wait to get away. You're too damned dismal, the lot of you. It's the tears and hushed voices and crepe and bombazine—that's what scares him. Everything's dark and grown-ups are crying. He wants to be with me because I'm big and noisy. Because I can scare away the monsters. Don't you see?"

Whether she saw or not, she gave in, and when she did, the others followed suit. It was only for a few weeks, after all. Even Vere Mallory couldn't corrupt a child's morals irrevocably in a matter of weeks.

He had no wish to corrupt the boy's morals, and he set out fully meaning to return Robin in a fortnight.

Vere could not be a father to him or any child, he was well aware. He was not a suitable role model. He hadn't a wife—and had no intention of getting one—to do the things females did, the soft things, to balance his rough, uncivilized ways. His household comprised one servant, his valet Jaynes, who possessed all the soft, maternal qualities of a dyspeptic porcupine. This "household," furthermore, had not occupied a fixed abode since Vere had left Oxford.

It was no way to rear a child, in short, especially one destined to assume the burdens of a great dukedom.

Nonetheless, the few weeks somehow stretched into a month, then another. From Brighton they traveled up into Berkshire, to the Vale of the White Horse, to view the ancient etching in a chalk hillside, thence to Stonehenge, and on to the West Country, following the coast and exploring smugglers' coves all the way to Land's End.

Autumn chilled into winter, which in turn warmed into spring. Then the letters came, from Dorothea and the others, with their gentle but not overly subtle reminders: Robin's education could not be ignored indefinitely, his sisters missed him, and the longer the boy wandered, the harder it would be for him to settle down.

It was all true, Vere's own conscience told him. Robin needed a real family, stability, a home.

Still he found it hard, returning Robin to Longlands, hard to part from him, though it was obviously the right thing to do. The household was not so dismal as before.

Dorothea and her husband were settled there now, with Robin's sisters as well as their own brood. The halls rang again with the children's songs and laughter, and in a defiance of convention Vere had to approve, the crepe and jet borders and black bombazine had already given way to the less lugubrious tones of half mourning.

It was also clear that Vere had done his job. He'd scared away the monsters, beyond question, for within hours, Robin was bosom bows with his boy cousins, Dorothea's sons, and joining them in tormenting the girls. And when it came time to say good-bye, Robin showed no signs of panic. He didn't take a temper fit or hit Vere, but promised to write faithfully, extracted his guardian's promise to come back in late August for his tenth birthday, then ran off to help his cousins reenact the Battle of Agincourt.

But Vere returned long before the birthday. Not three weeks after leaving Longlands, he was racing back.

The sixth Duke of Ainswood had contracted diphtheria.

The disease was not well understood. The first accurate account of the infection had been published in France only five years earlier. What was understood and not debated was that diphtheria was highly contagious.

Charlie's sisters pleaded with Vere. Their husbands tried to stop him, but he was bigger than any of them, and in a fury, as he was now, a regiment of soldiers couldn't have held him back.

He stormed up the great staircase and marched down the hall to the sickroom. He chased away the nurse and locked the door. Then he sat beside the bed and grasped his ward's weak little hand.

"It's all right, Robin," he said. "I'm here. I'll fight it for you. Let go of it and give it to me, do you hear me, lad? Throw off this curst ailment and let me tangle with it. I can do it, my boy, you know I can."

The cold little hand lay unmoving in his big, warm one.

"Give it up, please," Vere urged, choking back tears, stifling the useless grief. "It's too soon for you, Robin, you know it is. You've scarcely begun to live. You don't know a fraction of it—what there is to see, to do."

The young duke's eyelids fluttered and opened. Something like recognition seemed to flicker there. For an instant, his mouth shaped a ghost of a smile. Then the boy's eyes closed.

That was all. Though Vere went on talking, coaxing, pleading, though he clung to the little hand, he could not draw the disease away and into himself. He could do nothing but wait and watch, as he'd done so many times before. It was a short watch, this time, the shortest, hardest of all.

In less than an hour, as twilight slipped into night, the boy's life slipped away and fled . . . like a shadow.

1

London
Wednesday, 27 August 1828

"I'll sue 'em!" Angus Macgowan raged. "There're libel laws in this kingdom, and if that isn't libel, I'm a bull's blooming bollocks!"

The enormous black mastiff who'd been drowsing before the editor's office door lifted her head and gazed with mild curiosity from Macgowan to her mistress. Upon ascertaining that the latter was in no imminent danger, the dog laid her head down upon her forepaws again and closed her eyes.

Her mistress, twenty-eight-year-old Lydia Grenville, regarded Macgowan with similar dispassion. But then, oversetting Lydia wasn't easy. Fair-haired and blue-eyed, a few inches under six feet tall, she was about as delicate as the average Valkyrie or Amazon, and her body, like those of the mythical warriors, was as strong and agile as her mind.

When he slammed the object of his indignation down upon the desk, she calmly took it up. It was the latest edition of *Bellweather's Review*. Like the previous issue, it had devoted several columns of the first page to attacking Lydia's latest journalistic endeavor:

Like her namesake, the Argus's *"Lady Grendel" has once again launched a noxious assault upon an unsuspecting public, spewing her poisonous fumes into an atmosphere already thick with her pollutions. Her victims, still reeling from previous assaults upon their sensibilities, are hurled once more into the very abyss of degradation whence uprises the reek of foul and tainted creatures—for one can scarcely title as human the vermin she's made her subject—whose cacophony of self-pitying howls—for we cannot call these excretions language—the petticoated monster of the* Argus . . .

Here, Lydia stopped reading. "He has lost all control of the sentence," she told Angus. "But one cannot sue for bad writing. Or for lack of originality. As I recall, the *Edinburgh Review* was the first to title me after the monster in *Beowulf*. At any rate, I do not believe anyone owns a patent on the name 'Lady Grendel.' "

"It's a scurrilous attack!" he cried. "He all but calls you a bastard in the next to last paragraph, and insinuates that an investigation into your past would—would—"

" 'Would doubtless explain the virago of the *Argus*'s otherwise unaccountable sympathy with an ancient profession whose bywords are disease and corruption,' " Lydia read aloud.

"Libel!" Angus shouted, pounding his fist on the desk. The mastiff looked up again, uttered a deep canine sigh, then once more composed herself to sleep.

"He merely implies that I have been a prostitute," Lydia said. "Harriet Wilson was a harlot, yet her book sold very well. If she'd had Mr. Bellweather abusing her in print, I daresay she might have made a fortune. He and his fellows have certainly assisted ours. The previous issue of the *Argus* sold out within forty-eight hours. Today's will be gone before tea time. Since the literary periodicals began attacking me, our circulation has tripled. Rather than sue Mr. Bellweather, you should write him a note of thanks, and encourage him to keep up the good work."

Angus flung himself into the chair behind his desk. "Bellweather has friends at Whitehall," he grumbled. "And there're some in the Home Office who aren't exactly friendly to you."

Lydia was well aware that she had ruffled feathers in the Home Secretary's circle. In the first of her two-part series on the plight of London's younger prostitutes, she had hinted at the legalization of prostitution, which would enable the Crown to license and regulate the trade, as in Paris, for instance. Regulation, she had suggested, might at least help reduce the worst abuses.

"Peel ought to thank me," she said. "My suggestion stirred so much outrage that his proposal for a Metropolitan Police Force seems quite mild and sensible to the very same people who had been howling that it was a conspiracy to grind John Bull under tyranny's heel." She shrugged. "Tyranny, indeed. If we had a proper police force, that fiend might have been caught by now."

The fiend in question was Coralie Brees. In the six months since her arrival from the Continent, she had become notorious as the worst of London's procuresses. In order to get her employees' stories, Lydia had promised not to reveal the woman's name—not that revealing the bawd's identity would have aided the cause of justice. Eluding the authorities was a game with the whoremongers, and one at which they were highly skilled. They changed their names as often and as easily as Lydia's father had done, to elude his creditors, and scurried like rats from one lair to the next. Small wonder Bow Street couldn't keep track—and didn't feel compelled to do so. According to some estimates, London had more than fifty thousand prostitutes, all too many under sixteen years old. Insofar as Lydia had been able to determine, none of

Coralie's girls was older than nineteen.

"You've seen her, though," Angus said, breaking into Lydia's grim reflections. "Why didn't you sic that black monster of yours on her?" He nodded toward the mastiff.

"It's no good taking the woman into custody when there's no one brave enough to testify against her," Lydia answered impatiently. "Unless the authorities catch her in the act—and she takes care they don't—we've nothing to charge her with. No proof. No witnesses. There's little Susan could do for us except maim or kill her."

Susan cocked one eye open at the mention of her name.

"Since the dog would do so only at my command, I should be prosecuted for assault—or hanged for murder," Lydia continued. "I had rather not be hanged on account of a filthy, sadistic bawd."

She returned *Bellweather's Review* to her employer's desk, then took out her pocket watch. It had belonged to her great uncle Stephen Grenville. He and his wife, Euphemia, had taken Lydia in when she was thirteen. They had died last autumn within hours of each other.

Though Lydia had been fond of them, she could not miss the life she'd led with the feckless pair. While not morally corrupt—as her father had been—they had been shallow, unintelligent, disorganized, and afflicted with a virulent case of wanderlust. They were forever wanting to shake the dust of someplace from their feet long before dust could possibly have time to settle. The ground Lydia had covered with them reached from Lisbon in the West to Damascus in the East, and included the countries on the southern shores of the Mediterranean.

Still, she told herself, she would not have an editor to fume at present, or jealous publishing rivals to make him fume, if not for that life.

Something very near a smile curved her mouth as she rec-ollected the journal she'd begun—in imitation of her late and dearly loved mama—on the day her father abandoned her to Ste and Effie's incompetent care.

At thirteen, Lydia had been nearly illiterate, and her diary rife with spelling atrocities and horrific crimes against gram-mar. But Quith, the Grenvilles' manservant, had tutored her in history, geography, mathematics, and most important, lit-erature. Quith was the one who'd encouraged her writing, and she'd repaid him as best she could.

The money Ste had left her as a marriage portion, she'd converted into a pension for her mentor. It was no great sacri-fice. A writing career, not marriage, was what she wanted. And so, free of all obligations for the first time in her life, Lydia had set out for London. She'd taken with her copies of the travel pieces she'd previously had published in a few En-glish and Continental periodicals, and what remained of Ste and Effie's "estate": an assortment of bric-a-brac and trinkets and precious little coin.

The pocket watch was all that remained of their belong-ings. Even after Angus had hired her, Lydia had not troubled to redeem the other items she'd pawned during those first bleak months in London. She preferred to spend her earnings on necessities. The latest such purchase was a cabriolet and a horse to pull it.

She could afford the horse and carriage because she was earning more than satisfactory wages, far better than one might have reasonably expected. Certainly she'd expected to drudge for at least a year, writing for the newspapers, at a penny a line, accounts of fires, explosions, murders, and other accidents and disasters.

Fate, though, had sent a piece of luck her way in early spring. Lydia had first entered the *Argus*'s offices when the magazine was on the brink of failure, and its editor, Macgowan, desperate enough to do anything—even hire a female—that offered a chance of survival.

"Nearly half past two," Lydia said, returning the watch to her skirt pocket and her mind to the present. "I had better go. I'm to meet Joe Purvis at Pearkes's oyster house at three to look over the illustrations for the next chapter of the dratted story."

She moved away from the desk and started for the door.

"It isn't the blasted literary critics, but your 'dratted story' that's made our fortune," Angus said.

The story in question was *The Rose of Thebes*, whose heroine's adventures had been recounted in two-chapter installments in the biweekly *Argus* since May. Only she and Angus were aware that its author's name, Mr. S. E. St. Bellair, was also a piece of fiction.

Even Joe Purvis didn't know that Lydia wrote the chapters he illustrated. Like everyone else, he believed the author was a reclusive bachelor. Never in his wildest dreams would he have imagined that Miss Grenville, the *Argus*'s most cynically hardheaded reporter, had created a single word of the wildly fanciful and convoluted tale.

Lydia herself did not like being reminded. She paused and turned back toward Angus. "Romantic claptrap," she said.

"So it may be, but your fascinating claptrap is what hooked the readers—especially the ladies—in the first place, and it's what brings them back begging for more. Damnation, you've even got me wriggling on your hook." He rose and rounded the desk. "That clever girl, your Miranda—Mrs. Macgowan and I were talking about it, and my wife thinks the wicked, dashing fellow ought to come to his senses and—"

"Angus, I proposed writing that idiotish story on two conditions," Lydia said in a low, hard voice. "No meddling from you or anyone else was one condition. The other was absolute anonymity." She bent a glacial blue stare upon him. "If the faintest hint gets about that I am the author of that sentimental swill, I shall hold you personally responsible. In which case, all contracts between us shall be null and void." Her blue glare bore an alarming resemblance to one employed by certain members of the nobility, under which generations of their inferiors had quailed.

Lionhearted Scotsman though he was, Macgowan cowered under the frigid look as any other inferior would, his countenance reddening. "Quite right, Grenville," he said meekly. "Most indiscreet of me to speak of it here. The door is thick, but best to take no chances. You know I'm fully aware of my obligations to you and—"

"Oh, for God's sake, don't toady," she snapped. "You pay me well enough." She marched to the door. "Come, Susan." The mastiff rose. Lydia took up the leash and opened the door. "Good day, Macgowan," she said, then strode out the door without waiting for an answer.

"Good day," he said to her back and, "Your Majesty," he added under his breath. "Bloody damned queen, she thinks she is—but the bitch can write, confound her."

There were a great many people in England at this moment who would agree that Miss Grenville could write. Many of them, however, would have maintained that Mr. S. E. St. Bellair could write even better.

This was what Mr. Archibald Jaynes, valet to the Duke of Ainswood, was attempting to explain to his master.

Jaynes didn't look like a valet. Narrowly built and wiry, with beady black eyes sitting very close to his long, crooked—on account of being broken several times—nose, he looked more like the weasely sort of ruffian frequently encountered at horse races or boxing matches, taking bets.

Jaynes himself would have hesitated to use the term "gentleman's gentleman" on his own account. While, despite his unprepossessing features, he was exceedingly neat and elegant, his tall, handsome master was not what Jaynes would call a gentleman.

The two men sat in the best—which was not saying much, in Mr. Jaynes's opinion—dining room of the Alamode Beef House in Clare Court. The street, a narrow way off infamous Drury Lane, was hardly the most elegant in London, and the Alamode's culinary productions were scarcely calculated to appeal to discriminating palates. All of which suited the duke admirably, for he was no more elegant or discriminating than the average savage, and probably less so, from what Jaynes had read of the aboriginal races.

Having made short work of a tall heap of beef, His Grace had settled—or sprawled, was more like it—back in his chair and was watching a waiter replenish his tankard of ale.

The duke's chestnut hair, with which Jaynes had taken such pains only a short time earlier, had got raked into a tumbled disorder that declared it had never met comb or brush in its life. The neckcloth, once crisply starched and painstakingly knotted, with each crease formed at proper intervals and angles, had subsided into limp and rumpled disarray. As to the rest of His Grace's garments: In a nutshell, they looked as though he'd slept in them, which was how they usually looked, no matter what one did, and, *Really, I wonder why I bother,* Jaynes was thinking.

What he was saying was, "The 'Rose of Thebes' is the name given to a great ruby, which the heroine found some chapters ago when she was trapped in the pharaoh's tomb with the snakes. It is an adventure story, you see, and all the rage since summer."

The waiter having departed, the duke turned his bored green gaze upon the copy of the *Argus*. It lay as yet unopened—and it was only through a phenomenal exercise of willpower that Jaynes had resisted opening it—upon the table.

"That would explain why you hauled me from the house at dawn's crack," said His Grace. "And dragged me from one book shop to the next looking for it—and all of them thick with females. Mainly of the wrong sort," he added, grimacing. "I've never seen so many dowds in so many jabbering clumps as I have this morning."

"It's half past two," Jaynes said. "You never saw the morning. As to the dawn, it was cracking when you finally staggered home. Moreover, I discerned several attractive young ladies among the crowds of what you so callously dismiss as 'dowds.' But then, if their faces aren't thick with paint and their bosoms aren't bursting from their bodices, they are invisible to you."

"Pity they aren't inaudible as well," his employer muttered. "Twittering and simpering lot of nitwits. And meanwhile ready to claw one another's eyes out for—What is the curst thing?" He took up the magazine, glanced at the cover, and dropped it. "The *Argus*, indeed. 'The Watchdog of London,' it purports to be—as though the world is famished for more pontificating from Fleet Street."

"The *Argus*'s offices are in the Strand, not Fleet Street," said Jaynes. "And it is refreshingly free of pontificating. Ever since Miss Grenville joined the staff, the publication has become more like what its subtitle claims. The Argus of mythology, you may recollect—"

"I'd rather not recall my days in the schoolroom." Ainswood reached for his tankard. "When it wasn't Latin, it was Greek. When it wasn't Greek, it was Latin. And when it wasn't either, it was flogging."

"When it wasn't drinking, gaming, and whoring," Jaynes said under his breath. He ought to know, having entered Vere Mallory's service when the latter was sixteen, and the dukedom apparently safe, with several Mallory males standing between him and the title. But they were gone now. With the death of the last, a boy of nine, nearly a year and a half ago, Jaynes's employer had become the seventh Duke of Ainswood.

Inheriting the title had not mended his character a whit. On the contrary, he had gone from bad to worse, thence to unspeakable.

More audibly Jaynes said, "The Argus was reputed to possess a hundred eyes, you will recall. Its namesake's aim is to contribute to a well-informed populace by observing unflinchingly and reporting upon the metropolis as though it had a hundred eyes. For instance, Miss Grenville's article concerning the unfortunate young women—"

"I thought there was only one," said his master. "The addlepated chit who got herself trapped in the tomb with the snakes. Typical," he sneered. "And some poor sod must gallop to milady's rescue. Only to die of snakebite for his pains. If he's lucky."

Thickhead, Jaynes thought. "I was not referring to Mr. St. Bellair's story," he said. "Whose heroine, for your information, escaped the tomb with no outside assistance. However, I was speaking of—"

"Don't tell me—she talked the snakes to death." Ainswood hoisted the ale tankard to his lips and emptied it.

"I was speaking of Miss Grenville's work," Jaynes said. "Her articles and essays are exceedingly popular with the ladies."

"God save us from bluestockings. You know what their

trouble is, don't you, Jaynes? Due to not getting pumped regular, females take the oddest fancies, such as imagining they can *think*." The duke wiped his mouth with the back of his hand.

He was a barbarian, that's what he was, Jaynes thought. His Grace belonged among the Vandal hordes that had once sacked Rome. As to his views of women, those had rapidly regressed to antediluvian since his elevation to the title.

"Not all women are witless," the valet persisted. "If you would take the trouble to become acquainted with women of your own class, rather than illiterate whores—"

"The whores give me the only thing I want from a female, and don't expect anything from me but the fee. I can't think of one good reason to bother with the other kind."

"One good reason is, you'll never get yourself a proper duchess if you refuse to come within a mile of a respectable female."

The duke set down his mug. "Devil take you, are you going to start that again?"

"You'll be four and thirty in four months," said Jaynes. "At the rate you've been going lately, your chances of seeing that birthday are approximately nil. There is the title to consider, and its responsibilities, the foremost of which is to get an heir."

Ainswood pushed away from the table and rose. "Why the devil should I consider the title? It never considered me." He snatched up his hat and gloves. "It should have stayed where it was and let me alone, but no, it wouldn't, would it? It had to keep creeping on toward me, one confounded funeral after another. Well, I say let it go on creeping after they plant me with the others. Then it can hang itself on some other poor sod's neck, like the bleeding damned albatross it is."

He stalked out.

★ ★ ★ ★ ★

Some moments later, Vere had reached the end of Catherine Street and started west, intending to quiet his inner turmoil by the river, with the aid of a few more tankards of ale at the Fox Under the Hill.

As he turned into the Strand, he saw a cabriolet burst through the crush of vehicles at Exeter 'Change. The carriage narrowly missed spitting a pie seller on its shaft, veered perilously toward an oncoming cart, corrected in the nick of time, then swung aside sharply—straight toward a gentleman stepping off the curb to cross the street.

Without pausing to think, Vere hurtled forward, grabbed the fellow, and dragged him back to the footway—an instant before the carriage rocketed into Catherine Street.

As it thundered past, he caught a glimpse of the driver: a black-garbed female, with a black mastiff for a passenger, an obviously panicked horse under the ribbons—and no tiger on the platform behind to help her.

He set the fellow aside and hurried after the vehicle.

Lydia swore when she saw her prey dart into Russell Court. The cramped passageway was too narrow for the cabriolet, and if she made the long circuit round Drury Lane Theater, she was sure to lose them. She drew the carriage to a halt and leapt from it, Susan close behind. A ragged boy hurried forward.

"Mind the mare, Tom, and there's two bob for you," Lydia told the street urchin. Then, picking up her skirts, she ran into Russell Court.

"You there!" she called. "Release that child!"

Susan gave a low "Woof!" that echoed through the narrow passage.

Madam Brees—for it was she Lydia called to—threw one

quick glance over her shoulder, then darted left into a still narrower alley, towing the girl with her.

Lydia did not know who the girl was—a country servant by the looks of it, likely one of the countless runaways who made their way to London every day, only to fall promptly into the clutches of the bawds and pimps who loitered at every coaching inn from Piccadilly to Ratcliffe.

Lydia had spotted the pair in the Strand, the girl gawking at the sights like the average bumpkin while Coralie—garbed like a respectable matron, with an expensive bonnet perched upon her shoe-blacking-dyed curls—drew her relentlessly toward ruin: Drury Lane and its legion of vice pits, beyond doubt.

If they made it into whatever brothel Madam was aiming for, Lydia would not be allowed in, and the girl would never get out.

But as she turned into the alley, she saw the child dragging her heels and trying to shake off Coralie's grasp.

"That's it, my girl!" Lydia cried. "Get away from her!"

She was aware of masculine shouts behind her, but Susan's thunderous bark drowned out the words.

The girl was struggling in earnest now, but the stubborn bawd held tight, dragging her into Vinegar Yard. As Coralie raised a hand to strike the child, Lydia hurtled at them and backhanded the trull away.

Coralie staggered back against a dirty wall. "Murderous bitch! You leave us alone!" She flung herself forward again.

She wasn't quick enough to get to the girl, whom Lydia swiftly pushed out of the way. "Susan, guard," she told the mastiff. Susan moved close to the girl's drab brown skirts and let out a low warning growl. The fiend hesitated, her face twisted with rage.

"I recommend you crawl back into whatever hole you crawled out from," Lydia said. "Attempt to lay hands on this child again, and I'll have you taken up on charges of abduction and attempted assault."

"Charges?" the woman echoed. "You'll peach on me, will you? And what do you want with her, I wonder, you great Jack whore?"

Lydia looked at the girl, whose wide-eyed gaze shot from Lydia back to the trull, then back again. Obviously she didn't know which of them to trust.

"B-Bow Street," the child choked out. "I was attacked and r-robbed and she was taking me to—to—"

"Ruination," Lydia said.

A tall ruffian dashed into Vinegar Yard at that moment, with another fellow at his heels. Several other males were also emerging from divers taverns and alleys.

Lydia was well aware that, wherever a mob congregated, trouble usually followed. She was not about to abandon this waif, however, mob or no mob.

Ignoring the rabble, Lydia focused on the girl.

"Bow Street is that way," she said, gesturing westward. "The way this viper was taking you leads to Drury Lane, where all the lovely brothels are—as any of these elegant fellows can tell you."

"Liar!" Coralie screeched. "I found her first! Find your own girls, you overgrown hag! I'll teach you to come poaching in my yard."

She started toward her victim, but Susan's ominous snarl stopped her in her tracks. "You call that beast off!" she raged. "Or I'll make you sorry."

No wonder her girls were afraid of her, Lydia reflected. She must be half mad to dare move so close to Susan. Even the men—each and every one a gutter-spawned villain, beyond question—kept a respectful distance from the growling mastiff.

"You've got it wrong," Lydia told her calmly. "I shall give you to the count of five to make yourself scarce. Otherwise I shall make *you* exceedingly sorry. One. Two. Thr—"

"Ah, now, ladies, ladies." The tall ruffian shoved another clodpole out of the way and pushed forward. "All this daring and daunting will burst your stays, my fair delicates. And all for what? The smallest problem: one chick, and two hens wanting her. Lots of chicks about, aren't there? Not worth disturbing the King's peace and annoying the constables, is it? Certainly not."

He drew out his purse. "Here's what we'll do. A screen apiece for you, my dears—and I'll take the little one off your hands."

Lydia recognized the distinctive accents of the upper orders, but she was too outraged to wonder at it. "A screen?" she cried. "Is that the value you place on a human life? One pound?"

He turned a glinting green gaze upon her. Down upon her. He topped her by several inches, no common occurrence in Lydia's experience.

"From what I've seen of your driving, you place no value on human life whatsoever," he said coolly. "You nearly killed three people in the Strand in the space of a minute." His impudent gaze drifted over the assembled audience. "There ought to be a law against women drivers," he announced. "A public menace."

"Aye, Ainswood, be sure to mention it in your next speech in the House of Lords," someone called out.

"Next?" cried another. "More like the first—if the roof don't fall in when he staggers into Parliament."

"I'll be blowed!" came a voice from the back. "That ain't Ainswood, is it?"

"Aye, and playing King Solomon, no less," someone from the front shouted back. "And got the wrong mare by the tail, as usual. Tell His Grace, Miss Grenville. He's put you down as a Covent Garden abbess."

"No surprise," said one of his fellows. "Took the Marchioness of Dain for a tart, didn't he?"

That was when Lydia realized who the lout was.

In May, a drunken Ainswood had encountered Dain and the marquess's bride at an inn on their wedding night, and refused to believe the lady was a lady, let alone Dain's wife.* Dain had been obliged to correct his erstwhile schoolmate's misapprehension with his fists. The incident had been the talk of London for weeks afterward.

Small wonder, then, that Lydia had mistaken His Grace for another Covent Garden lowlife. By all accounts, the Duke of Ainswood was one of the most depraved, reckless, and thick-headed rakes listed in *Debrett's Peerage*—no small achievement, given the present lamentable state of the aristocracy.

He was also, Lydia saw, one of the untidiest. He'd apparently donned his expensively tailored garments days earlier and had debauched as well as slept in them. He was hatless, and a shock of thick chestnut hair dangled over one eye, which like its mate evidenced months of insufficient sleep and more than sufficient dissipation. His only concession to basic grooming had been letting someone shave him recently—probably while he was stupefied by drink.

She saw more than this: the hellfire sparking in the green depths of his gaze, the arrogant tilt of his nose, the hard lines of cheekbone and jaw . . . and the devil's own curve of a mouth, promising everything, ripe for laughter, sin, what have you.

* See *Lord of Scoundrels*, Avon Books, © 1995

She was not unaffected. The devil in her, one she normally kept well concealed, was bound to be drawn to its counterpart in him. But she was not a fool, either. She knew well enough that this was a rogue's own countenance, and she could sum it up in one word: trouble.

Still, this rogue was a duke, and even the worst of noblemen had more influence with the authorities than a mere journalist did, especially a woman journalist.

"Your Grace, you've mistaken only one of us," she said with stiff politeness. "I am Grenville, of the *Argus*. This woman is a known procuress. She was luring the girl to a brothel, under pretext of taking her to Bow Street. If you would take the bawd into custody, I shall gladly accompany you there and testify—"

"She's a false, scheming liar!" Coralie cried. "I was only taking the child to Pearkes's." She waved toward the oyster house opposite. "For a bite to eat. She got herself into a bit of trouble—"

"And will be in a great deal worse, in your hands," Lydia said. Her attention reverted to Ainswood. "Do you know what happens to the children unfortunate enough to fall into her clutches? They are beaten, starved, and raped until they are reduced to a state of abject terror. Then she puts them on the streets—eleven and twelve years old, some of them—"

"You false, filthy, Jack whore of a bitch!" the bawd howled.

"Am I impugning your honor?" Lydia asked. "Do you want satisfaction? I'll be glad to oblige. Here and now, if you wish." She advanced upon the procuress. "Let's see how you like being on the other end of a beating."

A pair of large hands clamped on her arms and pulled her back. "Enough, ladies. You're giving me the deuce of headache. Let's try to keep the peace, shall we?"

"Oh, that's rich," someone called. "Ainswood keeping the peace. Did hell freeze over when I wasn't looking?"

Lydia looked down at the big hand grasping her arm. "Take your paws off me," she said coldly.

"I will—as soon as someone fetches me a strait-waistcoat to tuck you into. Who let you out of Bedlam, I wonder?"

Lydia shoved her elbow backward, into his gut. It was not soft. Pain twanged down her forearm to her wrist.

Still, he'd felt something, for he muttered an oath and let go, amid the crowd's hooting and whistling.

Get out while you still can, an inner voice warned her, *and don't look back.*

It was the inner voice of reason, and she would have heeded it if the nerve his ridiculing comments had struck hadn't shrieked more loudly. Nature had not formed Lydia's character for retreat, and pride forbade any action hinting at weakness or, God forbid, fear.

Eyes narrowed, heart pumping furiously, she turned to face him. "Touch me again," she warned, "and I'll black both your eyes."

"Oh, do it, yer worship!" an onlooker urged. "Touch 'er again."

"Aye, my tenner's on you, Ainswood."

"And mine says she gives him a pair o' stinkers like she promised," another voice challenged.

The duke, meanwhile, was sizing her up, his green gaze boldly raking her from bonnet to half-boots.

"Big, yes, but not up to my weight," he announced. "I make her at five and three quarter feet. And ten stone, stripped. Which," he added, his glance skimming over her bodice, "I should pay fifty guineas to see, by the way."

Raucous laughter and the usual lewd comments greeted this witticism.

Neither the laughter nor the obscenities disconcerted Lydia. She knew this rough world; she'd spent most of her childhood in it. But the crowd's noise recalled her to the main issue. The girl she'd set out to rescue stood frozen in place, wearing the hunted expression of one who'd found herself in the jungle, surrounded by cannibals—which was not far off the mark.

Still, Lydia could not let this moron have the last word.

"Oh, that's well done," she told him. "Broaden the child's education, why don't you? Give her a pretty view of London manners—and the high moral tone of the peerage."

She had a great deal more to say, but she reminded herself that she might as well lecture a milestone. If this jackass had ever owned a conscience, it had died of neglect decades ago.

Contenting herself with one last, withering glance at him, she turned away and started toward the girl.

A swift survey of the crowd told Lydia that the bawd had vanished, which was frustrating. Still, it would not have made much difference if she'd stayed, when none of these loud-mouthed curs cared for anything but their own entertainment.

"Come, my dear," she said as she approached the girl. "We accomplish nothing amid this rabble."

"Miss Grenville," came the duke's voice from behind her.

Nerves jumping, Lydia swung about—and came up against a solid column of male. She retreated but half a pace, lifted her chin, and straightened her spine.

He did not back away, and she held her ground, though it wasn't easy. She could not quite see past his brawny torso, and at close quarters she was rivetingly aware of the muscular frame his garments hugged so snugly.

"Excellent reflexes," he said. "If you weren't a female, I'd take up your offer—of the stinkers, I mean. That is to say, the black—"

"I know what it means," said Lydia.

"Indeed, it's all very well to have an extensive vocabulary," he said. "In the future, however, I recommend you exercise a dash—the smallest sliver—of reason, my dove, before you exercise your tongue. You can manage that, I hope? Because another fellow, you see, might take your adorable little darings and dauntings as an amusing challenge. In which case, you might find yourself in a different sort of tussle than you bargained for. Do you take my meaning, little girl?"

Lydia opened her eyes very wide. "Oh, goodness, no," she said breathlessly. "You are much too deep for me, Your Grace. My tiny brain simply can't take it in."

His green eyes glinted. "Maybe your bonnet's squeezing it too tight." His hands came up to the ribbons and paused, inches away.

"I shouldn't, if I were you," she said, her voice even, her heart ricocheting against her rib cage.

He laughed and tugged at the bonnet strings.

Her fist shot up. He grabbed it, still laughing, and pulled her up against the hard column of his body.

She'd half expected that, sensed what was coming. But she wasn't prepared for the heat or the explosion of sensations she couldn't identify, and these threw her off balance.

In the next instant, her mouth was crushed under his, warm and firm and all too skilled, and she was sinking backward, disoriented and helpless under its deceitfully easy pressure. She was pulsingly aware of his big hand splayed against her upper back, its warmth seeping through stiff layers of bombazine and undergarments, and of more heat lower, where his brawny arm braced her waist.

For one perilous moment, her mind gave way as her muscles did, overpowered by heat and strength and the chaotic brew of masculine scent and taste.

But her instincts had been honed in a hard school, and in the next moment she reacted.

She sagged in his arms, making herself a dead weight.

She felt his mouth leave hers.

"By gad, the wench's faint—"

She slammed her fist into his jaw.

2

The next Vere knew, he was flat on his back in a pool of mud. Above the ringing in his ears he heard the crowd cheering, hooting, and whistling.

He pulled himself up onto his elbows and let his gaze travel from his vanquisher's black half-boots up over the heavy black bombazine skirts to the mannishly severe jacket that buttoned primly up to her chin.

Above the topmost button was a face so starkly beautiful that it had half blinded him when he'd first beheld it. This was a winter's beauty, of ice-blue eyes and snow-white skin, framed under the black bonnet by silken hair the color of December sunlight.

At present, those remarkable eyes directed a freezing blue stare down upon him. Such a look, he supposed, the mythical Gorgons might have bestowed. He little doubted that, had this been myth and make-believe instead of real life, he would be swiftly petrifying to stone.

As it was, he'd hardened only in the usual place, but very speedily, even for him. Her boldness as well as her face and lavish body had aroused him even before he'd hauled her into his arms and touched his mouth to hers.

Now, while he stared stupidly at the ripe mouth he'd so insanely hungered for, it curled into a contemptuous half-smile. The mockery he saw there recalled him to his senses.

The insolent wench thought she'd won—and so everyone

must think, he realized. Within hours everyone in London would hear that a female had knocked Ainswood—the last Mallory hellion—on his arse.

Being a hellion, Vere would rather be slow roasted on a spit than admit the damage to his pride or show anything of what he truly felt.

And so he answered her smug contempt with the provoking grin he was famous for.

"Well, let that be a lesson to you," he said.

"It speaks," she informed the onlookers. "I reckon it will live."

She turned away, and the rustle of her bombazine skirts against her legs sounded like the hissing of serpents.

Ignoring the hands reaching to help him, Vere swung up onto his feet without taking his eyes off her. He watched the arrogant sway of her rump as she sauntered away, coolly collected the dog and the girl, and turned into Vinegar Yard's southwest exit, out of sight.

Even then he couldn't bring his full attention to the men about him because his mind was churning with salacious scenarios that landed her on her back instead of him.

Still, he knew the trio about him—Augustus Tolliver, George Carruthers, and Adolphus Crenshaw—and they knew him, or thought they did. And so his expression remained the drunkenly amused one they'd expect.

"Let it be a lesson to her, eh?" Tolliver said, chuckling. "What lesson was that, I wonder? How to deliver a jawbreaker?"

"Jawbreaker?" Carruthers echoed indignantly. "And how could he be talking if it was? I vow, you must be half blind. It wasn't the uppercut that dropped him. It was that curious acrobatic trick of hers."

"I've heard of such things," said Crenshaw. "Something

to do with balance, I collect. All the rage in China or Arabia or some such—and about what you'd expect from those heathen inscrutables."

"About what you'd expect from Lady Grendel, then," said Carruthers. "I heard she was born in a Borneo swamp and reared by crocodiles."

"More like Seven Dials," Tolliver said. "You heard this lot, cheering her on. They know her. She's one of their own, spawned in the back-slums of the Holy Land, I don't doubt."

"Where'd she learn heathenish fighting tricks, then?" Crenshaw demanded. "And how is it no one ever heard of her before a few months ago? Where's she been keeping all this time that no one remarked a Long Meg like her? It isn't as though she's hard to see, is it?"

He turned back to Vere, who was swatting mud from his trousers. "You'd a close enough look and listen, Ainswood. Any hint of the Holy Land in her speech? London bred, would you say, or not?"

Seven Dials was the black heart of one of London's seamiest neighborhoods, St. Giles's parish, which was also known ironically as the Holy Land.

Vere doubted that the Grenville gorgon would have needed to travel beyond its boundaries to learn the kinds of dirty fighting tricks she employed. That he'd discerned no Cockney accent meant nothing. Jaynes had grown up in the back-slums, yet he'd lost all traces of the accent.

Perhaps she had sounded more like a lady than Jaynes did a gentleman. What did it signify? Plenty of lowborn wenches tried to ape their betters. And if Vere could not at the moment recall a single one who'd made it seem so natural, he could not, either, discern a single reason to stand here blithering about it. Covered with mud outwardly and simmering inwardly, he was in no mood to encourage this lot of morons to exercise their limited intellects upon this or any other point.

Leaving them, he made for Brydges Street in a storm of outrage, the likes of which he hadn't experienced in years.

He had hurried to the curst female's rescue and found her all but begging for a riot. His timely intervention had beyond question spared her a knife in the back. In reward, he'd received an earful of brimstone and taunting defiance.

Miss Insolence had actually threatened to black both his eyes. She'd threatened *him*—Vere Aylwin Mallory—whom even that great big-beaked brute Lord Beelzebub couldn't pound into submission.

Was it any wonder that a man so goaded should adopt the tried and true method of silencing a scold?

And if she didn't like it, why didn't she slap his face, as a normal woman would? Did she think he'd hit her—any woman—back? Did she think he meant to ravish her in Vinegar Yard before a mob of drunks, pimps, and whores?

As if he'd *ever* stoop so low, he fumed. As if he needed to take a woman by force. As if he didn't have to fight off their advances with cudgels, practically.

He was halfway to Brydges Street when a loud voice penetrated his indignation.

"I say—Ainswood, ain't it?"

Vere paused and turned. The man calling to him was the one he'd pulled out of the cabriolet's rampaging way.

"Couldn't place the name at first," the fellow said as he reached him. "But then they said something 'bout Dain and m'curst sister and then I recalled who you was. Which I should've done in the first place, him mentioning you more than once, but I'll tell you the truth: I been hurried and harried from pillar to post till I feel like what's-his-name the Greek fellow with them plaguey Fury things after him, and it's a wonder my brainworks ain't closed up shop permanent. So it's like as not if the tall gal did run me down I wouldn't know the difference, except maybe it'd be the first rest I had in weeks. All the same, I'm much obliged, since I'm sure it's a deuced awkward way to go, havin' your bones crushed under a wheel, and I'd be honored if you'd share a bottle with me."

He stuck out his hand. "Mean to say, it's Bertie Trent—me, that is—and pleased to make your acquaintance."

Lydia shoved the Duke of Ainswood to the darkest corner of her mind and focused on the girl. This was not the first damsel in distress she'd rescued. She usually took them to one of London's more trustworthy charitable organizations.

Early in the summer, though, Lydia had rescued a pair of seventeen-year-olds, Bess and Millie, who had run away from harsh employers. She'd hired them as maids of all work—or slaveys, as such servants were often called—because her intuition told her they'd suit her. Experience had proven her intuition correct. The same forceful inner voice told her this waif would also do better with her.

By the time Lydia had squeezed her and Susan into the cabriolet, she was certain the girl was not of the laboring classes. Though she spoke with a slight Cornish accent, it was an educated one, and practically the first words that came out of her mouth were, "I can't believe it's you, Miss Grenville of the *Argus*." Maidservants and simple country girls were unlikely to be familiar with the *Argus*.

The girl's name—definitely Cornish—was Tamsin Prideaux, and she was nineteen years old. Lydia had guessed fifteen at first, but on closer inspection the maturity was more evident.

Tamsin was a smallish girl, that was all, except for her eyes, which were enormous and velvet brown. They were also extremely shortsighted, it turned out. Apart from what she wore, her spectacles were the only belongings she had left. They were sadly mangled, with one lens cracked.

She had taken them off shortly after alighting from the coach, Miss Prideaux explained, in order to clean them, because by then they were thickly coated with road dust. There had been a great crush at the coaching inn, and someone had pushed her. The next she knew, someone tore her reticule and carpetbag from her hands so violently that she unbalanced and fell. When she got up from the ground, her box was gone, too. At this point, the bawd had come, feigning sympathy and offering to take her to the Bow Street magistrate's office to report the crime.

It was an old trick, but even hardened Londoners were assaulted and robbed daily, Lydia assured her.

"You mustn't blame yourself," she told the girl as they reached the house. "It could happen to anyone."

"Except you," Miss Prideaux said. "You're up to every rig."

"Don't be silly," Lydia said briskly while hustling her indoors. "I've made my share of mistakes."

She noticed that Susan showed no signs of jealousy, which looked promising. She had also resisted the temptation to play with the new human toy. This was considerate of the mastiff, since the girl had been terrified out of her wits already, and—misinterpreting affectionate canine overtures—might start screaming, which would upset Susan very much. Nonetheless, as they entered the hall, Lydia took precautions.

"This is a friend," she told the dog while lightly patting Tamsin's shoulder. "Be gentle, Susan. Do you hear? *Gentle*."

Susan licked the girl's hand, very delicately.

Gingerly, Tamsin petted her.

"Susan is highly intelligent," Lydia explained, "but you must communicate with her in simple terms."

"They used mastiffs to hunt wild boar in olden times, didn't they?" the girl asked. "Does she bite?"

"Devour is more like it," Lydia said. "Still, you've nothing to fear from her. If she grows too playful, tell her firmly, *'Gentle,'*—unless you'd rather be knocked down and drowned in doggy drool."

Tamsin chuckled softly, which was an encouraging sign. Bess appeared then, and in a little while the guest was borne off for tea, a hot bath, and a nap.

After a quick washing up, Lydia adjourned to her study. Only there, with the door closed, did she let her mask of unshakable confidence slip.

Though she'd seen a great deal of the world—more of it than the majority of London's most polished sophisticates, male and female—she was not altogether as worldly as the world believed.

No man had ever kissed Lydia Grenville before.

Even Great-Uncle Ste, kindly if misguided, had never done more than pat her on the head—or, when she started sprouting into a giantess, upon the hand.

What the Duke of Ainswood had done was very far from avuncular. And Lydia found she was very far from immune.

She sank into the chair at the desk and pressed her bowed head against the heels of her hands and waited for the hot inner tumult to subside and her neatly ordered, well-controlled world to settle back into place.

It wouldn't. Instead, the chaotically uncontrollable world of her childhood flooded her mind. The tide of images ebbed and flowed, to settle at last upon the scene most deeply etched in her memory: the time when her world and sense of who she was had changed irrevocably.

She saw herself as she had been then, a little girl sitting upon a battered stool, reading her mother's diary.

Though Lydia never would, she could have written the tale much in the same style she used for *The Rose of Thebes*.

London, 1810

It was early evening, several hours after Anne Grenville had been laid to rest in the parish burial ground, when her eldest daughter, ten-year-old Lydia, found the journal. It lay hidden under a shabby collection of fabric scraps intended for patches, at the bottom of her mother's sewing basket.

Lydia's younger sister, Sarah, had long since cried herself to sleep, and their father, John Grenville, had gone out to seek solace in the arms of one of his trollops or in a bottle—or both, most likely.

Unlike her sister, Lydia was awake and her blue eyes were dry. She had not been able to cry all day. She was too angry with God, who had taken the wrong parent.

But then, what would God want with Papa? *Lydia asked herself as she pushed away a stray lock of golden hair and searched for a patch for Sarah's pinafore. That was when she found the little book, its pages filled with her mother's tiny, precise penmanship.*

The mending forgotten, she sat huddled by the smoky hearth and read on through the night the vastly puzzling story. The diary was small, and her mama had not made entries faithfully. Consequently, Lydia reached the end before her father staggered home sometime after dawn.

She waited until midafternoon, however, when he was sober and the worst of his ill temper was abating, and Sarah was in the alley playing with a neighbor's child.

"I found something Mama wrote," Lydia told him. "Is it true she was a lady once upon a time? And you acted upon the stage

once? Or was Mama only making believe?"

He had started hunting in the clothespress for something, but paused and gave her a faintly amused look. "What does it matter what she was?" he returned. "It never did us any good, did it? Do you think we should be living in this hovel if she'd come with a dowry? What does it matter to you, Miss High and Mighty? Fancy yourself a great lady, do you?"

"Is it true that I take after Mama's ancestors?" Lydia asked, ignoring her father's sarcasm. She had learned not to let it upset her.

"Ancestors?" He opened a cupboard, shrugged at the meager contents, then slammed it shut. "That's a grand way of putting it. Is that how your mama explained it?"

"She wrote it in a book—a diary, it seems to be," Lydia persisted, "that she was a lady from an old, noble family. And one of her cousins was a lord—the Marquess of Dain. She wrote that she ran away with you to Scotland," Lydia continued. "And her family was very angry and cut her off as though she was 'a diseased branch of the Ballister tree.' I only want to know whether it's true. Mama was . . . fanciful."

"So she was." Papa got a crafty look in his eyes, much worse than the mockery and even the dislike he sometimes forgot to conceal.

Then, too late, Lydia realized that she shouldn't have mentioned the diary.

Then all she could do was want to kick herself. But she hid her feelings—as usual—when he said, "Bring me the book, Lydia."

She brought it and never saw it again, as she'd expected would happen. It vanished as so many of their belongings had vanished before and continued to do in the following months. Lydia had no trouble figuring out that he'd pawned her mother's journal and would never reclaim it, or had sold it outright. That was how he got money. Sometimes he lost it gambling, and sometimes he won, but Lydia and Sarah seldom saw much of it.

Neither did the people John Grenville owed.

Two years later, despite numerous changes of name and residence, his creditors caught up with him. He was arrested for debt and consigned to the Marshalsea Prison in Southwark. After he'd lived there for a year with his daughters, he was declared an insolvent debtor and released.

Freedom came too late for Sarah, though. She'd already contracted consumption, and died not long thereafter.

What John Grenville learned from the experience was that England's climate was unhealthy for him. Leaving thirteen-year-old Lydia with his uncle and aunt, Ste and Effie, and promising to send for the girl "in a few months," he set sail for America.

On the night of her father's departure, Lydia began her own journal. The first sadly misspelt entry began: "Papa has gonne—for ever, I fervantly hope—and good riddents."

Normally, Vere would have fobbed off Trent's offer of a drink as easily as he shrugged off the fellow's thanks.

But Vere was not feeling like his normal self.

It had started with the ferret-faced Jaynes's preaching about carrying on the line—when it was obvious to any moron that the Mallory line was cursed and destined for extinction. Vere had no intention of getting sons, only to stand by helplessly a few years later and watch them die.

Second, the virago of the century had to come rampaging across his path. Then, when Her Brimstone Majesty was done with him, his so-called friends had to debate who she was and where she came from and the technique she'd used to fell him. As though they actually considered her—a female —his *adversary*. At fisticuffs!

Trent, in contrast, offered a courteous and calm "much

obliged" and the sporting reward of a drink.

This was why Vere let Trent follow him home. Then, after a bath and change of clothes—with a sour-faced but mercifully silent Jaynes in attendance—Vere set out to give the younger man a taste of nightlife in London.

This taste couldn't include entering the abodes of Polite Society, where hordes of marriage-hungry misses pounced upon any male with money and a pulse. The Mallorys' last hellion would rather be disemboweled with a rusty blade than spend three minutes with a lot of simpering virgins.

The tour included instead establishments where drink and female companionship cost only coins. If this evening His Grace happened to choose places London's scribblers were known to frequent, and if Vere spent most of his time listening not to Trent but to the other customers, and if the duke came to taut attention on the two occasions he heard a certain woman's name mentioned, these matters easily escaped Sir Bertram Trent's notice.

They wouldn't have escaped Jaynes, but he was an annoyingly sharp fellow, while Trent . . . was not.

"The greatest nitwit in the Northern Hemisphere" was how Lord Dain had described his brother-in-law.

It didn't take Vere long to perceive that Beelzebub had put the case mildly, to say the least. In addition to getting himself into sentences the Almighty with the aid of all His angels would never find a way out of, Trent demonstrated a rare talent for getting under horses' hooves or directly beneath falling objects, for colliding with obstacles both human and inanimate, and for toppling from whatever he happened to be standing, sitting, or lying upon.

Initially, all Vere felt toward him—in the brief intervals when his mind took a breather from fretting and fuming about blue-eyed dragons—was amazement, mingled with amusement. Furthering their acquaintance was the farthest thing from his mind.

He changed his mind later in the evening.

Not long after exiting the Westminster Pit—where they'd watched Billy the Terrier perform the astounding feat of killing a hundred rats in ten minutes, as advertised—they met up with Lord Sellowby.

He had formed part of Dain's circle in Paris and was well acquainted with Trent. But then, Sellowby was acquainted with everybody and every single thing they did. He was one of England's foremost collectors and disseminators of gossip.

After they'd exchanged greetings, he sympathetically enquired whether "Your Grace had sustained any permanent injuries as a result of today's historic encounter with Lady Grendel? In glancing over the betting book at White's, I counted fourteen separate wagers regarding the number of teeth you had lost in the—er—altercation."

At that moment, Sellowby was in imminent danger of losing all of his teeth, along with the jawbone they were attached to.

But before Vere could initiate hostilities a red-faced Trent burst into an indignant rebuttal. "Broke his teeth?" he cried. "Why, it were only a tap on the chin, and anyone could see he were only playactin'—tryin' to make a joke and turn the crowd good-tempered. If you'd been there, Sellowby, you'd've seen what a mob of ugly-lookin' customers come rushin' in from everywhere, primed for head-breakin'. Not to mention you seen for yourself what my sister done in Paris, which shows how females are when they get worked up—and this one almost as tall as I am with the biggest mastiff bitch you ever seen. . . ."

Trent went on in this vein for several minutes, without letting Sellowby get a word in edgeways. When the baronet finally stopped to refill his lungs, His Lordship hastily took his leave.

For a moment—and the first time in years—Vere was rendered speechless himself.

He couldn't remember the last time anyone had leapt to his defense. But then, his behavior had never merited defending, he quickly reminded himself, for he was very far from saintly—about as far as a man could get without getting hanged. And so, he concluded, only a baconbrain like Trent would imagine that Vere Aylwin Mallory needed a champion . . . or even a loyal friend.

Since his heart had calcified long ago, the Duke of Ainswood couldn't possibly find Bertie Trent's blithering on his behalf touching—any more than His Grace could admit to any niggling doubts about his actions in Vinegar Yard. He would cheerfully submit to being flayed alive before confessing, even to himself, that more than one of Lady Grendel's verbal shafts had penetrated his thick hide.

Instead, the duke decided that Sellowby's blank bewilderment during Trent's diatribe was the most comical thing he'd seen in months, and that Trent was a most entertaining imbecile.

This, His Grace believed, was why he invited Bertie to move his bags from the George Inn to Ainswood House, and make himself at home there.

During dinner Lydia discovered that Miss Prideaux's table manners were faultless, her appetite good, her conversation intelligent, spiced with an agreeably wry humor. She had a musically sweet voice, which reminded Lydia of Sarah's, though this girl was much older and clearly more resilient.

Over cheese and fruit, Lydia commenced the interrogation.

"I collect you've run away from home," she said mildly.

The girl set down the knife with which she'd been paring an apple and met Lydia's gaze. "Miss Grenville, I know running away is foolish, and running away to London is probably insane—but there is a limit to what one can tolerate, and I had reached it."

Her story was not the usual thing.

Two years earlier, her mother had suddenly turned religious. Pretty frocks were forbidden. Dancing and music—except for hymns—were forbidden. All reading materials except Bibles, sermons, and prayerbooks were forbidden. Miss Prideaux's smuggled copies of the *Argus* constituted her sole link with the "rational world," as she put it.

"Having read your articles and essays," she said, "I was fully aware I'd face difficulties in London, and I came prepared, I assure you. If it were not for being robbed of everything, I should not have dreamt of imposing upon you. I had enough to pay for lodgings until I could find work, and I was ready to do anything honest."

Her face worked and her huge eyes began to glisten, but she quickly composed herself and continued. "Mama and her zealot friends have driven Papa out of the house. I hadn't seen him for a fortnight when she announced I must give up Aunt Lavinia's jewelry. The sect wanted to print up copies of Brother Ogbert's sermons. Unfortunately, all the printers turned out to be such tools of the devil as to charge for the work. Mama said I must contribute my late aunt's things to save souls."

"Whether they wanted to be saved or not," Lydia muttered. "There's plenty of that sort in London. Wasting money on Bibles and pamphlets when what people need is work, and a roof over their heads, and something to eat."

"That is exactly how I felt," Tamsin said. "I couldn't possibly give up my aunt's jewelry to those frauds. She'd left them to me in her will, and when I wore them, or simply looked at them, I thought of her, and how good she was to me and how often we had laughed together. I loved her very m-much," she finished shakily.

Lydia still possessed her sister Sarah's locket. If it hadn't been made of worthless metal, Papa would have pawned it or gambled it away. Then Lydia, who had no memento of her mother, would have had none of her sister, either.

Lydia couldn't wear the locket because it turned her skin green, yet she kept it in a box in her bedroom and took it out every night, and thought of the little sister she had so dearly loved.

"I'm sorry," she said gently. "The chances of getting your aunt's things back are not very good."

"I know it's hopeless," Tamsin said. "I shouldn't have minded if they'd taken everything else and left me those. But by now the thieves have torn everything apart and found them, and they're not likely to return jewelry, I'm sure."

Lydia began to calculate. "They were valuable, then?"

"I can't say precisely," said Tamsin. "There was a ruby necklace with a bracelet and earrings to match. Also a pretty amethyst set, rather old, in a silver filigree setting. And three rings. They were not paste, but I can't say what they're worth. I never had them appraised. The money value didn't matter to me."

"If they're not paste, there's a good chance they'll be fenced," Lydia said. "I have informants connected with the trade." She rang the bell and, when Millie appeared a moment later, asked for writing materials.

"We shall make a detailed list," Lydia told her guest when the maid was gone. "Can you draw them?"

Tamsin nodded.

"Good. That will improve our chances of tracking them down. Not that we can count on getting them back," Lydia warned. "You mustn't get your hopes up."

"I should not fuss about them at all," the girl said unsteadily. "But it's so horrid that I tried to save them from Mama's lot of pious thieves only to lose them to a lot of impious ones. If she found out, she'd say it was a judgment on me—but I shan't have to listen to that, or any of her galling sermons, ever again." She colored, and her lower lip trembled. "That is to say, you won't feel duty-bound to tell them where I am, will you? I left a note saying I'd run away with a lover. They think I'm upon the sea at present, en route to America. I was obliged to devise something desperately immoral and irrevocable, you see, to forestall pursuit."

"If you can't honor thy father and thy mother, that is your affair," said Lydia. "And their misfortune. It has nothing to do with me. If you want to make sure they don't get word of where you really are, though, I recommend you change your name to something less distinctive."

That wouldn't protect her from London's evils, however. She looked younger than she was and all too vulnerable.

After the briefest of pauses, Lydia went on, "It occurs to me that your present predicament is to my advantage. I'd been planning to hire a companion." She hadn't, but that hardly signified. "If you would be so good as to stay on with me, you'll spare me the bother of looking for one. The terms are room, board, and—"

The girl began to weep. "Please forgive me," she said, wiping her eyes futilely. "I don't mean to be v-vaporish, but you are so g-good."

Lydia rose and went to her, and stuffed a handkerchief into her hands. "Never mind," she said. "You've had an upsetting time of it. Another girl would have fallen into hysterics. You're entitled to bawl a little. It'll make you feel better."

"I can't believe you're not in the least overset," Tamsin said after wiping her eyes and nose. "You were the one who had to contend with everybody, yet you never turned a hair. I don't know how you did it. I've never seen a duke before— not that I could see him very well. Still, I shouldn't have known what to say to someone so grand, even if I had guessed what to make of him. But everything was a blur to me, and I could not tell whether he was truly joking or truly cross."

"I doubt he could tell, either," Lydia said, ignoring the hot prickling along her spine. "The man's a cretin. He belongs in Exeter 'Change with the rest of the menagerie."

The writing materials arrived then, and Lydia had no trouble turning her guest's mind away from Lord Ainswood.

Lydia's own mind was not so accommodating.

Hours later, alone in her bedroom, she still couldn't shake off the memory of the brief kiss, or altogether stifle the old yearnings it stirred.

She sat at her dressing table, holding Sarah's locket.

During the grim days in the Marshalsea prison, Lydia had entertained her sister with stories about Prince Charming, who'd one day arrive on a white charger. At the time, Lydia had been young and romantic enough to believe that one day a prince truly would come and she would live with him in a beautiful palace whose nursery would be filled with happy children. Sarah would also marry a prince, and live with her happy children in the castle next door.

In the real, grown-up world, unicorns were more plentiful than Prince Charmings.

In the real world, a duke—the next best thing to a prince —couldn't be bothered to take the wickedest of witches to the dungeon where she belonged.

In the real world, no kiss could turn a confirmed spinster

back into a dreamy-eyed girl. Especially not *that* kiss, which was obviously a substitute for the punch in the mouth His Grace would have given her if she'd been a man.

In any case, Lydia told herself, she had far more important issues to consider, namely, Miss Prideaux. Who was probably weeping into her pillow at this very moment, poor dear. Her clothes could be replaced, along with the spectacles, if they couldn't be repaired. And she wasn't alone and friendless, because she'd stay with Lydia.

But the jewelry, the precious keepsakes . . . oh, that loss must pain the child deeply.

If only that dolt of a duke had taken the bawd to Bow Street, they would have had an excellent chance of retrieving the girl's things. Obviously the thieves had been working for Coralie, because she'd played this game before. Several of her girls were adept pickpockets, and the bawd's bully boys had no scruples about assaulting defenseless girls.

But Ainswood hadn't been interested in Miss Prideaux's problems because he wasn't a noble and chivalrous hero. He only *looked* like Prince Charming, and a dissolute wreck of one at that.

If there were any justice in the world, Lydia told herself, he would have turned into the toad he was the instant his wicked mouth touched hers.

It would have soothed Miss Grenville's troubled spirit had she known that Lord Ainswood suffered worse indignities than turning into a toad.

He was used to causing talk. Being a born troublemaker, he was almost constantly at the center of one spectacle or scandal or another. Since he'd come into the title, the world —and especially the newspapers—followed his doings more avidly than before.

His contretemps with Dain on the latter's wedding night, an episode featuring Beelzebub's bastard son a week later, and a debacle of a carriage race in June had used up miles of paper and tons of ink. Vere's acquaintances had roasted him unmercifully as well.

The published satires and caricatures, along with the private jokes at his expense, had rolled off him as easily as he rolled off an endless series of harlots, and were as easily forgotten immediately afterward.

But on previous occasions, Vere's opponents had been men, and the affairs were conducted according to manly, sporting rules.

This time, his opponent had been a woman.

And now Vere didn't know which was worse: that he'd stooped to arguing with a female—when everyone knew they were the most irrational creatures on God's earth—or that he'd fallen, literally, for one of the oldest fighting tricks in history. What Lady Grendel had done was the same as playing dead, and he—who'd been scrapping since he was a toddler—had dropped his guard.

He was soon wishing he'd dropped *her*, right on her obstinate little head. That might have made up in some small way for the chaffing he endured in the following days.

Everywhere he went, his fellows couldn't resist exercising their limited wit upon him.

When he took Trent to the Fives Court in St. Martin's Street, for instance, someone had to ask why Vere hadn't brought Miss Grenville as sparring partner. At which every would-be pugilist in the place fell down laughing.

Everywhere Vere went, some sapskull wanted to know when the next match would be, or if His Grace's jaw had healed enough to allow him to eat soft foods, or if he reckoned so-and-so's grandmother was up to his weight.

Meanwhile, all the illustrators in London vied with each other for Most Hilarious Portrayal of the Great Battle.

Three days after the event, Vere stood, simmering, before a bookshop window. Displayed therein was a large print whose caption read, "Lady Grendel Gives the Duke of A_____ a Drubbing."

The artist had drawn him as a great, hulking brute wearing a stage villain's leer. He was reaching for the gorgon, portrayed as a dainty slip of a female. Above his caricatured head, the bubble read, "Why, my pretty, haven't you ever heard of *droit de seigneur?* I'm a duke now, don't you know?"

Miss Grenville was posed with her fists upraised. Her bubble said, "I'll show you a *droit*—and a *gauche* as well."

The feeble play on the French words for "right" and "left," he explained to a baffled-looking Trent, was intended to pass for wit.

"I got that part," Bertie said. "But that droy dee sig-new-er —ain't it French for two sovereigns? I thought you only offered a pound for the little gal."

The *droit de signeur,* Vere explained through stiff jaws, was the right of the feudal lord to deflower his vassals' brides.

Trent's square face reddened. "Oh, I say, that ain't funny. Virgins—and new-wed besides." He started for the bookshop door, doubtless intending to set matters straight in his own inimitable style.

Vere drew him back. "It's only a picture," he said. "A joke, Trent, that's all."

Recalling the adage "Out of sight, out of mind," he steered his would-be champion to the curb and started to cross the street with him.

Then he had to haul Bertie back, out of the way of the black vehicle bearing down upon them.

"Well, I'll be hanged!" Trent cried as he stumbled back to

the footway. "Speak of the devil."

It was she, the cause of the unceasing stale jokes and witless caricatures.

As she barreled past, Miss Boudicca Grenville saluted them in coachman style, touching her whip to her bonnet brim, and flashing a cocky grin.

Had she been a man, Vere would have hurtled after her, pulled her from the vehicle, and knocked that cocksure smile down her throat. But she wasn't a man, and all he could do was watch, smoldering, until she turned a corner a moment later . . . out of sight but far, perilously far, from forgotten.

3

The Duke of Ainswood's mood might have lightened had he known how close Lydia came to driving into the corner—and the shop standing there—rather than 'round it.

Though she collected her wits in time, it was in the very last tick of time, and she narrowly averted overturning as it was.

Not to mention she'd nearly run the two men down only seconds before.

This was because Lydia had no sooner recognized the tall figure at the curb than her brain shut down. Completely. No idea where she was or what she was doing.

It was only for a moment, but that was a moment far too long. And even afterward, she hadn't fully recovered. Though she'd managed the cool salute well enough, she had a horrible suspicion that her smile had been far too wide and . . . well, stupid, not to mince matters. A stupid, moonstruck smile, she reflected angrily, to match the idiotish pounding of her heart. As though she were a silly girl of thirteen instead of a hardened spinster of eight and twenty.

She lectured herself all the rest of the way to Bridewell prison.

When she entered the fortress of misery, though, she put her personal troubles aside.

She went to the Pass-Room. Here, pauper women claiming residence in other parts of England were held for a week before being sent back to their own parishes, the prevailing philosophy being, "Charity begins at home."

A row of low, narrow, straw-filled stalls lined the wall facing the door. The door and fireplace interrupted a similar line of stalls on that side. About twenty women, some with children, occupied the chamber.

Some had come to London to seek their fortunes; some had been ruined before they came and fled disgrace; and some had run away from the usual assortment of troubles: grief, poverty, brutality.

Lydia would describe the place for her readers in her usual style. She would sketch in plain and simple terms what she saw, and she would tell these women's stories in the same way, without moralizing or sentiment.

This wasn't all Lydia did, but she didn't think it was her reading public's right to know about the half-crowns she surreptitiously distributed to her interviewees, or the letters she wrote for them, or the people she'd later speak to on their behalf.

If, moreover, it frustrated Grenville of the *Argus* that she could do so little, or if her heart ached the whole time she listened to the women, these emotions would not enter her published work, either, for such feelings were nobody's business but hers.

The last interview was with the newest arrival, a fifteen-year-old girl who cradled an infant too weak and scrawny even to wail like the others. The boy lay limply in his mother's arms, now and then uttering a weary whimper.

"You must let me do something for you," Lydia told her. "If you know who his papa is, Mary, tell me, and I'll speak to him for you."

Pressing her lips together, Mary rocked to and fro upon her dirty heap of straw.

"You'd be amazed at how many fathers agree to help,"

Lydia said. *After I'm done with them,* she could have added.

"Sometimes their pas take 'em away," the girl said. "Jemmy's all I got now." She paused in her rocking and gave Lydia a troubled look. "You got any?"

"Children? No."

"Got a man?"

"No."

"Ever fancied one?"

"No." *Liar, liar, liar,* Lydia's inner devil mocked. "Yes," she amended with a short laugh.

"I was yes and no, too," Mary said. "I told myself I was a good girl and it was no use wishing for him, as he was miles above my touch and such like don't marry farm girls. But all the no was in my head, and every way else I fancied him something fierce. And so it ended up yes, and here's the tyke to prove it. And you'll be thinking I can't take care of him as he needs, which is true." Her bottom lip trembled. "All right, then, but you needn't speak for me nor write for me. I can write it myself. Here."

She thrust the child at Lydia, who stiffly exchanged her notebook and pencil for it. Him.

Lydia saw little ones all the time, for children were one commodity London's poor owned in abundance. She'd held them in her lap before, but none so young as this, none so utterly helpless.

She looked down at his narrow little face. The babe was neither pretty nor strong nor even clean, and she wanted to weep for him and the short, wretched future awaiting him, and for his mother, who was destitute and scarcely more than a child herself.

But Lydia's eyes remained dry, and if her heart ached as well from other causes, she knew better than to give those futile yearnings any heed. She was not a fifteen-year-old girl.

She was mature enough to let her head rule her actions, even if it couldn't altogether rule her heart.

And so she only quietly rocked the infant as his mother had done, and waited while Mary slowly dragged the pencil over the paper. When, finally, the very short note Mary took such pains with was finished, Lydia returned Jemmy to his mother with only the smallest pang of regret.

Even such a small regret was inexcusable, she chided herself as she left the Bridewell's grim confines.

Life was no romantic fable. In real life, London took the place of the palace of her youthful romantic imaginings. Its forgotten women and children were her siblings and offspring, and all the family she needed.

She could not be their Lady Bountiful and cure all that ailed them, but she could do for them what she'd been unable to do for her mother and sister. Lydia could speak for them. In the pages of the *Argus*, their voices were heard.

This was her vocation, she reminded herself. This was why God had made her strong and clever and fearless.

She had not been made to be any man's plaything. And she most certainly would not risk all she'd worked for, merely because a lout of a Prince Charming had raised a flurry in her unruly heart.

Three nights after she'd nearly run down Vere and Bertie, Lady Grendel tried to break Adolphus Crenshaw's skull in front of Crockford's club in St. James's Street.

Inside, Vere and Bertie joined the crowd at the window at the moment she took hold of Crenshaw's neckcloth and shoved him back against a lamppost.

With a grim sense of déjà vu, Vere hurried out of the club, advanced upon her, and firmly grasped her waist. Startled, she let go of the cravat, and Vere lifted her up off the pavement and set her back down well out of reach of the gasping Crenshaw.

She tried the elbow-in-the-gut trick again, but Vere managed to dodge it while still keeping a firm grip on her. He wasn't prepared for the boot heel crunching down on his instep, though he should have been, but he didn't let go then, either, even while pain shafted up his leg.

He grabbed her flailing arms and dragged her away, out of hearing of the group of men gathering at Crockford's entrance.

She struggled with him the whole way, and he struggled with a strong temptation to throw her into the street where an oncoming hackney could do London a favor and crush her under its wheels. Instead, Vere hailed the vehicle.

When it halted before them, he told her, "You can get in, or I can throw you in. Take your pick."

She muttered something under her breath that sounded like the synonym for "rectum," but when he pulled the door open, she climbed in quickly enough. Which was too bad, because he wouldn't have minded in the least hurrying her with a slap to her rump.

"Where do you live?" he asked when she'd flung herself onto the seat.

"Bedlam, where else?"

He jumped into the hackney and gave her a hard shake. "Where do you live, curse you?"

She mentioned a few other body parts he resembled before grudgingly admitting to a lair in Frith Street, Soho.

Vere relayed the direction to the driver, then settled onto the seat with her, where he made sure to take up more than his share of room.

After they'd traveled a good while in angry silence, she let out an impatient huff. "Lud, what a fuss you make," she said.

"A fuss?" he echoed, taken aback. "You were the one—"

"I wasn't going to hurt Crenshaw," she said. "I was only trying to make him listen. I had to get his full attention first."

For a moment, Vere could only stare at her in blank disbelief.

"There was no need to make a scene—and in St. James's, no less," she said. "But I suppose it's no use telling you. Everyone knows you delight in making a spectacle of yourself. You've been brawling from one end of England to the other for this last year at least. Sooner or later you were bound to bring your special brand of pandemonium back to London. Still, I did not think it would be this soon. It's only three months since your infamous carriage race."

He found his tongue. "I know what you're trying to do—"

"You haven't the least idea," she said. "But you are not interested in determining the facts of a situation before interfering. You jump to your own wild conclusions and leap in. This is the second time you've come in my way and caused needless complications and delay."

Vere knew what she was doing. The best defense is a good offense; this was one of his own modes of operation. He was not about to let her veer him off course.

"Let me explain something to you, Miss Gentleman Jackson Grenville," he said. "You can't rampage about London pummeling every fellow who crosses your path. So far you've been lucky, but one of these days you're going to try it with a man who hits back—"

"Perhaps I will," she cut in haughtily. "I don't see what business it is of yours."

"I make it my business," he said through clenched jaws, "when I see a friend in need of help. Since—"

"I am not your friend and I didn't need any help."

"Since *Crenshaw* is my friend," he went on doggedly, "and

since he is too much of a gentleman to fight back—"

"But not too much of a gentleman to seduce and abandon a fifteen-year-old girl."

That broadside took him unawares, but Vere quickly recovered. "Don't tell me the chit you tried to start a riot about is claiming Crenshaw ruined her," he said, "because I know for a fact she isn't his type."

"No, she's much too old," said the gorgon. "Quite ancient. All of nineteen. Whereas Crenshaw likes plump rustics of fourteen and fifteen."

From her pocket Madam Insolence withdrew a crumpled wad of paper. She held it out to him.

Very uneasy, Vere took it, smoothed it out, and read.

In large, round schoolgirl script, the note informed Crenshaw that he had a two-month-old son who currently resided with his mother, Mary Bartles, in Bridewell.

"The girl is in the Pass-Room," the virago said. "I saw the infant. Jemmy strongly resembles his papa."

Vere handed back the note. "I collect you announced this to Crenshaw in front of his friends."

"I gave him the note," she said. "He read it, crumpled it, and threw it down. I've been trying for three days to run him to ground. But every time I called at his lodgings, the servant claimed Mr. Crenshaw wasn't in. Mary will be sent back—to her parish workhouse, most likely—in a few days. If he will not help her, the child will die there, and Mary will probably die of grief."

The dragon lady turned her glacial gaze to the window. "She told me the babe was all she had. And there his father was, going to Crockford's, to throw his money away on cards and dice, when his son is weak and ill, with no one to care for him but a mother who's a child herself. You have some fine friends, Ainswood."

Though Vere considered it unsporting for a man of nearly thirty to seduce ignorant young rustics, and though he considered his crony's reaction to the forlorn note inexcusable, he was not about to admit this to Miss Self-Appointed Guardian of Public Morals.

"Let me explain something to you," he said. "If you want to get something out of a man, dashing out his brains against a lamppost isn't the way to do it."

She turned away from the window and regarded him levelly.

And he wondered what malignant power had created this shockingly beautiful monster.

You'd think the carriage's gloom would dull the impact of her extraordinary face. The shadows only lent intimacy, making it impossible for him to view her with detachment. He'd seen her in his dreams, but dreams were safe. This wasn't. He had only to lift his hand to touch the silken purity of her cheek. He had only to close the smallest distance to bring his mouth to hers, plum-soft and full.

If the impulse to touch and taste had been less ferocious, he would have surrendered, as he usually did to such impulses. But he'd felt this powerful pull before, in Vinegar Yard, and he wouldn't play the fool again.

"All you had to do was smile," he said. "And bat your eyelashes and thrust your bosom in his face, and Crenshaw would have done whatever you wanted."

She gazed at him unblinkingly for the longest time. Then, from a pocket hidden in her black skirts' heavy folds, she fished out a small notebook and a stump of a pencil.

"I had better write this down," she said. "I do not want to lose one priceless syllable of wisdom." She made an elaborate ceremony of opening the battered notebook and licking the pencil point. Then she bowed her head and wrote. "Smile," she said. "Bat eyelashes. What was the other thing?"

"Things," he corrected, leaning closer to read what she'd written. "Plural. Your breasts. You stick them under his nose."

Hers were right under his and mere inches from his itching fingers.

She wrote down his instructions with a ludicrous appearance of intense concentration: eyes narrowed, the tip of her pink tongue caught between her teeth.

"It'll be more effective if you wear something lower cut," he added. "Otherwise, a fellow might wonder whether you're hiding a deformity."

He wondered whether she had any inkling of the ferocious temptation the long parade of buttons represented, or of how the masculine cut of her garments only made a man more conscious of the womanly form they so rigidly encased. He wondered what evil witch had brewed her scent, a devilish mixture of smoke and lilies and something else he couldn't put a name to.

His head dipped lower.

She looked up at him with the smallest of smiles. "I'll tell you what," she said. "Why don't you take the pencil and notebook and jot down all your fantasies, in your own dear little hand. Then I shall have a keepsake of this delightful occasion. Unless, that is, you'd rather breathe down my neck."

Very slowly, so as not to appear disconcerted, he drew back. "You also need lessons in anatomy," he said. "I was breathing in your *ear*. If you want me to breathe down your neck, you shouldn't wear such high collars."

"Where I want you to do your breathing," she said, "is in Madagascar."

"If I'm bothering you," he said, "why don't you hit me?"

She closed the small notebook. "Now I understand," she

said. "You made the fuss in St. James's Street because I was hitting someone else, and you don't want me to hit anyone but you."

His heart sped from double to triple time. Ignoring it, he gave her a pitying look. "You poor dear. All this scribbling has given you a brain fever."

To his vast relief, the carriage halted.

Still wearing the pitying expression, Vere opened the door and very gently helped her out. "Do get some sleep, Miss Grenville," he said solicitously. "Rest your troubled brain. And if you don't recover your reason by morning, be sure to send for a doctor."

Before she could frame a retort, he gave her a light shove toward her door.

Then, "Crockford's," he told the driver, and quickly re-entered the hackney. As he pulled its door shut, Vere saw her glance back. She flashed him a cocksure smile before turning and sauntering, hips swaying, to the drab house's entrance.

Lydia had a natural talent for mimicry that allowed her to slip easily into another's personality and mannerisms. According to Ste and Effie, Lydia's father had possessed similar abilities. He'd failed as a thespian, apparently, because theatrical success required hard work as well as aping skills, and all he worked hard at was drinking, gaming, and whoring.

She'd put the gift to better use. It helped her capture on paper with vivid accuracy the personalities of those she wrote about.

It had also helped her develop fairly quickly a degree of camaraderie with her male colleagues. Her rendition of Lord Linglay's speech in the House of Lords months earlier had won her an invitation to her fellow writers' Wednesday night drinking bouts at the Blue Owl tavern. Nowadays, the weekly gatherings were considered incomplete if Grenville of the *Argus* wasn't there to do one of her hilarious impersonations.

This night, Lydia entertained Tamsin—whose new name, Thomasina Price, was eschewed in private—with a lively re-enactment of the encounter with Ainswood.

They were in Lydia's bedroom. Tamsin sat upon the foot of the bed watching Lydia perform before the fireplace.

Though Lydia's usual audience tended toward the latter stages of intoxication, and Tamsin was sober, she laughed as hard as the men usually did.

At least the girl was amused, Lydia thought as she took her bows. Lydia ought to be as well, but her customary detachment eluded her. It was as though her soul were a house in which nasty things had suddenly taken to crawling out of the woodwork.

Restless and uneasy, she moved to her dressing table, sat, and started unpinning her hair.

Tamsin watched her for a few minutes. Then, "Men are such odd creatures," she said. "And I begin to think the Duke of Ainswood is one of the oddest. I cannot quite make out what he's about."

"He's one of those people who can't abide peace and quiet," Lydia said. "If there isn't a stir, he has to make one. He constantly picks fights, even with his good friends. I'd thought people exaggerated about his troublemaking. But I've seen for myself. He can't let well enough alone. It wasn't enough to simply put me in the hackney and send me on my way, for instance. He must plague me all the way home as well. I'm not at all surprised that Dain pounded him a while back. Ainswood would try the patience of a saint."

"I had not heard Lord Dain was a saint," Tamsin said with a little chuckle. "From what I can gather, he and the duke are two sides of the same coin."

"That may be, but Ainswood had no business picking a fight with him on his wedding night." Lydia scowled into the small mirror. "The brute might have considered Lady Dain's feelings at least."

She didn't know why she was still so outraged about the mill in Amesbury.

Dain was nothing to her except a very distant relative. Her mother had come from a lowly cadet branch of the Ballisters, and they'd ceased to admit her existence once she had married John Grenville. So far as Lydia knew, no living person was aware of her connection to the Ballisters, and she was determined to keep it that way. The trouble was, she couldn't keep herself from caring about Dain, though he was, as Tamsin said, Ainswood's match in wickedness.

Lydia had stood outside St. George's Church, Hanover Square, on Dain's wedding day. Like her fellow journalists, she'd come only for the story. But when Dain had emerged from the church with his bride, his ebony eyes glowing in a most unsatanic way while his lady looked up so lovingly into his dark, harsh countenance . . . Well, the long and short of it was, Lydia had come perilously near bawling—in public, amid a crowd of her fellow reporters, no less.

It was absurd, but she'd felt an aching affection for him ever since, and an even more ludicrous protectiveness.

She'd been furious with Ainswood when she'd heard how he'd spoiled Dain's wedding night with the stupid brawl, and the anger lingered, against all reason.

Tamsin's voice broke into her thoughts. "But the duke was highly intoxicated, wasn't he?"

"If he could keep on his feet and utter coherent sentences, he couldn't have been as drunk as people seem to believe," Lydia said. "You have no idea the capacity such men have for liquor, especially overgrown louts like Ainswood." Her eyes narrowed. "He was only pretending to be blind drunk. Just as he pretends to be stupid."

"Yes, and that's what I meant about finding his behavior so odd," Tamsin said. "He isn't in the least inarticulate. Obviously, it wants a very quick intelligence to keep up verbal sparring with you, Lydia. If that had been a stupid man in the carriage, I'm sure you would have tied his tongue in knots. Instead . . ." She paused, frowning. "Well, it's difficult to say who won tonight's war of words."

"It was a draw." Lydia took up her brush and angrily dragged it through her hair. "He had the last word, but that was only because of the push he gave me before I could answer. And shoving me was so childish, I could scarcely keep a straight face, let alone trust myself to say anything without going off into whoops."

"Oh, look what you're doing!" Tamsin cried. "You'll be tearing out clumps of hair and making red welts in your skin." While she spoke, she came off the bed and crossed to the dressing table. "Let me do it."

"You're not my maid."

Tamsin took the brush from her. "If you're vexed with His Grace, you should not take it out on your own scalp."

"He let Crenshaw get away," Lydia said tightly. "And now he'll make himself scarce, the swine, and Mary Bartles will have to go home and be treated like filth. She isn't like the others—"

"I know, you told me," Tamsin said.

"She isn't used to hard treatment," Lydia went on angrily, despite the soothing strokes of the brush. "Men are so despicable. He will get away without doing a dratted thing for the poor girl."

"Perhaps the duke will speak to him," Tamsin said.

Lydia jerked away from the brush. "What the devil does he

care?" she cried. "I told you what he said after reading Mary's note. He went straight back to provoking me."

"Perhaps his pride would not allow—"

"I know all about his manly pride." Lydia left her chair and paced to the fireplace and back. "He saw his chance to get even with me tonight for what happened in Vinegar Yard. By now he's probably guzzled a dozen bottles of champagne celebrating his great victory over Lady Grendel. All he cared about was showing his friends I wasn't too big for *him* to handle—lifting me straight up off the pavement and carrying me halfway to the next street as though I weighed nothing. I struggled with him all the way to the hackney and the man wasn't even *winded,* curse him."

And her stupid heart had melted, and her brain with it, because he was so big and strong. Gad, it was enough to make one retch. She couldn't *believe* the rubbishy notions she'd got into her head.

"Then, after he's emptied Crockford's wine cellars and dropped several thousand pounds at the gaming tables," she fumed, "he'll stagger out of the club and into a high priced brothel in the neighborhood."

And he would take a harlot into his powerful arms, and nuzzle her neck and—

I don't care, Lydia told herself.

"He'll forget I exist, big and obnoxious as I am," she stormed, pacing on. "And so he's bound to forget all about a scrap of a note from a girl he probably believes *asked* for ruination. As though the child had any idea men could be so treacherous."

"Indeed, it's most unfair that the woman is punished and the man is admired for his virility," Tamsin said. "But we shan't let her be punished. I know you must attend an inquest tomorrow, but I can go to Bridewell—"

Lydia stopped short. "You most certainly cannot."

"I'll take Susan. All you need do is tell me how to get Mary and her baby out. If there's a fine to pay, you must take it out of my wages."

Tamsin advanced, took the bemused Lydia's arm, and led her back to the dressing table. "They can share my room until we contrive suitable arrangements for them. But the first priority is to get them out. Her week is up on Thursday, isn't it? And tomorrow is Wednesday." She tugged Lydia down onto the chair. "Write down what I must do, and I'll set out tomorrow morning. Where is your notebook?"

"By gad, what a managing creature you are turning out to be," said Lydia. But she reached into her pocket obediently—and somewhat amused at her docile obedience to a girl half her size and nearly ten years younger.

Lydia found the notebook in her pocket but not the pencil. She must have dropped it in the hackney. "There's a pencil in the drawer of the nightstand," she told Tamsin.

The girl quickly retrieved the pencil.

Lydia took it, then looked up to meet her companion's steady gaze. "Are you sure, my dear?"

"I managed to get from the other end of England to London on my own," Tamsin said. "And I only got into a scrape here because I couldn't see. This time, I promise not to remove my spectacles for anything. And I'll have Susan as a bodyguard. And I shall be so happy," she added earnestly, "to do something useful."

In six days it had become clear that Tamsin liked to be useful. The time had also proved her to be no fool.

A pity, Lydia thought as she began to write, the same couldn't be said for herself.

Early Wednesday morning, a hackney bearing Adolphus

Crenshaw, Mary Bartles, and the infant Jemmy drove away from Bridewell prison.

Bertie Trent should have departed at the same time, but he had fallen into a state of abstraction, which at the moment caused him to mutter, "Not Charles Two but somethin' to do with him. Only, What? is the question."

A short, feminine shriek broke into his cogitations, and he looked up to see an enormous black mastiff bearing down upon him, with a smallish, bespectacled female in tow.

The female was trying to slow the dog down. She might as well try slowing down a stampeding elephant, Bertie thought. Since she was having a hard time staying on her feet, he advanced to assist. He caught the dog by the collar, and she promptly turned on him, growling and baring her teeth.

Bertie gazed at her reproachfully. "Now, what did I do that you want to tear my head off? Ain't you had your breakfast yet?"

"Grrrrrrrrr," said the dog, backing toward the girl.

Bertie cautiously released the collar. "Oh, that's it, is it? Well, I ain't going to hurt her. It's only that you was pulling too hard on account of not knowing your own strength, my gal."

The mastiff paused in her growling to eye him warily.

Eyeing her in the same way, Bertie presented his gloved hand. The dog sniffed it, grumbled something to herself, and sat down.

Above the canine's huge head, Bertie met the girl's startled gaze. Behind the very little pair of spectacles perched on her tiny nose was a pair of very big brown eyes.

"Oh, I say, that were you, weren't it, in Vinegar Yard the other day!" Bertie exclaimed. "Only you wasn't wearin' gogglers then. I hope the tall gal didn't get in an accident afterwards and knock somethin' loose in your eyeballs."

The girl stared at him for a moment. "I'm shortsighted," she said. "I wasn't wearing them the—er—last time because they'd been broken. Miss Grenville was so kind as to have them repaired." She paused. "You were there when she rescued me, it seems. I thought you looked familiar, but I couldn't be sure. Without my spectacles, the world is rather a blur."

"She kept you, then." Bertie nodded approvingly. "Well, speak of the devil. I were thinkin' about her this minute. I seen her last night and she put me in mind of somebody, only I can't think who it is. Charles Two keeps comin' into my brain box, though it beats me why."

"Charles Two?" The girl stared very hard at him.

"Not the one they took the head off of, but the next one, when the fire was."

She stared some more. Then she said, "Ah, King Charles II. Perhaps it's because Miss Grenville is so majestic."

"Woof," said the dog.

Absently Bertie petted her.

"The dog's name is Susan," the girl said.

Bertie remembered his manners then and introduced himself. He learned the girl was Miss Thomasina Price, and she'd become Miss Grenville's hired companion.

After the introductions, she turned her keen gaze upon the building behind him. Her brow creased. "It isn't very welcoming, is it?" she said.

"Not the jolliest place I ever been in," said Bertie.

But it had to be less jolly for the girl Crenshaw had made the baby with—which was how Bertie had put the matter to the man last night.

After Ainswood had gone off to wrestle with Miss Grenville, Bertie had taken Crenshaw to a public house for a drink—"bein' ambushed by females bein' hard on the nerves," as Bertie had told him.

Finding a sympathetic ear, Crenshaw had poured out his troubles. At the end, though, Bertie pointed out that facts were facts, however disagreeable, and the fact was, the man was accused of fathering a bastard, and they had to look into it, didn't they?

And so Bertie had come with him to Bridewell this morning, where it became clear that Crenshaw was guilty as charged. Then there was a good deal of blubbering and the upshot was, Crenshaw said he'd take care of Mary and Jemmy. And that was that.

Though many wouldn't think so, Bertie could put two and two together. Here was Miss Price, companion of Miss Grenville, who had ambushed Crenshaw on Mary Bartles's account last night. There was Bridewell behind him, where Mary had been confined.

"You wouldn't be here to spring a gal and a baby from the Pass-Room, by any chance?" he asked. "Because if it's the ones Miss Grenville was in such a lather about last night, you can tell her Crenshaw came and got 'em. I were with him, and they went off not a quarter hour ago, the three of 'em, and —By Jupiter, what's he doing up at this hour?"

The girl turned in the direction Bertie was looking. The Duke of Ainswood was indeed up and about, though he hadn't come in, Jaynes had said, until daybreak—and drunk as a wheelbarrow.

Which would explain, Bertie thought, why His Grace was looking like six thunderclouds at once.

Though it took Vere a moment to place the girl, he recognized the black mastiff immediately. He would have turned and gone in the opposite direction then, because if the dog was here, the gorgon must be. However, the animal was staring fixedly at Vere, her teeth bared, and she was emitting a low, steady snarl. If Vere made an exit now, it would look as though she'd scared him off.

So he advanced and coolly gazed at the growling canine. She was splendidly muscled under the glossy black coat, and unusually large for a female. "I see she wasn't the runt of the litter," he said. "And such a charming personality she has."

The mastiff strained at the leash. Trent grabbed her collar. "Grrrrrrr," said the dog. *"Grrrrrrrrrr."*

"As amiable as her mistress," Vere went on above the hostile commentary. "Who has no business, by the way, leaving her puppy in the keeping of a slip of a girl who obviously can't control her. But that's typical of Miss Grenville's irresponsible—"

"Miss Price, this here's Ainswood," Bertie broke in. "Ainswood, Miss Price. And this one who's tryin' to tear my arm out of the socket is Susan. Beautiful mornin', ain't it? Miss Price, why don't I hail a hackney for you, and you can go back and tell Miss Grenville the good news."

Trent dragged the snarling mastiff away. Miss Price bobbed a hasty curtsy and followed. A short while later, girl and dog were safely tucked into a hackney.

When Trent came back, he gave Vere a searching look. "Why don't we go somewheres and find you some hair of the dog that bit you?" he said. "You ain't lookin' exactly flourishin' this mornin', Ainswood, if you don't mind my sayin' so."

"I already had Jaynes telling me how I look, thank you." Vere started down the street. "If I hadn't stayed in Crockford's forever waiting for you last night, I shouldn't have been obliged to swill a vat of bad champagne and listen to a lot of morons calling me Beowulf."

The truth was, Vere had been awaiting Crenshaw there in

order to complete the job the Amazon had started.

Thou shalt support thy bastards was the commandment the Mallorys substituted for the ones about not coveting others' wives and not committing adultery. Even Dain—who wasn't a Mallory, had no conscience to speak of, and lived entirely by his own rules—supported his illegitimate offspring.

Confronted by Mary's note, Crenshaw should have puffed out his chest and said, "By gad, I seem to be a father again. Much obliged for the information, Miss Grenville. I'll toddle down to Bridewell and collect them first thing tomorrow."

Then Miss Attila the Hun Grenville would have gone away, swaying her arrogant rump, and Vere wouldn't have seen her, let alone tangled with her and had to listen to her sarcasm and keep his hands to himself the whole aggravating way to the dragon's lair.

But Crenshaw hadn't done what he should, and hadn't turned up at Crockford's to get pummeled properly, and all those bottles of champagne hadn't been enough to flood away the aggravation.

Now, just in case Vere hadn't been plagued and goaded enough last night or didn't have cannon blasts going off in his head at present on account of getting up at an ungodly hour, Miss Guiding Light of Civilization would learn he'd come to Bridewell and would have no trouble figuring out why. And she'd think she'd won. Again.

"I should've asked one of the fellows to tell you not to wait for me," Trent said apologetically. "But I didn't figure you was comin' back, bein' more agreeably engaged for the night."

Vere stopped short and stared at him. "*Agreeably* engaged? With Lady Grendel? Have you lost your mind?"

Trent shrugged. "I thought she were deuced handsome."

Vere recommended walking. Only Bertie Trent, he told

himself, would imagine the Duke of Ainswood had made off with the blue-eyed dragoness for purposes of dalliance. The thought had never crossed the minds of the men with whom Vere had spent the evening. They thought—and rightly—that it would make as much sense to bed a crocodile.

It was merely one of the perverse jokes of the malign powers ruling his life that she should possess a long, lusciously feminine body instead of the humpbacked, shriveled, and scaly one that would have complemented her personality.

That's what he'd told himself through bottle after bottle last night, and what he'd told himself when he came home and couldn't sleep.

That's what he'd told himself this morning when he spotted the dog and his heart began to pound, even while he prepared to turn away to avoid meeting its owner.

And that was what he'd told himself moments ago, when he'd discovered the dragoness wasn't nearby and something mortifyingly like disappointment had entered his heart.

He told himself so again, for the troublesome feelings lingered there yet . . . under the breast pocket of his waistcoat . . . where he kept the stump of a pencil she'd left behind last night.

4

Entering the Blue Owl on this chill, damp night was like descending into the infernal regions.

Vere was used to inns and taverns filled with raucous, drunken men. Those, however, were normal human beings.

The Blue Owl was filled with writers, and the din of their voices was beyond anything he'd ever encountered in his life.

So was the smoke, roiling through the rooms like the heavy fog outside rolling in from the Thames. Every single customer in the place had a pipe or cigar in his mouth.

As Vere turned into the hall leading from the bar parlor, he half expected to see leaping flames, and the Old Harry poised on cloven hoofs in their midst.

But the forms Vere saw were unquestionably mortal. Under a lamp whose light the enveloping smoke had turned a sickly greyish yellow, a pair of young, reed-thin men shouted in each other's ears.

Beyond them a door stood open, from which clouds of smoke occasionally billowed forth, along with thunderous roars of laughter.

As Vere neared, the roar was subsiding to semideafening merriment, and above that noise he heard someone bellow, "Another! Do another!" Others took up the cry.

When he came to the threshold, Vere saw gathered about a few tables a crowd of some thirty men, most sprawled upon chairs and benches, a few slumped against walls. Though the smoke was thickest here, he saw her clearly enough. She stood before the great hearth, and the firelight behind sharply outlined her stern black attire.

The drama of her costume had not struck him before. It did so forcibly now. Perhaps it was the smoke and hellish noise. Perhaps it was her hair. She'd left off her bonnet, and without it she seemed troublingly unprotected, too exposed. Her thick hair, a soft pale gold, was coming loose from the untidy knot at the nape of her white neck. The tumbled coiffure softened her starkly beautiful features, made her look so young, so very young. A girl.

Above the neck.

Below was the dramatic contrast of her black armor, with the line of buttons sternly marching from waist to chin, ready to defeat and destroy all invaders.

He'd undone those buttons, again and again, night after night, in his dreams.

He wondered how many men here imagined undoing them.

All, naturally, since they were men.

She was the only woman, and there she was, parading herself in front of this mob of low-minded scribblers, every last one of whom was picturing her naked, in every lewd position known to the human species.

He watched her move forward to lean over one of the drunkards and talk to him while he gaped at her bodice.

Vere's hands fisted at his sides.

Then she moved away, and he saw she had a wine bottle in one hand and a cigar in the other. She'd taken only a few steps when he realized she was foxed. She swaggered unsteadily toward a group of men to her left, then paused, swaying, to direct a drunken leer at one of them.

"Big, yes, but not up to my weight," she said, her voice carrying easily over the hubbub. "I make her at five and three-quarter feet. And ten stone, stripped. Which I should pay fifty guineas to see, by the way."

It took Vere a moment to place the words, then another to place the voice, which wasn't hers. And because the audience exploded into laughter, it took him another moment to believe his ears.

Those were his words. In Vinegar Yard.

But that could not be . . . *his* voice?

"As much as fifty?" someone called out. "I didn't know you could count so high, Your Grace."

She stuck the cigar in the corner of her mouth and cupped her hand to her ear. "Was that a mouse squeaking I heard? Or was it—By gad, it *is*. It's little Joey Purvis. And here I thought you were still in the asylum."

It was something eerily like Vere's voice, deep and slurred with drink, coming out of her ripe mouth. And those were his gestures. It was as though his soul had entered this woman's body.

He stood frozen, riveted upon her, while the audience's laughter faded to the edges of his consciousness.

She withdrew the cigar from her mouth and beckoned to the heckler with it. "Want to know if I can count, do you? Well, come along, lad, and I'll teach you how I count teeth —while you pick yours up from the floor. Or would you rather a chancery suit on the nob? You know what that is, don't you, my little innocent? It's when I hold your head in place under one arm while I punch it in with the other."

There was little laughter this time.

Vere dragged his gaze from her to the audience.

Every head had turned toward the doorway where he stood.

When he looked back again, his impersonator's blue glance flicked over him. Evincing not the smallest quiver of

81

discomfiture, she raised the bottle to her lips and drank. Then she set the bottle down. After wiping her mouth with the back of her hand, she acknowledged him with a slight dip of her head. "Your Grace."

He made himself grin. Then he lifted his hands and clapped. The room grew quieter still, until the only sound was the steady slap of his palms.

She planted the cigar between her teeth again, doffed an imaginary hat, and made him an exaggerated bow.

For an instant he forgot where he was, as his mind darted from the present and caught on a memory. Something so familiar, but from long ago. He'd seen this before. Or experienced it.

But the feeling vanished as swiftly as it had come.

"Well done, m'dear," he said coolly. "Vastly amusing."

"Not half so amusing as the original," she answered, boldly eying him up and down.

Ignoring the heat her brazen survey generated, he laughed and, amid scattered applause, strode toward her. As he made his way through the crowd, he saw her beautiful countenance settle into a harder expression, while her evil mouth curled into the smallest fraction of a smile.

He'd seen that coolly mocking look before, but this time he didn't quite believe it. Perhaps it was the smoke and the sickly light, but he thought what flickered in her eyes was uncertainty.

And there again he discerned the girl within the beautiful monstrosity. And he wanted to pick her up and carry her away from this infernal place, away from these drunken swine with their roving eyes and lecherous thoughts. If she must mock and ridicule him, he thought, let her do it for him only.

. . . *you didn't want me to hit anyone else but you.*

He shook off the memory of her infuriating words along

with the absurd sense of foreboding they stirred, as they'd done last night.

"I've only one small criticism," he said, pausing a pace away from her.

She lifted an eyebrow.

About them he heard the low murmur of voices. A cough here. A belch there. Yet he'd no doubt their onlookers listened avidly. They were newsmen, after all.

"The cigar," he said. He frowned down at the one resting between her long, slightly ink-stained fingers. "The cigar is all wrong."

"You don't say!" She frowned down at it as well, mimicking his expression. "But this is a Trichinopoli cheroot."

From an inner pocket of his coat, he withdrew a slim silver cigar case. He opened it and held it out to her. "As you can see, these are longer and thinner. The tobacco's color indicates a higher quality. Do take one."

She shot him a quick glance, then shrugged, tossed her cheroot into the fire, and took one of his. She rolled it between her graceful fingers. She sniffed it.

It was a cool enough performance, but Vere was near enough to see what others couldn't: the barely discernible pink tinting the curve of her cheekbones, the quickened rise and fall of her bosom.

No, she was not so fully in command of herself as she made others believe. She was not so case-hardened and cynical and impudently self-assured as she seemed.

He was strongly tempted to lean in closer and discover whether the hint of a blush would deepen. The trouble was, he'd already caught her scent, and that, he'd discovered last night, was a mantrap.

He turned away from her and toward the audience, some of whom had found their tongues, which they employed in obligatory ribald witticisms about the cigar.

"I beg your pardon for the interruption, gentlemen," Vere said. "Do carry on. The drinks are on me."

Without a backward glance—as though he'd forgotten her already—he sauntered out the way he'd come.

He'd come this way, into this hellhole of a tavern in Fleet Street, intending to erase any wrong impressions she might be entertaining about his appearance at Bridewell this morning.

He'd planned to make a great production of returning her pencil—before an audience of nosy scribblers—while indicating with suitable innuendoes that the writing instrument wasn't all she'd lost in the hackney last night.

By the time he was done, she'd be convinced beyond any doubt that he was the obnoxious, conceited, conscienceless debauchee everyone—and rightly—believed he was. A few more hints would suffice to convince her that he'd only recently emerged from a bawdy house in the neighborhood when he'd come upon Trent and Miss Price, by which time His Grace had altogether forgotten Mary Bartles existed.

Consequently, it was logically impossible he'd come to obtain her release and send her to his man of business to make whatever arrangements were necessary to get her the hell out of London and settled comfortably so he wouldn't have to hear about her ever again or think about her and her bedamned sick baby.

If any good deeds had been done, Vere would have made clear, Bertie Trent alone was responsible.

As plans went, it had been a good one, especially considering he'd devised it while in the throes of a near-death experience, thanks to the swill Crockford passed off as champagne and a grand total of about twenty-two minutes' sleep.

But Vere had forgotten this very good plan the instant he'd

paused in the doorway and discerned the girl under the touseled mop of golden hair.

Now, recalling the faint blush and the quickened breathing, he abandoned the plan altogether.

He'd mistaken her. She was not, quite, what she made the world believe she was. She was not, quite, immune to him. The fortress was not impregnable. He'd perceived a chink. And being what he was—obnoxious, conceited, conscienceless, et cetera, et cetera—he was duty bound to get inside, if he had to dismantle her defenses brick by brick.

Or rather, he amended while his mouth curled into a dangerous smile, *button by button.*

Blakesleigh, Bedfordshire

On the Monday following Lord Ainswood's encounter with Miss Grenville at the Blue Owl, the Ladies Elizabeth and Emily Mallory, ages seventeen and fifteen respectively, were reading all about it in the pages of the *Whisperer.*

They were not supposed to be reading the scandal sheet. They were not allowed to peruse even the respectable newspapers that arrived daily at Blakesleigh. Their uncle, Lord Mars, allotted time every day during which he read aloud those portions he deemed fit for innocent ears. His ears, and his eyes as well, were not so innocent, for he'd been a politician all of his adult life. Privately, he read everything, including the scandal sheets.

The paper the young ladies were studying late this night, by the light of the fire in their bedroom, had been liberated from a large stack of periodicals belowstairs, awaiting the rag and bottle collector.

Like others liberated before, this one would be consigned to the flames as soon as they had gleaned as much as they could about their guardian's doings.

Their guardian was the seventh Duke of Ainswood. They were Charlie's daughters, Robin's sisters.

The firelight at present made fiery threads in the pair of auburn heads bent over the paper. When they finished reading the accounts of their guardian's encounter with Miss Grenville at Crockford's and the Blue Owl, matching pairs of sea-green eyes met, and both youthful countenances wore the same expression of mingled perplexity and amusement.

"Obviously something interesting happened in the hackney when he 'escorted' her from Crockford's," said Emily. "I told you Vinegar Yard wasn't the end of it. She knocked him on his arse. That had to get his attention."

Elizabeth nodded. "And obviously, she's pretty. I'm sure he wouldn't have tried to kiss her if she wasn't."

"Clever, too. I wish I had seen how she did that trick. I understand the pretending-to-faint part, and I can picture the uppercut, but I still can't picture how she dropped him."

"We'll figure it out," Elizabeth said confidently. "We simply have to keep trying."

"I'm not going to try smoking cigars," Emily said, making a face. "Not with Uncle John's cheroots, at any rate. I did it once and thought I should never eat again. I cannot think how she did it without puking all over Cousin Vere."

"She's a journalist. Only think of the filthy places she must enter to get her stories. She can smoke cigars because she has a strong stomach. If you had one, you wouldn't get sick."

"Will she write about him, do you think?"

Elizabeth shrugged. "We'll have to wait and find out. The next *Argus* comes out the day after tomorrow."

It wouldn't arrive at Blakesleigh, however, until Thursday at the earliest. Then it would pass through several hands, including the butler's, before it joined the stack of discards.

They both knew they must wait at least a week after its arrival. Their Uncle John never read aloud from the *Argus*, not even the fictional *Rose of Thebes*. Its hoydenish—and that was putting it mildly—heroine might have an unfortunate effect upon the suggestible minds of young ladies.

He would have been appalled if he had realized how closely the two young daughters of his wife's brother identified with the fictional Miranda. It was just as well, then, that he didn't know they considered the wicked Diablo the hero of the story, else Lord Mars would have concluded their minds were disordered by grief, and sent for a physician.

But Elizabeth and Emily had learned very young to live with heartache. They had grieved hard with each loss, and raged, too, because their father had told them it was natural to feel angry.

In time, the rage eased, and the painful grief subsided into quiet sorrow. Now, two years after losing their beloved father and nearly eighteen months after the death of the "baby" brother they'd doted upon, their natural zest for life was returning.

The world was no longer uniformly black. There were dark moments, to be sure, but there was sunshine as well. And one bright beam of sunshine was their guardian, whose doings afforded no end of vicarious excitement in what, at Blakesleigh, was a stultifyingly tame existence.

"I'll wager anything that half the letters Aunt Dorothea gets from her friends are about him," Elizabeth said, after a long sigh about the waiting period.

"I doubt the gossips know any more than the *Whisperer* does. They get everything secondhand. Or thirdhand." Emily looked at her sister. "I'm not sure Papa would approve of our nosing about in Aunt Dorothea's correspondence box. We should not think of it."

"I'm not sure he'd approve of no one telling us anything about our own guardian," said Elizabeth. "It's disrespectful of Papa, who named him guardian, isn't it? Remember how he would read his friends' letters, and laugh, and say, 'Only listen to what your Cousin Vere has done this time, the rascal.' "

Emily smiled. " 'A hellion,' he'd say. 'A true Mallory hellion, like your grandpa and his brothers.' "

" 'The last of the old, true breed,' " Elizabeth softly quoted her father. " 'Vere, as in *veritas*.' "

" 'Aylwin—formidable friend.' He was a friend to Robin, wasn't he?"

"And formidable." Elizabeth's eyes glistened. "They couldn't stop him. They kept us out when Robin was dying, because they were all afraid. But not Cousin Vere." She took her sister's hand. "He was true to Robin."

"We shall be true to him."

They smiled at each other.

Elizabeth put the *Whisperer* into the fire.

"Now, as to those letters," she said.

"Not so tight, drat you," Lydia snapped. "The thing's hard enough to move in. You needn't make it impossible to breathe in."

The thing in question was a corsetlike device ingeniously designed to transform a womanly shape into a manly one.

The person Lydia snapped at was Helena Martin.*

In the old days, when she and Lydia had played together in the London slums, Helena had a highly successful career as a thief. Nowadays, she was an even more successful courtesan.

* See *Captives of the Night*, Avon Books, © 1994.

The friendship had survived years of separation as well as changes in vocation.

At present they were in the elegantly cluttered dressing room of Helena's quietly expensive residence in Kensington.

"It must be tight," Helena answered, "unless you want your manly chest going in one direction while the rest of you goes another." She gave the lacing knot a final, brutal yank, then stepped away.

Lydia surveyed her reflection in the glass. Thanks to the contraption, she now had a chest like a pigeon's. The look was ultra-fashionable. Many men padded their chests and shoulders and squeezed their waists with corsets to achieve it. Except Ainswood. The manly form under his garments owed nothing to artifice.

For about the thousandth time in the week since the encounter at the Blue Owl, Lydia pushed his image from her mind.

She stepped away from the mirror and dressed. With the device secured, the rest of the masculine costume she quickly donned fit satisfactorily.

Months ago Helena had worn the ensemble to a masquerade and fooled everyone. Thanks to a few alterations—Helena was smaller—Lydia expected similar success, though she wasn't going to a masquerade.

Her destination was Jerrimer's, a gambling hell in a quiet way off St. James's Street. She had told Macgowan that she wanted to write a story about the place, the kind her female readers hungered for: a woman's inside view of a world normally forbidden to them—to the respectable ones, at any rate.

This was true. It wasn't the only reason, though, and it wasn't the reason Lydia had chosen Jerrimer's.

She'd heard rumors that the place did a side trade in stolen goods. Since none of her informants had thus far learned anything about Tamsin's keepsakes from the usual fences, it made sense to try other sources.

Tamsin had not agreed that it made sense. "You've already wasted a fortnight looking for my jewelry," she'd chided Lydia this evening. "You have much more important issues to pursue, on behalf of people who truly need help. When I think about Mary Bartles, I'm thoroughly ashamed of the tears I shed over a lot of stones and metal."

Lydia had assured her that the main project was getting the gambling hell story. If she happened upon news of the jewelry in the process, so much the better, but she would not actively pursue the matter.

Not that one could "actively pursue" much of anything in a stiff cage of buckram and whalebone, she thought as she turned to inspect the back of her disguise in the glass.

"You'll be in a good deal of trouble if anyone discovers you're not a man," Helena said.

Lydia moved to the dressing table. "It's merely a gambling club. The customers heed nothing but the cards, dice, or roulette wheel. And the owners and employees will be watching their money." From the jumbled assortment of cosmetics, scent bottles, and jewelry she unearthed the cigar Ainswood had given her and tucked it into an inside pocket. Looking up, she met Helena's worried gaze. "I was in more danger interviewing prostitutes in the Ratcliffe Highway, yet you weren't anxious then."

"That was before you began behaving so oddly." Helena moved to the chiffonier, upon which the maid had set a tray bearing a brandy decanter and two glasses. "Until very recently, you controlled your temper better. And used more finesse in handling those who dared disagree with you." She lifted the decanter and poured. "Your dust-up with Crenshaw, on the other hand, reminds me of the fight you had with a street arab because he called Sarah names and made her cry. You were eight years old at the time."

Lydia approached to take the glass Helena held out to her. "I overreacted with Crenshaw, perhaps."

"Thwarted desire can make one overemotional," Helena said with a small smile. "I've been irritable myself these last few weeks. I usually am, between lovers."

"I'll admit my desire to do murder to certain persons is thwarted by the present penal codes."

"I meant sexual desire, as you well know," Helena said. "The instinct to mate. And reproduce."

Lydia drank, eyeing her friend over the glass's rim.

"Ainswood is exceedingly handsome," Helena went on. "He has brains as well as brawn. Not to mention a smile that could make roses bloom in an Arctic winter. The trouble is, he's also the kind of libertine who despises women. We females have but one use, and once used, we're worthless. If he's awakened any thoughts of straying from virtue's path, Lyddy, I recommend you stray with a substitute. You might consider Sellowby. He doesn't hold women in contempt, and you definitely intrigue him. You've only to crook your little finger."

To Lydia's knowledge, no whore in London commanded a higher price than Helena did, and for very good reason. She could size up a man in an instant and respond accordingly, becoming the woman of his dreams. Her advice was not to be taken lightly.

Lydia couldn't consider the recommended substitute, however, because she knew why Lord Sellowby was "intrigued" with her.

London's champion gossip had noticed Lydia among the

crowd of journalists camped in front of St. George's on Dain's wedding day. Days later, Sellowby had told Helena about glimpsing a female who "might have stepped out of the ancestral portrait gallery at Athcourt." Athcourt, in Devon, was the home of the Marquess of Dain. Lydia had given Sellowby a very wide berth since then. A close look at her might lead him to make inquiries at Athcourt and dig up what her pride demanded remain buried.

"Sellowby's out of the question," Lydia told her friend. "A Society gossip and a journalist are bound to be competitors. In any case, this isn't a good time for me to get involved with any man. While scandal does sell magazines, whatever small influence I exercise over public opinion would vanish if I were known to be a fallen woman."

"Then maybe you should find another line of work," Helena said. "You're not getting any younger, and it would be a great waste—"

"Yes, love, I know you wish to be helpful, but can we discuss whatever's wasted and thwarted at another time?" Lydia emptied her glass and set it down. "It's growing late, and I do need to get back to Town."

She put on her hat, gave herself a final check in the mirror, picked up her walking stick, and started for the door.

"I'll be waiting up," Helena called after her. "So make sure you come back here and not—"

"Of course I'll come back here." Lydia opened the door. "Don't want the neighbors to see a strange man entering my house in the small hours of the morning, do I? Nor do I want to wake Miss Price or the maids to help me out of this beastly corset. That dubious pleasure will be all yours. I'll expect you to have a nightcap waiting for me."

"Be careful, Lyddy."

"Yes, yes." Lydia turned and threw her a cocky grin.

"Deuce take it, wench. Must you be forever pesterin' and plaguin' a fellow?"

Then she swaggered out, Helena's uneasy laughter trailing behind her.

This Wednesday night, the publishing hacks' gathering at the Blue Owl was a dull affair, for Grenville of the *Argus* was absent.

Joe Purvis was there, though, and returning from the privy when Vere met up with him in the hall.

It should have taken more than one glass of gin to loosen Joe's tongue regarding his co-worker's whereabouts. But the *Argus*'s illustrator was already the worse for drink, which exacerbated his sense of injury.

In the first place, he complained to Vere, the fellows had taken to calling him "Squeaky" ever since last week, when Grenville had pretended to mistake his voice for a mouse's. In the second, she'd as usual managed to hog a plum assignment all to herself.

"I should be at Jerrimer's with her," Joe grumbled, "seeing as it's to be the lead story next issue and wants a cover picture. But Her Majesty says there isn't a gambling hell in London doesn't know my face and I'll give the game away. Like anyone was likely to overlook a Long Meg like her in a poky little hole like that."

Small as Jerrimer's turned out to be, Vere very nearly did overlook her.

It was the cigar that caught his attention.

Otherwise, he would have walked by the young man with little more than a glance, noting only that he was dressed in the style young clerks aspiring to dandyism customarily affected, and seemed to be doing well at roulette. But as he passed behind the fellow, Vere caught a whiff of the cigar, and it stopped him in his tracks.

Only one tobacconist in London sold those particular cheroots. As Vere had pointed out to Mistress Thespian a week ago, they were unusually long and thin. He also could have told her that the tobacco was a special blend, and the limited stock was reserved exclusively for him. At certain social gatherings, among a select group of men who could appreciate them, Vere was more than happy to share.

He had not joined such a gathering in months.

And Joe Purvis had said she'd be here.

Swallowing a smile, Vere moved closer.

Roulette—or roly-poly, as it was commonly known—was all the rage in England.

It was certainly popular in Jerrimer's, Lydia discovered. The roulette room was thick with bodies, not all of them recently washed. Still, the air of the Marshalsea prison had been fouler, like that of many other places she'd known, and the cheroot clamped between her teeth helped mask the worst of the odors. Chewing on it also helped relieve her gnawing frustration while she pretended to watch the wheel.

While she was aware of the heap of counters growing in front of her, they hardly signified, compared to the prize dangling a table's length away.

Coralie Brees stood at the end of that distance.

Ruby drops hung from her ears. A ruby necklace circled her throat and a matching bracelet her wrist.

The set matched Tamsin's description and sketch perfectly.

The small room was packed to suffocation. Amid the general jostling and elbowing, Madam Brees was unlikely to notice the few deft moves that would strip her of her stolen valuables.

The problem was, those particular moves were not within Lydia's range of skills but Helena's, and she was miles away in Kensington.

While knocking the bawd down and ripping the jewelry violently from her poxy body was well within Lydia's repertoire, she knew this was neither the time nor the place for such methods.

Even if she hadn't been wearing a corset that severely hampered movement, she could list several excellent reasons for exercising self-restraint: dark, cramped quarters; no potential allies; a great many potential foes—especially if she were unmasked, which was bound to happen in a brawl—and the unmasking itself, which at best would result in humiliation and at worst severe, possibly fatal, injury.

Yes, it was infuriating to see Tamsin's jewelry adorning London's most villainous bawd. Yes, it made one wild to think of the girl, and her beloved aunt, and what the jewelry represented.

But no, Lydia was not going to let her temper get the better of her again. She most certainly would not let "thwarted desire" for the woman-despising Ainswood turn her into a temperamental eight-year-old.

Thrusting away his image, she made herself focus coolly and calmly on the problem at hand.

The wheel stopped at red, twenty-one.

The croupier, stone-faced, pushed Lydia's winnings toward her. At the same moment, she heard Coralie's shrill stream of oaths.

The procuress had been losing steadily for the last hour. Now, finally, she moved away from the roulette table.

If she was out of money, she might trade in her jewelry as others had done their valuables, Lydia thought. She'd already discovered where those transactions took place.

Swiftly she counted her winnings. Two hundred. Not much by the standards of some clubs—Crockford's, for instance, where thousands were lost in the space of minutes—but perhaps enough to purchase a set of ruby jewelry from a trull with gaming fever.

Lydia started pushing through the crowd.

Intent on keeping her quarry in sight, she reflexively dodged a red-haired trollop who'd tried to attract her notice before, and elbowed aside a pickpocket. What Lydia failed to notice, in her haste to close the distance between her and Coralie, was the boot in the way.

Lydia tripped over it.

A hand clamped on her arm and jerked her upright. It was a large hand with a grasp like a vise.

Lydia looked up . . . into glinting green eyes.

Vere wondered what it would take to crack her polished veneer of composure.

She only blinked once, then coolly withdrew the cigar from her mouth. "By gad, is that you, Ainswood? I haven't seen you in a dog's age. How's the gout? Still troubling you?"

Since he'd already spotted Coralie Brees—along with a pair of burly bodyguards—Vere dared not unmask Miss Sarah Siddons Grenville in the gambling hell.

She kept up the act, and he played along with it while he swiftly escorted her from the premises. Even after they were clear of the place, he kept a firm grip on her arm, and marched her up St. James's Street toward Piccadilly.

She continued to swagger along, the stub of the cheroot—*his* cheroot—clamped between her white teeth, the walking stick swinging from her free hand.

"This is getting to be a habit with you, Ainswood," she said. "Whenever matters are moving along smoothly, you

96

come along to muck them up. I was on a winning streak, in case you didn't notice. Moreover, I was working. Since gainful employment is not within your range of experience, let me explain a bit about basic economics. If magazine writers fail to perform their assignments, there are no articles for the magazine. If there are no articles, the customers won't buy it, because, you see, when they pay for a magazine, they expect it to have writing in it. And when the customers won't pay, the writers don't get paid." She looked up at him. "Am I going too fast for you?"

"You'd stopped playing roulette before I interrupted," he said. "Because you'd decided on a different game. While you were watching the bawd, I was watching you. I've seen that look in your eyes before and know what it bodes: mayhem."

While he spoke, she coolly puffed on the cigar, to all appearances the unflappable young Cit-about-town her costume declared her. He fought an irrational urge to laugh.

"Let me point out something you apparently failed to notice," he went on. "The bawd had a pair of bully boys in attendance. If you'd followed her outside, those brutes would have dragged you into the nearest dark alley and carved you up into very small pieces."

By this time they'd reached Piccadilly.

She tossed away the remains of the cheroot. "You refer to Josiah and Bill, I collect," she said. "I should like to know how anyone who wasn't blind could overlook that pair of gargoyles."

"Your eyesight is hardly reliable. You overlooked *me*." He signaled to a hackney leaving the water stand down the street.

"I trust you're summoning that carriage for yourself," she said. "Because I have an assignment to complete."

"You'll have to assign yourself someplace other than Jerrimer's," he said. "Because you're not going back there. If

I found you out, others might. If, as you suspect, any illegal activities are going on there, those conducting them will make sure Grenville of the *Argus* not only doesn't complete her assignment, but is never heard from again."

"How did you know I was looking for illegal activities?" she demanded. "This assignment was supposed to be a secret."

The hackney pulled up. It was not one of Mr. David Davies's compact new hackney cabriolets but a cumbersome vehicle which had evidently done service as a gentleman's town coach about a century ago. The coachman sat in front, not in back as in the modern cabs. At the back was a narrow platform upon which a pair of footmen—long dead and buried by now—would have stood.

"Where to, gentlemen?" the driver asked.

"Soho Square," Vere said.

"Are you mad?" she cried. "I can't go there in this costume."

"Why not?" He eyed her up and down. "Will you scare your sweet-tempered puppy?"

"Campden Place, Kensington," she told the driver. She yanked free of Vere's grip, adding in lower tones, "You've made your point. I'm not going back to Jerrimer's. If you figured out who I was, any moron might."

"But you live in Soho," he said.

"My clothes are in Kensington," she said. "And my carriage."

"Gentlemen?" the driver called. "If you ain't comin'—"
She stalked to the vehicle, pulled open the door, and climbed in. Before she could shut it, Vere caught the handle.

"It's been a dog's age since I've visited Kensington," he said. "I wonder whether the country air will heal my gout."

"Kensington is very damp at this time of year," she said in

a low, hard voice. "If you want a change of climate, try the Gobi Desert."

"On second thought, maybe I'll travel to a nice, warm brothel." He slammed the door shut and walked away.

5

By the time the hackney passed through the Hyde Park Turnpike, Lydia was well aware she had mainly herself to blame for
this evening's vexations.

At the Blue Owl last week, she'd spotted Ainswood the
instant he came to the doorway. Naturally, her pride
wouldn't let her exit the stage at that point. While only half a
Ballister by birth, she was every inch one by nature. She
couldn't possibly curtail her performance or feel in the least
embarrassed merely because a clodpole of a duke was watching.

Still, she might at least have resisted the inner devil urging
her to make sport of him, and chosen another target. Since,
instead, she had asked for trouble, she should have realized,
when it didn't come then, that it was sure to come sooner or
later. Like her, Ainswood had put on an act. He'd feigned
good humor because he hadn't wanted all those men to think
a mere female could upset him.

Lydia had upset him, though, and he must have returned
to the Blue Owl this evening to get even in some way. There,
someone who'd been at the last *Argus* staff meeting must have
let drink or a bribe loosen his tongue, and told Ainswood
where she was. His Grace had come to Jerrimer's merely to
disrupt whatever she was doing—whether it was work or play
was all the same to him. Then, having wrecked everything, he
could go on his merry, depraved way.

And so, thanks to her own childish behavior—and his

childish spitefulness—she'd lost a chance to get back Tamsin's ruby set.

Meanwhile, Ainswood would be congratulating himself for putting Lady Grendel in her place. He would probably make an amusing anecdote of the event, to entertain the company at the whorehouse he went to.

He would probably still be laughing while he wrapped his powerful arms round a voluptuous tart, and nuzzled her neck and . . .

I don't care, she told herself.

And perhaps the sensible and reasonable part of her truly didn't care what he did with other women, and considered it far better that he'd gone.

The devil inside her cared, though, because that part of her was as wild and wicked and shameless as he was.

And that part of her, at the moment, was making her want to leap from the hackney and hunt him down and tear him from the anonymous harlot's embrace.

That part of her fretted and fumed all the way to Campden Place—not about Tamsin's jewelry or an assignment interrupted, but about the taunting comment with which Ainswood had taken his leave and the way he'd slammed the coach door in Lydia's face.

Between composing a host of crushing setdowns she wished she'd administered and conjuring infuriating scenarios involving His Grace and painted harlots, it took Lydia a moment after the hackney halted to realize where she was.

Hurriedly she disembarked, paid the driver, and started toward Helena's house.

Then she froze, her churning mind belatedly registering what her eyes had taken in: the handsome equipage standing a few yards from the gate.

Helena had a visitor.

And Lydia knew who it was because she'd made it her business to recognize the vehicle, in order to avoid its owner, Lord Sellowby.

She glanced down the street, but the hackney was already beyond hailing distance.

She swore under her breath.

Then, after a furtive glance up at the house windows, she sauntered over to Sellowby's carriage, exchanged pleasantries with his tiger, obtained directions to the nearest public house, and ambled on, ostensibly in that direction.

Standing on the back platform of the ancient hackney for some three miles had not been the most comfortable mode of traveling. The sight before Vere at present, however, made up for the bone-shaking ride.

Since he'd had the presence of mind to disembark while the hackney was slowing, he'd managed to duck into the shadows before his prey emerged. Obviously, she hadn't the smallest suspicion that he'd followed her.

Admittedly, he hadn't had the smallest suspicion he'd be following her to the home of London's priciest courtesan. When the blue-eyed gorgon had said her clothes and carriage were in Kensington, Vere supposed she'd done her costume change at an inn, where her comings and goings would attract little attention. He had envisioned an interesting encounter at the inn.

But this, he decided, promised to turn out to be far more interesting.

From his hiding place in the tall hedges of the garden he was watching her struggle out of her coat. Though the moon wasn't full, it emitted enough light for him to observe the process.

The coat was fashionably snug, and the armor she'd

donned to conceal her shape hampered her movement to a comical degree. After a good deal of hopping, twisting, and jerking about, she finally got out of it and flung it down. Then she pulled off the hat, the wig underneath, and the skullcap under that, revealing the fair hair flattened and wrapped about her head.

She scratched her head.

Vere waited with bated breath for her to unpin her hair. It was thick, he knew, and must be long enough to tumble over her shoulders—and you'd think he was a schoolboy, to stand here breathlessly waiting for such a simple thing, as though he hadn't watched hundreds of women take down their hair and take off their clothes.

She was still fully covered, in shirt and pantaloons, yet his temperature climbed all the same. He told himself the hot reaction arose out of the depravity of what he was doing, hiding in the shadows watching her disrobe.

But she didn't take out so much as one hairpin or take off any more garments. What she did next was creep to the corner of the house, grasp the drainpipe, and swing herself up.

Vere blinked once in disbelief, then ran toward her, heedless of the gravel crunching underfoot.

Starting at the noise, she slipped and fell, landing with a soft thud upon the grass. Before she could scramble up, he grasped her upper arms and hauled her to her feet.

"What in blazes do you think you're doing?" he whispered.

She wrenched free of his grasp. "What does it look like?" She rubbed her bottom. "Plague take you, I might have broken a leg. What the devil do you mean by creeping up on me? You're supposed to be in a brothel."

"I lied," he said. "I can't believe you fell for that old going-to-a-brothel ruse. You didn't even look out the window to make sure I'd gone away."

She didn't try to hide her incredulity. "I don't believe this. You can't have hung on the back of the hackney the whole way."

"It's only three miles," he said.

"Why?" she demanded. "What score are you trying to pay now?"

He gave her a wounded look. "I was not trying to pay any scores. I was consumed by curiosity."

Her eyes narrowed. "About what?"

"How you did it." He let his gaze fall to her manly chest. "It isn't binding, is it? What have you done with your breasts?"

She opened her mouth, then shut it. She looked down at herself, then up at him. Then her jaw set and between her teeth she said, "It's a specially designed corset. The front is shaped like a man's torso. The back is like any other stays."

"Ah. Back lacing."

"Yes. Not in the least interesting. Nothing you haven't seen many hundreds of times before." She turned away and returned to the drainpipe. "If you want to make yourself useful, you could give me a boost up."

"I can't," he said. "I can't aid and abet your burgling a house."

"Since when have you become a champion of law and order?"

"Since you pointed out my failure to provide an example of high moral tone," he said. "I'm studying to become a saint."

"Then study someplace else. I'm not going to steal anything. I only want to get my clothes."

"If Miss Martin has them, why not go to the front door?"

"She has company," she answered in an impatient undertone. "A man. She didn't expect me back so early. My clothes are in the dressing room. The window is open." She pointed upward. "I only need to get in and out without disturbing the lovebirds."

Vere's gaze went to the window, then back to her. "That's a goodish climb."

"I can manage it," she whispered indignantly.

His gaze slid down the pantaloons lovingly hugging her long, shapely legs.

"I'll do it," he said. "Quicker that way."

Some minutes and a short, furious argument later, the Duke of Ainswood was pulling Lydia through the dressing room window. She wouldn't have needed to be pulled if it weren't for the dratted corset, which made it impossible for her to heave herself up from the ledge below.

He slid his arms under her shoulders and hauled her none too gently over the sill, then let her tumble in a heap on the floor.

But Lydia did not break easily, and being pushed and pulled and dropped didn't bother her. If she'd needed delicate treatment, she would not have become a journalist. If he really wanted to injure her, he could do much worse than this. He was cross, that was all, because she'd refused to do it his way.

He had expected her to wait in the garden. As though she had all night to wait while he bumbled about looking for her clothes in the dark, and collided with doors and knocked over furniture in the process, alerting everyone to the intrusion.

Besides, she didn't trust him to try to be discreet. More likely, he'd think it a good joke to break in on Helena and her guest. Lydia could easily picture Ainswood wandering into the bedroom, carrying a handful of undergarments. "Sorry to interrupt, Miss Martin," he'd say, "but could you tell me which of these drawers belong to Miss Grenville?"

The image made Lydia's mouth twitch. Then, recalling who Helena's guest was, she sobered. If Sellowby got a close look at her, a lot of dirty family linen would soon be displayed for the titillation of the public.

She scrambled up from the carpet, thanking heaven it was a thick one. Otherwise, the entire household would have heard the thump when she went down. She went to check the door to the bedroom.

"What the devil are you doing?" came Ainswood's angry whisper. "Can't you keep still?"

Ignoring him, Lydia listened at the door for a moment before cautiously cracking it open. Her anxiety easing, she quickly closed it again. "They're not in the bedroom," she softly informed Ainswood. "They're in the sitting room."

"How disappointing for you. If they'd been considerate enough to fornicate in the bedroom, you might have watched."

"I wish you would be considerate enough to be quiet," she returned. "Can't you find things without all that rustling and snorting?"

"I can't see a bleeding thing. Stay by the window, confound it, so I'll know where you are. Do you want me to trip over you?"

"Why can't you stay at the window and let me look for them?"

"I know what bombazine feels like—what it smells like, curse it. I've been to enough funerals."

Lydia moved to the window, where a feeble shaft of moonlight made a narrow rectangle of visibility. Thickly draped and crammed with garments and furniture, the dressing room was several degrees darker than the outdoors.

She could just barely make out his form, one disturbingly large, blacker shape against the surrounding darkness. She saw him bend and snatch up something, heard him sniff it.

"Found 'em," he whispered. He advanced and shoved them at her. "Let's go."

"You go first," she said. "I'll catch up in a minute. I have to . . . change." And she preferred to do it here, where it was good and *dark*.

There was a silence.

She lifted her chin. "It will be easier to climb down once I get the corset off. I had the deuce of a time getting up, and it'll be harder to climb down." That certainly was true.

Another, longer pause ensued. She hoped the thick corset muffled the erratic thumping of her heart.

"Miss Grenville, you seem to have overlooked a minor detail."

"I can climb in skirts," she assured him. "I've done it many times."

"The corset," he hissed. "It fastens in *back*, remember? How do you propose to get it off?"

For an instant her mind went utterly blank. Then heat shot up her neck and suffused her face. She'd forgotten: Lacing and unlacing this corset was not a one-woman maneuver.

"I'll jump from the ledge." She turned to look down at the garden below. Very far below. And bathed in too much moonlight. "It isn't so very far."

He muttered something under his breath, which she doubted was a prayer. "You're not going to jump," he said evenly. "You are going to step away from the window. Then you will take off the shirt. In the dark. Can you manage that?"

"Of course I—"

"Good. Then I'll undo the bleeding, damned corset—if you can contrive to keep still for two minutes."

Lydia's hands began to sweat.

"Thank you," she said composedly. And very calmly she stepped away from the window and moved to the opposite—and very darkest—corner of the dressing room.

She heard him approach. Felt it.

Clutching the clothing tightly to her stomach, she murmured, "With your vast experience, I'm sure you can unlace a corset in a few seconds." And she would not have time to do anything foolish, she told herself, as her mind dragged up a memory of wild sensations, of heat and power and large, sure hands. She would not listen to any inner devils. She would not make an error she'd spend the rest of her life paying for.

She forced her stiff fingers to relinquish the garments. As quickly as her rigid muscles would let her, she pulled off the shirt.

She swallowed a gasp as his fingers touched her shoulder.

He snatched them away almost in the same instant. "Jesus," he hissed. "You've nothing underneath."

"A man does not wear a chemise."

"You're not a man."

She heard a faint grating sound, as though he was grinding his teeth.

"I have to find the lacing first," he told her, his whisper rough.

He meant that he had to do it by touch, because he couldn't see. She swallowed. "Down," she directed. "Under my right shoulder blade."

His fingers touched her shoulder again and trailed downward, leaving a burning trail of sensation.

He found the place quickly enough, yet even with his hands on the stays instead of her flesh, the heat continued to prickle. A thin thread of moisture trickled between her breasts.

She could feel his warm breath on her neck, on her taut spine, while he unlooped the lacing, systematically working his way down, and the confining garment loosened.

It should have been easier to breathe then, but it wasn't.

When he was halfway down, the corset sagged to her hips, and she couldn't stop herself from grabbing the front and holding it up to shield her breasts.

The hands at her back paused, and her breath jammed in her lungs.

The pause lasted but two pulsebeats before he returned to his work, which he completed with disconcerting efficiency.

He stepped away.

Then what Lydia felt was all too easy to identify, and shame scorched her from the top of her head to the ends of her toes. What had she expected him to do? Go mad with passion for her simply because she was half naked?

He was a rake, a champion libertine. He'd seen hundreds of women completely naked.

While she silently raged at her idiot self, she speedily donned her chemise and mannish shirt, and pulled her skirt up over the pantaloons. Not that there was any point in modesty when he couldn't see and had made it plain that he wasn't interested in seeing. All the same, she felt less vulnerable exposing her hindquarters under the shelter of her skirt.

She got her drawers on, then had to take them off again because she'd pulled them on backward. Swearing under her breath, she got them right—finally—and hastily pulled on and tied her petticoat.

She could hear him breathing—or snorting was more like it—while she continued dressing. The harsh expulsion of breath made it clear he was impatient to be gone.

She quickly shrugged into her spencer. "You can go," she told him. "I have to find my boots."

He uttered a low, guttural sound. It was very like the sound Susan made when she felt ill used: when one denied the greedy creature an extra biscuit, for instance, or ordered her to stop leaping on the maids.

Something in the analogy made Lydia's nerve endings twitch. Ignoring the feeling, she got down on her hands and knees to hunt for her half-boots.

She found them close by, under the sofa wedged against the chiffonier. Before she could get them on, she heard footsteps and Helena's voice approaching.

"I'm sure it's the neighbors' cat," Helena was saying. "Rosa must have left the window open."

Lydia's glance darted to the window, but Ainswood had already moved away. In the next instant, he was down on the carpet next to her.

She heard the doorknob's faint click as it turned.

Lydia hastily scrambled aside, pushed him down, and shoved him under the sofa. She had pulled the deep flounce back into place by the time the door opened fully.

Helena entered. "Here, kitty," she called. Then, after she'd closed the door, her voice dropped to a whisper. "Is that you, Lyddy?"

"Yes."

"I didn't expect you back so early."

"I know. It's all right. Go back to your guest. I'm fine."

Lydia was not fine. A portion of Ainswood's overgrown anatomy pinned down a section of her skirt. She couldn't get up without his moving, too, and given the limited space available, she doubted he could lift a muscle without overturning the sofa.

"Here, kitty," Helena repeated in carrying tones. Then, very softly, she went on, "Do try to be quieter. Sellowby isn't that drunk, and he heard something. Doubtless he suspects

110

I've another man hidden in the house, and is dying to know who it is. You'd make a more agreeable surprise for him. Are you sure you don't want to come out and—"

"He's all yours," Lydia whispered tightly.

"Do you need help with the corset?"

"*No.* I'm nearly dressed. Please go, Helena, before he decides to investigate."

There was a long pause. Lydia hoped Ainswood had sense enough to hold his breath. She couldn't tell. Her heart was thumping too loudly.

"Lydia, I'd better warn you." Helena's whisper held a worried note. "Sellowby said he heard that Ainswood was seen entering the Blue Owl in Fleet Street this evening. Sellowby thinks you've piqued His Grace's interest. Perhaps, to be on the safe side, you ought to contrive assignments far from London for the next few weeks."

Lydia was aware of movement under the sofa. Any minute now, Ainswood would overturn it, she was sure, and rush upon Sellowby to correct the man's assumptions with his fists.

"Yes, of course, but do go," she urged. "I think I hear Sellowby."

It worked. Helena hastened out. "Coming," she called. "It was only the tiresome cat. She . . ."

Lydia didn't listen to the rest. Her attention reverted to Ainswood, who released a pent-up breath. She expected a stream of profanity to follow as he wriggled out from under the sofa—trapping more of her skirt in the process. Instead, she discerned a more ominous sound.

She told herself it couldn't be what she thought it was, and tried to concentrate on untangling her skirt from his limbs. She couldn't, and he wasn't helping.

His shoulders shook, and his chest heaved, and the strangled sounds he emitted confirmed her first suspicions.

She twisted about and clamped her hand over his mouth. "Don't," she whispered furiously. "Don't you dare laugh. They'll hear you."

"Mmmmmmph. Mmmmmmmmmph." Ainswood's mouth moved spasmodically against her hand. She snatched it away.

A slap, she thought frantically. That would—no—too much noise—and he wouldn't feel it. A knee to the groin—no—impossible—she could barely move her legs—but—yes—her hands were free. She made a fist and struck—his belly, drat him—and it was made of brick. Aim lower, she told herself.

Before she could act, he did, and in an instant she was flat on her back, her hand pinned to the carpet and Ainswood on top of her. "Get off me, you—"

His mouth fell upon hers, stifling the words and driving the breath back into her lungs.

She had one hand free, and should have pushed or clawed at him with it, but she didn't. Couldn't.

He'd kissed her before, but that had been in public before a restive audience, and their lips had scarcely met before she recovered her reason.

This time there was no audience to remember, to keep her mind cool and focused. This time there was only darkness and silence and the warm, insistent pressure of his mouth upon hers. She wasn't quick enough reacting, and this time the devil inside her took over.

She couldn't get her mind to think past the potently masculine taste and scent of him. She couldn't rouse her body to struggle against the warmth and hard, muscular power of his. He was so big, so beautifully, warmly big, and his mouth tasted like sin, wild and dark and irresistible.

The hand he held to the carpet curled 'round his, and her

free one, the one she should have fought with, curled and tightened upon his coat, holding him instead. Her mouth clung to his in the same way, silently answering Yes when it should have been No, and following his lead, when he would only lead her to disaster.

She knew this. In the depths of her swamped consciousness she knew right from wrong, safe from dangerous, but she couldn't summon her weapons, her hard-won wisdom. For this dark moment, all she wanted was him.

It lasted but a moment, and a lifetime too long.

He broke away, done with her when she had scarcely begun to comprehend what she wanted from him.

Even then, though hotly aware of her folly, she could still taste the sin of him on her lips and feel the need he'd stirred rippling in the pit of her belly. And when his body lifted from hers, she felt the loss of his warmth and strength and whatever else it was that he made her need. And she felt regret, as well, because she didn't know how to draw him back, so that she could find out what it was she needed and what it was she'd been missing.

From a distance came the tinkle of feminine laughter. Helena's laughter, from two rooms away, where she lay in the embrace of . . . another rake.

Like the tinkle of a bell, it summoned Lydia to sanity. She thought of the career she'd prepared and waited so long for, the small but precious influence she'd gained and could, with diligence, increase. She thought of the women and children whose voice she was.

And she reminded herself what kind of man this was.

The kind of libertine who despises women.

Once used, we're worthless.

"Are you all right?" came Ainswood's rough whisper.

No, she wasn't. She doubted she'd be altogether right for a

long time. Forbidden fruit left a bitter aftertaste.

"Get off my skirt, curse you," she said. "How am I to get up with you sitting on it?"

The relation between Vere and his conscience had never been amicable. For the last year and a half, they had not been on speaking terms.

Consequently, he was far from feeling any pangs of guilt for his plans to seduce Grenville of the *Argus* or entertaining any scruples about how he'd accomplish this. On the contrary, he'd been having a jolly old time, jollier than he'd had in ages. This night's adventures brought back fond memories of long-ago escapades with his two partners in crime, Dain and Wardell.

It had been a long time since Vere had last stolen a ride on the back of a coach or committed absurdities in pursuit of an attractive wench.

And even though matters thereafter had not gone quite as he'd expected, the novelty of the experience made up for the occasional irritation. While climbing in and out of windows for illicit purposes was a familiar activity, this was the first time he'd made a clandestine entry into the home of a known Cyprian.

He'd thought it hilarious that Miss Damn Your Eyes Grenville didn't want her harlot friend to know the depraved Duke of Ainswood was on the premises. As though there were anything this side of the house exploding that could shock Helena Martin.

To make it more amusing, there was Sellowby, also on the premises, suspecting Helena had a man hidden—and Helena thinking she didn't—and the dragoness fretting and twitching the whole time. And there was the added farce of Vere hiding under a sofa when the room was as black as a privy hole, and their hostess couldn't see her own hand in front of her.

He'd nearly choked to death, stifling laughter.

And then . . .

Well, of course. How could he resist? After all the difficulty Madam Dragon had had wriggling into all those layers of underwear and overgarments, Vere couldn't resist showing her how little trouble he'd have taking them off again. After all her fretting about being discovered with him, he thought she ought to have something more interesting to think about.

And there, matters had taken a very odd turn.

In Vinegar Yard, Vere had hardly touched his mouth to hers. This time, he'd settled in for a long, slow siege of a resistance-killing kiss.

And he'd met with the shock of his life.

She didn't know how to kiss.

It had taken a moment for this anomaly to sink in, and before he'd quite digested it, she had caught on to the basics. Meanwhile, he could hardly be unaware of the lushly curving body under his, or the mantrap of scent. And so he had heated far too quickly to quibble with himself about whether or not she was a virgin and whether or not this was supposed to matter to him. And since he hadn't been engaged in any soul-searching, it was very strange that he should pause. But he did, because something . . . bothered him.

That was when he lifted his head and asked, "Are you all right?"

Which was evidently a tactical error, because she pushed him off with surprising strength and got her boots on and her body up off the floor and out the window while he was still trying to understand what had happened.

He had no trouble at the moment, however, comprehending that she was getting away. Pushing everything else from his mind, he swung over the windowsill and swiftly descended.

A quick scan of the garden offering no sign of her, he hurriedly retraced the route she'd taken to get in, through the back gate. In her departing haste, she'd left it ajar, sparing him the trouble and precious seconds of fiddling with the latch.

He ran down the passageway leading to the street, which he reached in time to hear her rapidly retreating footsteps.

A glimpse of skirt told him she'd just turned the next corner.

He picked up his pace and followed . . . and saw his mistake in the half second before the walking stick slammed against his shins.

He heard the crack of splintering bone and felt the pain shaft up his legs and saw the ground come up to meet him, all in the same instant.

6

First he swore.

Then he laughed.

Then he swore some more.

Fists clenched, Lydia stood glaring down at the Duke of Ainswood. For one horrifying moment, she thought she'd done him a serious injury. She should have known better. It would want a herd of stampeding bulls to do this great lout any significant damage.

"Don't expect any sympathy from me," she said. "You can lie there until Judgment Day, for all I care. You've made me break my favorite walking stick, drat you." Not his legs, as she'd feared.

Groaning, he lifted his head. "That was a damned dirty trick," he said. "You *ambushed* me."

"And it wasn't a damned dirty trick you played me in the dressing room?" she returned. "When you knew I dared not make any strong protest? And don't tell me a simple no would have sufficed, because words never suffice with you."

"Can we argue about this later, Grenville?" Releasing a series of low profanities, he laboriously rolled onto his side and heaved himself up onto one elbow. "You might give a fellow a hand up."

"No." Smothering a stab of conscience, she backed away, out of reach. "You interfered with an assignment and could have endangered my life," she said, as much for her unreasonable conscience's enlightenment as his. "You also wrecked my chance to perform a service for a friend. This makes the third time you've complicated everything by blundering in my way. Not to mention you might have cost me my position. If Sellowby had burst into the dressing room and found me in a compromising position with England's most notorious debauchee, he would have spread the news all over London—and I should lose the precious small measure of respect I've earned after months of unremitting labor."

She bent and snatched up the remnants of her walking stick. "I know a great many more dirty tricks than this," she added as she straightened. "Bother me again, Ainswood, and I'll *really* hurt you."

Then, before he could point out the flaws in her sermon, she turned away and strode out of the alley without once looking back.

"Behold, the dragon stalker returneth," Jaynes announced as Vere limped in the door at three o'clock in the morning.

Trent, who'd hurried out into the hall clutching a billiard cue, stood mute, eyeing Vere up and down with a pained expression.

Vere had told them he was going to the Blue Owl this evening, "dragon hunting."

Jaynes had lectured and Trent had babbled and Vere had not heeded a syllable.

Now he saw "I told you so" written plainly on their faces. His coat and trousers were torn and filthy, his face scraped and bruised. He'd fallen face first, hard, and though his nose wasn't broken, it felt as though it was. The same applied to his shins, which throbbed like the very devil.

He managed a grin. "I can't remember when I've had so much fun," he said. "You missed a great lark. When I tell you—"

"I'll have a bath drawn," said Jaynes in martyred tones. "And I suppose I'd better fetch the medicine case."

Vere watched him march away, then turned to his houseguest. "You'll never guess what happened, Trent."

"I reckon not," his guest said sadly.

Vere started limping toward the staircase. "Come along, then, and I'll tell you."

The *Argus* arrived at Blakesleigh on Friday morning. Not until the following Friday did Elizabeth and Emily get their hands on it.

Fortunately, their aunt and uncle were entertaining a large party of guests, which kept the maids too busy to pop into the girls' bedroom unexpectedly to chase them back into bed.

They had all night to pore over the magazine's pages. This time, however, they did not go directly to *The Rose of Thebes*, but to Miss Lydia Grenville's account of her collision with their guardian in Vinegar Yard.

At the end, they were curled up on the floor, clutching their bellies, choking out quotes from the tale in between convulsive laughter.

When, finally, they could sit up again, they gazed at each other, mouths quivering.

Elizabeth cleared her throat. "Droll. I should say she was droll."

Emily arranged her features in a fair imitation of her uncle's "judicial" one. "Yes, Elizabeth, I believe one might reasonably infer as much." The judicial mask dissolved and her eyes danced. "I think it's the best thing she's ever written."

"You haven't read *everything* she's written. We never have time. Besides, it's unfair to compare serious work with comedy."

"I think he's inspired her," said Emily.

"It *is* quite wicked," Elizabeth admitted.

"He does bring out the devil in people. Papa said so."

"He brought out the devil in Robin." Elizabeth smiled. "Lud, how naughty he was when he came back. And how he made us laugh, poor baby."

Emily's eyes filled. "Oh, Lizzy, how I miss him."

Elizabeth hugged her. "I know."

"I wish we were at Longlands," Emily said, wiping her eyes. "I know they're not there. What's in the mausoleum isn't them. But Longlands is home, and it's where their spirits are, all of them. There aren't any Mallorys here. Not even a ghost. Aunt Dorothea's been married so long she's forgotten how to be a Mallory."

"I shall contrive to marry a younger son," Elizabeth said, "because they almost never behave properly. Perhaps, since Cousin Vere isn't living at Longlands, he'll let us stay there. I shall try to get a husband in my first Season—and it's only six months away. Then you'll come to live with us. And you'll never wed, so that you can stay at Longlands forever. And look after the children."

Emily nodded. "I suppose that will have to do. But you must not marry anyone like Uncle John. I know he's good, but I'd rather you found someone not quite so stuffy."

"Like Diablo, you mean?"

Lizzy pressed her hands to her chest. Nature had not yet gifted her with what one could properly call a bosom. "Yes, like Diablo."

"Well, let's study him, then, so I'll know exactly what to look for." Elizabeth took up the *Argus* and turned to *The Rose of Thebes*.

On the following Wednesday, Vere and Bertie sat in the Alamode Beef House, fortifying themselves after a grueling few hours of Miranda's latest adventures in *The Rose of Thebes*.

"Miranda tricked the snakes to get out of the tomb," Vere was telling his dining companion. "She'll trick a guard, or Diablo himself, to get out of the dungeon, you mark my words."

Bertie speared another forkful of beef. "I dunno," he said. "I figure they'll be on a sharp lookout for tricks now, because she already tried one and it didn't work."

"You can't believe that useless court card Orlando is going to get her out of it."

Chewing, Bertie shook his head.

"Then how?"

"The spoon," Bertie said. "You forgot about the spoon. What I figure is, she'll dig a tunnel."

"With a spoon—out of a dungeon?" Vere took up his tankard and drank.

"Mean to say, she'll sharpen it first, on the stones, you know," Bertie said between mouthfuls.

"Oh, yes, one can do anything with a sharpened spoon. She could even saw her way through the iron bars, I daresay." Vere eyed the magazine, which lay at Bertie's elbow.

Vere had not, initially, intended to become acquainted with the fictional Miranda. The day after his collision with the walking stick, he had started reading Jaynes's back issues of the *Argus* solely in order to learn how Miss Devious Sneak Attack Grenville's twisted mind worked. He'd begun with the first issue to which she'd contributed. On the page facing her article about a prosecution for debt was an illustration for *The Rose of Thebes*. From the picture, his gaze had drifted downward to the text.

The next he knew, he'd come to the end of Chapter Two and was tearing through the piles of magazines Jaynes had left on the library table, looking for the next issue.

In short, he, like half the world, apparently, was hooked on St. Bellair's story. Though he hadn't shown it, Vere had been as eager this morning as Bertie was to grab the latest issue, fresh off the presses.

Today's cover depicted a mob of men and women crowded about a roulette table. It was titled "Miss Fortune's Wheel." By now familiar with the dragoness's style, Vere was certain the caption wasn't her doing.

Though she wasn't above perpetrating puns, she wouldn't have used one so hackneyed. Moreover, the feeble play on words hardly measured up to the sly humor and acid-edged commentary of her accompanying article.

In which, incidentally, the Duke of Ainswood did not figure.

In the previous issue, his caricatured image had adorned the cover in a two-panel illustration. In the first, he had his arms stretched out and lips puckered, beseeching a kiss of the dragoness. She was depicted, arms folded and nose aloft, with her back turned to him.

In the second panel, he appeared as a toad wearing a ducal coronet, looking forlornly after her departing figure. Above her head, the bubble read, "Don't blame me. It was *your* idea." The picture caption read, "Lady Grendel's Kiss Breaks the Spell."

She'd written the accompanying article in a parody of the style of *Beowulf*, titling it, "The Battle of the Titans in Vinegar Yard."

That was just like her impudence, Vere thought. Because she'd henpecked a lot of weak-livered scribblers and doodlers, she fancied herself a Titan.

Bother me again, and I'll really hurt you.

Oh, yes, and he, the last of the Mallory hellions, had been

quaking in his boots. Yes, and wasn't he terrified?—he, who'd stood up to Lord Beelzebub, all six and a half murderously brutal feet of him. How many times had Dain uttered similar threats in the same low, deadly tones? As though threatening tones were likely to set Vere Mallory a-tremble.

Did Miss Ivan the Terrible Grenville actually believe she could intimidate *him?*

Very well, let her think it, he'd decided. He would give her plenty of time. Weeks. He'd let her enjoy her apparent triumph, while his miscellaneous gashes and bruises healed. As the days passed, her vigilance would relax while her conceited head swelled. And then he'd teach her a lesson or two, such as "Pride goeth before destruction, and a haughty spirit before a fall," and "the bigger they are, the harder they fall."

She was long overdue for a fall from her vainglorious pedestal. She was long overdue for a sharp awakening from her delusion that she was more than a match for any man, that donning trousers and aping males made her invulnerable.

He knew she wasn't.

Under the disguises and bluster, she was a girl playing Let's Pretend.

And since he found this amusing—and rather adorable, when you came down to it—he'd decided to go easy on her.

He would not humiliate her publicly.

He would be the only witness to her downfall.

Which would involve, he'd decided, her falling into his arms and down onto a bed with him.

And she would like it, and admit she liked it, and beg for more. Then, if he happened to be feeling charitable, he would give in to her pleadings. And then—

And then a boy burst into the dining room.

"Oh, help, help, please!" the child cried. "There's a house fell in—and people inside."

★ ★ ★ ★ ★

Not one, but two houses had fallen in: Numbers Four and Five in Exeter Street, Strand. More than fifty men had rushed over from their work on the sewer excavations in nearby Catherine and Brydges Streets, and quickly begun clearing away the debris.

The first victim they uncovered was a dead carman, who'd been taking in a load of coal when the house collapsed. Half an hour later, they found an elderly woman, alive, her arm fractured. An hour afterward, there was a seven-year-old boy, scarcely injured, and his infant sibling, dead. Then their seventeen-year-old sister, bruised. Their nine-year-old brother was one of the last to be rescued. Though they found him at the bottom of the rubble, he was alive and babbling deliriously. The mother hadn't survived the accident. The father was away from home.

Lydia obtained most of the details from one of the penny-a-liners who contributed occasionally to the *Argus*. She had arrived late at the scene, having been in the Lambeth Road at an inquest. But she had not come too late to witness Ainswood's role in the rescue.

He did not see her.

From what Lydia observed from her discreet post amid a group of reporters, the Duke of Ainswood was conscious of nothing but the heap of rubble he attacked with steady, ferocious purpose, Trent working at his side. She watched His Grace heave away bricks and timbers, clearing a way to the boy, then bracing a joist on his broad shoulder while others pulled the child out.

When the mother's mangled corpse was freed at last, Lydia saw the duke go to her weeping daughter and press his purse into her hands. Then he pushed his way through the crowd and fled, dragging Trent with him, as though they'd done something to be ashamed of.

Since one of Ainswood's lighter pushes could throw the average-sized human several feet, the other journalists retreated from him and returned to the disaster victims.

Lydia was not so easily put off.

She chased Ainswood and Trent to the Strand, reaching the street at the moment a hackney, in response to Ainswood's shrill whistle, was drawing to a stop.

"Wait!" she shouted, waving her notebook. "A word, Ainswood. Two minutes of your time."

He pushed the hesitating Trent into the carriage and leapt in after him.

In response to his command, the vehicle promptly started, but Lydia wouldn't give up.

The Strand was a crowded thoroughfare. She had little trouble trotting alongside the cab, which couldn't make rapid progress in the crush of vehicles and pedestrians.

"Come, Ainswood," she called. "A few words on your heroics. Since when have you become so shy and modest?"

This was one of the newer-model hackneys, with merely a hood, leather apron, and curtains to shield passengers from the elements. Since he hadn't drawn the curtains, he could hardly pretend to neither see nor hear her.

He leaned out from under the hood to glare at her. Above the street's din—the rattle of wheels, the cries of drivers and pedestrians, the snorts and whinnies of horses, the yapping of stray dogs—he shouted back, "Damn you, Grenville, get out of the street before someone runs you down."

"A few words," she persisted, still jogging alongside. "Let me quote you for my readers."

"You may tell them for me that you are the plaguiest cocklebur of a female I ever met."

"Plaguiest cocklebur," she repeated dutifully. "Yes, but

about the victims in Exeter Street—"

"If you don't get back to the walkway, *you'll* be a victim —and don't expect me to scrape up what's left of you from the cobblestones."

"May I tell my readers that you're truly studying to become a saint?" she asked. "Or shall I ascribe your actions to a transitory fit of nobility?"

"Trent made me do it." He turned back to roar at the driver, "Can't you make this accursed plod of a horse *move?*"

Whether the driver heard or not, the beast picked up its pace. In the next instant, an opening appeared in the crush of vehicles, which the cab promptly darted through, and Lydia had to jump back to the curb as those behind the hackney hastened toward the break in traffic.

"Plague take her," Vere said after a backward glance assured him she'd given up. "What the devil was she doing here? She was supposed to be at an inquest in the Lambeth Road. And that was supposed to take all day."

"There's no tellin' how long them things'll take," Trent said. "And speakin' of tellin'—if she finds out Joe Purvis been spyin' for you, there's goin' to be an inquest on his dead body." He leaned out and peered 'round the carriage's hood.

"She's given up," Vere said. "Settle back, Trent, before you tumble out."

Grimacing, Trent settled back. "Now she's gone and planted Charles Two in my brain box again. What do you reckon it means?"

"Plague," Vere said. "You associate them both with plague."

"I can't think why you'd say that to her face," Trent said. "She were bound to think well of you, after what you done back there. And why you should tell her it were me made you do it when you were the one who rushed out of the Alamode first—"

"There were fifty other men at it with us," Vere snapped. "She didn't ask them why they did it, did she? But that's just like a female, wanting to know why this and why that and imagining there's some deep meaning to everything a fellow does."

There wasn't any deep meaning, he told himself. He hadn't brought the nine-year-old boy back to life, merely freed him from a premature burial. And that boy's plight had nothing to do with anything else. He was only one of several victims. Saving him had meant no more to Vere than had rescuing the others.

The lump in His Grace's throat was merely dust, and it was dust that made his eyes smart and his voice hoarse. He wasn't thinking of anyone else . . . such as a nine-year-old boy he'd been unable to save.

Nor had he felt tempted in the slightest to talk of what he felt. He had nothing burdening his heart, and most certainly had no idiotish wish to unburden himself to her. He had no reason to fear he'd be tempted to do so simply because he'd learned, in reading her work, that she was not so cynical and stony-hearted, not so much the dragon on a rampage, when it came to children. This couldn't possibly matter to him, because he was cynical and stony-hearted about everything.

He was the last Mallory hellion, obnoxious, conceited, conscienceless, et cetera, et cetera. And because he was, he had only one use for her, and seeking a sympathetic ear wasn't it. He did not confide in anyone because he'd nothing to confide, and if he had, he'd rather be staked under a broiling sun in the Sahara than confide in a female.

He told himself this, in several different ways, during the journey home, and not once did it occur to the Duke of

Ainswood that he might be protesting too much.

"Trent made him do it, indeed," Lydia muttered to herself as she strode down the hall to her study. "A regiment of infantry with bayonets at the ready couldn't make that obstinate boor cross the street if he didn't want to."

When she entered the small room, she tossed her bonnet onto the desk. Then she moved to the bookshelves and took out the latest edition of Debrett's *Peerage*.

She found the first clue quickly. Then she turned to her *Annual Register* collection, which covered the last quarter century. She drew out the 1827 edition and turned to the "Appendix to the Chronicle." Under "Deaths, May," she found the epitaph.

"At his seat, Longlands, Bedfordshire," she read, "aged nine, the right hon. Robert Edward Mallory, sixth duke of Ainswood." It went on from there for four columns, an unusually long death notice for a child, even for one of the nobility. But there was a poignant story here, and the *Register* could be counted upon to focus on it, as it did on other of the year's curiosities and dramas.

I've been to enough funerals, Ainswood had said.

So he had, Lydia found. Moving from one information source to the next, she counted more than a dozen funerals in the last decade alone, and these were only the near kin.

If Ainswood was the callous pleasure seeker he was supposed to be, the relentless parade of deaths couldn't have affected him.

Yet would a callous pleasure seeker bestir himself for a lot of peasants in distress, and labor alongside laboring men, at no small physical risk to himself?

She wouldn't have believed it if she hadn't seen it herself: Ainswood ceasing only when assured there were no more to rescue, coming away ragged and dirty and sweating. And stopping to press his purse into a grieving girl's hands.

Lydia's eyes stung, and a tear plopped onto the page she'd been reading.

"Don't be a ninny," she scolded herself.

The scold produced no sensible result.

A minute later, though, what sounded like an elephant's thundering approach dispelled all symptoms of ninnyness. The thunder was Susan's. She and Tamsin were back from their walk.

Lydia hastily wiped her eyes and sat down.

In the next moment, Susan was bounding into the room and trying to bound into Lydia's lap, and responding to the firm, "Down!" by slobbering on her skirts instead.

"It seems someone's in a good temper," Lydia said to Tamsin. "What happened? Did she find a plump, juicy toddler to snack on? She doesn't smell much worse than usual, so she can't have been rolling in excrement."

"She has been a dreadful hussy," Tamsin said while she untied her bonnet. "We met up with Sir Bertram Trent in Soho Square, and she made a complete spectacle of herself. As soon as she spotted him, she shot off like a rocket—or cannonball, rather, for she knocked him flat on his back. Then she stood over him, licking his face, his coat, and sniffing—well, I will not say where. She was utterly deaf to my remonstrances. Fortunately, Sir Bertram bore it all good-naturedly. When he finally got her off and himself up, and I tried to apologize, he wouldn't have it. 'Only playful,' says he, 'and don't know her own strength.' And then Susan—"

"Woof!" the mastiff cheerfully acknowledged her name.

"She had to show off her tricks," Tamsin went on. "She gave her paw. She teased him with a stick until he played tug-of-war with her. She played dead as well, and rolled on her back to get tickled and—oh, you can imagine."

Susan laid her big head in her mistress's lap and regarded her soulfully.

"Susan, you are a puzzle," Lydia said, petting her. "The last time you saw him, you didn't like him."

"Perhaps she sensed he'd been doing good deeds this afternoon."

Lydia looked up to meet the girl's gaze. "Trent told you about it, did he? Did he happen to explain what he was doing in Soho Square instead of Ainswood House, recovering from his herculean labors?"

"When he saw you, Charles Two came into his brain box, he told me. The king bothered him so, he got out of the hackney a few streets away and walked to the square to look at the statue."

In Soho Square's sadly neglected patch of greenery stood a crumbling statue of Charles II.

After their first encounter, Tamsin had reported Trent's associating Lydia with the Restoration-era monarch. It made no sense to Lydia, but she didn't expect it to. She was aware that Lord Dain's brother-in-law was not noted for intellectual acumen.

"Speaking of herculean labors," Tamsin said, "I daresay you had a shock in Exeter Street. Do you think the Duke of Ainswood is reforming, or was this a momentary aberration?"

Before Lydia could respond, Millie came to the doorway. "Mr. Purvis's here, Miss. With a message for you. Urgent, he says."

At nine o'clock that night, Lydia entered a small, heavily draped room in the Covent Garden Piazza. The girl who let her in quickly vanished through the curtained doorway opposite. A moment later, the woman who'd summoned Lydia entered.

She was nearly as tall as Lydia, but shaped on broader lines. A large turban crowned her head. The face below was thickly painted. Despite the paint and dim light, Lydia discerned clear signs of amusement.

"An interesting choice of costume," said Madame Ifrita.

"It was the best I could do on short notice," Lydia said.

The older woman signaled Lydia to take a chair at the small table near the curtained doorway.

Madame Ifrita was a fortune-teller, and one of Lydia's more reliable informants. Normally the two women met at a discreet distance from London, because Madame would soon be out of business if her clients suspected that she shared any of their confidences with a journalist.

Since a disguise was necessary, and there wasn't time for transforming into a man, Lydia had gone with Tamsin to the secondhand shops in Greek Street. There they'd hastily assembled the alleged "gypsy" costume Lydia was wearing.

The result, in Lydia's opinion, was more tartlike than gypsylike. Though she wore half a dozen petticoats, in different colors, she hardly felt decently clothed. Since none of the previous owners had been Amazons like her, the hems stopped well above her ankles—as did those of virtually every streetwalker in London. But she hadn't time for alterations.

The same difficulties of fit applied to the bodices. The one finally decided upon was scarlet, and as tight as a tourniquet—which was just as well, for Lydia's breasts would have tumbled out of the obscenely low neckline otherwise. Fortunately, the night was cool enough to require a shawl.

Unwilling to risk a secondhand wig, which was bound to be infested with several forms of insect life, Lydia had used colored scarves to fashion a turban. With her hair tightly bound underneath and the ends of the scarves artfully draped, it not only concealed her betraying blond hair but helped camouflage her features.

She wasn't worried about anyone noticing the color of her eyes, since she was going out after dark in the first place, and wasn't going to let anyone get close enough to notice they were blue in the second.

A generous application of paint, powder, and cheap jewelry completed the gaudy ensemble.

"I'm supposed to be one of your gypsy relatives," Lydia explained.

Madame settled into the chair opposite. "Clever," she said. "I knew you'd contrive something. I regret the hasty summons, but the information came only this afternoon, and you may have very little time to act upon it—if my crystal ball can be believed," she added with a wink.

Madame Ifrita's powers of divination stunned the credulous. They didn't stun Lydia, who knew the fortune-teller operated in much the same way she did, with regular assistance from a network of informants, some of them unwitting.

Lydia was also aware the information was expensive. She produced five sovereigns and set them down in a row upon the table. She pushed one toward Ifrita.

"The girl Coralie brought with her from Paris came to me today," the fortune-teller said. "Annette wishes to return to France, but is afraid. With good reason, as you may know. One of Coralie's runaways was pulled from the river ten days ago, her face cut to pieces, and the mark of the garrote on her throat. I told Annette about this and a few other things she thinks are secrets. Then I look in my magic crystal and tell her I see Coralie, and there is a curse upon her. Blood drips from her ears and droplets circle her throat, her wrist."

Lydia lifted her eyebrows.

"You were not the only one who saw Madam Brees wearing rubies in Jerrimer's," Ifrita said. "The one who told me about them described them much as you had done." She paused briefly. "I heard more than this: how the Duke of Ainswood appeared, and met up with a beautiful young man he knew, though no one else did. The duke saw through you, did he?"

"It was his bloody damned cigar," Lydia said. "That's what gave me away, I'll wager anything."

"And he gave himself away today, in Exeter Street," the fortune-teller said.

"Did he?"

"Does it matter?"

It did, but Lydia shook her head. "At the moment, it's Coralie I want to know about." She pushed another coin toward the older woman.

"The bawd keeps the jewelry her minions steal," Ifrita said. "She has a weakness for sparkling trinkets, like a magpie. While Annette feels this is very foolish, it is not the reason she means to run away. She says she has bad dreams about the murdered girl. Yet the little runaway wasn't the first they've made an example of. I think Annette's trouble is that she either saw or participated in the killing—"

"And it distressed her delicate sensibilities," Lydia put in with heavy irony. "Annette is hardly an innocent lamb, as we both know."

"That's why I was in so great a hurry to talk to you. If she has nightmares, it is most likely her own pretty face she sees cut up, and the wire or rope circling her own pretty throat. Perhaps she saw what she was not meant to see. Perhaps there is another reason. Whatever the cause for her alarm, it is genuine. I have no doubt she will make a run for it. What matters is, she isn't fool enough to do it as other girls do—on foot and penniless. She'll steal as much as she can carry."

"So she can hire the fastest post chaise to take her to the coast."

Ifrita nodded. "Tonight she helps Coralie and the bully boys break in a new girl, so there is no opportunity to slip away. Tomorrow night she must service a special client. She might be able to run away afterward, depending on how long the customer requires her. The only time she can rob Coralie with any degree of safety is between nine o'clock at night, when the bawd goes out, and the early morning hours, well before the bawd's return. Annette will need a good head start of them, and their pursuit will be more difficult if she travels under cover of darkness."

The fortune-teller paused. "I cannot say absolutely that she will take the jewelry. I told her the rubies were cursed. But if she can't put her hands on enough money, she'll probably overlook the curse."

"Then I'd better get to the jewelry before she does," Lydia said, showing none of the uneasiness she felt. She would have to enlist Helena's help on very short notice, and she doubted Helena would be enthusiastic.

Lydia pushed another coin forward.

Ifrita pushed it back, shaking her head. "There's little left to tell you. Coralie at present lives at Number Fourteen, Francis Street, off the Tottenham Court Road. She usually leaves about nine o'clock with her two brutes. One servant, Mick, also a brute, remains to guard the house. Often, a girl stays as well, to entertain him or one of a select group of clients."

Helena definitely was not going to like this, Lydia thought. Too many people on the premises. But she was the only professional thief Lydia knew intimately, and there wasn't time to locate someone else with the necessary expertise. This job was not one for an amateur. Lydia couldn't risk bungling it. If she got killed, Tamsin, Bess, and Millie would be on their own—and likely on the streets in very short order.

It had to be done right, and Helena was the one to see that it was. She only had to be talked into it, and that would want a lot of talking. Which meant Lydia had no time to waste.

A few minutes later, she took her leave of Madame and hurried out.

She slowed down when she emerged from the building. Though she had a hackney waiting only a few streets away, she did not allow herself to make a mad dash for it.

While it was too early for the demimonde to be out in full force, the denizens of the night were beginning to gather. A hasty departure was too liable to invite pursuit by drunken bucks. Lydia forced herself to stroll casually through the piazza.

She was stepping out from under the portico and turning away from the marketplace into James Street when a tall figure emerged from the shadows of the portico opposite and turned in the same direction.

It wanted but one glance to ascertain his identity, and exactly two seconds to decide against traveling the same route.

Pretending to recognize someone in the marketplace, Lydia redirected her steps thither.

7

The Duke of Ainswood was about to give up searching Covent Garden for his prey. Even if the Grenville gorgon had come out alone, as Purvis claimed, that didn't mean this was the one and only opportunity to snare her. There was no hurry, Vere reminded himself. He could bide his time, choose the perfect moment for the lesson he meant to teach her. It wasn't as though he lacked ways to amuse himself in the interim.

Seeing her today hadn't made him impatient. It wasn't as though he missed her pestering, provoking company. Or the sound of her haughty voice. Or the sight of her exasperatingly beautiful face. Or that body, that devil-designed, curvaceous, long-legged . . .

The thought hung uncompleted and he stopped midstride, stunned, as a wench strolled out from the shadowy piazza, hips swaying, petticoats lapping her shapely calves. As she turned away from James Street and started into Covent Garden—apparently having spied someone who took her fancy—the night breeze lifted her rainbow-colored shawl, revealing a mouth-watering expanse of generously rounded bosom.

For an instant, all Vere could do was stare, dumbfounded, and wonder if he'd got drunk without knowing it. But he hadn't had time to get drunk this night, and his eyesight was in working order.

Which meant that the wench sauntering through Covent

Garden in the middle of the night was Lady Grendel, very much in the flesh.

Instantly he was on the prowl, weaving in and out of the shifting clusters of men and women on the east side of the marketplace. He saw her slow, then pause, at the passageway next to Carpenter's Coffee House. Then the turban disappeared from view.

Believing she must have entered the passage, he was turning that way when he happened to glance to his left.

Before a crippled flower girl who sat on a rotting upended basket, the would-be gypsy crouched, holding the girl's hand and studying the palm.

Vere drew nearer. Intent on their conversation, the two women didn't notice his approach.

"My future's all crooked, isn't it?" he heard the flower girl say. "Like me. All twisted and crooked. I heard of a doctor in Scotland who might help me, but it's very far, and the coach fare is ever so dear. And all the fancy doctors come dear, too, don't they? Last night, a gentleman said he'd give me a guinea to go into a room in the piazza with him. I said no, but after, I kept thinking maybe I was foolish. He'll come again tonight, he said. I wish he wouldn't, because it's easier to be good when no one promises you money to be wicked. And a guinea is so very much."

Vere did not want to think about the sort of cur who tried to seduce defenseless cripples. He hadn't time for it, anyway. He had only a moment to devise his tactics.

Then it flashed in his mind: an image of Mistress Melodrama impersonating him at the Blue Owl, pretending to be drunk.

"Only a guinea?" he exclaimed, his voice slurred. "For such a beauty?" Two lovely, startled faces—one painted, one not—looked up at him.

Swaying woozily, he advanced. "By gad, I'd give"—he pulled out his purse—"twenty, simply for the privilege of looking at you, little blossom. Here." He bent and clumsily pushed the purse into the flower girl's hands. "Now give me your posies. Poor things are embarrassed, don't you know? Next to you, they look like weeds. No wonder no one's buying 'em."

Miss Gypsy Queen Grenville rose, while the little flower girl remained huddled upon her rotting basket, the purse clutched to her belly, her wide-eyed gaze riveted upon him.

"Best go home," Vere told the girl, "before someone comes along to relieve you of your profits."

With the exaggerated care of the catastrophically intoxicated, he helped her up and onto her crutch. While Miss Half-Naked Painted Harlot Grenville assisted the bewildered girl in secreting the purse in her clothing, he added, "You go tomorrow to Mr. Hayward. He's a very good doctor." He gave the address, then fished a crumpled card from his waistcoat pocket. "Give this to him, and tell him I'll answer for you."

A moment later, after a stammered thanks, the flower girl was limping away. Vere watched until she'd rounded the southeast corner of the marketplace and disappeared from view.

Then his gaze came back to his prey—or, rather, to where he'd last seen her, for she was gone.

After a moment's frantic survey of the marketplace, Vere spotted the gay turban bobbing among some scattered groups of idlers. The turban was heading northward.

He caught up with her near Russell Street. Planting himself in her path, he withdrew the cluster of straggling bouquets from under his arm, where he'd absently stowed them, and held them out to her. " 'Sweets to the sweet,' " he quoted from *Hamlet*.

With a shrug, she took the crushed flowers. " 'Farewell,' " she said, and started to move away.

"You mistake me," he said, following. "That was the beginning."

"So it was," said she. "But the line ends with 'farewell.' Then Queen Gertrude scatters the flowers." Suiting action to words, she strewed the posies about her.

"Ah, an actress," he said. "This gypsy garb is to advertise a new play, I take it."

"I've been an actress in better times," she said without slowing her pace. "A fortune-teller in harder ones. Like the present."

Once again she'd adopted someone else's voice. This one was higher and lighter than her own, its accents coarser. If Purvis hadn't told him she'd be here incognito, or if Vere had been as drunk as he pretended to be, she might have taken him in.

He couldn't tell whether his act was taking her in, whether she truly believed he was too drunk to penetrate her disguise or she was simply playing along until she could find a way to escape without attracting attention.

As though her attire—what there was of it—wasn't screaming, "Come pump me!" to every male in the vicinity.

"You passed any number of well-breeched swells who could have crossed your palm generously with silver, if not gold," he said. "Yet you stopped for a crippled child who'd scarcely a copper to bless herself with. I very nearly mistook you for an angel."

She shot him a glance from under her lashes. "Not likely. You acted the part so well, I could only play supernumerary."

If she'd directed that sidelong come-hither look at another

man, she'd be up against an alley wall in nine seconds with her skirts over her head. The image made his temples throb.

"It was the easiest way to get rid of the chit," he said carelessly. "And to bring myself to your notice. You'd already brought yourself to mine, you see. Forcibly," he added, ogling her lavish bosom. "And now I must have my fortune told. I strongly suspect that my love line has taken a turn for the better." He pulled off his glove and waved his hand in her face. "Would you be so kind as to look?"

She swatted his hand away. "If it's love you want, you need only look in your pockets. If you find a coin there, you might pluck any of the flowers of the night blooming here about you."

While one of the other lechers plucked *her?* Not likely.

Heaving a deep sigh, he pressed to his breast the hand she'd swatted. "She touched me," he said soulfully, "and I am transported to heavenly spheres. Gypsy, actress, angel—I know not what she is, or how I came to be worthy of her touch, but I—"

"Mad, quite mad, alas!" she cried, startling him. "Oh, good people, hearken and pity him!"

Her cry seemed so genuine that several whores and customers paused in their negotiations to stare.

" 'Mad as the sea and wind, when both contend/ Which is the mightier,' " she declaimed.

Vere vaguely recalled the lines as Ophelia's. If she thought he was going to play *Hamlet*—who lost the girl—she had another think coming.

"Mad for you," he cried poignantly. A harlot nearby giggled. Nothing daunted, he announced to the onlookers, "Into the desolate darkness of my weary existence she came, all burning color, like the Aurora Borealis—"

" 'O heavenly powers, restore him!' " she wailed.

"And lit me ablaze!" he went on in stirring accents. "Behold me burning for but a smile from these ruby lips. Behold me consumed in the sweet fire of undying devotion—"

" 'O what a noble mind is here o'er thrown!' " Back of her hand to her forehead, she plunged into a cluster of laughing tarts. "Shield me, fair ladies. I fear this ecstatic fool will be driven to desperate acts."

"Only the usual one, dearie," said an older harlot with a laugh. "And it's Ainswood, don't you know, as pays handsome."

"Fair Aurora, take pity on me," Vere cried beseechingly. He elbowed his way through the crowd of men gathering round the knot of females. "Flee not from me, my blazing star, my sun and moon and all, my galaxy."

"Yours? When, how, why yours?" The turban disappeared briefly in a forest of top hats, but when she emerged from the cluster of laughing men, Vere darted to her side.

"By love's decree," he told her. He fell to his knees. "Sweet Aurora, behold me prostrate before you—"

"That isn't prostrate," she said reproachfully. "Truly prostrate is out flat, face down—"

"Bung upwards, she means, Your Grace," a tart called out.

"I should do anything for my goddess," he said above the male segment of the audience's raucous suggestions of various acts he might perform in his present position. He would kill them all later, he decided. "I wait only for you to bid me rise from this decaying earth. Only summon me, and I shall lift up my soul to join yours in celestial realms. Let me drink the ambrosia of your honeyed lips, and wander the sweet infinity of your heavenly body. And let me die in ecstasy, kissing your . . . feet."

" 'O shame! Where is thy blush?' " Gesturing at him while

her gaze swept the audience, she went on, "He feigns to worship, yet you hear him. He dares to sully my ears with talk of lips, of—of"—she shuddered—*"kisses."*

Then she flounced away in a rustle of petticoats.

He was caught up in the game, but not so caught up—or drunk, as she believed—to let her escape so easily. Almost as soon as she moved, he was on his feet, hurrying after her.

Vere saw the collision coming.

Grenville changed direction and glanced over her shoulder as she darted toward the piazza's columns—at the same moment a woman in spangled black hurried out from its shadows.

Even as he was calling, "Look out!" his "Aurora" crashed into the woman, knocking her back against a pillar.

He reached them before they'd fully recovered their balance, and drew the dragoness away.

"Why'n't you look where you're going, you bean pole slut!" the woman in black screeched.

It was Coralie Brees. Vere would have recognized her shrill tones from a furlong away.

"It was my fault," he said quickly as his glance took in the pair of bully boys trailing behind her. "A lovers' quarrel. She was so vexed with me that she couldn't see straight. But you are better now, are you not, my sun and moon and stars?" he inquired of Aurora while he straightened her turban, which had slipped askew.

She pushed his hand away. "A thousand apologies, miss," she told Coralie contritely. "I hope I caused you no injury."

Vere would wager fifty quid that the bawd had not been addressed as "miss" in some decades, if ever. He would also wager that Grenville had caught sight of the two brutes as well, and wisely decided in favor of pacification.

Madam Brees was not looking remotely mollified, however, which boded ill for peace.

That should have been agreeable to Vere, for he was in the habit of looking for trouble, and the pair of bully boys would have suited him admirably. Tonight, however, he must make an exception. Having spent the afternoon heaving bricks, stones, and timbers, he preferred to reserve his remaining energies for Her Highness. Besides, she might easily wander into another fellow's greedy hands while Vere was busy pummeling the brutes.

He pulled the jade stickpin from his neckcloth and tossed it to the procuress. Coralie caught it neatly, her expression softening during a quick examination.

"No hard feelings, m'dear, I hope," he said.

He did not wait for her answer, but turned a drunken grin upon Grenville. "What now, my peacock?"

"It's the male of the species that's colorful," she said with a toss of her head. "The female's dull. I'll not stay to be called your drab, Sir Bedlam." In a swirl of petticoats she turned and started away.

But he was turning, too, laughing, to scoop her up in his arms.

She let out a gasp. "Put me down," she said, wriggling. "I'm too big for you."

"And too old," Coralie said acidly. "A great lump of mutton, Your Grace—while I can give you dainty young lambs."

But Vere was carrying his lively burden into the shadows and away from the bawd's shrill litany of her youthful employees' attractions.

"Too big?" he asked the alleged gypsy. "Where, my treasure? See how neatly my head fits upon your shoulder." Nuzzling her neck, he let his gaze linger upon the luscious territories below. "It will fit as comfortably upon your breast,

I'll warrant. And I can tell," he went on as he dexterously shifted his hand toward her derriere, "there is precisely enough here—"

"Put me down," she said, squirming. "The game is over."

Not by a long shot, he thought as he carried her to the door of an establishment with which he was more than passing familiar, where the first-floor rooms might be rented by the hour.

"Listen to me, Ain—"

He stopped her speech with his mouth, while he kicked the door open and carried her into a dimly lit corridor.

She squirmed harder and wrenched her mouth away, and so he had to let her down, to free his hands to hold her head still while he kissed her again, in heated earnest, as he'd wanted to do from the moment she'd begun teasing him.

He felt her stiffen while her lips compressed, rejecting him, and anxiety bubbled up inside him.

She didn't know how to kiss, he remembered.

She's innocent, an inner voice cried.

But it was the voice of conscience, and he'd stopped listening to it a year and a half ago.

She was acting, he told himself. She was impersonating an innocent. She was no green girl but a grown woman with a body made for sin, made for him, blackhearted sinner that he was.

Still, if she wanted to play the skittish maiden, he was willing to play along. He gentled his kiss, from lusty demand to patient persuasion. He gentled his touch as well, cradling her head as one might hold a moth captive.

He felt the shiver run through her, felt her rigidly unyielding mouth soften and tremble under his. He felt, too, a sharp ache, as though someone had stabbed him to the heart.

He called the ache lust and wrapped his arms about her.

He drew her close, and she didn't resist. Her mouth, blissfully soft in surrender, seemed to simmer under his. He was simmering, too, on fire, though for him this was the chastest of embraces.

What made him burn, he believed, was the novelty of playing at innocence. It was that and impatience to take what, usually, he didn't need to work or even coax for.

He'd never had to work at winning women. A glance, a smile, and they came—for a coin or out of mutual desire—and always knew, all of them, what to do, because knowing women were the only kind he chose.

She wanted to pretend she didn't know, and so he played the role of tutor. He taught her what to do, coaxing her soft mouth to part for him, then tasting her little by little while her scent swam about him and in his mind until scent and taste mingled and simmered in his blood.

He was aware of his heart pumping furiously, though this was merely a deepening kiss, no more than the titillating prelude.

The wild heartbeat was only impatience with this game of hers. And it was for the game's sake he let his hands move slowly down from the innocuous realms of her shoulders and back, down along the supple line of her spine to the waist his big hands could easily span. Then slowly, caressingly, he continued down, to the realms no innocent would let a man touch. And it was the perverse game they played that made his hands tremble as they gently shaped to the lavish curve of her derriere. It was the perversity that made him groan against her mouth while he pressed her against him, where his swollen rod strained against confining garments.

Too far, the rusty voice of conscience cried. *You go too far.*

Not too far, he was sure, for she didn't pull away. Instead, her hands moved over him, tentatively, as though it were the first time she'd ever held a man, the first time she'd ever let her hands rove over masculine shoulders and back. And still playing the game, she pretended to be shy, and went no lower than his waist.

He broke the kiss to tell her she needn't be shy, but he couldn't make his mouth form the words. He buried his face in her neck instead, inhaling her scent while he trailed kisses over silken skin.

He felt her shudder, heard her soft, surprised cry, as though it were all new to her.

But it couldn't be.

She was breathing hard, as he was, and her skin was hot against his mouth. And when he slid his hand up to cup her breast, he felt the hard bud against his palm through the woefully inadequate bodice. There was little enough fabric shielding her skin, and he pushed down what there was and filled his hands with her, as he'd dreamed so many times.

"Beautiful." His throat was tight, aching. He ached everywhere. "You're so beautiful."

"Oh, God, don't." Her body stiffened. "I can't—" She reached up, grabbed his hands. "Damn you, Ainswood. It's *me*, you drunken idiot. It's *me—Grenville*."

To Lydia's astonished dismay, Ainswood did not recoil in horror.

On the contrary, she was having the devil's own time prying his hands from her breasts.

"It's me—Grenville," she repeated five times, and he went on fondling her and kissing an exceedingly sensitive place behind her ear that until now she hadn't known was sensitive.

Finally, "Stop it!" she said in the firm tones she usually employed with Susan.

He released her then, and instantly changed from the ardent lover telling her she was beautiful—and making her feel she was the most beautiful, desirable woman in all the world—into the obnoxious lout he usually was . . . with an added dose of surliness she might have found comical if she hadn't been so disgusted with herself.

She had not put up even a reasonable facsimile of resistance.

She knew he was a rake, and the worst kind—the kind who despised women—yet she'd let him seduce her.

"Let me explain something to you, Grenville," he growled. "If you want to play games with a man, you ought to be prepared to play them through to the conclusion. Because otherwise you put a fellow in a *bad mood*."

"You were born in a bad mood," Lydia said as she jerked up her bodice.

"I was in an excellent humor until a minute ago."

Her glance fell to his hands, which ought to have warning signs tatooed on them. With those evilly adept hands he'd stroked and fondled and half undressed her. And she hadn't offered a whisper of protest.

"I'm sure you'll cheer up again soon," she said. "You've only to step out the door. Covent Garden is rife with genuine harlots eager to raise your spirits."

"If you don't want to be treated like a tart, you shouldn't go out dressed like one." He scowled at her bodice. "Or should I say 'undressed'? Obviously, you're not wearing a corset. Or a chemise. I suppose you haven't bothered with drawers, either."

"I had a very good reason for dressing this way," she said. "But I'm not going to explain myself to you. You've wasted enough of my time as it is."

She started for the door.

"You might at least fix your clothes," he said. "Your turban's crooked, and your frock is every which way."

"All the better," she said. "Everyone will think they know what I've been up to, and I should be able to get out of this filthy place without having my throat cut."

She opened the door, then paused, looking about. She saw no signs of Coralie or her bodyguards. She glanced back at Ainswood. Her conscience pinched. Hard.

He did *not* look in the least lonely or lost, she told her fool conscience. He was sulking, that was all, because he'd mistaken her for a whore and gone to all the bother of pursuing her and seducing her for nothing.

And if he wasn't so curst damned good at it, she would have stopped the proceedings before they truly got going and he could have found someone else . . .

And wrapped his powerful arms about that someone and kissed her as sweetly and ardently as any Prince Charming might have done, and caressed her and made her feel like the most beautiful, desirable princess in all the world.

But Lydia Grenville wasn't a princess, she told her conscience, and he wasn't Prince Charming.

She walked out.

Only after she'd closed the door behind her did she say, under her breath, "I'm sorry." Then she hurried out from the piazza and turned the corner into James Street.

Vere was furious enough to let her go. As she'd so snidely reminded him, Covent Garden was rife with whores. Since he hadn't got what he wanted from her, he might as well get it from someone else.

But an image hung in his mind's eye of the lechers ogling her, and the vision set off a host of unpleasant inner sensations he didn't care to identify.

Instead, he swore violently and hurried out after her.

He caught up with her at Hart Street, halfway to Long Acre.

When he reached her side, she glared at him. "I don't have time to entertain you, Ainswood. I have *important* things to do. Why don't you go to the pantomime—or a cock fight—or whatever else appeals to your stunted mind?"

A male passerby paused to leer at her ankles.

Vere caught her hand and tucked it into the curve of his elbow. "I knew it was you, Grenville, all along," he said, walking on with her.

"You say so now," she said. "But we both know you would never have done . . . what you did if you'd realized it was plaguey cocklebur Grenville instead of a nice, friendly slut."

"That's like your conceit," he said, "to fancy your disguise was so clever I'd never see through it."

She threw him several sharp glances.

"You were only pretending to be drunk," she accused. "That's even worse. If you knew it was me, you could have only one reason for—for—"

"There's only one reason for it."

"Revenge," she said. "You're nursing a grudge about what happened in the alley two weeks ago."

"I wish you would look at yourself," he said. "You've hardly any clothes on. What more reason does a fellow need than that?"

"You'd need more reason," she said. "You hate me."

"Don't flatter yourself." He frowned down at her. "You're merely irritating."

There was the understatement of the year.

She'd teased him, got him all stirred up and randy . . . and made him stop, just as they were getting to the good part.

Worse than that, she'd made him doubt.

Perhaps she wasn't acting.

Perhaps no other man had touched her.

Not in that way, at least.

In any case, he had to know. Because if she truly was a novice, he was not going to bother with her again.

He had no use for virgins. He'd never had one and never intended to. This had nothing to do with moral scruples. The simple fact was, a virgin was too damned much work for too little reward. Since he never bedded any female more than once, he was not about to waste his time on a beginner. He was not going to go to all the trouble of training her so that some other fellow could enjoy all the benefits.

There was only one way to settle this matter, once and for all: the direct way.

He set his jaw, closed his hand a bit more firmly over hers, and said, "You're a virgin, aren't you?"

"I should think it was obvious," she said, chin up.

And cheeks blazing, most likely, though he couldn't be certain in the gaslight's shifting shadows. He almost lifted his hand to touch her cheek, to find out for sure whether it was hot, whether she blushed.

He remembered then how miraculously smooth her skin was, and how she'd trembled under his touch. And he felt the stabbing in his heart again.

Lust, he told himself. What he felt was simple lust. She was beautiful and lavishly shaped, and her ripe breasts had filled his hands, as he'd dreamed, and she had yielded so sweetly and warmly, and let her hands roam over him . . . as far as shyness would let her.

That was the maddest of incongruities, to connect the word "shy" with a woman who drove hell for leather through London's streets as though it were the Coliseum and she were Caesar's chief charioteer. Shy, indeed, this woman, who climbed up the sides of houses, who sprang upon a man in a dark alley, swinging her walking stick with the accuracy and power of a champion batsman.

Shy, she.

A virgin, she.

It was ridiculous, insane.

"I've shocked you," she said. "You're speechless."

He had been, he realized. Belatedly, he discovered that they'd reached Long Acre.

He also realized his death grip would probably leave bruises on her arm.

He released her.

She stepped away from him, tugged at her bodice—for all the good that did, when there wasn't enough to cover more than her nipples—and rearranged her shawl more modestly. Then she put her fingers to her lips and let out an eardrum-shriveling whistle.

A short distance down the street, a carriage started toward them.

"I hired him for the evening," she said, while Vere rubbed his ear. "I know I look like a tart, and I did know better than to walk far in this costume. I wasn't trying to invite trouble, whatever you think. I was leaving Covent Garden when I saw you. I only went back into the marketplace to avoid you. Otherwise—"

"Two steps is too far for an unescorted female, especially in this neighborhood, after dark," he said. "You should have found someone to play bully boy. One of the fellows you work with, for instance. Surely there must be one big enough or ugly enough to keep off the lechers."

"A bully boy." Her expression grew thoughtful. "A big, intimidating fellow, you mean. That's what I need."

He nodded.

The hackney was pulling up at the curb, but she didn't

seem to notice. She was eyeing Vere up and down, rather as one would size up a horse at Tattersall's.

"Do you know, Ainswood, you may be right," she said meditatively.

He remembered her saying she had a very good reason for dressing as she had. He hadn't asked what the reason was. He didn't need to know, he told himself. He'd asked the only pertinent question, and having obtained his answer, had no earthly reason to linger.

"Good-bye, Grenville," he said firmly. "Have a pleasant journey to wherever it is you're going." He started to turn away.

Her hand clamped on his forearm. "I have a proposal to make," she said.

"Your driver's waiting," he said.

"He'll keep on waiting," she said. "I bought him for the night."

"You are not buying me, for any period of time." He picked her hand off his arm, rather as one would pick off a slug.

She shrugged, and her shawl slipped, baring one white shoulder and all of one breast except for the fraction concealed by the scrap of red cloth. "Very well, have it your way," she said. "I'm not going to beg you. And perhaps, after all, it would be wrong of me to ask. The venture would be far too dangerous for you."

She turned and moved to the hackney. She said something in a low voice to the driver. While she exchanged secrets with him, her shawl slipped further.

Vere swore under his breath.

He knew he was being manipulated.

She showed a bit of skin and said the magic words, "too dangerous"—which anyone who knew him had to know were irresistible to him—and expected him to run after her.

Well, if she thought she could whip Vere Mallory into a frenzy of excitement with such a paltry, tired old trick as that . . .

. . . she was right, confound her.

He went after her, pulled the carriage door open, "helped" her in with a firm hand to her hindquarters, and climbed in after her.

"This had better be good," he said as he slammed down onto the seat beside her. "This had better be bloody damned dangerous."

8

Lydia gave him an abbreviated version of the tale of Miss "Price's" keepsakes, starting with the assault and robbery at the coaching inn and ending with this night's discoveries.

Lydia didn't reveal Tamsin's true identity or Helena's previous career in theft. She merely told him she'd intended to enlist someone else's aid and would return to the original plan if Ainswood preferred not to burglarize the lair of killers who liked to carve up their victims' faces before or after strangling them.

His Grace only grunted.

He sat, arms folded, making no more articulate comment throughout her recitation. Even when she was done, and paused for his questions—for surely he had many—he remained silent.

"We're nearly there," she said after a glance out the window. "Perhaps you'd rather have a look at the place before committing yourself."

"I know the neighborhood," he said. "Shockingly respectable for Coralie Brees. I'm amazed, in fact, that she can afford it. The goods she sells are hardly prime quality. Far below Miss Martin's level." He threw Lydia a quick glance. "I daresay you employ your own unique criteria in selecting your intimates. You seem to go to extremes. One is a high-priced harlot. The other is hardly more than a schoolgirl. You've known Miss Price for only a few weeks, yet you mean to risk your neck to recover her baubles."

"The value is mainly sentimental," Lydia said. "You wouldn't understand."

"Don't want to," he said. "Females are always fretting about one triviality or another. I'm aware that a stocking rent is a catastrophe. You're welcome to 'understand' all you want. I'll take care of the dreary practical matters, such as how to get in and out undetected. Otherwise, I'll probably have to kill somebody, and Jaynes will nag the daylights out of me. He always gets in a foul mood when I come home with bloodstains on my clothes."

"Who is Jaynes?" Lydia asked, momentarily diverted.

"My valet."

Lydia turned to study him.

His thick, dark hair looked as though a drunken gardener had combed it with a rake. His rumpled neckcloth was coming unknotted. His waistcoat was unbuttoned and a corner of his shirt hem dangled from his waistband.

She was hotly aware that she'd done some of the rumpling. But not all of it, she fervently hoped. She did not remember unbuttoning or untucking anything. The trouble was, she couldn't be sure her memory was any more reliable than her powers of reason and self-control had been.

"Your valet ought to be hanged," she said. "He ought to consider your title, if nothing else, before allowing you out of the house in that disorderly condition."

"You're a fine one to talk," he said. "At least I have all my clothes on."

He didn't so much as glance down at his attire. He did not lift a finger to button a button or tuck in his shirt or straighten his neckcloth.

And Lydia had to fold her hands tightly in her lap to keep from doing it for him.

"The point is, you are the Duke of Ainswood," she said.

"That's not my bloody fault, is it?" He turned away to glare out the window.

"Like it or not, that's who you are," she said. "As Duke of Ainswood, you represent something greater than yourself: a noble line that hearkens back centuries."

"If I want a lecture about my obligations to the title, I can go home and listen to Jaynes preach," he said, still watching the passing scene. "We're nearing Francis Street. I had better be the one to get out and survey the premises. You're far too conspicuous."

Without waiting for her acquiescence, he directed the driver to halt at a safe distance from the house.

As Ainswood started to open the door, she said, "I hope you will not think of trying anything by yourself. This will need careful planning. We don't know how many are there tonight, and so you are not to go barging in with any impetuous notions of—"

"Perhaps the pot would be so good as to leave off calling the kettle black," he said. "I know what to do, Grenville. Stop fussing."

He pushed the door open and alit.

Lydia was very late rising on the day of the crime.

This was partly because she'd come home very late. She'd spent more than an hour arguing with Ainswood after he returned from studying the prospective crime scene. He had got the maggoty idea in his head of doing it with his incompetent valet instead of her, and she'd had to waste a good deal of energy eradicating that imbecile notion before they could get to the crucial matter of planning the burglary.

Consequently, she hadn't got to bed until nearly three o'clock in the morning. She should have fallen asleep quickly, her mind easy, for the plan they'd finally agreed upon was simple and straightforward, and the risks were considerably smaller with him along than with Helena.

Lydia's conscience was quiet as well. She did not have to ask Helena to jeopardize all she'd achieved—not to mention life and limb—for a girl she didn't know. Instead, it would be Ainswood, who constantly courted danger and thought nothing of risking his worthless neck for a bet.

It was neither her conscience nor qualms about what lay ahead that kept Lydia awake, but her inner devil.

The images filling her mind were not of the dangers she'd face in the coming night, but of those she'd already experienced: powerful arms crushing her against a rock-hard body; slow, thorough kisses that drained away her reason; and big hands that stole her will while they stole over her, and left her only the power to yearn for more.

She argued with the devil: One would have to be self-destructive to wish for a liaison with Ainswood. He used and discarded women; she would lose all her self-respect if she went to bed with a man who didn't respect her; she would lose the world's respect as well, since he'd be sure to let the world know.

She reminded herself how much she stood to lose. Even the most open-minded of her readers would have to doubt her judgment, if not her morals, in taking England's most notorious debauchee as a lover. She told herself it was insane to sacrifice her influence, limited though it was, upon the altar of physical desire.

Yet she could not quiet the inner devil urging her to do as she wanted, and to hell with the consequences.

As a result, day was already breaking when Lydia finally drifted into a fitful sleep, and it was past noon before she came down to breakfast.

Tamsin, who'd been asleep when Lydia came home, had

risen hours before. She entered the dining room soon after Lydia sat down, and started the interrogation promptly after Lydia took her first sip of coffee.

"You should have wakened me when you came in," the girl chided. "I tried to keep awake, but I made the mistake of taking a volume of Blackstone's *Commentaries* to read in bed, which was rather like taking a large dose of laudanum. What did Madame Ifrita want to talk about that was so urgent?"

"She's uncovered some dirt on Bellweather," Lydia said. "If it's true, we've a delicious exposé of our archrival for the next issue. I'll find out tonight whether it's true or not."

The truth was that she couldn't tell Tamsin the truth. The girl would raise as much of a fuss as Ainswood had done last night. Worse, Tamsin would spend the night worried frantic.

With the big lie out of the way, Lydia went on to an edited version of her encounter with Ainswood.

She left out all references to the planned crime, but she did not leave out the torrid embrace in the dark corridor of the piazza. It was one thing to shield Tamsin from needless worry. It was altogether another to pretend to be any less a fool than one was.

"Please don't ask me what I did with my brain," Lydia said at the conclusion of the tale, "because I've asked myself the same question a hundred times."

She tried to eat the food she'd mainly been pushing around her plate, but she seemed to have lost her appetite along with her mind.

"It was most inconsiderate of him," Tamsin said, frowning at the neglected breakfast, "to behave nobly twice in the same day—first in Exeter Street, then with the flower girl—and both times under your observation."

"Three times," Lydia corrected tightly. "He stopped when I told him to, remember. If he hadn't, I'm not at all sure

I should have made much of a struggle to preserve my maidenhead."

"Perhaps there's a decent man inside him, struggling to get out," Tamsin said.

"If so, the decent fellow has an uphill battle." Lydia refilled her coffee cup and drank. "Did you have a chance last night to look over that lot of books and notes I left on my desk?"

"Yes. It was very sad, especially the last funeral, for the little boy who died of diphtheria—only six months after his papa."

The boy's father, the fifth duke, had died of injuries sustained in a carriage accident.

"That papa appointed Ainswood guardian to three children," Lydia said. "What do you reckon possessed the fifth duke to leave his children in the care of England's prime profligate?"

"Perhaps the fifth duke was acquainted with the decent fellow."

Lydia set down her cup. "And perhaps I'm only looking for excuses, trying to justify succumbing to the handsome face, strong physique, and seductive skills of a practiced rake."

"I hope you're not hunting excuses on my account," Tamsin said. "I shan't think ill of you if you go to bed with him." Behind the spectacles, her brown eyes twinkled. "On the contrary, I should be vastly interested to hear all about it. Purely for information, of course. And you needn't act it out."

Lydia tried a majestic glare, but her quivering mouth spoiled the effect. Then she gave in and laughed, and Tamsin giggled with her.

She was a darling, Lydia thought.

With a few words she'd dispelled Lydia's black gloom—

and this wasn't the first time. One could tell Tamsin just about anything. She had a quick understanding and an open heart and a delicious sense of humor.

Her parents hadn't appreciated what they had. Her father had abandoned her and her mother had driven her away, when it could have been so easy to keep her. She asked for nothing. She was so eager to be of use. She never complained about the long hours she spent alone while Lydia worked. The girl was thrilled when asked to help with an assignment. The most tedious research task was an adventure to her. The maids loved her. So did Susan.

Though Lydia had learned long ago not to place any dependence upon Providence's assistance, she could not help viewing her young companion as a gift from heaven.

Tonight, if all went well, Lydia would be able to give a small but precious gift in return.

That was what mattered, she reminded herself.

She rose, still smiling, and ruffled Tamsin's hair.

"You ate hardly anything," the girl said. "Still, at least you've recovered your spirits. I wish it were as easy to cheer up Susan."

Belatedly, Lydia noticed that the dining room contained no canine pretending to be in the last stages of starvation.

"She turned up her nose at her breakfast," Tamsin said. "She dragged me out to Soho Square, then dragged me back home three minutes later. She didn't want to walk. She went into the garden and lay down with her head on her forepaws and ignored me when I tried to tempt her with her ball. She didn't want to chase sticks, either. I was looking for her pull-along duck when you came downstairs."

Susan had several toys. The battered wooden duck with its frayed pull string was her favorite.

If she was sulking, though, as it seemed she was, the duck

wouldn't cheer her, Lydia knew.

"Either she ate something that disagreed with her—a stray Pekingese, for instance—or she's in a sulk," Lydia said. "I'll go out and have a look at her."

She left the dining room and started for the back of the house. Before she'd taken more than a few steps, she heard paws thundering up the stairs from the kitchen.

The servants' door flew open and Susan burst through. In her blind rush through the hallway, she bumped into Lydia and nearly overturned her.

The knocker sounded, and Bess hurried out from the parlor to answer the door.

Lydia recovered her balance and hastened after the excited dog. "Susan, *heel*," she ordered. To no avail.

The mastiff thundered on, sideswiping the maid. Bess stumbled and caught the door handle. The door swung open, Susan pushed through, knocking Bess aside, and leapt upon the man standing on the doorstep. Lydia saw him stagger backward under the mastiff's weight a moment before her foot struck something.

Lydia toppled forward, saw the wooden duck skid sideways while she headed downward. An instant before she could land, she was jerked up and hauled against a large, hard torso.

"Plague take you, don't you ever bother to look where you're going?" an all too familiar voice scolded above her spinning head.

Lydia looked up . . . into the laughing green eyes of the Duke of Ainswood.

A quarter hour later, Lydia was in her study, watching His Grace inspect her books and furniture as though he were the broker's man, come to assess the property for a debt action.

Meanwhile, Trent—he was the one Susan had tried and failed to knock over—Tamsin, and Susan had departed for Soho Square—because Ainswood had told them to go for a walk.

"Ah, *Life in London*, by Mr. Pierce Egan," the duke said as he took the book from the shelf. "It's one of my favorites. Is this where you learned what a chancery suit on the nob was?"

"I am waiting to learn why you have invaded my house," she said frigidly. "I told you I would come to collect you at nine o'clock this evening. Do you want the whole world to know we're acquainted?"

"The world found that out a month ago in Vinegar Yard. The world witnessed the introduction." He did not look up from the book. "You really ought to get Cruikshank to illustrate for you. Purvis is too Hogarthian. You want Cruikshank's slyer touch."

"I want to know what you mean by strolling in here as though you owned the house—and bringing Trent with you."

"I needed him to draw Miss Price out of the way," he said, turning a page. "I should think that was obvious. He will keep her busy trying to fathom the mystery of Charles Two, which will prevent her speculating about my unexpected arrival."

"You could have achieved that purpose by not arriving at all," Lydia said.

He closed the book and returned it to the shelf. Then he eyed her, slowly, up and down. Lydia felt a hot prickling at the back of her neck that spread downward and outward. Her gaze slipped to his hands. The longing they'd stirred in her last night rippled through her again, and she had to back away and busy her hands with tidying her desk, to keep from reaching for him.

She wished she'd experienced a schoolgirl infatuation when she'd been a girl. Then she would have been familiar with the feelings, and disciplined them as she'd disciplined so many others.

"I've asked Trent to take Miss Price to the theater tonight," he said.

That brought Lydia back to business with a jolt. Trent. Tamsin. To the theater. Together. She made herself think. She must have an objection.

"Jaynes won't be available to fleece him at billiards," Ainswood continued, distracting her. "And I can't leave Trent to his own devices. I considered drawing him into our conspiracy—"

"Into our—"

"—but the prospect of having Trent's unique brand of help—as in tripping, breaking things, walking into doors, knives, and bullets—made my hair stand on end."

"If he's so troublesome, why in blazes have you adopted him?" Lydia asked, while she tried to get her mind off the absurd images Ainswood painted and back onto the right track.

"He entertains me."

Ainswood moved to the fireplace. The study being small, he had no great distance to travel. It was more than enough, though, to display the easy, athletic grace with which he moved, and the form-fitting elegance with which his garments hugged his muscular frame.

If he'd been merely handsome, she could have viewed him with detachment, Lydia was sure. It was the sheer size and power of his frame that she found so . . . riveting. She was hammeringly conscious of how strong he truly was, and how easily he wielded his strength. Last night he'd carried her in his arms effortlessly, and made her feel like a mere slip of a girl.

She'd never felt that way before, even when she was a girl.

At present he made her feel stupid as well, like a besotted

adolescent. She hoped she was not looking as idiotishly entranced as she felt. She dragged her gaze away, to her hands.

"You needn't be uneasy."

The deep voice called her attention back to him.

Ainswood rested his elbow on the mantel and his jaw upon his hand, and gazed at her. "I told him you'd asked me to help you with a difficult assignment of a highly confidential nature," he went on. "I asked him to take Miss Price to the theater, to 'allay suspicions.' He didn't ask whose suspicions had to be allayed or inquire why going to the theater would allay them." Twin devils danced in the green eyes. "But then, a man who imagines a girl can dig her way out of a stone dungeon with a sharpened spoon can imagine just about anything. So I left him to it."

"A spoon?" she said blankly. "Out of a dungeon?"

"Miranda, of *The Rose of Thebes*," he said. "That's how she'll escape, Trent believes."

Lydia came out of her fog with a jolt. Miranda. Bloody hell. She gave the desk a quick survey. But no, she hadn't left the manuscript out. Or if it had been left out, Tamsin must have locked it away. Letting her in on the secret had been an act of trust—not to mention less complicated than subterfuge would have been, with so quick and perceptive a young woman in the house.

Tasmin had also put away the *Annual Register* and *Debrett's Peerage*. But Lydia's notes and the Mallory family tree she'd begun lay square in the center of the desk. She casually pushed them under a copy of the *Edinburgh Review*.

"You're not going to stab me with a penknife, are you?" Ainswood asked. "I didn't give the game away. I know you wanted to surprise her tonight. I collect you've already fabricated an assignment."

"Yes, of course." Lydia shifted position to perch on the

edge of the desk, her derriere resting on the *Edinburgh Review*. "I'm supposed to be digging up dirt on a literary rival. There's no chance of their comparing stories. She would never disclose my doings."

"Then what's got your back up?"

He came away from the fireplace and made a circuit of the desk. Lydia stayed where she was. "I suppose the possibility of her declining Trent's invitation hasn't occurred to you," she said.

"I heard they had an interesting encounter yesterday." Ainswood rounded the corner of the desk and paused a pace away from her. "It seems she bore Trent's blithering for rather a long while." He bent his head and in lower tones said, "Maybe she fancies him."

She felt his breath on her face. She could almost feel his weight upon her, and the lashing strength of his arms.

Almost wasn't enough. Her hand itched to reach up and grab his pristinely starched neckcloth and pull his face down to hers. "I doubt it," she said. "She . . ." Lydia trailed off, belatedly realizing that his neckcloth was indeed crisply starched and that, moreover, those form-fitting garments fit without crease, wrinkle, rips, or stains.

"Good grief, Ainswood," she exclaimed softly. "What's happened to you?" Her astonished gaze moved up to his head. "Your hair is combed." Her attention drifted downward. "You haven't slept in your clothes."

His powerful shoulders lifted in a shrug. "I thought we were discussing Miss Price and Trent, not what I wear to bed."

Lydia would not be diverted from her subject. "I collect you took my suggestion and hanged your valet, and found a responsible replacement."

"I did not hang him." He leaned in closer, and Lydia

caught a tantalizing whiff of soap and cologne. "I told him—"

"That's a most agreeable scent," she said, tilting her head back. "What is it?"

"I told him," Ainswood went on tautly, "that you did not approve of my manner of dressing." His big hands settled upon the desk on either side of her. "I told him my life was henceforth rendered weary, stale, and profitless."

She closed her eyes and sniffed. "Like a pine forest . . . far away . . . the faintest trace carried on the wind."

She opened her eyes. His mouth was but an inch from hers.

He drew back, retreated out of reach, and brushed something from his cuff. "I'll tell him you were transported and burst into poetical raptures. I'll tell him you were rendered utterly useless for intelligent discussion. Still, you haven't argued about my arrangements for Trent and your companion—which ought to be marked down as a miracle of some kind. Until tonight, then."

He turned away and started toward the door.

"That's all?" she asked. "That's all you came for—to tell me about your plans for Trent?"

"Yes." He didn't look back, didn't pause, but strode through the door and slammed it behind him.

Grenville had very sensibly stuffed her thick golden hair under a battered cap. The trousers were supposed to be sensible, too. As she'd told Vere, she was stripped for action—in a dark-colored masculine shirt tucked into the waistband of the trousers and a spencer over that—with no skirts or loose garment ends to catch or tangle in anything.

And so, because the spencer reached only as low as her waist, and because the secondhand trousers were worn tissue-thin in the rump and the fit there was a tormenting fraction too tight, Vere's own nether regions were stirring for action.

The wrong kind.

Keep your mind on the job, he commanded himself as her foot left his laced fingers and she swung up onto the privy.

They were in the backyard of Coralie's house.

Vere adjusted the dark kerchief—slit, like hers, for seeing and breathing—that hid his face, and climbed after her. From the roof of the outdoor necessary, it was an easy reach to the ledge outside Coralie's back window. The window was closed only, not bolted, so Vere had no trouble prying it open with his pocketknife.

Coralie had long since left, and moments earlier, Vere had checked on the remaining occupants. A pair of servants were belowstairs having a row, by the sounds of it. Nonetheless, he checked again for signs of first-floor occupancy before climbing in. Grenville followed close behind him, swinging her long legs over the sill.

"Light closet," she murmured, the words barely audible. "Unused, evidently."

That was unsurprising. Coralie had moved to Francis Street very recently.

Grenville's study was a converted light closet, he recalled. The cramped space at the back of the house had one small window to let in daylight, and a doll-size fireplace. With the desk and chair and wall-to-wall books, it was an open invitation to conflagration.

That wasn't the fire he'd been worried about at the time. It was the way she'd looked at him. The blinking astonishment—as though his combed hair and clean, unrumpled clothes constituted one of the world's wonders—should have been comical, but he'd been too irritated to laugh. He'd felt hot and uncomfortable, like a schoolboy in his Sunday best, trying to impress the object of his calf-love.

That wasn't the worst of it, though. He'd discovered moments later that a pair of ice-blue eyes could transmit heat and drive a man's temperature up to the danger point. He'd had to hurry out then, before he lost control.

In his haste, he'd failed to inform her of other changes in plans. Doubtless she would play him one of her rotten tricks, to pay him back for sneaking in her servants' entrance at half past eight and bullying her into the carriage he'd hired.

She'd wanted to take a hackney. It was more anonymous, she said. She apparently believed him stupid enough to arrive in one of his own vehicles—complete with ducal crest screaming his identity from the door.

She truly did believe his mind was stunted, Vere brooded as he felt his way through the tiny back room.

As though her brain were infallible.

It hadn't dawned on her that Coralie's house was but a few streets from Soho Square, which made it logical for Vere, who was coming from farther away, to collect his partner-in-crime en route, instead of her going out of her way and having to backtrack.

Not that there would have been any point in telling her. He was sure she hadn't attended to more than a word in twenty of what he'd said to her in the study. She'd been too busy staring at him, watching every move he made, as though she had him under a microscope.

In his misspent life, he'd undressed any number of women with his eyes. If they'd returned the favor, he hadn't paid much attention. Today he'd been pulsingly conscious of the blue gaze that seemed to penetrate layers of immaculately tailored clothes as though they'd been transparent.

Naturally, his rod had started swelling for sport, and then she'd got that dazed, dreamy look and started talking poetry, and . . . well, then, as you'd expect, his brain had closed up shop and left the thinking to his breeding organ.

It was a miracle he hadn't thrown her down on the desk and relieved her of her maidenhead then and there, he reflected irritably as his fingers settled upon the door handle. Again he listened. No signs of life. Cautiously, he cracked the door open.

One small lamp feebly lit the room, casting uncertain shadows. "Bedroom," he said in an undertone.

"You take the left side, I'll take the right," she whispered.

He slipped into the room and moved noiselessly to the opposite door. She trailed close on his heels. Starting from the door, they began to search their assigned territories for jewelry.

The room was a mess: gowns, underthings, footwear strewn everywhere.

In his mind's eye, Vere saw a similar scene, but in his own bedroom, and in his fancy it was dragon's wear scattered about: a wanton trail of discarded black garments ending in a tangled heap of chemise, corset, and stockings, beside the bed. Upon the bed lay a luscious expanse of woman, smoky hot, and . . .

"Good God."

Vere's glance shot toward his companion. For one mortifying moment, he feared he'd said what he was so lewdly thinking. But no. Her masked countenance was not turned toward him. She was on her knees, staring into an open hatbox.

He dropped the petticoat he'd just fished out from under a footstool, crossed the room, and knelt beside her.

In the flickering lamplight, bracelets, earrings, rings, necklaces, seals, chains, and brooches winked up at him from the box. The hopeless tangle looked like a magpie's nest, with pieces knotted and woven with one another. That, however, was not what had elicited Grenville's breathless exclamation.

She took up an object from the top of the glittering heap. It was a silver stickpin. The head was artfully carved to depict two body parts conjoined in a manner expressly prohibited by both church and state.

He snatched it from her. "Never mind puzzling over that," he whispered. "Are Miss Price's things in there?"

"Yes—along with, apparently, every piece of jewelry in the Western Hemisphere. Separating them will be like untying the Gordian knot. She's hooked rings through chains and necklaces and—oh, everything is either attached to or tangled with everything else."

She crawled away, searched through a heap of clothing, and drew out a chemise. She came back, laid it on the floor, and dumped the hatbox's contents onto it. Then she gathered up the edges of the garment and fashioned a bundle.

"Find me a garter," she said.

"Are you mad? We can't take everything. You said—"

"We have no choice. We can't stay here all night trying to work loose the pieces we want. Find me a—Never mind. There's one."

She snatched up a stray garter and tied the bundle with it.

Vere relieved his feelings by jamming the obscene stickpin into a nearby bonnet.

She started to rise, then froze.

Vere heard it, too, in the same instant: footsteps and voices approaching . . . rapidly.

He lunged at her, pushed her down, and shoved her under the bed. He flung a heap of gowns and petticoats onto the hatbox and pushed it into a corner, then dove under the bed, in the same moment the door opened.

9

It seemed to go on for hours: the mattress jerking violently above, the French girl alternately crying out in pain and begging for more while her partner alternately laughed and threatened in a vaguely familiar voice that seemed to slither over Lydia's skin and into her belly, leaving her chilled and faintly nauseated.

She could not stop herself from edging nearer to Ainswood. She would have burrowed under his big body if she could, but the tight vertical fit prevented her from carrying out that inexplicable act of cowardice. Even flat on her stomach, she occasionally felt the mattress sag onto her head. She prayed it wouldn't collapse. She prayed that neither of the acrobatic lovebirds would tumble off and happen to look under the bed.

It wasn't the easiest corner to fight one's way out of, and she would not be able to fight very effectively while keeping a firm grip on the precious bundle.

Devil take them, would they never stop?

Finally, after about two more minutes that felt like two decades, the tumult subsided.

Leave, Lydia silently commanded. *You've had your fun. Now go away.*

But no, now they had to exchange pillow talk.

"Lovely performance, Annette," said the man. "But you may tell your mistress that one accommodating slut is not enough to appease me."

The mattress shifted and a pair of stockinged masculine

171

feet descended to the floor, inches from Lydia's head. She felt Ainswood's hand slide over her back and press her down firmly.

She comprehended his silent message: Keep still.

She remained still, although it seemed that every muscle in her body was twitching. From her vantage point, it was evident that the fellow was conducting a search similar to theirs. She stifled a gasp when he unearthed the hatbox she'd emptied.

But he flung it aside and snatched up a bonnet. "Here's my silver stickpin," he said. "Now, do you know what this looks like? It looks like adding insult to injury. After keeping what she knew was mine, and lying when I asked her whether I'd left it here, she has the effrontery to flaunt the thing in public—adorning her garish bonnet, no less."

"I did not know," came the girl's uneasy voice. "I never saw it before, I promise you, monsieur."

The stockinged feet advanced to the bed, then disappeared as he climbed onto it, the mattress sinking under his weight. The girl let out a shriek.

"Do you like that, Annette?" the man asked, his voice tinged with amusement. "Would you like to be my pincushion for an hour or so? I can think of many interesting places to—"

"Please, monsieur. It was not me. I did not take it. Why do you punish me?"

"Because I am very cross, Annette. Your mistress stole my wicked little stickpin—one of a kind, and it cost me plenty. And she's stolen—or driven off—the little flower girl I'd set my heart on. A pretty little cripple, all alone in the world. She wasn't in her usual place in Covent Garden last night, but Corrie was there, all smiles. The girl wasn't there tonight, either." The mattress moved violently and the girl cried out.

Lydia felt Ainswood's body tense beside her. She, too, was tensing, eager to spring out and beat senseless the foul thing above them. But the girl began to giggle, and Lydia reminded herself what sort of girl Annette was: second only to Madam Brees in ruthlessness and brutality, Annette was the one who usually helped Josiah and Bill break in new girls.

Lydia found Ainswood's hand and pressed hers upon it, willing him to remain where he was.

"No, this isn't the way to punish her, is it?" the man was saying. "What does she care what I do to you?"

Once more his feet descended to the floor. This time, he collected the garments he'd discarded so hastily.

"Get dressed," he said. "Or stay undressed, whatever you prefer. But you're going on a treasure hunt, Annette, and I hope for your sake it's successful."

"But I do not know what has become of the jewelry."

Lydia's heart tried to crawl into her throat.

The girl knew the jewelry was missing. Evidently her client had either returned or arrived unexpectedly, and interrupted her ransacking of Coralie's bedroom. It must have been Annette and this vile man they had heard arguing downstairs.

The man laughed. "What good is that rat's nest to me? It would take weeks to untangle it, and for what? A very few items of any value, mixed with a prodigious lot of worthless gewgaws. Corrie has no taste, no discernment, only greed. No, my little pincushion. I want the silver, gold, and banknotes. The box. I know what it looks like, but I'm not in a humor to hunt for it."

"Monsieur, I beg you. I am the only one she tells where it is. If it is gone, she will blame me, and she—"

"Tell her I made you do it. I *want* you to tell her. I *want* her to know. Where is it?"

After a brief pause, Annette answered sullenly, "In the cellar."

Her swain moved to the door. "I'll wait at the back while you fetch it. Make it quick."

The mattress bounced as the girl alit from the bed. Muttering in French too low for Lydia to understand, Annette picked up her garments and hurried out after him.

The door had scarcely closed behind Annette, and Lydia had hardly begun breathing normally again, when Ainswood gave her a push. "Out," he whispered.

Lydia obediently wriggled out from under the bed, the hand on her hindquarters hastening her exit. He didn't wait for her to scramble up from the floor, but dragged her up and pushed her toward the light closet door.

They were obliged to wait at the window while a servant exited the privy. A moment after the menial had departed, Lydia was climbing down from the building's roof. Ainswood reached the ground at the same time and grabbed her shoulder. "Stay here," he murmured in her ear. "I've something to do. It won't take long."

Lydia tried to do as she was told, but after several tense minutes, curiosity got the better of her. She edged cautiously along the wall of the outdoor necessary and peeped 'round the corner.

She saw Ainswood's big form leaning against the house wall near a stairway leading belowground. As she watched, a man ascended, bearing a small box. He paused when he caught sight of the masked idler, then started to descend again, but Ainswood moved very quickly.

While Lydia watched, dumbstruck, the duke dragged the man up the stairs and flung him against the wall. The box clattered to the ground at the same instant Ainswood's fist crashed into his prey's gut. The man doubled over. The big fist smashed again—into his face, this time—and he toppled to the ground.

"You shit-eating maggot," Ainswood said in low, hard tones Lydia scarcely recognized as his. Turning from his unconscious victim, the duke untied his mask. He cast it aside as he strode toward her.

Numbly, she pulled off her own mask.

He took her arm and steered her out of the narrow yard and into Francis Street.

Not until they reached the Tottenham Court Road did Lydia find her voice. "What in blazes was that for?" she asked breathlessly.

"You heard him," he said in the same dangerously low tones. "The flower girl. He was the one who tried to lure her—and now you can deduce what he would have done to her."

Lydia came to a stop and looked down at his hands, then up into his hard, angry face.

"Oh, Ainswood," she cried softly. She reached up and grasped his shoulders. She meant to shake him, because he was such a fraud—pretending, last night, that he'd thrown money at the girl merely to get her out of the way.

Lydia did start to shake him. But then her arms circled those massive shoulders, and she hugged him instead. "Thank you. It's what *I* wanted to do—smash him." *And I could kiss you for it,* she thought as she tilted her head back to look again into his grimly set countenance.

But thinking it wasn't enough.

She kissed him.

Still, she wasn't altogether lost to reason. She meant the kiss to be quick, a brief salute to his chivalry. Her lips would touch his cheek lightly, a friendly gesture for a job well done.

But he turned his head and caught the kiss on his mouth,

and when his arms lashed about her, she understood what a fraud *she* was, pretending she'd wanted anything less.

The mouth crushing hers wasn't gentle and persuasive as it had been last night, but angry and insistent.

She should have broken away, but she didn't know how to resist what she wanted so badly, bad as it was to give in. She curled her arms 'round his neck and drank in greedily the wild heat and anger. Like some dangerous liquor, it raced through her veins, stirring the devil inside to mad joy.

She should not feel so happy, as though it were she who'd conquered instead of being conquered. But she was glad, feverishly so, because the iron bands of his arms crushed her, molding her to him as though he would crush her into his skin. This was where she wanted to be: part of him, as though he had a piece missing and she was the only one that fit.

His mouth pressed for more, and she parted to him, and shivered with guilty pleasure when his tongue tangled with hers in sinful intimacy. His big hands moved over her, boldly, as though she belonged to him, as though there was no question about it. And in that moment, it seemed inarguable to her.

She let her own hands move down to slip under the edge of his waistcoat, over his shirt, and she shivered again as the powerful muscles tautened under her touch. Then she understood she had power over him as well. She searched until she found the place where he couldn't hide the truth from her, where she could feel the furious beat of his heart against her palm.

She felt him shudder under her touch, as she did under his, heard the low, hungry sound he made as he boldly grasped her bottom and pressed her pelvis to the hard swell of his.

She hadn't layers of petticoats to insulate her this time,

and the size and pulsing heat of him made her recoil reflexively. It was no more than an instant's startled reaction, but he must have felt it, because he broke away.

He pulled his head back, grasped her upper arms, and said thickly, "Dammit, Grenville, this is a public byway."

He released her, stepped aside, and picked up the bundle she hadn't realized she'd dropped. Then he took firm hold of her arm with his free hand and marched her down the street to the waiting carriage.

Annette had not quite closed the cellar door when she heard the hurried footsteps—returning, not departing. She hadn't looked, only listened. She'd heard the thud against the wall and a clatter and grunts.

Annette had walked the streets of some of Paris's most unsavory neighborhoods. She could not fail to recognize the sounds of a back-alley attack. She'd lured any number of drunks into ambush in her misspent youth.

She heard an angry English voice and knew it wasn't her repellent client's. She waited, listening, until retreating footsteps told her the angry voice's owner had exited the narrow yard.

Then she slipped out and cautiously ascended the stairs. The space was little more than an alley, unlit except for what feeble light filtered down from a few overlooking windows. Nonetheless, she had sufficient light to discern whose body lay upon the ground.

She drew nearer. To her disappointment, the pig was still breathing. She looked about for something to finish him off with, but no satisfactory weapon lay within reach, not even a stray brick. This neighborhood was all too tidy and respectable, she thought, frustrated. Then her eye lit upon the box. She started toward it. The man groaned and moved. Annette kicked him in the head, snatched up the box, and ran.

At about this time, Vere was watching Grenville climb into his carriage and wishing someone would kick him in the head.

He scowled up at Jaynes, who sat in the driver's seat, wearing a villainously knowing smile.

The blackguard had seen.

So might anyone passing along the Tottenham Court Road have done. Unlike Jaynes, however, they wouldn't know it was a female Vere had wrapped himself about like a boa constrictor, trying to crush and devour her simultaneously.

He tossed the bundle to her, then flung himself inside and onto the seat.

The carriage jolted into motion with an abruptness that threw Grenville against him. She hastily righted herself, and that, for some reason, incensed him.

"You've left it rather late to play propriety," he snapped. "The gossips could banquet on the morsel for the next twelvemonth. If anyone saw us, it'll be all over London by noon tomorrow that the Duke of Ainswood fancies *boys*."

"You've left it rather late to worry about scandal," she said coolly. "You've been giving the gossips an endless series of banquets for years. Suddenly, tonight, you decide to become sensitive to public opinion." She shot him a blasting look of blue sleet.

He didn't need better light to know it was blue or a thermometer to ascertain the temperature. "Don't give me any of your deadly looks," he fumed. "You're the one who started it."

"I didn't hear you screaming for help," she said contemptuously. "I didn't notice you putting up any sort of struggle. Or am I supposed to believe that the two blows with which you dispatched that pervert left you too weak to fend off my assault?"

He hadn't even thought of resisting. If she hadn't started it, he would have, which was stupid, when he'd only get himself worked up for nothing. Even if he was humiliatingly randy for this infuriatingly arrogant female, he could hardly slake his lust in a public thoroughfare. And it would not be satisfactory anywhere else, because she was a novice.

But he wasn't randy for her in particular, he told himself. It was the circumstances. Danger could be sexually arousing.

Yet he hadn't been excited in the usual way during those moments under the bed. He'd been sick with dread while he listened to the nauseating maggot, and imagined everything horrible that could possibly happen: a knife in Vere's back, a cudgel to his head, and Death coming for him finally, at the one moment Vere couldn't afford to go, because then there would be no one to protect her from the slug and his perverted bedmate, and they would do terrible, sickening things to his partner in crime. And Vere had prayed, fervently, desperately: *Only let me live through this, long enough to get her safe away—only that, and I'll be good, I promise.*

An image flickered in his mind of himself, holding a child's hand and silently pleading, trying to bargain with an unseen Power. He hastily blocked out the image, and ignored the painful tightness in his chest.

"I don't want you," he said.

"Liar," she said.

"You're so conceited," he said, turning away. "You, Miss Vestal Virgin Grenville, think you know everything. You didn't even know how to kiss until I taught you."

"I don't recollect begging for the lesson," she said.

"And so you conclude you're irresistible."

"To you, yes. I should like to know what else I should

logically conclude from your behavior. And I should like to know why you have to make such a fuss about it."

"I am not making a fuss—and I wish you would stop using that patronizing term."

"I wish you'd stop lying," she said. "You do it very ill. I don't see why you can't admit you find me attractive, and it mortifies you—because I annoy you, and because I'm an ignorant virgin, and whatever other 'becauses' are troubling your manly dignity. Doubtless it hasn't occurred to you that I'm mortified, too. Finding you attractive is no compliment to my taste and judgment. Fate has played me any number of provoking tricks, but this beats them all."

He turned back to look at her.

She sat rigidly erect, staring straight ahead, her hands tightly folded upon the bundle in her lap.

"Confound you, Grenville," he said, his own hands fisting on his lap. "There's no need to get all pinched up like that, as though I hurt your feelings."

"As though you could," she said scornfully. "As though I'd let you."

"Then what?" he demanded. "What do you want me to do? Bed you? You've lived to this great age—"

"Eight and twenty," she said, her jaw stiff. "I am not a crone."

"You've managed to guard your virtue for all this time," he went on, his voice rising. "You are not going to make me responsible. You are not going to make me believe I've corrupted your morals."

"I don't give a damn what you believe."

"You knew what I was when you met me! Even your harlot friend warned you against me! She told you to get out of London, didn't she?"

"London is a large place. There was no reason for our

paths to cross, again and again." She shot him a sidelong glance. "No reason for you to turn up at the Blue Owl, which all the world knows is a publishing trade haunt. No reason for you to turn up at Jerrimer's, or to pursue me to Helena's, or to turn up at Covent Garden last night, on the only night I've gone there alone. Am I to believe that was all mere happenstance, that you haven't someone spying on me? Tell me you haven't, that this is more of my conceit, imagining you've gone to so much trouble on my account."

The corner of her mouth turned up ever so slightly. "Then tell me another, why don't you, Ainswood, because that cock won't fight."

"Plague take you, Grenville, I wouldn't have done it if I'd known you were a curst damned *virgin!*"

She did not answer right away, and the damning words he'd uttered seemed to hang in the tension-fraught air between them.

Then he was mortified, truly, as the meaning sank in and he saw what he'd done. He was a liar, just as she said, and he'd been lying to himself for weeks. Pitiful, childish lies. She was a beautiful monster and he wanted her, he was afraid to think how much. Rarely had he ever wanted anything badly, and never a woman. He had only one use for women, and no one woman had ever been worth taking any trouble for, not when there were so many, and the next would do as well.

He had a horrible suspicion that this time, no one else would do. If that wasn't the case, why hadn't he found someone else? It wasn't as though London had suddenly run out of whores, was it?

It was a short drive to Soho Square, not nearly long enough for him to decide what to do. A glance out the window told him they'd already reached Charles Street.

"It seems you're in the grip of one of your sporadic fits of nobility," the beautiful monster said.

"I'm not noble," he said tightly. "Don't make me out to be what I'm not. I made a mistake, that's all, and it's no surprise, since I make this sort often enough. I mistook Dain's lady for a ladybird, didn't I? If you'd had someone at hand as she did, to pound the facts into me in the first place, none of this would have happened. I was ready to go, as soon as I understood my error, last night. You were the one who called me back and asked for help. If you'd kept your distance a little while ago, I would have kept my hands to myself. But you can't expect—"

He broke off as his gaze drifted downward, over the long stretch of wickedly curving trousered leg. Then upward it strayed again over the perfect contours of hip and waist, the waist his big hands could easily span, and on to the glorious swell of her bosom while longing tore at him, shredding pride and a lifetime's accumulation of cynicism.

And so, when he lifted his gaze to her beautiful arrogant face, he began to comprehend, whether he wanted to or not, what the thing was that kept stabbing at his heart.

"I understand," she said. "I've turned out to be a disappointment to you. You might have set aside your personal dislike if I'd been a woman of experience. But to have to tolerate my odious personality as well as play tutor is asking too much." She looked out the window. "It isn't your responsibility, as you said. Merely because you started something, unintentionally, you aren't obliged to finish it. Merely because you introduced me to a neglected part of my education, I shouldn't assume you must complete my training. The subject is hardly esoteric. It isn't as though I can't find someone else to continue my lessons."

"Someone else? Who the devil do you—But you're not serious." He essayed a laugh while he recalled how Helena

Martin had invited her friend to come out and make "a more agreeable surprise" for Sellowby the scandalmonger.

"There's no accounting for tastes," she said. "Some men enjoy my company."

"That lot of drunken lowlife scribblers in the Blue Owl, you mean," he said. "Well, let me explain something to you about men, Miss Messalina Grenville: It isn't your personality they appreciate. Or your intellect."

"We're entering Frith Street." She turned away from her window. "Not a minute too soon for you, I'm sure. Still, you can bear my thanks, I hope? I was exceedingly glad to have you along this night. I found that man very disturbing. It was comforting to know you'd have no trouble dispatching him. As you demonstrated."

The carriage stopped before her house.

Vere was still staring at her, the "someone else" blaring in his head like a bugle in time to the furious drumbeat of his heart. "There isn't going to be anyone else," he choked out above the inner roar. "You only said that to make me—" Not jealous, it was ridiculous to be jealous of a man he only imagined. "To make me do what you want. The way you manipulated me last night. It's a taunt, that's all."

The carriage door opened. Jaynes could be quick enough, curse him, when it suited him—which usually happened when it was least convenient for Vere. But Jaynes was in a fearful hurry to get home, before any of his acquaintances spotted him in the ignominious role of coachman.

"I beg your pardon," she said ever so politely. "I did not mean to taunt. Would you kindly step out of the vehicle, Your Grace? Or would you rather I crawled over you?"

Jaynes stood there, taking in every word, obviously, for he'd both black eyebrows lifted nearly to his hairline.

Vere threw him a threatening look and climbed out. Before he could put out his hand to help her, Grenville nimbly alit, and without pausing moved swiftly to her door.

"Wait," Vere told Jaynes, then hurried after her.

"What are you telling me?" Vere demanded as she paused to fish out her key from a pocket of her spencer. "I've corrupted your morals, is that it, Grenville?" He moved to block the door. "Is that what I've done?"

"Don't be ridiculous," she said. "I'm not a lady, but a journalist, and everyone knows we haven't any morals." The slim hand holding the key waved impatiently. "Do get out of the way, Ainswood. I'm not blaming you for anything. There's no need to make a scene."

"Not blaming me?" His voice rose. "Oh, no, certainly not. All I did was start you on the road to ruin. No harm done, no, indeed. Only that you've taken it into your hollow little head—"

"Keep your voice down," she said. "You'll upset the dog. She doesn't like it when strange men shout at me."

"Devil take the curst dog! You can't dare and daunt me with someone elses—"

"I was not—Oh, there, now you've done it."

Vere heard it, the muffled thumping from somewhere within the house, and then the unmistakable bark of a mastiff, and not one in a friendly mood. The sound appeared to emanate from the bowels of hell. Even with house walls between them, Vere could feel the vibrations in his teeth. The windows rattled.

"Oh, yes, I've done it." Vere stepped back from the door and shouted above the animal's din. "And you're too late, Susan. I've started it, and now there's no holding her back. You'd better get used to strange men, my girl, because—"

"Devil confound you." Grenville pushed the key into the lock and pushed the door open. Then she grabbed his arm, pulled him inside, and slammed the door behind them.

The next thing Vere heard was a furious roar.

It all happened in the blood-chilling space of a heartbeat: He saw the dog leap—Death, black, hurtling toward them with fangs bared—and tried to push Grenville out of the way. But she flung herself against him, shielding his body with hers.

"*Down,* Susan!" she shouted.

"DOWN, DAMN YOU!" he roared as the beast lunged.

Vere sagged back against the door, his arms wrapped tautly about his would-be savior, while he waited for his heart to recommence beating and his gut to unknot itself.

He saw the dog trot back down the hall, where a flustered maid grabbed her collar. With an apologetic glance at the pair at the door, the maid took Susan away.

The mistress's last scream—or possibly Vere's bellowed command—had evidently penetrated Susan's homicidal brain, for they both seemed to be in possession of their limbs.

Vere didn't know how the dog had managed to stop herself mid-attack. He hadn't been watching, but moving, trying to turn to take the brunt of the assault.

He understood mastiffs. He'd grown up with them at Longlands. They were not vicious or high-strung by nature. Unless ill-treated, they were, generally speaking, even-tempered. They could be trusted with children. Still, they were dogs, unamenable to reason and deaf to even the master's command when their blood was up.

His gorgon might have been mauled . . . killed.

It was a damn fool thing to do, getting in the way of a maddened mastiff.

To shield *him.*

Vere brought his hand up to the back of her neck and tunneled his fingers into her hair. The cap, knocked askew when she'd flung herself upon him, fell to the floor.

"You'll be the death of me, Grenville," he whispered raggedly.

She tilted her head back and her blue eyes flashed.

"If you had kept still, she wouldn't have tried to knock you down." She raised her hand and pushed at his chest. "She was only trying to scare you away." She pushed again. "You're crowding me, Ainswood."

Crowding her. Vere had lost about ten years of his life in the horrifying moment when the dog sprang, and he was certain he'd simultaneously sprouted a large crop of grey hairs.

His hands slid down to her shoulders. He wanted to shake her. He started to. But her eyes shot sparks and her mouth was parting, preparing to deliver more brimstone, and he bent and clamped his mouth upon it so he wouldn't have to hear it, whatever it was.

She still pushed at his chest, and her other hand beat against his lower ribs: slow, hard, angry blows . . . once, twice, thrice. But even while she struck, her mouth softened under his, and she returned his kiss in a slow, sensuous surrender that melted his knees. His brain melted, too, along with all the excuses he'd piled there: Innocents were too much trouble; this one was impossibly arrogant and headstrong and fancied herself a match for any man; she was a bluestocking, the most loathsome of female species, et cetera, et cetera.

He was no saint. He'd never learned how to resist temptation. He had an armful of it now, and neither the wit nor the will to let go.

She circled his tongue with hers, and pressed her ripe body to his, moving against him to the slow beat of her hand, this time upon his back.

He'd taught her too well, or she understood him too well. The door to his heart was thick; one needed a battering ram to get in.

She hit him, and not gently, while she offered herself to him.

He didn't know how to shut her out.

He caught her punishing hands and brought them down to his waist and held them there. Slowly, through the deepening kiss, her fists uncurled. Then her hands began to roam, over his waist and up over his back, and down over his buttocks and hips, and up again.

She was no longer shy, and that unbashful touch burned through his garments and seared the skin beneath. Refusing to burn alone, he caressed her in the same deliberate way, dragging his hands up to rove over her back and down her proud spine to the waist his hands so easily spanned and downward, over the luscious arc of her derriere. His heart beat to the sensuous rhythm she'd set, driving the blood through his veins at the same throbbing tempo.

In a distant corner of his mind, a beacon flashed in warning, but it couldn't penetrate the thickening heat of desire.

He wanted. Nothing else mattered. He wanted the scent and taste of her and the silken purity of her skin and the voluptuous curves of her long body. The wanting pulsed in nerve and muscle, in every fiber, a fierce hammering need, like physical blows.

He dragged his hands over her, as though his touch were enough to mark every cell of her as his.

When she broke the kiss at last, the beacon flashed again, only to flicker out as she trailed her mouth along his jaw and down to his neck. He branded her in turn with his mouth, along her smooth cheek and down the silken arc of her throat. He drank in the taste of her and the skin-scent of smoke and lilies and something else. "Dragon scent," he murmured. "My beautiful dragon."

She shifted against him, and he felt her hands tugging at the buttons of his waistcoat.

No longer shy; far from it.

She stroked over his shirt and laid her hand over his heart, where there was no hiding the truth from her, no concealing its wild hammering.

He was past wanting to hide the truth, even if he'd known how. He was past reasoning in any way.

Mindless, he was pulling at buttons, drawing back fabric warm with her warmth. It whispered as he pushed it away. He found the hot silk of her skin, and teased himself, lightly stroking over the swell of her breast, letting his thumb play over the tight bud while he heard her catch her breath and let it out with a faint cry she couldn't keep back.

She pushed nearer until her pelvis pressed against his rod, swollen and all too eager to accommodate.

The beacon flashed once more, but he buried his face in her neck and dragged her scent deep into his lungs. The warning light went out, smothered by sensation: Her skin was velvet against his cheek, warm silk under his lips.

He was aware, searingly aware of her hands, tugging at his shirt, then scorching over his skin.

His own were busy, too, searching for the waistband of her trousers, for the buttons, the flap opening. He found it—and in the same instant, a jab of sensation darted from his elbow to his shoulder.

It jolted him into a moment's consciousness. He blinked stupidly, like a drunkard, sotted with lust. And in the next instant he focused and saw that it was a doorknob his elbow had struck, and it was attached . . . to a door.

The door.

He had her against the bedamned *front door*.

"Jesus." He lifted his head and dragged in a lungful of air, then another and another.

He felt her hands slip away, heard her shuddering breath.

"Grenville," he began, nearly choking on his thick tongue.

He saw her hands move unsteadily to her garments and clumsily refasten what he'd undone. "Don't say a word," she said, her voice as thick as his. "I started it. I'll take the blame, the responsibility, whatever you like."

"Grenville, you—"

"I'm out of my depth," she said. "That's obvious. I should be thankful, I suppose. Only I can't quite get to that yet. I understand now what you meant last night about getting in a bad mood." She shut her eyes, opened them. "You didn't mention anything about one's vanity being hurt, but that's just as one deserves, isn't it?"

"Damnation, Grenville, don't tell me I've hurt your feelings." His voice was too sharp, too loud. He tried to level it. "For God's sake, we can't do it against the *front door*."

She pushed away from the door, picked up her bundle, and started down the hall.

He started after her. "You don't really want me," he said. "It was the heat of the moment. The excitement. Danger is arousing. You shouldn't come within a mile of me, Grenville. I'm a bad influence. Ask anybody."

"I'm not exactly a model of goodness myself," she said. "If I were, I should never be attracted to a worthless degenerate like you."

She punctuated the statement with an elbow to his ribs. "Go away," she said. "And *stay* away."

He stopped then and let her go. He watched her march, spine straight and arrogant rump swaying, the last few paces to her study door.

She opened it and without a backward glance at him went in and shut it behind her.

He stood unmoving, unsure, his mind the churning mess it usually was in her vicinity. This time it roiled with "someone else" and all the lies he told himself and whatever stray bits of truth managed to survive in the hellhole that was his brain.

In that seething pit, he discerned one glaring truth, the most humiliating: It was the "someone else" he couldn't bear.

This was the most unfortunate truth for her, but it couldn't be helped. She'd been so unlucky as to cross his path, and more unlucky still to pique his interest, and now . . .

He shouldn't even think it because, of all the depraved things he'd ever done or thought of doing, what he contemplated at this moment took the prize.

Still, he was the last Mallory hellion, dissolute, conscienceless, et cetera, et cetera.

What was one more crime in a lifetime of sins and outrages?

He advanced to the study door, pushed through it.

He found her dumping the chemise's contents onto her desk.

"I told you to go away," she said. "If you have one shred of consideration—"

"I don't." He pulled the door closed. "Marry me, Grenville."

10

Ainswood stood before the door, looking like a shipwreck. His coat and waistcoat, both rumpled and dirty, hung unbuttoned. He'd lost his neckcloth—probably with Lydia's help—and his shirt had fallen open, revealing the powerful lines of neck and shoulder and a tantalizing V of masculine chest. His snug trousers were stained, his boots scuffed.

"Marry me," he repeated, drawing her gaze back to his face. His eyes were dark and his countenance had taken on the hard-set expression she'd seen before. It signified his mind was closed and she might as well talk to the door he was blocking.

She wasn't absolutely certain what had put wedlock into his head, but she could guess: a belated attack of conscience, a misguided notion of duty, or the simple male need to dominate. Most likely it was a random mess of all three, with a dose of charity and probably several other noxious ingredients thrown in.

In any event, regardless what he meant by asking, she knew that marriage *meant* male dominance—with the unquestioning support of all forms of societal authority: the law, the church, the Crown. By everyone, in short, but the dominated gender, the women, whose enthusiasm for this state of affairs ran from strong (among the misguided few) to nonexistent (among the enlightened). Lydia had in her late teens taken her place among the latter and had not budged from that position since.

"Thank you," she said in her coolest, most resolute tones, "but marriage is not for me."

He came away from the door to take up a position across the desk from her. "Don't tell me," he said. "You've some high-flown principle against it."

"As a matter of fact, I do."

"You don't see, I suppose, why a woman has to behave differently than a man does. You don't see why you can't simply bed me and leave me. After all, this is what men do, so why can't you?"

"Women do it, too," she said.

"Whores." He perched on the edge of her desk, his back half turned to her. "Now you're going to tell me that calling them 'whores' is unjust. Why should women be vilified for doing what men do with impunity?"

This, in fact, was what she had been thinking and what she was about to say. Lydia darted him a wary glance. His face was averted. She couldn't read its expression.

She grew uneasy. She would have wagered a large sum that he hadn't the remotest idea of what she thought or believed in.

He was not supposed to have any idea at all about what went on in her head. He was supposed to view all women as objects of varying degrees of physical attractiveness who had but one use, thus only one purpose for existing at all.

"I should like to know why I am the only woman who has to marry you," she said, "merely to get what you pay to give other women. Thousands of other women."

"Leave it to you," he said, "to make it sound as though you've been singled out for punishment—cruel and inhuman, no doubt." He left the desk and moved to the fireplace. "You think I'm a bad bargain. Or, more likely, it's worse than that: It isn't me specifically, but all men."

He took up the coal bucket and replenished the dying fire while he spoke. "You're so blinded by contempt for men in general that you can't see any of the advantages of marrying me in particular."

As though she hadn't spent most of her life seeing for herself wedlock's so-called advantages, Lydia thought. As though she didn't see, almost daily, women wedlocked in heartbreak, helplessness, instability, and all too often, appallingly, in violence.

"What particular advantages do you have in mind?" she asked. "Your great wealth, do you mean? I have all the money I require and enough left over to save for a rainy day. Or is it the privileges of rank you refer to? Such as shopping for the latest fashions to wear to grand social affairs where the main entertainment is Slander My Neighbor? Or do you mean admittance to court, so that I may bow and scrape to the king?"

He didn't look up from his work but took his time, arranging the coals just so with the poker, applying the bellows to set the tidy stack aglow.

He did it with the smooth competence of one who'd been doing it for ages, though this was lowly work, beneath a footman's dignity, let alone that of a peer of the realm.

Lydia's gaze strayed over his broad shoulders, down over the strong back that tapered to lean waist and hips.

She felt a surge of longing. She beat it down.

"Or perhaps you call it a privilege," she continued, "to be obliged to live within an exceedingly narrow set of rules dictating what I may and may not say, do, or think?"

He rose finally and turned to her, his expression infuriatingly calm. "You might consider Miss Price, for whose precious trinkets you risked your life," he said. "As Duchess of Ainswood, you could dower her, which would allow her to wed to her liking."

Lydia opened her mouth to point out the fallacy of assuming that Miss Price needed to be wed any more than Miss Grenville did. But her conscience sprang up and shrieked, *How do you know?* And Lydia found herself staring speechlessly at Ainswood while her mind churned.

What if Tamsin did fancy Trent? His funds were very limited, everyone knew. If they wed, they'd have nothing to live on. But no, Tamsin wasn't interested in him in that way, Lydia argued with her conscience. He was odd, and the girl was no more than curious, as she was about everything and everyone.

Then what of Tamsin's future? her conscience asked gloomily. *If you contract a fatal disease or have a fatal accident, what becomes of her?*

"You write constantly about London's unfortunates," Ainswood went on, while she was still wrestling with the problem of Tamsin. "About injustice, generally. I daresay it hasn't occurred to you that the Duchess of Ainswood could, if she chose, wield considerable political influence. You'd have the opportunity to browbeat any number of members of Parliament into passing Peel's bill for a Metropolitan Police Force, for instance."

He wandered to the bookshelf and studied her *Annual Register* collection. "Then there's the issue of child labor. That's one of your pet causes, isn't it? Along with public hygiene and the appalling conditions of the back-slums. And prison conditions. 'Breeding places of vice and disease,' you've called them."

Lydia remembered Sarah in her shabby, patched pinafores, playing in the stinking alleys, and the children she played with, many worse off than she.

Lydia remembered the Marshalsea: the stench, the dirt, the diseases that spread unchecked through the squalor . . .

the disease that had spread to her sister and killed her.

Her throat tightened.

"Education," his deep voice went on, like a scourge, flaying her. "Medicine." He turned toward her. "Did you know that Trent's cousin, the Earl of Rawnsley's young bride, is building a modern hospital in Dartmoor?"* Schooling . . . which Lydia had hungered for, and the books she'd craved. What would have become of her education, if not for Quith? Thanks to him, she'd had an education and discovered a means of making her way in the world independently. She was strong and determined, though. What of those who weren't? And what of the weak and sickly, needing medicine, doctors, hospitals?

"You could *do* something," Ainswood said, "instead of simply writing about what is wrong."

If he'd spent years studying maps of her sore spots he couldn't have targeted them more accurately or shot his verbal darts with more devastating impact.

Lydia didn't know when or how he'd studied her. All she knew was that, at that moment, she felt like the most selfish woman in all the world, rejecting the power and wealth to do good, merely to preserve her personal freedom.

There had to be a flaw somewhere in this terrible logic of his, she told herself. There was an answer she could give him, surely, a proper setdown. Because he could not be entirely right and she entirely wrong. She knew the answer—the escape route—was there, somewhere in her agitated brain. She could almost—

The thump at the door sent the elusive wisps in her mind scattering. The second thump knocked them away alto-

* See "The Mad Earl's Bride," *Three Weddings and A Kiss*, Avon Books, © 1995.

gether. Lydia glared at the door, silently reviewing every oath she knew.

"Kitchen," she said in firm, carrying tones. "Back to the *kitchen,* Susan."

Outside the door, the dog began to whimper.

"I collect Susan wants her mama," Ainswood said. He went to the door.

"You'd better not," Lydia said as he grasped the handle.

"I'm not afraid of a dog," he said. He opened the door. Susan pushed past him as though he didn't exist, and trotted to Lydia.

She sniffed Lydia's hand, then licked it. "You don't have to make nice," Lydia said, striving for patience. "It isn't your fault he upset you."

"Did I upset you, Susan?"

Lydia's gaze swung back to him.

Ainswood was watching the dog, his brow furrowed, his wicked mouth turned down. "You're much too big a creature to be cooped up in a little kitchen of a little house. No wonder you're so high-strung."

"She is not high-strung!" Lydia snapped. "Everyone knows that mastiffs—"

"At Longlands, she'd have acres and acres to run and play in. And other mastiffs to play with. Would you like that, Susan?" he asked, his voice gentling. He crouched down. "Wouldn't you like to have a lot of playmates, and acres and acres to explore with them?" He gave a low, musical whistle.

Susan's ears pricked up, but she refused to turn.

"Su-san," he crooned. "Su-u-san."

Susan circled her mistress, then paused, her gaze settling on him. "Gr-rr-rr," she said.

Lydia knew that growl. It wasn't in the least threatening. It was Susan's sulky growl.

Don't you dare, Lydia commanded silently. *Don't you succumb to him, too.*

"Come, Susan." He patted his knee. "Don't you want to come and bite my face off? Your mama wishes you would. Su-u-u-san."

"Grrr-rr-rrr," said Susan.

But she was only playing hard to get, the wicked creature. After a moment, she started meandering toward him, feigning interest in a corner of the desk first, then studying a corner of the rug. She took her time, but she went to him.

Lydia watched her in utter disgust.

"I thought you had taste, Susan," she muttered.

The dog looked back, briefly, at Lydia, then started sniffing at His Grace. He remained crouched, his expression ostensibly sober while Susan sniffed his face, his ears, his neck, his mangled clothes, and—of course—his crotch.

Lydia's neck burned, and the heat spread upward and downward. Susan was bound to be intrigued because her mistress's scent must be all over him, as his was all over Lydia. Ainswood obviously realized this. The amusement in his eyes when his glance caught Lydia's told her so.

She was already heated. That green glint of humor merely ignited a temper already smoldering.

"I should like to know why, suddenly, you're concerned with unfortunates, including my sadly abused dog," she said tartly. "Since when have you become Saint Ainswood?"

He scratched behind Susan's ears. Susan grumbled and looked away, but she bore it well enough.

"I merely pointed out a few matters you couldn't be bothered to think about," he said innocently.

Lydia came 'round the desk and strode to the fireplace. "You've been playing on my sympathies as though they were harp strings. You—"

"What do you expect me to do?" he cut in. "Play fair? With a woman who makes up her own rules as she goes along?"

"I expect you to take no for an answer!"

He rose. "I should like to know what you're afraid of."

"Afraid?" Her voice climbed. *"Afraid? Of you?"*

"The only reason I can think of for your rejecting an opportunity to run the world as you see fit is fear that you can't manage the man offering the opportunity."

"You can think of only one reason because your mind is too narrow to fit any other in." She took up the poker and stabbed at the coals. "Ever since I admitted I was a virgin you've developed a virulent case of chivalry. First you decided to nobly forsake me." She straightened and shoved the poker back onto its rack. "Now you've decided to save me from ruin—which would be mildly amusing if you were not so curst obstinate and underhand about it."

"You find my behavior mildly amusing?" he asked. "What do you think is my reaction when I hear Miss Queen of Playactors, Miss Fraud of the Century, accuse me of being 'underhand'?"

She swung away from the chimneypiece. "Whatever else I've done, I haven't used tricks or playacting to make you follow me. You're the one who's been spying on me, dogging my footsteps. Then, when I'm ready to give you what you want, you decide it isn't enough. I have to give up my freedom, my career, my friends, and vow unswerving devotion until death us do part."

"In exchange for wealth, rank, and power to do what you've been trying to do anyway," he said impatiently.

Susan looked at him, then at Lydia. She ambled to her mistress and nuzzled her leg. Lydia ignored her. "The price is too high!" she raged. "I don't need your—"

"You needed me tonight, didn't you?" he interrupted.

"You admitted as much, or have you forgotten?"

"That doesn't mean I want to be attached to you permanently!"

Susan sank down before the hearth, grumbling.

Ainswood leaned back against the door, folding his arms. "You might not have lived to engage in tonight's enterprise if I hadn't been about last night," he said levelly. "You might not have lived to sashay about Covent Garden last night if I hadn't taken you out of Jerrimer's before Coralie and her cutthroat minions penetrated your disguise. And if I hadn't come along in Vinegar Yard, one of Coralie's cohorts might have planted a knife in your back while you were daring and daunting the rest of the world. Not to mention that you might have killed Bertie Trent if I hadn't been on the spot to pull him out of the way."

"I came nowhere near killing him, you blind—"

"You drive in the same unthinking, headstrong way you do everything else."

"I've been driving for years and never once caused injury to human or animal," she said coldly. "Which is more than you can say. That demented hell-for-leather race of yours on the king's birthday ended with two fine animals having to be destroyed."

That dart penetrated.

"Not *my* animals!" He jerked away from the door.

Having finally found Lord Superior Male's sore spot, Lydia ruthlessly pressed her advantage.

"It was your doing," she returned. "That mad race on the Portsmouth Road was your idea, according to Sellowby. He told Helena that you challenged your fellows—"

"It was a fair race!" His color darkened. "It was not my fault that ham-fisted idiot Crenshaw abused his cattle."

"Ah, so he was incompetent *despite* being a superior male.

Yet I cannot be considered a capable whip simply because I'm a woman."

"A whip? *You?*" Ainswood laughed. "Is that what you fancy yourself—a candidate for the Four-in-Hand Club?"

"You fancy I'm no match for you or any of your clodpole friends?" she returned.

"If you attempted that course, you'd land in a ditch before the second stage."

Lydia covered the distance between them in three angry strides. "Oh, would I?" she asked, her voice taunting. "How much would you care to wager?"

His green eyes flashed. "Anything you name."

"Anything?"

"Name it, Grenville."

Lydia thought quickly, assessing his previous assault on her unreasonable conscience. Here was the solution.

"Five thousand pounds for Miss Price," she said, "and a thousand each to any three charitable causes I name—*and* you agree to take your seat in the House of Lords and exert your influence to pass the police bill."

He stood, hands clenching and unclenching.

"Are the stakes too high for you?" she asked. "Perhaps you are not so sure, after all, of my incompetence."

"I'd like to know how sure you are of mine," he said. "What will *you* stake, Grenville?" He advanced another pace to loom over her, his mocking green gaze slanting down his nose as though she were ever so small and inferior. "How about your precious freedom? Are you confident enough to risk that?"

Well before he'd finished speaking, Lydia saw what she'd done: the corner she'd let pride and temper box her into.

She paused but a moment as the realization struck, yet it was enough for Ainswood to assume she was entertaining doubts, for the world's most patronizing smile curved his wicked mouth and the world's most aggravating glints of laughter lit his green eyes.

Then it was too late for second thoughts. The inner voice of reason was no match for the roar of Ballister pride, fueled by centuries of Ballister drive to conquer, crush, and in general pound whatever stood in its path into abject submission.

Lydia could not back down. She could not do or say anything that looked like doubt, because that was the same as admitting weakness or, God forbid, fear.

"My freedom, then," she said, her voice low and hard, her chin high. "If I can't beat you, I'll marry you."

They would set out from Newington Gate at eight o'clock sharp next Wednesday morning, regardless of weather, illness, or Acts of Parliament or of God. Backing out, for any reason, would equal losing—with the same consequences. They would each take one passenger to alert tollgate keepers and hostlers and pay tolls. They would drive single-horse vehicles, commencing the first stage with their own cattle. Thereafter, they would take the best available at the changes. The finish line was the Anchor Inn in Liphook.

It took less than half an hour to settle upon the terms. It took a fraction of that time for Vere to comprehend the enormity of his error, but even then it was already far too late to retreat.

The June race was a sore point with him. It was Fate's own perversity that had put the goading words in her mouth. And he, provocateur par excellence, had let himself be provoked. He'd lost his self-control along with his temper, and so lost control of everything.

In June, at least, he'd had the excuse of being three sheets in the wind when he'd challenged a roomful of men to reenact the chariot races of ancient Rome upon a busy English coaching road. By the time he came to his senses—to sobriety, in other words—it was the next morning and he was sitting in his phaeton at the starting line with nearly a dozen other vehicles arrayed on either side of him.

The race had been a nightmare. Drunken observers as well as drivers caused property damage totaling several hundred pounds; four competitors suffered broken limbs; two carriages were demolished; and two horses had to be put down.

Vere had paid for everything, and certainly hadn't forced his idiot friends into racing. Nonetheless, the papers, politicians, and preachers held him personally and solely responsible—not simply for the race in particular but, judging by their extravagant oratory, for the downfall of civilization in general.

He was well aware that, loud, rude, and crude, he made a prime target for reformers and other pious hypocrites. Unfortunately, he was also well aware that there wouldn't have been an insane race and consequent public uproar if he'd kept his big mouth shut.

At present, he hadn't even the excuse of inebriation. Stone-cold sober he'd flapped his fool tongue, and in a few moronic words undone what he'd so carefully constructed while tending the fire: the logical and virtually irresistible—for her—argument for matrimony.

And now he could scarcely see straight, let alone think straight, because his brain was conjuring images of smashed-up carriages and mangled bodies and screaming horses, and this time it was *her* carriage, *her* screaming horse, *her* mangled body.

The nightmarish images accompanied him as he exited the study and headed down the hall, and crashes and screams rang in his head as he jerked open the door . . . and nearly trod down Bertie Trent, who had his hand upraised to grasp the knocker.

In the same instant, Vere heard heavy doggy paws thundering behind him, and swiftly moved aside, to avoid being knocked aside, as Susan leapt upon her beloved.

"I should like to know what is so irresistible about him," Vere muttered.

The mastiff stood on her hind legs, her forepaws on Bertie's chest while she tried to lick his face off.

"Drat you, Susan, get down," His Grace commanded irritably. *"Down."*

To his amazement, she obeyed, releasing Bertie so abruptly that he would have fallen over the threshold if Miss Price hadn't grabbed his arm and jerked him upright.

"Oh, I say, much obliged." Bertie grinned at her. "By gad, you've a strong grip for such a little female—mean to say, not little, exactly," he added quickly, the grin fading. "That is—" He broke off, his gaze alighting on Vere in what seemed to be belated recognition. "Oh, I say. Didn't know you was here, Ainswood. Anything amiss?"

Vere grasped Susan's collar and pulled her back from the doorway so that the pair could enter. "Nothing amiss," he said tightly. "I was just leaving."

He released Susan, bade the decidedly curious Miss Price a terse good night, and hurried out.

As he was yanking open the carriage door, he heard Bertie calling to him to wait.

Vere did not want to wait. He wanted to make for the nearest tavern posthaste, and start drinking and continue drinking until Wednesday morning. But he hadn't been able to make anything happen as he wanted since the day he'd first collided with Miss Nemesis Grenville, and so he supposed he was getting used to it, and only swallowed a sigh and waited for Bertie to make his adieu to Miss Price.

It seemed to Lydia that Ainswood had scarcely sauntered out of the study before Tamsin was hurrying in, Susan at her heels.

The girl raised her eyebrows at Lydia's trousers. Then her keen gaze went to the tangle on the desk. "Good grief, what is it?" She leaned over, pushed her spectacles up her nose, and peered closely at it. "Pirate's treasure? What an odd—Oh, my!" She blinked up at Lydia. Her face worked. "Oh, d-dear." She swallowed and bit her lip, but a sob broke from her, then another. She flung herself at Lydia and hugged her fiercely.

Lydia returned the hug, her throat tight. "Please don't make a fuss," she said as the girl began to weep. "I've always wanted to be a jewel thief. This was the only way to do it more or less legally." She patted Tamsin's back. "It's no crime to recover stolen goods."

Tamsin drew back and stared, her tear-filled eyes as big as an owl's. "You wanted to be a jewel thief?"

"I thought it would be exciting. And it was. Come along and I'll tell you all about it." She beckoned the bewildered girl. "You'll want tea—and I'm starving. These knock-down, drag-out rows with thickheaded noblemen do stir up the appetite."

Tamsin listened to the tale in a daze. She nodded and shook her head and smiled in the right places, but Lydia was sure her companion wasn't entirely present in spirit. "I hope I haven't shocked you witless," she said uneasily, as they ascended the stairs from the kitchen.

"No. It's Sir Bertram, who's *talked* me witless," Tamsin said. "He has muddled my brain with Charles II. The king kept wandering into the conversation on the way to the theater, during the intervals, and all the way home. I'm sure I've mentioned all the significant events of His Majesty's reign, but nothing helps. We cannot discover the connection, and now I cannot make my mind work on anything else. Please forgive me, Lydia."

They had reached the ground-floor hallway.

She thanked Lydia again for recovering the keepsakes, and hugged her again and kissed her good night and went up to her room, murmuring to herself.

Coralie Brees was not happy when Josiah and Bill carried a battered Francis Beaumont—whom they'd found slumped against the privy—into the house shortly before daybreak.

Once upon a time she had worked for Beaumont in Paris, ruling over the brothel that formed a part of his elaborate pleasure palace, Vingt-Huit. They'd had to make a speedy exodus from Paris in the spring, and the move to England had been a downward one for her. Beaumont had been the brain behind Vingt-Huit's operations. That brain, however, was at present rotting from large quantities of opium and drink—and likely pox as well.

Why it was rotting did not interest Coralie. She counted only results, and the result for her was no grand pleasure palace in London, but a more laborious and much poorer-paying job peddling young flesh upon the streets.

Coralie wasn't clever enough to build grand enterprises on her own. Her mind was small and simple. Uncorrupted by schooling, unbroadened by experience, incapable of learning by example, it was also too barren to support alien life-forms such as conscience or compassion.

She would have cheerfully killed Francis Beaumont, who was nothing but a nuisance these days, if she'd believed she could get away with it. She had more than once cheerfully garroted recalcitrant employees—but these were mere whores, whom nobody missed or mourned. To the authorities, they were anonymous corpses pulled from the Thames, causing a lot of paperwork and the bother of pauper burial, using up time and labor without recompense to the laborers.

Beaumont, on the other hand, had a famous artist wife who traveled in aristocratic circles. If he were found dead, an investigation would be ordered and rewards offered for information.

Coralie didn't trust any of those who worked for her to resist the temptation of a reward.

This was why she didn't step behind Beaumont while he sat slumped in a chair, and wrap her special cord 'round his neck.

Deciding against killing him was a mistake. Unfortunately, it was a mistake other people had made, and this time, as on previous occasions, the error had grave consequences.

By the time Beaumont had, with the aid of the gin bottle, recovered his zest for villainy, Coralie was in a screaming fit. She'd found the house servant, Mick, insensible on the kitchen floor, her bedroom ransacked, and Annette as well as money box and jewelry gone.

She sent Josiah and Bill to hunt the girl down—and bring her back alive, so that Coralie could have the pleasure of killing her very slowly.

Only after the boys had gone did Beaumont remark that it was a waste of time, since Annette had fled hours before—with a bully of her own who would easily make mincemeat of Josiah and Bill.

"And you only thought of it now they're gone?" Coralie shrieked. "You couldn't open your mouth before, while they was here? But no, you had the bottle in it, didn't you?"

"That's the second time in six months I was obliged to eat a large fist," Beaumont said, wincing as he spoke. "It was the same as Dain did to me, in Paris, remember? If I didn't know he was in Devon, I'd swear he was my accoster. Big fellow," he explained. "More than six feet, easily."

His bleary gaze drifted to the jade stickpin fastened to Coralie's bodice.

Instinctively, Coralie's hand went up to cover it.

"The French trull stole my stickpin, along with the rest of your magpie's nest," he lied. "I'll take your new acquisition as restitution. It's small enough payment, considering I nearly got killed trying to stop the bitch from robbing you. The devil only knows why I didn't help her instead, considering the tricks you've played me. You stole my stickpin. You made the flower girl disappear, too. What brothel have you stowed her at? Or did the little cripple fight your bullies off with her crutch and escape their loving attentions?"

"I never went near the little crookback!" Coralie cried. "Didn't anyone tell you what happened last night? That's all them sluts was talkin' about in Covent Garden—how Ainswood was throwin' money about, and chasin' some Jack whore gypsy—"

"Ainswood?" Beaumont said. "With a tall female?"

"That's what I said, didn't I? It were him give me the pin." She stroked the new treasure. "On account she knocked me over against a pillar post."

Beaumont's bruised mouth twisted in an ugly smile. "There's one tall female he's been chasing for weeks. Ever since she knocked him over. In Vinegar Yard. Don't you recall how she stole the little dark-haired chit from you?"

"I remember the bitch," Coralie said. "But she was in widow weeds. The one last night was one of them filthy, thievin' gypsies—some kin to the fat sow who pretends she can tell fortunes."

Beaumont gazed at her, then shook his head, took up the gin bottle and applied it to his swollen lips. When he'd emptied it, he put it down. "I do believe there isn't a stupider woman than you in all of Christendom, I truly do."

"I'm clever enough not to get my face smashed in, though, ain't I?"

"Not clever enough to see that it was Ainswood who helped your little French tart rob you blind last night."

"A dook? Takin' to forkin'? When he got more money than he knows what to do with and runs about London givin' purses full of sovereigns away, like they could burn him if he held on to 'em too long?"

"What I like about you, Coralie, is your refreshing freedom from all processes of logic. If you tried to put two and two together, it would hurt your head excessively, wouldn't it, my little charmer?"

Coralie had no more idea what he meant than if he'd spoken to her in Latin, Greek, or Chinese. She ignored him, went to the cupboard and took out another bottle of gin, opened it, and poured it into a grimy, smeared glass.

Watching her drink, Beaumont said, "I can't think why I should enlighten you. Ignorance is bliss, they say."

In fact, one would wonder why he tried to speak at all, since it hurt acutely. The trouble was, when Francis Beaumont was in pain or in trouble or experiencing anything in any way disagreeable, his favorite treatment—which was usually mixed with opium and/or alcohol—was making someone else much more miserable than he was.

Consequently, he did enlighten Coralie.

"Let me guess," he said. "That rat's nest of baubles you hoard contained, along with everything else that didn't belong to you, something belonging to the dark-haired chit Miss Lydia Grenville relieved you of."

Coralie slumped into a chair, her eyes filling. "Yes, and very nice they was, too. Rubies and emmyfists." A tear splashed onto the hand clutching the gin bottle. She refilled her glass. "And now all I've got left is the dook's stickpin and you want it."

"Amethysts, not emmyfists, you illiterate cow," Beaumont said. "And they must be gemstones, not paste, else no one would trouble to get them back. Don't you see? The tall female got Ainswood to help recover them for her precious little chick, and they enlisted Annette. She'd never have the nerve to do it on her own. She'd already dosed Mick with laudanum when I got here, and she was none too pleased to see me an hour ahead of time. I practically had to drag her upstairs by her feet. When I saw what she'd done to your room, I understood why. That's when she panicked and ran—and chasing after her, I ran straight into Ainswood. I'll wager anything they split the take and helped her get out of London. And he and Miss Lydia Grenville are laughing themselves sick. Well, why shouldn't they? They've stolen two girls from you, all your sparkly treasures, and all your money."

Having emptied one bottle and noticing Coralie's jealous hold of the other, Mr. Beaumont left her to brood over what he'd said.

He was not, in any case, the kind to watch over the poison seed he'd planted. He didn't need to. He knew exactly what to say, and chose his remarks according to the nature of his listener. He left the listener to fertilize the noxious garden and reap the evil he had sown.

On Friday, Elizabeth and Emily read in the pages of the *Whisperer* of their guardian's heroics in Exeter Street, which included the very interesting fact that Miss Grenville had chased him into the Strand.

On Saturday, a letter arrived express from London, while the family were at breakfast. The girls had time to recognize the exceedingly bad penmanship, along with the Duke of Ainswood's seal, before Lord Mars left the breakfast table and took the letter with him into his study. Lady Mars followed him there.

Her shrieks, despite the thickness of the study door, were audible. A maid hurried in, moments later, with smelling salts.

On Saturday night, the eldest of Dorothea's three older sisters arrived with her husband. On Sunday, the other two came with their spouses.

By this time, Elizabeth and Emily had already sneaked into their uncle's study, read the missive, and sneaked out.

Through numerous ingenious contrivances, Elizabeth and Emily managed enough eavesdropping in the course of the day to grasp the essentials of the family crisis. After dinner, they had only to open their bedroom window a crack and, concealed in the drapery, listen to the men talking on the terrace while smoking—and answering the call of nature, by the sounds of it. The eldest uncle by marriage, Lord Bagnigge, being well into his cups, held forth longest.

"It's a pity," he was saying, "but one must think of Lizzy and Em. United front, that's what one wants. Can't lend the thing countenance. Scandal's bad enough. Can't be a part of it, looking on. Drat the boy. Ain't it like him? A gel with no connections to speak of, and probably not fit to be spoken of, else someone would've heard of 'em by now. And a race. He'll win her in a race, like a purse. Poor Lizzy. Ready to make her comeout, and how's she to hold her head up? A common scribbler, the Duchess of Ainswood—and won in a race, no less. Even that old rip, Charlie's pa, must be turning in his grave."

Elizabeth beckoned her sister away from the window.

"They're not going to change their minds," she whispered.

"It isn't right," said Emily. "Papa would go."

"Cousin Vere was there for Papa, when it mattered."

"He was there for Robin, when no one else dared."

"Papa loved him."

"He made Robin happy."

"One little thing. Cousin Vere has asked his family to be with him at his wedding." Elizabeth's eyes flashed. "I don't care about her connections. I shouldn't care if she was the Whore of Babylon. If he wants her, that's good enough for me."

"Me, too," said Emily.

"Then we'd better make it clear, hadn't we?"

11

Wednesday, 1 October

The sun had heavy going in its climb from the horizon. It struggled through the fog rolling from the river, sparkled fitfully through the mist, then was swallowed up in a grey morass of clouds.

Thanks to the morning fog and a last-minute—and futile—attempt to talk Tamsin out of accompanying her, Lydia arrived at Newington Gate with only a quarter hour to spare.

Despite the early hour, not all of the small crowd gathered there was of the hoi polloi. Along with the expected reporters, miscellaneous ruffians, and streetwalkers, she spotted half a dozen male members of the Beau Monde—all drunk, apparently. They were accompanied by representatives of the aristocracy of whoredom—minus Helena, who had a cold and would rather be hanged than seen in public with a red nose.

The bulk of Ainswood's associates, however, would be in Liphook. According to Helena, Ainswood had sent notes inviting all his friends to help celebrate his victory.

"Sellowby claims that His Grace has obtained a special license, and a ring, and that there will be a minister waiting at the inn to perform the ceremony," Helena had reported on Saturday.

Lydia had been seething ever since.

Now, however, she wondered whether Sellowby had merely passed on idle rumor.

212

It was a quarter to eight and Ainswood wasn't here.

"Perhaps he has come to his senses," Lydia said as she steered her carriage into position. "Perhaps someone has made him recollect his position and responsibilities. If his curst family cared anything about him, they would not let him make such a ridiculous spectacle of himself. Only think of those two girls, his wards, and how mortified they must be by his methods of winning a wife. He doesn't consider how the eldest must face Society when she makes her comeout in the spring. He never considers how his scandals affect others, and they're mere females, after all," Lydia added tartly. "I doubt he even recollects their names."

Elizabeth and Emily. Seventeen and fifteen respectively. They lived with their paternal aunt, Lady Mars, at Blakesleigh in Bedfordshire. Lord Mars was one of Peel's staunchest allies in the House of Lords.

Lydia did not want to think about the two girls, the elder on the brink of entering the social whirl, with all its pitfalls. Unfortunately, she had already opened Pandora's box last Wednesday, when she'd opened *Debrett's Peerage*.

By now she'd collected almost as much information on the Mallory family as she had on her mother's. While Lydia worked on *The Rose of Thebes* and the articles and essays needed for the next issue of the *Argus*, Tamsin had continued what Lydia had begun. After exhausting *Debrett's*, the *Annual Register*, and the standard genealogical resources, Tamsin had turned to the numerous Society publications.

The Mallorys were not Tamsin's sole research project. She was also becoming knowledgeable on the subject of Trent's family.

Initially, she'd been trying to discern an event or persons, past or present, that would explain his obsession with Charles II. In the process, she'd discovered that his family had more than its share of unusual characters. She found them fascinating, and regaled Lydia with stories about them during mealtimes.

This took Lydia's mind off the Mallorys, but never for long. Her thoughts kept returning to Robert Edward Mallory, the young duke, and she found herself grieving for a little boy she'd never met. Soon her reflections would move on to his orphaned sisters, and that was worse, because she often caught herself fretting about them, as though she knew them personally and was somehow responsible for them.

Worrying about them was absurd, Lydia tried to persuade herself. While Lord and Lady Mars had a large family of their own, that didn't mean the wards Ainswood neglected weren't happy and properly looked after.

Lydia told herself this scores of times. Her mind was convinced; her heart was not.

She took out Great Uncle Ste's pocket watch and frowned. "Less than ten minutes to starting time. Drat him, if he means to default, he might at least send word. Bellweather will claim I made it all up. A shameless bid for publicity, he'll call it." She put the watch away. "As though it wasn't Ainswood who blabbed about the race first, to all his idiot friends. As though I wished all the world to know I let that obstinate, patronizing brute goad me into this ridiculous situation."

"It was very bad of His Grace to bring me into it," Tamsin said, smoothing her gloves. "No matter how desperate he felt, he should not have been so unscrupulous—not to mention completely unreasonable—as to work upon your too-kind feelings towards me. One tries to understand, but there is a limit, as I told Sir Bertram." She let out an impatient huff. "A dowry, indeed. I can well understand why you became so incensed with His Grace, for Sir Bertram did not at all comprehend the principles at issue, and I was strongly tempted to box his ears. Charles II or no Charles II, he might grasp the simple and obvious fact that I can earn my keep. But they will see. They will eat our dust, Lydia, and my ludicrous five thousand will be used to aid those who *need* help, which I most certainly do not."

Once Tamsin had recovered from an evening of Bertie Trent—and Charles II—and the shock of getting back jewelry she'd philosophically given up for lost, she'd taken umbrage at the part of the wager connected to her. With what must be the same singleminded determination that had taken her from her Cornwall village to London, she had insisted upon accompanying Lydia. Moreover, Tamsin remained as vexed with Trent today as she'd been on Friday, the last time she'd spoken to him.

"It seems the gentlemen have decided to breakfast on something other than our dust," Lydia said. She took out the watch again. "A few minutes more and—"

A cacophony of shouts and whistles from the crowd cut her off. An instant later, a smart tilbury with a powerful chestnut in harness whisked through the gate and up to the starting line. When he pulled up on the left alongside her, Ainswood tipped his hat—for once, he was wearing one—and flashed a crooked grin.

Lydia wished she'd positioned her vehicle nearer the edge of the road, so that he would have been stationed to her right. Then Trent's big form would have blocked her view of the duke.

But only Tamsin sat between them, and Lydia easily saw over her head the cocky assurance in Ainswood's hard-edged countenance, the wicked glint in his green eyes, the arrogant angle of his jaw. She saw as well that his elegant garments might have been sculpted to him. She could almost smell the starch in his neckcloth, could almost feel the linen's crispness . . . and she remembered, all too vividly, the warmth and power of his big frame, the muscles bunching at her touch, the beat of his heart against her palm.

She felt her heart lurch against her rib cage. Then it came, the flood of unwanted recollections: the boy he'd lost . . . the two orphaned girls . . . the children he'd rescued in Exeter Street . . . the flower girl . . . the cold, brutal rage while he finished off a villain in two ferocious blows . . . the big, rugged body . . . the strong arms that could lift her as though she were a slip of a girl . . . the husky whisper, "You're so beautiful."

Yet she gave him only a regal nod, clicked the watch case closed, and put it away.

"Impatient for my arrival, were you, Grenville?" the duke called above the whistling, cheering crowd.

"Delayed by an attack of nerves, were you, Ainswood?" she returned.

"I'm trembling," he said, "with *anticipation*."

"I'll anticipate you—to the finish line," she said. "With a mile to spare."

On the sidelines, the blacklegs who infested every sporting event were taking last-minute bets, but Lydia couldn't make out what the latest odds were above the tumult in her mind.

Still, tumult or not, there was no turning back. She could not give up all she'd worked for—her very identity, for that's what it came to—without a battle. And Lydia Grenville never entered a battle she wasn't determined to win.

"One minute," a voice called out above the crowd's roar.

The onlookers fell silent.

Lydia's own inner uproar stilled.

Someone raised a handkerchief aloft. She focused on it, grasping the whip firmly. Then the bells of the parish church rang out, while the square of white linen fluttered to the ground. She cracked her whip . . . they were off.

The old Portsmouth Road started at London Bridge, wended through Southwark past the Marshalsea and King's Bench prisons, on through Newington and Vauxhall turnpikes down to Wandsworth, and on through Putney Heath to the Robin Hood Gate.

This was the route Lydia had chosen, for several sound reasons. By eight o'clock, the slower Portsmouth coaches would have already set out, leaving this, their usual route, a fraction less congested. Meanwhile, the fast coaches departing from Piccadilly at the same hour would gain a considerable lead over the racers maneuvering through Newington and Lambeth parishes. Consequently, there would be less of a crush, Lydia hoped, at Robin Hood Gate, the first change, and the point at which slow and fast coaching routes joined.

The slow route would also suit Cleo, Lydia's black mare, who was accustomed to negotiating busy streets and could be counted on not to take fright or fly into a fit at vehicles or humans darting into her path.

Unfortunately, it turned out that sturdy, fearless Cleo was no match for Ainswood's powerful gelding. Though the tilbury was nearly as heavy as Lydia's cabriolet, and though the men's weight more than compensated for their slightly lighter vehicle, Ainswood overtook Lydia a short distance past the Vauxhall Turnpike and rapidly lengthened the lead thereafter. By the time Lydia changed horses at the Robin Hood Inn, the tilbury was out of sight.

Lydia was aware of Tamsin's worried gaze upon her as they sped past Richmond Park.

"No, it doesn't look promising," Lydia said in answer to the unspoken question. "But it's not hopeless. I only want an-

other minute or so to make sure this creature and I understand each other."

The bay in the harness was not so cooperative as Cleo, and
tended to shy at every passing shadow. By the time they
passed through Kingston Market Square, however, the
horse's will was obliged to submit to Lydia's. Once clear of
the town, Lydia told her companion to hang on.

A sharp crack of the whip—a hairsbreadth from touching
the horse—was enough, and the bay thundered over the next
four miles at a punishing pace.

After a speedy change at Esher, Lydia plunged into the
next stage, and they finally caught sight of the tilbury at the
Cobham Gate.

Trent was clinging to the side of the tilbury, watching the
road behind them.

"By Jupiter, there she is again," he said hollowly. "Dash it,
Ainswood, it don't look like they mean to give up."

Vere glanced upward. Heavy masses of grey clouds rolled
above their heads, and the same wild currents driving the
thunderclouds beat against his face. The wind whipped
through Pains Hill to tear fading leaves from the trees and
drive them in mad eddies over the rolling countryside.

He'd already pushed two horses to the very edge of their
endurance to gain a lead sufficient to discourage any rational,
sober human being.

Not only had Grenville not given up, but she was inching
up on him.

Meanwhile a storm straight from the bowels of hell was
brewing, and the worst of the route lay ahead.

For the thousandth time in five days, he cursed himself for
goading her into this bedamned race—or letting himself be
goaded. He still wasn't altogether certain who had provoked

whom, though he'd replayed their row in his mind any number of times. All he knew was that he'd lost his temper over nothing and made a thorough muck of matters. He wished she'd thrown something at him or hit him. That would have given her satisfaction, and maybe knocked some sense into him.

But it was too late. These reflections were merely the most recent in a long series of If Onlys.

Ockham Park had faded behind them and the first straggling houses of Ripley were coming into view under the ominously darkening sky. The wind was sharpening, and Vere wanted to believe that was why he felt so chilled.

He knew better.

He was insensitive to weather. Torrid heat, freezing cold, downpour, sleet, and snowstorm had never caused him any discomfort worth noticing. He never fell ill. No matter how he abused his body, no matter what ailments he was exposed to, no matter how contagious . . .

He pushed away the memory before it could fully form, and focused on his competitor, and the road ahead.

They had some twenty-five miles yet to cover in what promised to be the worst weather over the most treacherous terrain. He could see clearly half a dozen places where she could come to grief . . . and he would be too far away to save her.

Too far away, as always, when he was needed.

He pulled into the yard of the Talbot Inn and minutes later pulled out again, a fresh animal in harness, and all the while the refrain tolled like funeral bells in his mind.

Too far away. Too late.

He snapped the whip over the horse's head and the beast lunged and thundered through the wide village street.

In the same way, not so very long ago, had he raced

through countryside and village streets. . . .

But he wouldn't think of it, of the spring that had made him hate springtime ever since and spend the blossoming season blind drunk.

They flew past Clandon Park and entered the long stretch—almost deserted on their near side—of Meroe Common, and Vere drove on, harder than before, and prayed his competitor would come to her senses. She couldn't hope to win. He was too far ahead. She must give up.

Trent again turned back to look.

"Is she still there?" Vere asked, dreading the answer.

"Gainin' on us."

They plunged into Guildford, hurtling over the cobbled street, gaining speed down the incline.

Yet the cabriolet drew ever closer.

Over the River Wey they went, and up St. Catherine's Hill, the horses slowing, laboring through the steep ascent, and too tired to increase their pace as they crossed Pease Marsh Common.

And all the while the cabriolet drew nearer, until Vere could practically feel its horse breathing down his neck.

But he was more aware of the furious wind, the lowering skies, the warning rumble in the distance. He thought of the brutal stretch to come: twelve miles of punishingly steep ascents and treacherous descents. He saw in his mind's eye the storm breaking over them . . . panicked horses, screaming, hurtling over the road edge . . . the cabriolet smashed to pieces.

He tried to make himself believe she'd give up, but with each passing mile his doubts grew.

When had he ever seen her back down?

Rescuing Miss Price in Vinegar Yard . . . bashing Crenshaw in front of Crockford's . . . mocking Vere to his

face in the Blue Owl . . . masquerading as a man in Jerrimer's
. . . climbing up the back of Helena Martin's house . . . sa-
shaying half naked through Covent Garden . . . playing jewel
thief in Francis Street. . . . Grenville was game for anything,
afraid of nothing. And when it came to pride, Vere could
think of but one person who could match her for pure, over-
weening arrogance, and that was Lord Beelz himself.

With the thought, he became aware of something beckon-
ing at the far fringes of memory—a wisp of an image, a recognition. It had appeared before, more than once, and it
vanished this time as on previous occasions, in the way,
sometimes, a word or phrase stays tantalizingly out of reach.
He let it go because memory, the past, didn't matter so much
as the present.

At present, he could no longer believe the woman would
give way, come forty-day flood or apocalypse. To back down
was no more in her nature than it was in his. The difference
was, what happened to him didn't matter.

By the time he pulled into the yard of the inn at
Godalming, he'd made his decision.

The cabriolet followed close on his wheels.

The clouds spat chill droplets and the warning rumbles
grew louder.

"We'll never outrun this storm, Grenville," he called to
her over the stable yard hubbub. "Let's call a halt—and no
forfeit. We're as near a draw as makes no difference."

"Thank God," Bertie muttered beside him. He drew out
his handkerchief and mopped his brow.

Grenville only stared at him, in the cold, deadly way Vere
found so intolerably provoking. Even now, though he was
drawing perilously near the edge of panic, he was provoked
and wanted to shake her.

"Lost your nerve, have you?" she returned, her tones as

cool and level as the vexatious look.

"I can't let you kill yourself on my account," he said. A stable man led her horse up. It was a large, black gelding with a wild look in its eye. "Take that beast back," he snapped at the man. "Any idiot can see he's a bolter."

"Put him in the traces," Grenville commanded.

"Grenville—"

"Look to your own animal, Ainswood," she said. "I'll see you in Liphook."

"A draw, I said, drat you! No forfeit. Are you deaf, woman?"

She only shot him another gorgon glare and turned to raise the cabriolet's hood.

"You don't have to marry me!" he shouted. "It's done, don't you understand? Over. You've proved you're a competent whip."

"Obviously, I haven't proved a dratted thing. You there," she called to a yard man. "Give us a hand with the hood, and never mind gawking."

While Vere watched in numb disbelief, the cabriolet's hood went up, and the beast from hell was wrestled into harness.

Before Vere could summon the presence of mind to leap from the tilbury and pull her from her seat, the black gelding lunged forward, knocking aside the startled stable man, and throwing Miss Price back against the seat. In the next heartbeat, the cabriolet was hurtling out of the yard. Above the shouts and curses of the grooms, Vere heard Grenville's laughter.

"Oh, Lord, Lydia, this animal is insane," Tamsin gasped. She was clutching the side of the carriage with both hands—an intelligent response, given the gelding's breakneck speed. "The duke will go off in an apoplexy, you know he will. I'm sure he's worried to death, poor man."

"Are you worried?" Lydia asked, keeping her eyes on the road. The gelding was a lively brute, to be sure, and strong enough to take them up Hindhead Hill at a good pace, but he did have a mischievous tendency to pull to the left.

"No. This is too exciting." Tamsin leaned forward and peered 'round the hood. "They're starting to catch up again. Sir Bertram's face is very red."

Thunder reverberated over Witley Common. Lydia caught a flash of light in the distance. Another rumble followed after a short interval.

The girl sat back. "I can't think how you summoned the strength of will to refuse His Grace. He was so terribly upset. I know he's dreadfully provoking, and he might have put his offer of a draw more tactfully—"

"He believes I'm so addlepated and irresponsible as to get myself killed—and take you with me," Lydia said tightly. "That's why he's upset, and that's what's intolerable."

Out of the corner of her eye she glimpsed another shaft of light. A low boom of thunder followed. "If he had his way, I should finish sitting tamely beside him," she went on. "While gazing up adoringly into his deceitful face. But he is not going to make me his private property and tie me to him until death us do part, if I can help it."

They were more than halfway up the long hill. The black gelding was beginning to slow, but he showed no signs of wishing to rest.

"It wouldn't be so bad if he would gaze back adoringly," Tamsin said.

"That's worse," Lydia said. "Ainswood's adoring looks can be lethal. I had a sample in Covent Garden, recollect. His Grace, on his knees, looking up worshipfully into one's face, is a devastating sight."

"I wish I had seen it."

"I wish I hadn't," Lydia said. "I had to fix my mind on Susan, and her soulful gazes, which are motivated by greedy doggy concerns such as food or playing or petting. Otherwise, I should have melted into a puddle on the spot."

"Poor Susan. How wicked the duke was to use her against you."

"Poor Susan, indeed. Her behavior was disgraceful."

"She may have simply felt sorry for him," Tamsin said. "You know how she seems to sense when one is unwell or out of sorts or distressed. Only yesterday, Millie was upset because she'd scorched an apron. Susan went to her and dropped her ball at Millie's feet and licked her hand just as though—Oh, my goodness, there's the gibbet."

They'd nearly reached the top of the hill. On the near side stood the Hindhead gibbet. The spitting rain beat down upon the carriage hood, and the shrieking wind mingled eerily with the gallows' creaking chains. Lightning blasted at the distant edges of the Devil's Punchbowl, on the far side, and the thunder rolled, adding its ominous drumbeat to this satanic concerto.

At the crest of the hill, Lydia drew the horse to a halt, for he was steaming and clearly needed a rest. But within minutes he was fretting and straining in the traces, impatient to go on.

"By gad, you're a game 'un, aren't you?" Lydia said. "Still, my fine fellow, you shan't plunge us headlong down this hill."

She heard behind her—close behind—the rattle of wheels and clatter of hoofbeats.

Ahead and below stretched the perilous decline, with packhorse tracks as deep as a Devonshire lane on either side. The only sign of habitation in this bleak terrain was the smoke coiling upward from the Seven Thorns Inn, an unsavory place in which she didn't fancy taking refuge.

This stretch of the usually busy Portsmouth Road was virtually deserted, thanks to the storm. This, clearly, was not the time or place to have an accident.

The rain drummed angrily upon the hood—which, thanks to the wind, did little to keep them dry. But Lydia had no energy for considering her discomfort, having her hands full with the gelding. He fought her efforts to slow him while obstinately—and in typically self-destructive male fashion—aiming for the road edge.

By the time they reached the bottom of the hill, her arms were aching, and still the gelding showed no sign of tiring.

Lydia glanced guiltily at Tamsin. Her skirts were drenched and she was shivering.

"Two more miles." Lydia had to raise her voice to be heard over the pounding rain and rolling thunder.

"I'm only wet," Tamsin said through chattering teeth. "I won't melt."

God forgive me, Lydia thought, her conscience stabbing. She should never have let Tamsin come, should never have agreed to this fool race. At the very least, she should have accepted Ainswood's offer of a truce. If Tamsin took a fatal chill—

A blast of lightning nearly jolted her from the carriage seat, and the thunderous clap following in the next heartbeat seemed to shake the road beneath them. The gelding rose up on its hind legs with a terrified whinny, and her arms and hands burned as she strained to bring him down and away from the road edge before he capsized them into a ditch.

The world went dark for an instant, then blindingly bright again as lightning bolted over the commons, accompanied by deafening crashes.

It took a moment to register the other sounds: shouts, the shriek of a horse in pain or panic, the clatter of carriage wheels.

Then she saw it, hurtling down the road inches away from her wheels. Lydia pulled the cabriolet back to the left, saw the tilbury jerk crazily to the right as it rumbled past, narrowly missing her. Lightning flared again and she glimpsed Ainswood's taut silhouette, saw him work the ribbons in the instant before the crash of thunder and the next, more frightening crash as the tilbury went down, over the far side of the road.

Lydia was aware of the sheeting rain, of the blasting light, and of shuddering thunder, and voices, too, but only as something distant, in another world eons away.

All the world she knew at this moment lay in a too-still form at the edge of the wreckage, and an eternity seemed to pass as she scrambled down into the track to him.

She sank down on her knees, in the mud, where he lay facedown.

Behold me prostrate before you.

She remembered him kneeling before her in Covent Garden and the sound of his theatrically pleading voice and the glint of laughter in his rogue's eyes belying his soulful expression.

A terrible, mad laughter surged up inside her. But she was never hysterical.

She pulled at his coat. "Get up, drat you. Oh, please." She was not crying. It was the rain, filling her eyes, and the sting in her throat was the cold. It was so cold, and he was so heavy. She tore his coat trying to turn him onto his back, and then she could not let him lie there in the mud, and so she yanked him up by the lapels. "Wake up, you stupid, stubborn brute," she cried. "Oh, wake up, please."

But he wouldn't wake up and she couldn't hold him up. All she could do was cradle his head and wipe the mud from his face and order and argue and beg and promise, anything.

"Don't you die on me, you beast," she choked past the burning thing in her throat. "I've grown . . . attached to you. Oh, come. I never meant . . . Oh, I shall be wretched. How could you, Ainswood? This is not fair—not sporting of you. Come. You've won." She shook him. "Do you hear me, you thickheaded cockscomb? You've won. I'll do it. The ring. The parson. The whole curst business. Your duchess." She shook him again. "That's what you wanted, isn't it? Make up your mind. Now or never, Ainswood. This is your last chance. Wake up, damn you, and m-marry me."

She choked back a sob. "Or I'll leave you as I found you." She bowed her head, despairing. "Here. In the mud. In a ditch. I knew you'd come . . . to a b-bad end."

Vere was very bad. A hopeless case.

He should have opened his eyes sentences ago, but he was afraid he'd wake up and find it was only a dream: his dragon-girl scolding him and grieving for him.

But it wasn't a dream, and she must be soaked to the skin, and he must be the greatest brute in Christendom to risk her falling ill on his worthless account.

And so Vere reached up and brought her beautiful, stubborn face close to his. "Am I dead and are you an angel, or is it only you, Grenville?" he whispered.

She started to pull back, but he was not so enfeebled—or noble—as to let her off without a kiss. He cupped the back of her head and held her down, and she yielded, as always, in an instant. Then he knew it was no dream.

No dream ever tasted so plum-sweet as her soft, ripe

mouth, and he savored it, lengthening and deepening the kiss, drinking her in while the storm broke about them.

But this time when he released her—reluctantly, so very reluctantly that he should be canonized for self-restraint —the truth slipped past his guard and he said thickly, "I'd rather you, wicked girl, than all the seraphs in heaven. Will you have me, sweet? Do you mean it?"

She let out a shaky sigh. "Yes. I mean it, plague take you. And I am not *sweet*. Get up, you great fraud."

It was not Bertie's first accident. It was, however, the first time he hadn't been driving when the smash-up occurred. Still, as he told Miss Price moments after Miss Grenville had hurried down to Ainswood, even the most skilled whip could not have prevented the accident. Taking fright at the lightning, the horse had reared up with enough force to break one of the tilbury's shafts. The other one broke when the carriage overturned. The horse had bolted, dragging the remains of its draft gear with it.

Bertie had leapt clear in the nick of time and only taken a tumble on the road. He would have rushed down to Ainswood's side if Miss Grenville hadn't already abandoned her cabriolet to do the same. Then Bertie's first thought was "ladies first," and he had hurried to aid Miss Price, left in charge of a clearly mettlesome gelding.

As Bertie explained to her, if Ainswood was dead, no one could help him. If he wasn't, assistance would likely be needed to haul him up from the track and take him to Liphook. Since the tilbury was in splinters and the cabriolet could not carry four, Bertie had dashed off in the vehicle with Miss Price to summon aid from the village.

This had not taken long. The Anchor Inn was scarcely a mile from the accident scene, and it was filled to the rafters with Ainswood's friends, all eagerly awaiting the race's conclusion. Within minutes, somebody's carriage was readied and on its way to the rescue.

Bertie wasn't sure whose carriage it turned out to be, because by that point he'd fallen into a profound state of distraction.

The confusion had started en route to the inn, when Bertie spotted a signpost indicating the direction and distance of several villages in the general vicinity.

"Oh, I say," he said, blinking. "Blackmoor. That were the one."

Miss Price had been a little stiff until now, though considerably more thawed than when he'd last spoken to her, on Friday. Then, she'd stalked off angry about something or other which he was hanged if he had any idea what it was.

When he'd taken charge of the cabriolet, she hadn't seemed quite so vexed, yet she wasn't altogether as talkative and friendly as usual during the short drive to the village.

When he mentioned Blackmoor, however, she turned to him with the keen, studying look he was more used to. "You know the village?"

He shook his head. "No. It were a picture. Charles Two, only not him, but his friend, and I dunno what he did to get the title, on account of them long, pale yellow curls made me wonder why a fellow'd want to look like a female. And so I weren't listening with all ears at the moment, but he's the one I wanted. Not the king at all, you see."

Miss Price stared at him for a moment. "Long, yellow curls," she said. "A friend of King Charles II. A cavalier, then, most likely. You saw a picture of a courtier, a friend of the king."

"And he could've been Miss G's brother," Bertie said, as he halted the carriage at the inn's entrance. "Only he couldn't, bein' dead some centuries. The first Earl of Blackmoor, which m'curst sister likes the best of all the men in the pictures, she says, on account of—By Jupiter, there he is, when I never thought he'd come on such short notice, and only pray he didn't bring m'sister with him."

Miss Price turned her enormous brown gaze to the door of the Anchor Inn, where the Marquess of Dain stood wearing one of his famous deadly stares, which Bertie was well aware took some getting used to.

Miss Price clearly wasn't used to it because she gasped, "Oh, my goodness," and fainted dead away. This was the point at which Bertie fell into an acute state of distraction.

12

"Of course I shall stand up for you," Tamsin said as she deftly pinned up Lydia's hair. "I am perfectly well now. It was the excitement, coupled with hunger, that made me faint. But I am not in the least unwell. This is the most exciting day I've ever had, and I refuse to miss a minute of the conclusion."

The two women were in a bedchamber of the Anchor Inn.

Lords Dain and Sellowby had arrived in a private drag as Lydia and Ainswood were starting the wet trek to Liphook. They had mentioned Tamsin's swooning—in terror at the sight of Dain, was how Sellowby explained it—but Lydia had been in too much of a tumult then to fret about her companion.

Her tumult hadn't to do with Ainswood exclusively, though her softhearted—or softheaded—agreement to wed caused her no little turmoil. But Dain, too, had thrown her world into confusion.

Though Lydia was supposed to be the mirror image of Lord Dain's father, neither the present marquess nor Sellowby had shown the smallest glimmer of recognition during the short drive to the inn or in the moments after their entering it, when it was settled that the wedding would take place as soon as the bride- and groom-to-be had washed and changed into clean clothes. At the time, Lydia had been incapable of composing any coherent objection to the duke's urgings for a prompt shackling.

Even now, after a hot bath, tea, and pampering under

Tamsin's hands, Lydia still felt at sea. The sense of upheaval, of matters careening out of her control, was not agreeable.

"I should have insisted on time to rest, at least," she said. "But Ainswood . . . oh, he is so insistent and impatient and he makes such a bother of himself when one says no."

"It would have made little sense to put off the wedding, when he had everything ready," said Tamsin. "Is it not amazing how organized he can be when strongly motivated?"

"Smug and cocksure is more like it," Lydia said. "Still, he had everything in hand, and his friends were already gathered, and so it seemed we might as well get it over with."

Tamsin stepped back to admire the tidy coiffure she'd created.

A few soft, wavy gold tendrils framed Lydia's face, and the knot she usually pinned any which way at the base of her neck was neatly gathered atop her head.

" 'If it were done when 'tis done, then 'twere well/ It were done quickly,' " Tamsin smilingly quoted from *Macbeth*. "Lady Dain said that the longer a man is obliged to wait, the more likely he is to work himself into an irrational state. She said it happened to Lord Dain, and he was nearly impossible to deal with by the time they were married. The weeks of wedding preparations nearly drove her mad as well, she told me, though she isn't the sort to be easily overset."

"Organizing that wedding must have been like preparing for Waterloo," Lydia murmured. "It was very grand. The church was packed to bursting, and there were even more people at the wedding breakfast."

"And she has expensive tastes, according to His Lordship."

"Well, we shan't be very grand." Lydia studied her reflection in the glass. "Except for my hair. How elegant you've made me—from the neck up."

But that was only appearances, she thought. And now even she wasn't sure who she really was.

Fancy yourself a great lady, do you? Papa had asked so mockingly all those years ago. That's all it had been, evidently: a fantasy on Mama's part that she was a Ballister. Otherwise, surely, Lydia would have detected something—surprise, annoyance, even amusement—in Dain's dark countenance. But all he'd done was look her over very briefly, reserving his attention for his erstwhile schoolmate Ainswood.

Obviously, when Sellowby had made the comment, after Dain's wedding, about spying a female who might have stepped out from the Athcourt portrait gallery, he'd merely discerned a vague resemblance from a distance, Lydia decided. Up close, the resemblance must have proved vague indeed, since this day he'd seemed no more struck by her features than Dain had been.

Maybe that was it. Perhaps Mama had seen the previous Lord Dain at a procession or stepping out from his carriage. At a distance, she might have perceived a resemblance to Lydia, and subsequently built a long fictional story upon it. Lydia could hardly be surprised. Her own inspiration for *The Rose of Thebes* had come from a gossipy newspaper article describing Lady Dain's betrothal ring, a large cabochon ruby surrounded by diamonds.

"I don't think the duke cares what your hair looks like," Tamsin said, drawing Lydia back to the present. "I'm sure he would have wed you on the spot, as you were, your sopping hair in your mud-spattered face and your bonnet a wet lump dangling from your neck."

"He was hardly Beau Brummell himself," Lydia said, rising from her chair at the dressing table. "In any event, he was wetter than I and bound to fall ill standing about in dripping clothes during the ceremony. I didn't wish to spend my first days of marriage nursing him through a lung fever." She turned to meet Tamsin's gaze. "You must think me mad, or at least capricious."

"I think it was a mistake to call your feelings for him 'a schoolgirl infatuation' or 'mating instinct' or 'the delirium of lust,' as you've done." Tamsin chuckled softly. "I had the feeling he might be beginning to grow on you—"

"Like a fungus, you mean."

"It's no use pretending you don't care for him," Tamsin went on. "I saw you leap from the carriage without a thought for the storm, that deranged gelding, or anything but the Duke of Ainswood." She grinned. "It was ever so romantic."

"Romantic." Lydia scowled. "I shall be ill."

"That's bridal nerves." Tamsin moved to the door. "I daresay he's in a worse state than you are, and undergoing agonies. We had better let the minister put the pair of you out of your misery."

Lydia lifted her chin. "I am not subject to nervous fits, Miss Impertinence. I am not in any sort of misery. I am perfectly composed." She stalked to the door. "In a short while I shall be the Duchess of Ainswood, and then"—she glared at Tamsin—"the rest of you peasants had better look out."

She swept from the room, a laughing Tamsin following.

Thanks to Dain, Sellowby, and Trent, Vere was in a fair way to being driven distracted. None of them could hold his tongue for half a minute and let a fellow think.

They were gathered in the small dining parlor reserved for the nuptials.

"I'm telling you, it's the oddest thing," Trent was saying, "and how you can't see it is beyond me only maybe it were on account she were the worse for the rain and mud and her own mother wouldn't recognize her—"

"Of course I recognized her," said Sellowby. "I had seen her outside the church after Dain's wedding. One could hardly fail to notice a handsome young woman of such statuesque proportions. She seemed a fair flower among the weedy clump of journalists. Not to mention that female scribblers are scarcely thick on the ground, and there could be only one Lady Grendel. Even at a distance, her appearance was striking."

"That's what I mean," Trent persisted. "The tall fellow with the golden curls I seen—"

"I shouldn't call it gold," Dain interrupted. "I should say flaxen. And not a curl in sight."

"A pale gold," Sellowby agreed. "Reminded me of—"

"That fellow, the cavalier one which m'sister—"

"The Comte d'Esmond," Sellowby continued. "Not the same eyes, though. Hers are a lighter blue."

"And she can't be French," said Dain.

"I didn't say she were French, only that were the word they used for 'em which has something to do with horses, Miss Price says, bein' *cheval*—"

"The rumor I heard," Dain went on, as though his brother-in-law weren't there, "was that she was born in a Borneo swamp and reared up by crocodiles. I don't suppose you know the facts about her background, do you, Ainswood? I am not certain Borneo has crocodiles."

"What the devil do I care about her background?" Vere snapped. "What I want to know is where the curst parson's got to—and whether the bride means to come down to the wedding sometime in this century."

It had taken him but half an hour to bathe and dress, snarling at Jaynes the whole time. That had left His Grace another hour and a half to cool his heels waiting for his duchess-to-be, and fretting all the while that she'd taken ill and was quietly expiring of a putrid sore throat while his friends nattered on about the precise color of her hair and eyes and whether there were crocodiles in Borneo.

"Maybe she's having second thoughts," Dain said with a mocking half-smile Vere was itching to punch off his arrogant countenance. "Maybe she agreed to wed you while in a state of shock, and has since come to her senses."

"I agreed to wed him out of pity," came a cool feminine voice from the doorway. "And out of a sense of civic duty. We can't allow him to run amok upon the public byways, breaking up carriages and alarming the horses."

The four men turned simultaneously toward the speaker.

Vere's dragoness stood in the doorway, garbed from neck to toe in black, and buttoned within an inch of her life. When she entered, the bombazine rustled suggestive whispers.

Miss Price trailed behind her, and the preacher brought up the rear.

"I'd better find my wife," Dain said, heading for the door. "And you are not to so much as think of starting without us. I must give the bride away."

Grenville's eyebrows went up.

"They drew straws," Vere explained. "Trent is groomsman, and Sellowby is charged with guarding the door, to keep out the crowd of noisy drunkards."

The crowd had been herded into the large public dining room, where they entertained themselves by singing ribald songs and terrifying the hapless travelers who'd paused here for shelter from the storm.

"Your friends were denied the entertainment of witnessing your spectacular race finish," said his dragoness. "I cannot believe you mean to deprive them of this spectacle as well."

"I promise you, Grenville, they're in no state to appreciate it," he said. "Half of them couldn't tell the bridegroom from a wine barrel at this point—and the majority would rather be near the wine barrel."

"It is a solemn occasion," the minister added sternly. "The holy state of matrimony is not to be entered into lightly, nor—" He broke off as Grenville's glacial blue gaze settled upon him. "That is. Well." He tugged at his collar. "Perhaps we might take our places."

The nagging, frustratingly faint thought or memory or whatever it was teased Vere once more. But Dain and his wife entered in the next moment, and Lord Beelzebub took charge, as he was everlastingly wont to do, and ordered this one to stand here and that one there and someone to do this and another to do that.

And in another moment, the ceremony began, and then all Vere could think about was the woman beside him, about to become his, absolutely . . . and forever.

The bride and her attendants had withdrawn hours earlier, but it was midnight before Vere's friends allowed him to escape from the post-wedding orgy, and this was only because someone—Carruthers or Tolliver—had a bevy of trollops delivered. At that point, Dain decided the married men were free to depart if they chose. Though Trent wasn't a married man, he left with them, still trying to make Dain listen to some incomprehensible theory or story or whatever it was about Charles II and courtiers and cavaliers and Lucifer only knew what else.

"I know it were at your place," Trent was telling his brother-in-law as the three men ascended the stairs. "In the picture gallery, which must be at least a mile long, and he were in the alcove and Jess said he were her favorite—"

"The gallery is one hundred eighty feet long," Dain said.

"As Ainswood will attest. On the day of my father's funeral, I set up one of the portraits of my sire upon an easel and proposed an archery contest. You recall, don't you, Ainswood? Using my dear Papa for target practice was sophomoric, you claimed. You assured me that I would find more satisfaction rogering that evil redhead, Charity Graves, in the master bedchamber. Having tested her yourself, you deemed her worthy of my efforts." He clapped Vere on the shoulder as they reached the top of the stairs. "Ah, well, my lad, those days are over. No more sharing trollops for us. We must make do with ladies, and only one apiece." He turned to Bertie. "Good night, Trent. Pleasant dreams."

"I say Dain, but you—"

Dain's deadly black stare cut him off.

Bertie tugged at his neckcloth. "That is. Well." He backed away from Dain. "Mean to say, congratulations, Ainswood, and good night and much obliged, you know—groomsman. Honored." He shook Vere's hand, nodded at Dain, then fled to his room.

In the recesses of Vere's brain, the wispy something teased again, but his glance stole down the hall to the last door, behind which his duchess waited, and that hot awareness blotted out the vexing will-o'-the-wisp.

"My lady's expecting our brat sometime in February or March," Dain said, recalling Vere's attention to him. "It wants godparents. Perhaps you and your bride will accept the position."

It took Vere a moment to believe his ears, then another to digest the implications. Then his throat tightened. Despite time, separations, misunderstandings, and mills, he and Beelzebub were friends, still. "So that's why you were so eager to see me wed," he said, not altogether steadily.

"I was eager on several counts," said Dain. "But I will not

make you stay and listen to my reasons. You have . . . responsibilities." He smiled faintly. "I will not keep you from them."

To his horror, Vere felt the heat rise in his face.

"You are blushing, Ainswood," said Dain. "Today is truly
a day of miracles."

"Go to the devil," Vere muttered, starting down the hall.

Behind him, he heard Dain's low chuckle. "If you find
yourself stumped what to do, Your Grace," he called, "feel
free to knock on my door."

"Stumped what to do, indeed," Vere answered without
turning around. "I taught you everything you know, Beelz—
and not half what *I* know."

He heard another of the satanic rumbles that passed for
laughter, then the sound of a door opening and closing.

"Knock on your door," Vere went on under his breath.
"Very amusing. Hilarious. As though I'm not the elder and
wasn't the one who brought you your first trollop." He
rapped impatiently at the portal to his room. "Bloody
damned know-it-all. Always was. Always will be. I should
break his big beak for—"

His bride opened the door.

He was vaguely aware that she was still fully dressed, but
he didn't pause to wonder about it. He entered, kicked the
door shut behind him, caught her in his arms, and crushed
her to him.

He buried his face in her neck. Her soft, thick hair tickled
his cheek while her scent stole into him, and he drank it in
greedily. "Oh, Lord, Grenville," he murmured. "I thought
I'd never get away from them."

Her arms came up about him, but stiffly, and her long
body vibrated tension. He lifted his head to gaze at her. Her
face was pale and hard. Her eyes gave him back his own reflection and something else. Something dark and troubled.

"You're weary," he said, loosening his boa-constrictor grip. "It's been a very long and tiring day."

"I'm not weary." Her voice throbbed. "I came straight here, and fell onto the bed and asleep before my head touched the pillow." She eased out of his arms. "I woke an hour ago. I've had plenty of rest. And time to think."

"Which left no time for changing into something more appropriate for the wedding night," he said, resolutely ignoring a fierce jab of the conscience he wasn't speaking to. He had rushed her into matrimony. He'd taken advantage of a moment of weakness. Very well, then. He was unscrupulous—along with depraved and obnoxious and the other et ceteras. That was his nature. "That's quite all right. I'll be happy to help you out of your armor." He brought his hands to the topmost button.

"I'm not prepared to consummate the marriage," she said stiffly.

"No problem." He unbuttoned the first button. "I'll prepare you."

She swatted his hands away. "This is serious, Ainswood. We must talk."

"Grenville, you know we can't converse for more than two minutes without quarreling," he said. "Let's not talk tonight, what do you say?" He started to work on the second button.

Her hand, very cold, clamped upon his. "My conscience will not allow me to be your wife," she said. "I want an annulment."

"Your conscience has lost its mind," he said. He kissed her straight, haughty nose. "This is merely bridal nerves."

"I am not a nervous person." Her voice climbed, grew shakier. "I am not hysterical, and you are not to patronize me. All I have done is come to my senses." She paused, setting her jaw and lifting her chin. "The fact is, I am not a lady, not even half a lady. You are the Duke of Ainswood. You must wed a lady. You owe it to your family."

"I've wed you," he said impatiently. "I don't want a lady. I shouldn't know what to do with one." He grasped her shoulders. "I hope you're not turning missish on me."

"We cannot go to bed." Twin spots of pink appeared in her cheeks. "You must not be fruitful and multiply with me. I cannot allow you to take such a risk."

"A *what?*"

"My family." She choked out the words. "You don't know about my family. I should have told you before, but I was too agitated. I had been so alarmed that you were killed, and then . . ." She pulled away. "It is so absurd. I wanted to make you happy, and you were so set upon marrying without delay. I do not know why I wanted to make you happy, why I fancy I can."

"It's easy to make me happy, Grenville. All you need to do is take off your—"

"My mother was sickly from the time my sister was born." Her words came out in a rush. "My mother died when I was ten. My little sister took consumption and died barely three years later. My father was a third-rate actor and a drunkard and a gambler. He possessed not one redeeming quality." Twisting her hands together, she walked to the fireplace. "Mine is bad blood. Your family deserves better. You must consider them—the line you represent."

"A pox on my line," he said, but without heat. She was obviously overset, on the edge of hysteria. The strain of the day's events was telling. He went to her. "Come, Grenville, only listen to yourself. You're a worse snob than Dain. The line I represent, indeed. What's become of Miss *Liberté*, *Égalité*, and *Fraternité?* What's become of Madam Vindication of the Rights of Women? Where has my dragon-girl gone?"

"I'm not a dragon," she said. "I am merely a lowborn scribbler with a foul disposition."

"I see that you're not in a humor to listen to reason," he said. "We'll have to settle this in sporting fashion."

He stepped away from her and shrugged out of his coat. Then he tore off his neckcloth. A few swift yanks released his waistcoat buttons. He pulled off the waistcoat and tossed it aside. He kicked off his shoes.

He assumed a fighting stance, fists upraised.

She stared at him.

"Hit me," he said. "I'll give you three tries. If you can't connect, *I* get three tries."

"To hit me?" she asked, plainly bewildered.

He relaxed his stance. "Grenville, if I hit you, you'd drop stone cold on the floor," he said patiently. "What bloody good would you be to me then? Use your head."

He resumed his pugilistic pose. "If you can't hit me, *I* get three tries to make you fall onto the bed, panting with lust."

A martial light sparked in her blue eyes. "Devil confound you, Ainswood, haven't you heard a word I've said? Can't you take your mind off your breeding organs for a moment and consider your future—and your ancestors—and your position?"

He shook his head. "Sorry. Not that civilized. Come, Grenville." He stuck out his chin. "Aren't you itching to break my jaw? Or how about my nose?" He pointed there. "Wouldn't you like to plant me a conker? Not that you've a prayer, but it'll be amusing to see you try."

She glowered at him.

He danced a bit, jabbing the air with his right, then his left. "Come, what are you afraid of? Here's your chance to give me the pair of stinkers you promised in Vinegar Yard. Or was that all boasting? Did the tap on my jaw hurt your little hand too much, my delicate flower? Did you learn your lesson then?"

It came from nowhere. Lightning fast and low, her fist shot toward his privates.

He nipped aside in the nick of time. "Not there, Grenville," he said, swallowing his astonishment. "Think of our children."

She stepped back, her eyes narrowed, assessing him from head to toe, looking for the chink in his defenses. "You didn't say I had to fight fair," she said.

"You wouldn't have a prayer if you did," he taunted.

She brought her arms up, holding them at strange angles, while her body began swaying side to side, like a cobra preparing to strike. Her hair was coming undone, tumbling about her shoulders. It was a glorious sight, and he ached to tangle his fingers in it. But he could not let his mind wander. She had any number of tricks in her repertoire, and she was devilish unpredictable. Not to mention quick.

He waited, bracing for the strike, wondering where it would come from, and aware she was playing with him, staying in motion to distract him while she waited for an opening.

He caught it half a pulsebeat before she moved: the merest flicker of a glance downward. Her skirts hitched up as her foot shot out, but he moved in the same instant, spinning to the side. The miss threw her off balance and she started to topple. Reflexively, he reached for her—and pulled back an instant before her outthrust elbow could connect with his groin.

"Sweet Jesus," he gasped. He was not so much winded as stunned. If he'd been an eyeblink slower, she would have had him singing High C.

He waited, braced, not daring to relax his guard, even though she'd turned away and was working her way through the standard list of profanities.

"That's three tries, Grenville," he said. "My turn now."

She swung about to face him. "What happens if you—*when* you fail?" she demanded.

"You get another three tries. Then I do. Until one of us wins. The winner gets what he wants."

And I'll make bloody damned sure you want what I want, he added silently.

She folded her arms and lifted her chin. "Very well. Do your worst."

He eyed her up and down, assessing her as she'd done him. He began to circle her. She stayed where she was, only her head turning as her wary gaze followed him. He paused close behind her.

For a long moment he simply stood there, making her wait, building tension. Then he bent and lightly traced with his parted lips a meandering path from her ear to her creamy cheek. "So soft," he murmured while he let his fingers skim down her arms, drawing them away from her chest and down to her sides. "Your skin is like rose petals."

She inhaled sharply. "That's one," she said, her voice strained.

He brushed his cheek against hers. "I love the scent of your skin." He drew his outspread hands ever so lightly—barely touching the fabric—and slowly down over her lavish bosom to her waist and lower still, to gently press her belly, drawing her back against him, her lush derriere just touching his trousers front, under which his rod eagerly swelled for business.

Her eyes closed and she swallowed. "That's t-two."

He did nothing, letting the moment stretch out while he remained still, his cheek to hers, his hands resting on her belly. His touch remained light, only enough to keep her in place and inescapably aware of his aroused masculinity and its heat.

A tremor went through her.

Still he waited. It was killing him, but the hot tension was working on her as well. He could feel it, the struggle within her, intellect warring with feeling, abstract principle fighting for supremacy in a nature fiercely physical and sensual.

She squirmed, ever so little, pressing just a fraction nearer.

He brushed his mouth at the corner of hers.

With a little moan, she sank back against him, turning her head for the kiss he teased her with.

He teased her still, letting his lips play lightly and lazily over the soft fullness of her mouth.

Her hands covered his, holding him to her.

"That's three," he said thickly. "Your turn now."

"You beast," she hissed. "You know I can't fight you." She tried to turn to him, but he held her where she was, letting her sweet rump torment his loins.

"Ah, no, not so quickly, dragoness." He nipped her ear and crushed her closer. "I had planned to go easy on you—this being your first time and all—but that would be patronizing, wouldn't it? You're not afraid to fight me—and not shy about where you aim, I noticed. Delicacy would be wasted on you."

He lashed one arm 'round her waist to keep her against him while with his free hand he undid the long parade of buttons.

He pulled the frock down to her waist. The sleeves bunched at her elbows, trapping her arms.

Soft, creamy flesh beckoned from the borders of petticoat and corset. He made a carpet of hurried kisses over the fragrant skin behind her ear and down to the nape of her neck and over her shoulders. She shivered.

He undid tapes and hooks, released her arms from the sleeves, and pushed the frock down over her hips. It slid to the floor, making a rumpled heap at her feet. He nudged her to step out of its tangle and went immediately to the corset, his fingers working swiftly at the lacings. The stiff garment at last gave way, sagging to her hips. He drew it away and tossed it aside.

He swung her up in his arms and carried her to the bed. He let go, dropping her on the mattress. She swore, but before she could scramble up and strike him, he fell upon her. He dragged his fingers through her hair and held her while he covered her mouth with his and kissed her, fiercely.

She struggled but a moment before yielding, as she always did, as she ought to understand by now she must do.

"No annulment," he growled when at last he freed her mouth. "No someone else. Ever. So put it out of your mind."

"You idiot." Her voice was husky. She grasped his shirt front and pulled him back to her. She took her revenge, her ripe lips smoldering against his, her tongue stirring a devil's brew inside him.

He rolled onto his back, taking her with him, his mouth clinging hungrily to hers, his legs tangling in her petticoats.

He pulled up the skirts of the frothy garments and groaned as his fingers touched stocking and traced the sleek outline of her thigh. Inches above the garter, there was only warm, silken skin . . . all the curving way up to the wicked arc of her rump.

Her utterly bare naked rump.

"Sweet Jesus." His voice was a thick whisper. "Where are your drawers, you hussy?"

"I forgot to pack them," she said in suffocated tones.

"Forgot." It was the last articulate word he uttered, the last clear thought he had.

With a low, animal growl, he pushed her off him and onto her back. It took him but a few feverish seconds to tear off the last of his garments. Before they reached the floor, he was untying the ribbons of her petticoat's bodice.

The neckline gatherings loosened and he pushed the fabric down. Her skin was as pale as moonglow, a miracle of softness and lavish curves. He drew his hands down over the creamy swell of her breasts, let his thumbs play over the pink buds, taut even before he touched them.

With a soft cry, she arched up, pushing against his hands, reaching for his shoulders, even as he bent to take one rosy pearl into his mouth.

Her fingers tangled in his hair to hold him to her while he suckled, drawing helpless little cries from her that made his heart drum and his insides tighten and ache.

He stroked down over her belly, felt it tighten under his touch. But the petticoat's fabric tickled his skin. Impatient, he pulled it off and flung it away. He made himself pause to drink in the sight of her, so perfectly formed, his beautiful amazon. Then he let his hands and mouth touch and taste boldly, and reveled in her hot answering caresses, in the soft sounds she uttered, of surprise and pleasure.

She'd been made and meant for him, every velvet-smooth, dragon-scented inch of her. And, as his fingers stole into the soft mound of curls between her legs and he felt the tiny recoil, he found her ready for him.

She was already damp, passionate dragoness, and his first gentle caresses in that intimate place had her squirming against his hand.

In his power. Under his control. At last.

He'd wanted to bide his time, pleasure her into madness before he pleasured himself. He'd wanted to make her wild and helpless. He'd promised himself that he would, that he'd make her beg, and he had more reason now, after what she'd put him through this hellish day.

Her quick, hot answer to his touch burned up all those promises and wishes.

His masculine pride was no match for the need tearing through his veins like liquid hellfire.

He stroked her, parted her, and pushed himself into her . . . and she screamed.

13

What sounded like a scream to the more-nervous-than-he'd-admit bridegroom was only a small, startled exclamation.

When therefore, he stopped abruptly, Lydia's own nervousness mixed with embarrassment.

She opened her eyes. His were dark, his face set in rigid lines.

"What?" she said. "What did I do wrong?"

"Did I hurt you?"

The embarrassment ebbed. Lydia shook her head.

"I was too hasty." His voice was harsh. "You weren't ready."

"I didn't know what to expect," she admitted. "I was surprised." She shifted position, pulling her knees up slightly. He inhaled sharply. She gasped, too, at the strange sensations within.

The part of him inside her was not only large, but seemed to have a throbbing life of its own that radiated waves of heat. "Oh," she whispered. "I had no idea."

His expression softened.

Her muscles also began to relax, adapting to his size.

He hadn't really hurt her. It stung a little at first, and she'd felt an uncomfortable friction and tightness. She was more comfortable now—physically, at any rate.

"I'm such a ninny," she said. "I thought something was wrong with me, that you wouldn't fit."

"There's nothing wrong with your body." He moved inside her, and her breath caught again.

No, there wasn't anything wrong with her body. With him, she didn't feel like a giantess. But her body was all she was sure of.

She wasn't a lady, not even half a lady. No Ballister blood ran in her veins. She was no longer sure who she was, what she was.

He lowered his head. "Grenville."

"I hate not knowing what to do."

His mouth covered hers.

She reached up, tangled her fingers in his hair.

She wanted him. She wasn't unsure about that. She drank in the sinful taste of him, inhaled the scent of his skin.

She'd learned how to kiss him, how to stop thinking, and swim in sensation instead.

She'd learned how easy it was for control to slip away and longing to take its place.

She'd learned that longing dug deep, a dagger to the heart.

She ached now, though he was inside her, part of her. She ached because she knew what he was and knew better than to hope he'd change. She knew that what she yearned for was more than he could ever give.

She became aware again of his hands moving over her, caressing, moving down to the place where they were joined. He touched her there as he'd done before to prepare her. This time, though, he was inside her as well, and the stroke of his fingers, combined with the vibrating inner heat, made her squirm. The ache spread, beating through her like a pulse.

She felt him withdrawing, and, "No, wait," she begged. She dug her fingers into his shoulders, to hold him.

The muscles under her hands knotted, taut as whipcords, and he thrust inward. Pleasure reverberated in vein and muscle.

"Oh, God," she gasped. "Sweet Jesus."

Again he stroked, and this time she arched up, instinctively, to meet it. The ache swelled, mingling with pleasure to sweep through her like a hot incoming tide. Another stroke came, and she met it. And again and again, while pleasure pounded against doubt and despair until they shattered.

She surrendered then, body, soul, will—all—to him. She clung to his sweat-slicked skin, rocking with him while the rhythm built, inexorably, faster and wilder, like the storm that had borne down upon them while they raced.

And this time, too, the climax took her unawares. She heard his low cry, an animal sound, felt his fingers grasping her buttocks, lifting her. She felt the last, fierce thrust . . . and a bolt of joy, searingly bright, tore through her. And then another and another, until she shattered, like a bursting star, and darkness enveloped her.

For a long while afterward she lay stunned.

For a long while, she couldn't find her tongue. No surprise, when she couldn't find her brain.

When, finally, she forced her unwilling eyes open, she found herself staring straight into his.

Before she could read their expression, he blinked and looked away. Carefully he withdrew from her. He rolled onto his back and lay silent, staring at the ceiling.

She also kept silent for a while, telling herself it was ridiculous to feel lonely and rejected.

It wasn't personal, she reminded herself. That was the way he was. Helena had warned her. *Once used, we're worthless.*

Only worthless to him, though. She wasn't a worthless woman, Lydia told herself, and she shouldn't feel that way simply because he moved away and wouldn't look at her.

"It's not my fault," she burst out. She sat up. "Marrying me was your idea. You could have bedded me. I offered myself to you. It is completely unreasonable to sulk about it now, when I gave you every opportunity to change your mind."

He rose up from the pillows, firmly cupped her face in his hands, and kissed her, hard.

She melted instantly, her arms wrapping about him. He sank back onto the pillows, taking her with him. His long legs tangled with hers while he drained her doubts and loneliness with a deep, mind-melting kiss.

She understood, then, that whatever was wrong, it hadn't to do with his desire being sated. He wasn't finished with her yet. When, finally, he released her mouth, his hands still moved over her, lazily caressing.

"If you had regrets, I suppose you're too obstinate to admit it," she said.

"You're the one who was blithering about your unworthiness," he said. "You're the one who was looking for a way out."

Lydia had no way out now. For better or for worse, she was tied to him. She wouldn't have minded if she could perceive some good she could do him.

She would not let herself worry about the harm he could do her. She could bear that, whatever it was. Life had taught her that she could bear anything.

She drew back, lifting herself onto one elbow for a better view of his long, leanly muscled body. "I shall simply have to make the best of matters," she said. "On the physical side, at least, I've nothing to complain about."

She hadn't realized how tense he was until now, when his expression eased and his mouth slowly curved. She had never seen this smile before. If she had, she would have remembered.

Crooked, disarmingly boyish, it was, as Helena had said, a smile that could make roses bloom in an arctic wasteland.

Lydia felt it spread over her like the warmth of the sun. Her pulse, which had finally returned to normal, began to hurry again, and she could actually feel her brain softening, ready to believe anything.

"Do you know what, Grenville?" he said. "I think you're besotted with me."

"There's a brilliant insight," she said. "Do you think I would have married you if I were not? If I were fully rational?"

"Are you in love with me, then?"

"In love?" Lydia stared at him. She was a writer, and words were her life. "Besotted" and "in love" were not synonyms. "In *love?*" she repeated incredulously.

"In the ditch, you said you'd become attached to me."

"I am attached to my dog," she said in the crisp tones of a schoolteacher. "I make allowances for Susan's inferior intelligence and humor her to an extent that seems reasonable. I should be sorry if anything happened to her. Does it follow that I'm in love with her?"

"I see your point, Grenville, but she's a *dog.*"

"Apart from my belief—based on experience—that the masculine brain appears to function much in the way of the canine brain—"

"You're so prejudiced against men," he chided, still smiling.

"Love involves the heart and mind—the soul, if you will. 'Besotted' indicates an altered state of physical being, similar to that induced by overindulgence in drink. Both—"

"Do you know, Grenville, you're rather adorable when you're pedantic?"

"Both infatuation and intoxication are physical states," she went on doggedly. "Both often lead to gross errors of judgment."

"Or perhaps it's the combination of 'pedantic' and 'naked.' " His green gaze drifted lingeringly downward from her face to the ends of her toes, which she could barely keep from curling.

Since he would not listen to anything a woman said in ordinary circumstances, it was absurd to expect him to concentrate on what a naked woman said, she told herself.

On the other hand, his gaze was admiring, and Lydia was certainly woman enough to enjoy that. She returned the smile, to reward and encourage the admiration. Then, because she turned away to climb out of the bed, she didn't see his smile fade or the uncertainty that passed over his face like a shadow.

"Where are you going, Grenville?"

"To wash." She headed for the washstand, which stood behind a folding screen.

"Do you know, duchess," he said reflectively, "the back view is as magnificent in its own way as the front. You have a . . ."

His voice trailed off as she stepped behind the screen.

Though she would have liked to hear the rest of the compliment, Lydia turned her attention to practical matters.

She had scarcely bled at all, which was not surprising in an athletic young woman, and more common, she was aware, than the prevailing wisdom maintained. Still, there were a few faint smears and she was definitely sticky. With his seed.

She washed herself, well aware that any number of incipient Mallorys had spilled into her and did not require any special cultivation to sprout to life.

Still, she had warned him that she was not prime breeding stock. Not that one could expect him to reflect upon the consequences. He cared no more about how his children turned out than he cared what a shambles he'd make of her existence if she let herself fall in love with him.

"Grenville."

"I'll be done in a minute," she said.

There was a silence broken only by the slosh of water in the basin.

"Grenville, what's that on your rump?"

"On my—" Then she remembered. "Oh, the birthmark, you mean. I know it looks like a tattoo, but it isn't."

She speedily completed her ablutions and stepped out from behind the screen . . . and came up against a tall, hard column of naked male.

"Turn 'round," he said. His voice was very mild, his expression unreadable.

"Do you know, Ainswood, you become even more annoying than usual after sexual intimacy. I should—"

"Turn, please."

She set her jaw and did as he asked, though she did not like being examined as though she were a curious biological specimen. She resolved to return the favor at the earliest opportunity. About one minute from now.

"I thought so," he murmured. He touched her shoulder, gently turning her back to him. "My dear, do you know what that is?"

The endearment made her wary. "A birthmark, as I said. And a very small one at that. Hardly disfiguring. I hope you don't have some sort of morbid aversion to—"

"You're beautiful," he said. "And the mark is . . . fetching." He lifted his hand to stroke her tense jaw. "You don't know what it is, do you?"

"I am on pins and needles to find out what it is to you," she said, every instinct stirring, sensing trouble.

"Nothing." He stepped back. "Nothing at all. Nothing to bother yourself about." He turned away. "I'm simply going to kill him, that's all."

He strode back to the bed. Muttering to himself, he snatched up from the floor near the bedpost his dressing gown and flung it on. Like hers, it had been neatly laid out upon the bedclothes. His had slipped to the floor in the tumult of lovemaking. Hers was a rumpled clump wedged between mattress and bedpost.

She did not even try to figure out what he was about, but ran to the bed and tugged her robe free. As she pulled it on, he marched to the door, yanked it open, and stormed out. She hurried after him, tying her sash as she went.

"Facts about her background," Vere snarled under his breath. "Crocodiles in Borneo. And there was Trent trying to tell me."

"Ainswood," his wife's voice came from behind him.

He paused and turned. She stood in the open doorway of their room. "Go back to bed," he said. "I'll deal with this." He swung 'round and went on walking.

He stopped at Dain's door, raised his fist and pounded, once, twice, thrice. "Lord Almighty know-it-all. Portrait of his sire. 'You recall, don't you, Ainswood?' Very amusing. Hilar—"

The door swung inward and six and one-half feet of dark, arrogant, half-Italian so-called friend advanced to fill the doorway. "Ah, Ainswood. Come for instructions, have you?" Beelzebub regarded him with a mocking half-smile.

Her smile. Why hadn't he seen it?

Vere let his mouth curl in mimicry. "Shouldn't call her hair gold, should you? Couldn't be French, could she? Crocodiles in Borneo. You *knew*, you big-beaked macaroni bastard."

Beelzebub's black gaze shifted to Vere's left. An impatient

glance that way showed Vere that his wife had not gone peaceably back to bed, but was swiftly approaching. Barefooted, he discovered to his dismay. She would catch her death.

"Grenville, I said I'd deal with this," he told her, irritably aware of Beelzebub's amused regard.

The bride only planted herself at Vere's side, folded her arms, and waited, mouth set, eyes narrowed.

By this time, Lady Dain had elbowed her way into position beside her spouse. "Let me guess," she said to him. "You didn't tell Ainswood, though you promised me you would, before—"

"Plague take it!" Vere snapped. "Does all the world know? Devil rot your soul, Beelz, I don't mind a joke—but you might have considered *her* feelings. The poor girl—"

"I hope you are not referring to me," Grenville cut in icily. "I don't know what maggot is eating at your brain at the moment, Ainswood, but—"

"Ah, you don't know," said Dain. "The bridegroom flew into a fit and thundered out without troubling to explain what had thrown his innards in an uproar. This is typical, I'm afraid. Ainswood has a lamentable tendency to leap first and think later. That is because he cannot keep more than one idea at a time in his very thick head."

"Hear, hear," said Lady Dain. "Pot calls kettle black."

Dain turned to her. "Jessica, go to bed."

"Not now," answered she. "Not for a thousand pounds." Her grey gaze moved to Vere. "I'm dying to learn how you found out."

"It was precious difficult," said Dain. "Sellowby and I only dropped about a thousand hints, amid Trent's demented driveling about the Earl of Blackmoor—Charles II's bosom bow—the cavalier with the golden curls."

Vere heard his wife's sharp intake of breath.

Dain shifted his attention to her. "You bear a strong resemblance to my pretty ancestor. If Trent had seen the portrait of my father as well, his remarks might have made more sense. Regrettably, the more recent painting had an encounter with the Demon Seed—my son, Dominick—and came out the worse," he explained. "It was being repaired when Trent visited. If he'd seen it, he would have come nearer the mark, for if my late, unlamented sire had been a woman, he should have been you . . . cousin."

If Bertie had been sleeping as he normally did, cannon fire would not have wakened him. But his sleep was fitful, agitated by visions of crocodiles snapping at the dainty feet of bespectacled maidens attempting to flee from leering cavaliers who wore nothing but the golden sausage curls clustering about their heads and shoulders.

This was why the hubbub in the hall penetrated his consciousness and shot him up from the pillows and, in short order, from the bed.

He found his dressing gown and slippers and, decently covered, opened his door in time to hear Dain's remarks about family portraits and the last, intriguing word: *cousin.*

Before Bertie could fully digest these revelations, the quartet had filed into Dain's chamber and the door closed behind them.

Bertie was about to retreat to his room to ponder what he'd overheard when out of the corner of his eye he spied a flash of white, at the hallway's corner near the top of the stairs.

An instant later, a bespectacled feminine face, surrounded by white ruffles, peeped out from the corner. A small white hand, also surrounded by ruffles, beckoned.

After a moment's inner debate, Bertie went whither he was summoned.

"What's happened?" Miss Price enquired—for it was she in the bewildering concoction of white ruffles. The silliest froth of a nightcap covered her dark hair. Ruffles encircled her neck and fluttered downward along the borders of her wrapper, which encasing cloud of a garment left absolutely everything to the imagination except her face and her fingers.

"I ain't exactly sure," Bertie said, blinking at this vision. "I only heard the last of it. Still, it looks like I were on the right trail but come by the wrong direction. It weren't the cavalier fellow but Dain's father. Only Dain called her 'cousin,' which were a jolt to me. I figured she were his sister—mean to say . . ." His face heated and his hand went up to tug on his neck-cloth. He found he wasn't wearing one, and the discovery made his face several degrees hotter. "Mean to say, half-sister, only without the parson's blessing, if you know what I mean."

Miss Price stared at him for a full twenty seconds by his count. "Not the cavalier," she said slowly. "Who was the Earl of Blackmoor, you mean. Instead, Lord Dain's father. Is that it?"

"She looks like him," Bertie said.

"Miss Gren—the Duchess of Ainswood, I mean, resembles the previous marquess."

"And Dain said 'cousin.' That were all. Then they went in his room." He gestured that way. "The lot of 'em. What do you make of it? If Dain recognized her, why didn't he say so before? Or were it a joke, do you think, which I can't figure what else, bein' as how if he didn't want to know her, he wouldn't say 'cousin,' would he?"

Her sharp brown gaze strayed toward Dain's door. "A joke. Well, that would explain. I discerned a resemblance

—that remarkable stare—but I thought my imagination had run away with me." Her attention returned to Bertie. "It's been a most exciting day. And this makes a splendid conclusion, do you not think? That Miss Grenville—that is to say, Her Grace—turns out to be a relative of the duke's good friend."

"Best of friends," Bertie corrected. "Which is why I were so surprised when Dain said I was to be groomsman, not him, and told Ainswood we drew straws, when we never did. It were Dain who decided he'd give away the bride, and no one argues with him usually—except Ainswood, but he weren't there at the moment."

Behind the spectacles, Miss Price's enormous eyes glistened ominously. "I thought she hadn't anyone and was quite alone in the world, but she wasn't, was she? Her kinsman gave her away." She blinked a few times and swallowed. "I'm glad I didn't know. I should have made a watering pot of myself. It is so . . . affecting. Such a kind gesture, to give her away. And she deserves it, you know. She is the kindest, m-most generous . . ." Her voice broke.

"Oh, I say." Bertie gazed at her in alarm.

She withdrew a scrap of a handkerchief from somewhere in the voluminous froth of her wrapper and hastily wiped her tears away. "I beg your pardon," she said shakily. "It is simply that I am happy for her. And . . . relieved."

Bertie was also relieved—that she'd stopped short of waterworks. "Yes, well, like you say, it were an exciting day and I reckon you could do with some rest. Not to mention there's a draft, and even if there wasn't no danger of you takin' a chill you oughtn't be wandering about in your unmentionables at this hour. Most of the fellows're half-seas over at the very least, and no tellin' what ideas they could take into their heads."

She stared at him for a moment, then her mouth turned up and parted and a soft laugh came out. "Oh, you are so droll, Sir Bertram. Ideas in their heads. Those tipsy fellows should grow faint with exhaustion trying to find me in all these yards and yards of . . . unmentionables," she finished with another small chuckle.

Bertie wasn't tipsy, and he was sure he could find her easily enough, considering she stood well within easy reach. Her eyes were sparkling with humor now, as though he were the wittiest fellow on earth, and a pink glow was forming in her cheeks, and he thought she was the prettiest girl on earth. Then, realizing he was the one with ideas in his head, he told himself to make a bolt for it.

Only he moved in the wrong direction and somehow there was a great deal of white froth in his arms and a soft mouth touching his and then colored lights were dancing about his head.

At this same moment, Lydia was strongly tempted to make her cousin see stars. He had flummoxed her utterly.

"Dain could lecture on family history for weeks," Lady Dain was saying. She and Lydia sat in chairs by the fire, glasses recently filled with champagne in their hands. "He pretends to find it boring or makes a joke of it, but it is one of his hobbyhorses."

"It isn't as though I can escape it," said Dain. "We've rows upon rows of books, boxes of documents. The Ballisters never could bear to discard anything of the slightest historical value. Even my father could not bring himself to wipe your mama's existence altogether from the records. Still, Jess and I wouldn't have known to look if Sellowby hadn't whetted our curiosity. He'd spotted you after our wedding and noted the resemblance to my sire and his ancestors. It wasn't until after your Vinegar Yard encounter with Ainswood made the gossip rounds, though, that Sellowby wrote to us. Everything he'd heard, coupled with his occasional glimpses of Grenville of the *Argus*, inclined him to suspect a Ballister connection."

"If you only knew how careful I was to avoid Sellowby," Lydia said. "And all for naught. I vow, he must be part bloodhound."

"By gad, Grenville, was that why you climbed up to the first floor of Helena's house instead of going in by the door, like a normal person?" Ainswood said in soft incredulity. "You risked your neck to avoid Sellowby?"

"I didn't want the past raked up," Lydia said.

Their keenly alert expressions told her they expected more of an explanation, but she couldn't bear to say more. Those who'd known about her mother's elopement and its sordid consequences were dead and buried. Anne Ballister's was a lowly cadet branch of the family tree. To the Great World, they were virtually unknown. Her sad story had commenced and ended out of the glare of the Beau Monde's stage, where more sensational dramas with more important principals—most notably, the Prince of Wales—riveted attention.

Lydia had kept the secret, determinedly, because she did not want her mother's folly thrust upon that stage, her degradation the topic of tea table conversations.

"Some of it must come out now," Ainswood said. "I'm amazed Sellowby held his tongue for this long. We can't expect him to keep quiet forever."

"He doesn't know the details," said Dain. "Grenville is hardly an uncommon surname. It's enough to say her parents quarreled with the family, and no one knew what had become of them or had the least idea they'd produced a daughter until now. Even that is more explanation than the world deserves."

"I should like something explained," said Lady Dain to

Lydia. "We still haven't learned how His Grace made his amazing discovery."

"It followed directly upon his discovering my birthmark," Lydia said.

Her Ladyship's lips quivered. She looked up at Dain, who had gone very still.

"It isn't possible," he said.

"That's what I told myself," said Ainswood. "I couldn't believe my eyes."

Dain's dark glance darted from his cousin to his friend. "You're sure?"

"I should know that mark from a furlong away," Ainswood said. "The 'mark of the Ballisters,' you told us at school—the one incontrovertible proof that your mother did not play your father false. And when Charity Graves started pestering you about the brat Dominick, I was the one who went down to Athton to make sure he was yours, not mine. There it was in the same place, the same little brown crossbow."

He glowered at Dain.

"I had no idea my cousin bore that mark, I assure you," said Dain. "I was under the impression that it appeared only in males of the family." He smiled faintly. "A pity my dear papa didn't know. The holy badge of the Ballisters appearing on a female—product of the union between a nobody and a young woman he doubtless assisted in permanently ejecting from the family. He'd have gone off in an apoplexy the instant he heard—and I should have been one delighted young orphan."

He turned to the duke. "Well, then, are you done working yourself into a lather over my little joke? Or are you appalled to find yourself connected with me? If you don't want a Ballister for your wife, we shall be happy to take her."

"The devil you will." Ainswood drained his glass and set it

down. "I haven't endured five weeks of trials unimaginable in their horror only to turn her over to you, long lost family or not. As to you, Grenville," he added irritably, "I'd like to know why you haven't offered to break his big nose. He played you for a fool as well—and you were upset enough a while ago about your peasant blood contaminating mine. You're taking this precious calmly."

"I can take a joke," she said. "I've married you, haven't I?" She set down her nearly empty glass and rose. "We must not keep Lady Dain up all night. Mothers-to-be require a reasonable amount of sleep."

Lady Dain rose. "We've scarcely had a chance to talk. Not that one could hope to carry on an intelligent conversation with a pair of noisy males at close hand, competing for precedence. You must return to Athcourt with us tomorrow."

"Certainly you must," said Dain. "It's the ancestral home, after all."

"I have an ancestral home as well." Ainswood advanced to place a possessive arm about Lydia's shoulders. "She's only your cousin, Dain, and a distant one at that. And she's a Mallory now, not a Ballister, no matter what's stamped upon her—"

"Another time, perhaps," Lydia cut in smoothly. "Ainswood and I have a great deal to sort out—and I have work to complete for the *Argus*, which—"

"Yes, as you said, a great deal to sort out," her spouse said, his voice tight.

He made quick work of the good nights, and they'd started down the hall when Lady Dain called to them. They paused. She hurried up to them, pressed a small oblong package into Lydia's hand, kissed her cheek, then hurried away.

Lydia waited until they'd reentered their own room to unwrap the parcel.

Then a small, startled sob escaped her.

She heard Ainswood's voice, alarmed. "Good God, what have they—"

She turned in his arms, felt them close, warm, and strong about her. "My mother's diary." The words were muffled in the folds of his dressing gown. "They've given me back Mama's d-diary."

Her voice broke, and with it, the composure she'd so determinedly maintained with her newfound family.

Pressing her face to his chest, she wept.

14

Anne Ballister's Diary

I can scarcely believe it is my nineteenth birthday. It seems twenty years since I left my father's house, rather than twenty months.

Does my father remember what day this is, I wonder? He and his cousin, Lord Dain, have between them obliterated my existence by all means available, short of actual murder. But memory is not so easily blotted out as a name in a family Bible. It is easy enough to rule that a daughter never again be mentioned; yet memory submits to no will, even a Ballister's, and the name and image persist long after death, literal or figurative.

I am alive, Father, and well, though your wish almost came true when my dear baby girl was born. I had no expensive London accoucheur to preside over my labor, merely a woman no older than I who has borne three children already, and is in a family way again. When Alice Martin's time comes, I shall return the favor and play midwife.

It was a miracle I survived the childbed fever, all the wise matrons of this humble neighborhood agree. I know it was no miracle, but an act of will. I could not submit to Death, however much he insisted. I could not abandon my infant daughter to the false, selfish man I married.

John is sorry now, I don't doubt, that both I and Lydia survived. He has been obliged to take whatever minor roles come

266

his way, and exert himself to study his handful of lines. I have arranged for his wages to be put directly in my hands. Otherwise, every farthing of the little he earns would go to drink and women and gaming, and my Lydia would starve. He complains, bitterly, that I make his life hardly worth living, and rues the day he set out to win my heart.

For my part, I am heartily ashamed that he succeeded, that I had been such an utter fool. Still, I was a green girl when I ran away from home. Though ours is merely an insignificant cadet branch of the Ballister tree, I had been pampered and sheltered as much as any duke's daughter, and was, as a result, no less naive. For a handsome, silver-tongued rogue like John Grenville, I was all too easy a mark. How was I to realize his stirring speeches and tear-filled declarations of love were merely . . . acting?

He was not so wise, either. He viewed me as a ticket to a life of wealth and ease. He believed he understood the English aristocracy because he'd played noblemen upon the stage. It was inconceivable to him that so proud a family as the Ballisters would abandon to penury and degradation a daughter who'd never known a day of hardship in all her seventeen and a half years. He truly believed they would accept him: a man who could not by any stretch of definition claim the title "gentleman," and compounded his infamy by belonging to that subhuman species labeled "actor."

Had I been aware of John's delusions, I should have enlightened him, confused and ignorant though I was. But I assumed he understood, as I did, that my elopement severed all ties to the Ballisters, reconciliation was out of the question, and we must make our way on our own.

I should live contentedly with him in a hovel, so long as we were of the same mind, and would strive together to better our lot. But striving is alien to his nature. How I regret that I was *never taught a profitable trade. My neighbors pay me to write letters for them—there's scarcely one who can write his own name. I do some sewing. But I'm no artist with the needle, and who hereabouts can afford, let alone see the value of, a private tutor? Except for the odd penny I earn here and there, I must depend upon John.*

I must stop—and in good time, too, for I see I've done little but complain. My Lydia stirs from her nap, and will soon grow bored with babbling to herself in her comical baby language. I should have written instead of her, how beautiful and clever and good-natured she is—a prodigy and paragon among infants. How can I complain of anything, when I have her?

Yes, sweet, I hear you. Mama comes.

Lydia paused at the end of the first diary entry because her control was slipping again, her voice too high and quavering. She sat upon the bed, pillows heaped behind her. Ainswood had arranged them. He'd also drawn up to the bed a small table whereupon he'd collected most of the room's candles, so that she'd have better light to read by.

He had started out standing at the window, looking down into the courtyard. He had looked back, surprised, toward her, when she began to read aloud. She was surprised, too, when she realized she was doing it.

She had started reading hurriedly, silently, turning and skimming pages, hungry for the words she'd read so long ago, so poorly understood then and so faintly remembered since. Phrases stood out, not because she remembered the words but because they captured her mother's way of speaking. She began to hear Mama's voice, so clearly, in the same way others' voices seem to sound in her ears, even when the speaker wasn't there. She had only to open her mouth, and her voice became someone else's. It wasn't something she consciously tried to do. It simply happened.

And so she must have forgotten Ainswood for a time or been too much immersed in the past to think of the present. Calmed, reassured it was all there, the little story, Lydia had returned to the first page, and read in the voice lost for so many years, and now returned to her—an unexpected gift, the recovery of a treasure she'd believed forever lost.

Yes, sweet, I hear you. Mama comes.

She had always heard, always come, Lydia remembered vividly, palpably, now. She'd understood what Mary Bartles felt for her baby: pure, fierce, unshakable love. Lydia knew there was such a thing. She had lived within that securest of all havens, her mother's love, for ten years.

Her throat ached. She couldn't make out the words through the mist in her eyes.

She heard him move, felt the mattress shift as he climbed onto the bed.

"Lud, what a way to spend your w-wedding night," she said shakily. "Listening to me b-blubber."

"You might be human now and then," he said. "Or is there a Ballister law against it?"

A warm wall of male moved into place beside her, and a muscular arm slid behind her back, to draw her close. She knew this wasn't the securest of havens, yet for the moment it seemed so, and she saw no great harm in pretending it was.

"She doted upon me," Lydia told him, her blurry gaze still upon the page.

"Why shouldn't she?" he said. "In your own dreadful way, you can be adorable. Furthermore, being a Ballister, she could appreciate the more appalling of your personality traits as an outsider couldn't. As Dain does. He doesn't seem to believe there's anything wrong with you." He uttered this last in sorrowful amazement, as though his friend must henceforth be considered certifiably insane.

"There's nothing wrong with me." She pointed to the page. "Here it is in black and white: I am 'a prodigy and paragon.' "

"Yes, well, I should like to hear what else she has to say," he answered. "Perhaps she'll proffer valuable advice on how to manage such a paragon and prodigy." He nudged her with his shoulder. "Read on, Grenville. If that's her voice, it's a most soothing one."

It had been, Lydia recalled. She was soothed, too, by his nearness, and his teasing, and the strong arm holding her.

She read on.

A wavery morning light was mingling with the room's shadows when Grenville finally closed the book and sleepily returned his share of the pillows before sinking down onto hers. She didn't turn to him, yet she didn't object, either, when Vere made more comfortable adjustments, drawing her up close against him, spoon fashion. By the time he had her snugly tucked up as he wanted her, she was breathing evenly, sound asleep.

Though he customarily took to his bed at the time respectable citizens were waking, if not already up and at their work, he was aware of fatigue weighing upon him more heavily than usual. Even for a man accustomed to live hard, who craved excitement and danger and all their accompanying batterings upon his mind and body, this long day and night had proved a strain.

Now, while there was silence and what should have been peace, he felt as though he'd been both captain and crew on a vessel tossed upon the rocks after a day and night of battling a furious tempest.

He might have managed to put into a safe harbor, if it

hadn't been for the little book.

Its contents were the rocks he seemed to have foundered upon.

At least a dozen times while he'd listened to the voice—his wife's, yet not his wife's—he'd wanted to tear the book from her hands and throw it in the fire.

It was horrible, hearing the cool courage and irony with which Anne Grenville described the hell her life was. No woman ought to need such courage and detachment; no woman ought to live a life that demanded so much. She lived from day to day, never knowing when she might be evicted or see her few shabby possessions borne away by the broker's man, or whether this night's supper would be the last. Yet she made jokes of the privations, converted her husband's infamies into satiric anecdotes, as though to mock at Fate, which dealt so brutally with her.

Only once, at the very end, had she made anything like a plea for mercy. Even then, it wasn't on her behalf. Those last, barely legible lines, written days before her death, stood stark and blazing in his brain as though burned there with an iron: *Dear Father in Heaven, look after my girls.*

He'd tried to blot out her story, as he'd banished so much else from his mind, but it stuck and rooted there, like the stubborn gorse that grew on the inhospitable moors her Ballister ancestors had made their home.

The words of a woman eighteen years dead had dug into him as few others' words could do, and made him feel like a cur and a coward. She'd borne her lot with courage and humor . . . while he couldn't face what had happened on his wedding night.

He'd leapt at the chance to quarrel with Dain, eagerly used anger to blot out the other thing.

As though what he had to bear, one disagreeable realization, were the most excruciating thing in the world.

It wasn't. The joke was on him, that was all.

He'd wanted Grenville, hadn't he, as he'd never wanted any other woman. Why then should he be so amazed that when he'd finally bedded her, it wouldn't be like bedding any other woman?

With the others, he'd merely coupled.

With his wife, he'd made love.

She was a writer. In his place, she'd have found streams of metaphors to describe the experience, what it was like, how it was different.

He hadn't metaphors. But he was a libertine, with more experience than any man ought to have. Experience enough to discern the difference. And wit enough to understand his heart was engaged, and to know the word for that.

Are you in love with me? he'd asked, smiling, as though the possibility amused him. And he'd had to go on smiling and teasing, all the while aware what the thing was that stabbed his heart, and why it hurt, as no physical injury had ever hurt him, when she didn't give the answer he wanted.

Hurt, that was all. In love, that was all.

What was that to what Anne Grenville had endured? To what her daughter had endured?

Not to mention, he knew only a fraction of the tale. The slim volume scarcely covered the palm of his hand. Its few pages held so little—most of it appalling—with great gaps in time between entries. He was sure it told only the smallest part of the story.

He didn't want to know more, didn't want to feel smaller than he did already. Small and petty and selfish and *blind*.

But if Grenville could live it, whatever that life had been, he could certainly bear learning about it.

Not from her. She hadn't wanted the past raked up, she'd

said, and he wasn't going to make her relive it.

Dain would know more of the tale, and he'd tell, like it or not. He had a lot to answer for. The least he could do was answer a few questions, Lord All-Wise and All-Knowing.

He would seek Dain out first thing, Vere resolved, and pound the facts out of him if necessary.

With that agreeable prospect in mind, the Duke of Ainswood finally drifted into sleep.

As it happened, Vere didn't have to seek Dain out. Mid-afternoon, upon learning from Jaynes that the master and mistress were up and about, Dain arrived to bear Vere off to the private dining parlor, while the ladies enjoyed a late breakfast in Dain's chambers.

"Jessica is nigh exploding," Dain said as they descended the stairs. "She must have a private tête-à-tête with my cousin, in order to share her experience in the art of torturing husbands. Trent's taken Miss Price to Portsmouth to shop for some fripperies my lady insists your lady can't do without, so he shan't pester us with his blithering while we eat. Jess and I will take the pair of them with us to Athcourt. You will need to reorganize your household to accommodate a wife, and you won't want Trent about. Not that I want him, either, but he shouldn't be too much underfoot—at least not under my feet. He will trot after Miss Price, and show a degree of intelligence for once in his life, in falling head over ears in love with the only female in all the known universe who has any idea what to make of him."

Vere paused on the stairs. "In love?" he said. "Are you sure?"

"Certainly not. How should I know? To me, he sounds and looks as imbecilic as usual. But Jessica assures me he has fixed his minuscule brain upon Miss Price."

They continued on, Dain calculating aloud the amount he'd settle upon Miss Price if she would take pity on Trent and marry him, while Vere heard "in love" echo in his mind and wondered whether Lady Dain had noticed symptoms of the same ailment elsewhere.

"You are abnormally quiet," Dain said as they settled into their chairs. "We've passed a full five minutes together, with nary one belligerent remark passing your lips."

A servant entered then, and they ordered. When the man had left, Vere said, "I want you to tell me everything you know about Grenville."

"As it happens, that was what I intended to do, whether you wanted to hear or not," said Dain. "I had prepared myself to beat you senseless, revive you, and drop your broken body into the chair. In that agreeably spongelike state you would absorb the tale, and perhaps even the occasional tidbit of advice."

"Interesting. I had something like that in mind for you, in case you chose to be your usual aggravating self."

"I'm in charity with you this once," said Dain. "You've made my cousin a duchess, restoring her to her proper place in the world. Furthermore, you wed her with, if not noble motives, at least not entirely ignoble ones. I was touched, Ainswood, I truly was, by your serene unconcern for her origins." The mocking half-smile played about his lips. "Perhaps 'serene' is not precisely the word I want. Still, I was affected—not to mention deeply astonished—by your evidencing taste, for once in your misbegotten life. She is a wonderfully handsome girl, is she not? They are appallingly handsome, most of the Ballisters. She gets her looks from her maternal grandfather, you know. Frederick Ballister and my father were much alike in their youth. But Frederick contracted smallpox in his late teens, and the disease disfigured him. That must be why Anne compared her daughter to my father, instead of her own. She mustn't have been aware that Frederick had been one of the beautiful Ballisters. We haven't yet discovered a portrait of Anne. However, if one exists, you may be sure Jessica will find it. She has an alarming genius for finding things."

Vere was aware that one of the "things" Lady Dain had found—and made Dain keep—was his bastard son, Dominick. The thought stirred a chill wave in the dark area of Vere's mind, the distant shores where orphaned and outcast thoughts huddled.

He labeled the feeling "hunger" and looked impatiently toward the door.

"Where's the servant got to?" he said. "How long does it take to draw a tankard of ale?"

"They've all been run off their feet, attending to the wedding guests this morning," Dain said. "Or collecting the corpses is more like it. When I first came down at midday, the public dining room was strewn with bodies. It brought back fond memories of our Oxford days."

The servant appeared then, and another behind him. Both staggered under the weight of the trays, though the meal was for only two men. Still, they were two very large men, with commensurate appetites.

It was a while, therefore, after the servants had gone, before Dain launched into the story. Still, he didn't linger over the telling by adding literary embellishments or, worse yet, sentimental ones. He told it as Vere wanted it told, as a man would tell it, keeping to the plain facts and putting them in order, without wandering into whys and wherefores and that most profitless of all digressions, if onlys.

Still, it was as unpleasant a tale as Vere had expected, and he lost his appetite before he'd emptied his plate of the first helping, because by then he'd heard about the Marshalsea.

He pushed his plate away. "She told me her sister had died, that was all. She said nothing of how it happened. She said nothing of debtors' prison."

"The Ballister nature is not confiding," said Dain. "Lydia is obviously like the rest of us. 'Didn't want the past raked up' was all her explanation for telling nobody anything about her origins. Did you know she was at my wedding—on the very church steps—and never made herself known? What the devil was she thinking? That I gave a damn what her mother did?" He scowled at his mug. "My own mother ran off with a sea merchant. The brat I got with the prime whore of Dartmoor lives in my house. Did the girl think I fancied she wasn't good enough for us?"

"Don't ask me," said Vere. "I haven't the least idea what goes on in her head."

The scowl shifted to Vere. "I am well aware your interest lies elsewhere. You did not marry her for her mind. It is inconceivable to you that she—any woman—has one. Well, let me tell you something, Ainswood. They do. They are always thinking, women are, and if you don't wish to be outmaneuvered at every turn, I recommend you exercise your very thick and sluggish brain in comprehending your wife's. I know this is hard for you. Thinking upsets the delicate balance of your constitution. I am trying to make it easier, by telling you what I know. We men must stick together."

"Then get back to telling, why don't you?" said Vere. "You've scarcely buried her sister."

Dain took up the tale where he'd left off, but hadn't much to say about Grenville's life from the time after her father had gone to America, when she went to live with her great-uncle and -aunt. The father had died in '16, of injuries sustained in a beating. He'd tried to run off with a rich American girl. This time, though, they were pursued, and the girl's brothers rescued her and meted out their own justice to John Grenville.

"It appears that my cousin traveled abroad with Stephen and Euphemia Grenville," Dain said. "They died last autumn. I had learned the name of one of their servants, who lives in Marazion, Cornwall. We were planning to go down to talk to him when we received your wedding invitation." Dain took up his tankard and emptied it.

When he set the mug down, his dark gaze shifted to Vere's plate. "I shall send Mr. Herriard to meet with your solicitor in London. You will not deny me a small act of belated revenge upon my sire, I hope. To spite the dear departed, I should like to dower Lydia, and Herriard can be counted upon to entangle you in settlements sufficiently exorbitant and complicated to stifle any shrieks of your manly pride. Lydia, of course, is perfectly capable of taking care of herself, as she's proven. Yet I'm certain she would not object to having her offspring's future secured."

"If she does, I'll tell her to quarrel with you about it," said Vere. There would be offspring, of course, he told himself, and Dain asked nothing more than what was customary. Dowry and settlements tied up certain issues neatly and legally, and provided a degree of material security for the future. If other aspects of the future troubled Vere, and if he was having rather more difficulty than usual in obliterating fresh anxieties, only his gut—currently in an annoying state of mal de mer—offered a hint, and that was on the inside, where Dain couldn't see.

"You won't leave me to it without ammunition," Dain said. "I've told you what you didn't know. It's your turn to satisfy my curiosity. I've had Sellowby's version of recent events, but even he, it seems, does not know all. I'm on tenterhooks to hear about this business of climbing to the first floor of Helena Martin's house. He was there at the time?"

"It's a long story," said Vere.

"I'll order more ale," said Dain.

The waiter was summoned, the tankards replenished, and Vere took his own turn, telling his tale from the start, in Vinegar Yard. He did not tell everything, naturally, and he made a joke of what he did tell—which it was, and what did it matter that the joke was on him?

He wasn't the first man who'd run blindly into matrimony without realizing where he was headed. It was rather, as Dain so succinctly put it, like walking into a door in the dark. Dain certainly should know. He, too, had walked into the door.

And because he had, Dain had no qualms about laughing at his friend's errors, discomfitures, and defeats, or about calling him a "precious cretin" and other like endearments. Dain was merciless, but then, they had always been merciless to each other. They had always traded insults and blows. That was how they communicated. That was how they expressed affection and understanding.

And because this was the way it had always been between them, Vere soon relaxed. If the uneasiness did not altogether vanish, he forgot it for the time he remained in the dining parlor, talking with his friend.

It was all so much like old times that Vere could be excused for failing to understand that times had changed. He didn't know that in six months of marriage, Dain had come to know himself better, and had no trouble applying this sharpened awareness elsewhere.

Consequently, Lord Beelzebub was strongly tempted to take his bosom bow by the neckcloth and bang his head against the wall. He resisted the temptation, though, as he later told his wife. "He has Lydia," Dain said. "Let her do it."

★ ★ ★ ★ ★

"Oh, Lizzy, I'm so sorry," Emily moaned.

"There's nothing to be sorry about," Elizabeth said briskly, as she wiped her sister's forehead with a cool cloth. "If it had been something worse than dyspepsia, then you must be sorry, because it would frighten me out of my wits. But I'm not afraid of mere puking, however prodigious."

"I ate too much."

"You'd gone too long between meals, and the food was ill prepared. I was queasy myself, but then my stomach's tougher than yours."

"We've missed it," Emily said. "We've missed the wedding."

That was true. It was Thursday evening. They occupied a chamber of an inn near Aylesbury, many miles from their destination. They might have reached Liphook in time for the wedding, if Emily had not become violently ill half an hour after a hurried midday meal on Wednesday. At the next stage, they had to disembark. Emily had been so sick and weak that an inn servant had to carry her up to the chamber.

They were traveling as governess and charge. Elizabeth had donned one of her old mourning dresses, because black made her look older. She'd also "borrowed" a pair of reading spectacles from the Blakesleigh library. She had to look over them, since she couldn't see through them, but that, Emily assured her, made her appear all the more stern.

"You must stop fretting about the wedding," Elizabeth said. "You didn't get sick on purpose."

"You should have gone on without me."

"You must be delirious to say such a thing. We're in this *together*, Lady Em. Mallorys stick together." Elizabeth plumped the pillows behind her sister. "They'll be sending

the broth up soon, and tea. You have to concentrate on getting strong again. Because as soon as you are, we'll set out."

"Not for Blakesleigh," Emily said, shaking her head. "Not
until we've made our position clear. He has to know. That we
tried."

"We can write a letter."

"He never reads them."

The Longlands servants communicated regularly with
those at Ainswood House, and Longlands' housekeeper
wrote every quarter to the Ladies Elizabeth and Emily. Consequently, the girls were aware the present Duke had not
opened his personal correspondence in a year and a half. At
Longlands, the house steward dealt with His Grace's business correspondence. At Ainswood House in London, the
butler Houle performed the same service.

"We could write to *her*," said Elizabeth. "And she could
tell him."

"Are you sure they're married? News travels fast, but it
isn't always accurate. Maybe she won the race and he'll have
to try something else."

"It'll be in tomorrow's paper," Elizabeth said. "Then we'll
decide what to do."

"I'm not going back to Blakesleigh," Emily said. "I shall
never forgive them. *Never.*"

There was a tap at the door. "There's your dinner," Elizabeth said as she rose from the chair. "And in the nick of time,
too. Perhaps your temper will improve when you've something in your belly."

Though Lydia and Ainswood arrived at Ainswood House
very late on Thursday, all the household awaited them.

By the time the housekeeper had relieved Lydia of her
outer garments, the rest of the staff had filed in to the ground-

floor hall and stood at attention—or their version of it.

Lydia understood what Wellington had felt before Waterloo when he surveyed his "infamous army"—the ramshackle lot with which he must overcome Napoleon.

She noted wrinkled aprons and tarnished livery, wigs and caps askew, haphazardly shaven chins, and most of the range of human expression from terror to insolence, embarrassment to despair.

She withheld comment, however, and concentrated on memorizing names and positions. Unlike Wellington, she had a lifetime to make a satisfactory domestic fighting unit of this demoralized mob.

As to the state of the house itself: Even without seeing much of it, she perceived that it was in even sorrier condition than its staff.

She was not surprised. Ainswood rarely spent much time in residence and, like so many of his sex, lacked the faculty for perceiving dust, dirt, or disorder.

Only the master bedchamber turned out to be in neat order. This, doubtless, was due to Jaynes. She had discovered earlier in the day that, contrary to appearances—which was to say Ainswood's appearance—Jaynes was a prodigious fussbudget. He simply had the misfortune to be working with an uncooperative subject.

Since Ainswood had dismissed the others with an impatient wave as soon as the butler and housekeeper, Mr. Houle and Mrs. Clay, had introduced everyone, it was Jaynes who showed Lydia her apartments. They adjoined Ainswood's. No one, evidently, had entered them in years.

Ainswood certainly didn't want to enter them. As Jaynes opened the door to Her Grace's quarters, the duke went in the opposite direction, into his dressing room.

"On such short notice, I collect Mrs. Clay was unable to

tend to my rooms," Lydia said mildly, once Ainswood was out of earshot.

Jaynes glanced about him, his mouth pinching up as he took in the cobwebs dripping from the ceiling corners, the film frosting mirrors and glass, the dust that lay as thick as the volcanic ash upon Pompeii. "She might have done something," he said, "if she dared."

Lydia peered into the gloomy, cobwebbed cavern Jaynes had called her dressing room. "I understand that bachelors—some bachelors—dislike having their things disturbed."

"Many of the servants have been here since the fourth duke's time," said Jaynes. "We've some from families who've served the Mallorys for generations. Loyalty's a fine thing, but when you've nothing to do, day in and day out on account of not knowing what to do or not daring—" He broke off, and pinned his mouth shut.

"Then it will be easier to bring the staff 'round to my methods," Lydia said briskly. "We shall commence with a blank slate. No housekeepers set in their ways. No interfering mothers-in-law."

"Yes, Your Grace," said Jaynes. Then he screwed his mouth shut again.

Lydia could tell he was nigh bursting with revelations. While she was curious, she was, however, also aware of the protocol forbidding her to encourage him. She had noticed he was not so restrained in dealing directly with the master. Earlier in the day, she had heard the valet muttering—not always under his breath—while assisting His Grace with his toilette.

"In any case, whatever changes will be effected must wait until tomorrow," Lydia said, moving back to the door leading to the master chamber.

"Yes, Your Grace." Jaynes trailed behind her as she entered the bedchamber. "But you will want a maid. I had better go down—"

"There you are," Ainswood said, stomping out of his dressing room. "I was wondering if you meant to stay gossiping with my lady all night. What the devil have you done with my clothes?"

"Your clothes are in your dressing room, sir." Jaynes added something in an undertone, which Lydia couldn't make out.

"Not those clothes, you smug rascal," Ainswood snapped. "The ones I wore yesterday. The ones in my bags. All I can find is damned shirts and neckcloths. Where's my waistcoat?"

"The waistcoats you wore yesterday are in my quarters, to be cleaned," said Jaynes.

"Curse and confound you! I hadn't emptied the pockets!"

"No, Your Grace. I took that liberty. You will find the—er—contents in the lacquered box on the—That is to say, I shall find it for you, sir." Jaynes started toward the dressing room.

Ainswood backed toward the doorway, blocking it.

"Never mind. I can find the bleeding box. I'm not blind."

"In that case, if you will pardon me, sir, I was about to go down for one of the maids. I should ring, but no one will know who's to come or what for."

Ainswood, who had been about to reenter the dressing room, turned back. "A maid? What the devil do I want with a maid?"

"Her Grace requires—"

"Not in my room."

"Her Grace's chambers are not fit for—"

"It's past midnight, confound you! I won't have a pack of females clucking and fussing and disrupting everything." At last Ainswood seemed to recollect Lydia's existence. He shifted his glower to her.

"Dash it, Grenville, must we start that nonsense tonight?"

"No, my dear," she said.

The green glare flashed back to Jaynes. "You heard her. Go to bed. You'll have all day tomorrow to toady."

Mouth screwed tight, Jaynes bowed and departed.

After the door had closed behind him, Ainswood's expression softened marginally. "I can undress you," he said gruffly.

" 'Can' is not the same as 'want to.' " She went to him, pushed back a lock of chestnut hair from his forehead. "I had supposed the excitement had palled. You've done it once already."

He edged back, his green eyes wary. "Grenville, you are not going to be . . ." His gaze shifted away while he sought the word he wanted. "Kind," he tried, and frowned. "Patient." That word didn't satisfy, either, apparently, for his brow furrowed. "I should like to know what you and Lady Dain talked about. Dain said it had to do with torturing husbands."

"What did you and Dain talk about?"

"You." He essayed half a grin. "I must meet with lawyers, and sign away my life, and accept a dowry."

"Lady Dain told me. I had meant to discuss it with you on the way home." Instead, she had slept most of the way.

The half-grin faded. "Gad, Grenville, are we going to have to *discuss?* Is that why you're humoring me? Because if it is, you're wasting your time. You'll have to quarrel with Dain about it."

She studied him. He'd discarded his coat, waistcoat, and neckcloth without Jayne's assistance. Which probably meant those garments were lying on his dressing room floor. Along with his boots. His left shirt cuff was buttoned. The button was gone from the right, and a large tear told her why. She grasped his wrist and pointed to the tear.

"If you had trouble getting it unbuttoned, why didn't you bellow for help?" she asked. "We were only in the next room."

He shook her off. "Don't take care of me. I don't need taking care of."

Her temper flared. She banked it and retreated a pace. "No, and you don't need a wife, either, I'm sure." She walked away to the window. "This should be interesting—watching you try to figure out what to do with me."

He stomped back into the dressing room and slammed the door.

15

Ten seconds later, there was more stomping, and the door flew open. "I didn't think!" he shouted. "Are you happy now? I admit it. I didn't think past the wedding night. And now you're going to turn everything inside out, and—and there'll be *maids* parading in and out of *my room*—and I won't have a minute's peace!"

"That is correct," Lydia said calmly. "I am going to turn this house upside down and inside out, from garret to cellar. Because it is a disgrace. I cannot abide disorder. I will not have it." She folded her arms. "What do you propose to do? Shoot me? Chuck me out the window?"

"Of course I won't! Damnation, Grenville—" He stormed to the fireplace, slammed his hand against the mantel, and glared at the fire.

"Even if I could abide dirt and disorder," she went on steadily, "it is very bad for morale. This is a fine house. It is a shame to let it go to rack and ruin, and a good staff with it. I will not compromise on this matter, Ainswood. You must like it or lump it."

"Bloody hell."

"Perhaps I had better dispel all illusions at once," she said. "It is very unlikely I shall compromise on any matter. I am not at all sure I possess the capability."

He lifted his head, glanced briefly at her. "You married me. That was a compromise. Of your curst damn principles."

"It was not a compromise, but a complete overthrow of my

286

principles," she said. "The only way I can restore my equilibrium is by arranging everything precisely as it ought to be."

His gaze returned to her and settled accusingly. "You said you wanted to make me happy."

She opened her mouth to retort, then shut it.

She paced the length of the room instead. It was a considerable length, and minutes passed. He said nothing. All he did was straighten away from the fireplace and watch her.

She had an idea of what the fundamental problem was, and since it was her habit to confront problems straight on, her instinctive reaction was to confront him.

The trouble was, it wasn't Ainswood's nature to confront his troubles straight on, else he wouldn't have the problem in the first place.

She had to choose her words carefully.

She covered the room's length once more. Then she went to the window and looked down into the garden. A light rain had begun falling. She heard it rather than saw it. With starlight and moonlight blotted out, the world outside the window might as well have been an abyss.

"Devil roast me," his exasperated voice broke the silence. "It isn't your fault I didn't consider the consequences. You gave me every chance."

She turned from the window. He stood not far from the fire, behind a chair whose back he grasped. He was staring at his hands, his handsome countenance as rigid as a death mask.

"Dain told me I must reorganize my household to accommodate a wife," he continued. "What the devil is it to me? It's not as though I give a bleeding goddamn about this pile."

He didn't, obviously. He wished it didn't exist, she supposed. Since it did, the next best thing was to pretend it didn't, to pretend nothing had changed, and he wasn't the

Duke of Ainswood. He shut his eyes and mind to the house and staff he'd inherited, in the same way he shut out all the other responsibilities of the dukedom.

That's not my fault, is it? he'd said so bitterly when, not many days ago, Lydia had reminded him of the title he bore.

"A most astute observation," she said, strolling toward the bed. "Since you don't give a bloody goddamn, it makes no sense for you to roar and rage about what I do with the household. If you find the reorganization process trying to your nerves—and I will admit, there will be tumult and apparent confusion for perhaps as much as a fortnight—you will be so good as to take your fits elsewhere. Out of the house."

"Out of the—"

"I don't want you upsetting the servants. How can one expect them to develop enthusiasm for their work—not to mention their mistress—if you are stomping about, snarling and snapping at everyone?"

"You are throwing me out of my *own house?*"

She met his stormy gaze. She preferred it stormy, the bleak look wiped out by indignation. "You rarely visit it. You don't care what becomes of it. I should think you'd be happier elsewhere."

"Damnation, Grenville, we were married only yesterday—and—and you're chucking me?" He let go of the chair, advanced upon her, and grabbed her shoulders. "I *married* you, dammit. I'm your husband, not a lover you can discard after one tumble."

His mouth came down hard on hers.

It was quick, fierce, and devastating, an erotic rampage, demanding what she'd never intended to withhold.

She tasted anger and power, but more than that was the sin of it, the diabolical knowing of it, the way he made love words inside her mouth with his tongue.

He released her before she was ready. Unbalanced, she caught a fistful of his shirt. "Good God, Ainswood." A few seared syllables; that was all she could get out.

"Vere," he growled. "You said my name when we said our vows. Say it, Lydia."

"Vere." She reached up, cupped his face to tilt it toward hers. "Do it again."

"You're not throwing me away," he said. With a flick of his fingers he unfastened the topmost button of her bodice. With the quick assurance of a concert pianist performing arpeggios, he undid the rest.

She brought her hands down, let them hang uselessly at her sides. "You've got it all wrong," she said.

"I'll make it right." He unfastened hooks and tapes with the same ruthless efficiency.

In a moment, her black frock was a heap on the floor. He kicked it aside.

He started on the petticoat.

"I never said I don't want you," she tried.

"You don't want me *enough*." He paused, though, his fingers brushing over lace and silk ribbons. His grim expression softened a degree. "Pretty."

"A gift from Lady Dain."

He bent his head and drew his tongue over the intricate, gossamer-light edging of the petticoat's bodice.

She sucked in her breath, dug tense fingers into his hair, to stop him. "What are you doing?" She heard the uncertainty and anxiety in her voice and hated it, but couldn't help it. He was a rake. He'd committed acts of depravity she, completely inexperienced, could scarcely begin to imagine.

He turned his head and nipped the skin of her forearm.

She let go.

"You put on lovely new underthings, just for me," he said. "It's sweet."

They were lovely. And ghastly expensive, no doubt. But it would have been churlish to refuse Lady Dain's gifts, even though she had gone overboard and given Lydia enough lewd underwear to dress a dozen harlots. "Does that mean you're not cross anymore?" she asked warily.

He lifted his gaze to hers. She saw twin slits of green, dark and glinting. "Was I cross? I've completely forgotten." He smiled then, that dreadful, brain-bone-muscle-melting smile. It was lethal, the lazy curve of his dissolute mouth, and he most certainly knew it. No wonder he despised women. He'd only to turn that smile upon them to topple them like ninepins.

She toppled, too, inwardly, while outwardly she reached for him, brought his face to hers, and trailed her lips over that wicked curve.

He simply let her do it. He didn't move, didn't respond. His hands remained at her waist, where they'd come to rest a moment before.

She drew her tongue over his mouth, in the same teasing way he'd done to the lace of her bodice.

The grip on her waist tightened.

She nipped at his lower lip, as he had done to her arm.

He nipped back, then, and parted for her.

It was long and deep and dark this time, a kiss that was like falling off a precipice.

And while she fell, so did her petticoat, so smoothly and easily that she was scarcely aware it was happening. His big hands ran over her like water while tapes and buttons gave way and hooks lost their mates.

Her petticoat cascaded to a whispering heap at her feet. He knelt and gently pushed it away. He put her hand on his shoulder and took off her shoes and set them neatly aside.

He held up his hands and she took them, and came down to kneel on the carpet in front of him.

"That's the prettiest corset I've ever seen," he whispered. "Too pretty to take off in a mad rush. Turn around, Lydia."

It *was* pretty, embroidered with pink twining vines and tiny leaves. From behind, he drew his fingers over the edge of the corset, where the lacy chemise veiled her breasts. He spread his hands over the front of the garment while he kissed the back of her neck and her shoulders.

She was weak with longing already. All she could do was stroke his wonderfully wicked hands and swim in sensation.

He drew the corset away. She heard his sharp inhalation.

"Oh, Lydia, this is . . . *evil*." His voice was a rough whisper. He stroked over the back of the chemise.

It was made of silk as thin as a butterfly's wing, in the palest blush of pink.

"Turn around," he said.

She turned, resisting the temptation to cover herself. He'd seen her naked before, hadn't he?

"It doesn't conceal much, does it?" she said, fighting down a nervous giggle.

"I forgive you," he said thickly. His green gaze dwelt lingeringly upon her breasts.

"For what?"

"Everything."

He pulled her into his arms and bore her down with him to the carpet.

He forgave her with deep, wild kisses that hurtled her over the precipice and dragged her up again. He forgave her with his hands, with caresses rough and tender by turns.

She had no control. The slow undressing had awakened in

her something deeper and darker than what, before, she'd called lust, infatuation.

He was big and strong and beautiful and diabolically knowing, and everything he was, every pore and cell of him, she wanted for herself alone.

The drive to possess and conquer was in her Ballister blood, and it was a hot blood, wild and greedy.

She had no patience to be further undressed, and pushed his hands from her drawer strings. She pushed him onto his back and dragged off his shirt. He let out a low, short laugh that turned into a groan when she unbuttoned his trousers. She was not so smooth as he had been, but she was quicker. She peeled them off and tossed them aside, and sat back on her haunches.

He was a magnificent man, long and leanly muscled. The broad chest tapered to a tautly slim waist and hips. She drew her hand over the dark, silky hair feathering his chest, and down where it arrowed to his pelvis, lighter and tinged with red. "I hadn't the presence of mind last night to look," she said huskily as her fingers stole down to that forbidden place.

"Look, touch," he said with a choked laugh.

She grasped his rod, swollen and hot. It pulsed in her hand. He made a low, aching sound.

"You said I could touch," she told him.

"Yes, I *like* torture."

She bent and touched her tongue to it.

"*Jesus.*" He pulled her hand away, pulled her on top of him. He found the opening of her drawers, slid his fingers in, and cupped her.

The climax took her unawares. She was quivering under the strokes of his fingers when it speared through her, one sharp shock of joy that set off rippling aftershocks.

Another came, and another . . . and then he pushed in, and

she lifted instinctively, and came down to take him inside, deep.

"*Yes.*" A ragged cry of triumph she couldn't keep back.

He pulled her down to him. She took his mouth, and stroked with her tongue, shamelessly mimicking his quickening thrusts.

He rolled her onto her back and, breaking her greedy kiss, wrenched her hands from his neck and held them down on the carpet. He held her so, and she watched him, watching her, while the last stormy strokes spasmed through her body. Her eyes closed and she saw firebursts behind them. And one long, shuddering moment later, she heard a choked sound that was her name as he sank down, spent, on top of her.

At half past ten the following morning, Her Grace met in Vere's study with Mrs. Clay.

At half past eleven, pandemonium erupted.

What seemed like thousands of maids and footmen spilled out of baize doors, all armed with cloths, dusters, mops, brooms, pails, and some fearful implements Vere could not identify.

He fled to the billiard room, only to be ambushed by another lot of servants.

He escaped to the library, only to find yet more close on his heels.

He went from room to room, looking for refuge, only to meet invasion time and time again.

At last he skulked into his study, closed the door, and shoved a chair against it.

"Oh, my dear," came his wife's amused voice behind him. "That isn't necessary."

He swung toward the sound, his face hot. She was sitting at the desk, trying very hard not to laugh.

"They're *everywhere*," he reproached.

"They won't come in here today," she said. "I told Mrs. Clay I needed to work."

"Work?" he cried. "They're tearing the house to pieces. Thousands of them. They tear rugs out from under your feet. They pull the drapery—rods and all—down on your head. They—"

"Do they?" She smiled. "Mrs. Clay means to make a thorough job of it. I thought she would." She set down her pen and folded her hands upon the desk.

"And you're mightily pleased with yourself," he grumbled. He started to move the chair from the door, then changed his mind and left it as it was. He advanced to the desk, pushed aside a tray piled with correspondence—his, neglected—and perched on the corner, half turned toward her. "They're so terrified of you that they scarcely know I'm there."

"Why *are* you there? Or here, rather. I'd thought you'd have run screaming from the house long since."

"I couldn't decide where to go," he said. "China seemed far enough away. But then, New South Wales may be more appropriate, being a penal colony and all."

"May I suggest Bedfordshire?" she said.

He didn't move, by not so much as a muscle twitch. His gaze remained fixed upon the untidy pile of letters and cards, while in his mind's eye images played, of how they'd made lazy, sleepy love this morning, while the rain softly pattered at the windows . . . and of how she'd left the bed before he did, and he'd dozed, and wakened to her scent—in the pillows, the bedclothes, on his skin—and the musky scent of their coupling.

"Yes, well, I did not expect you to leap eagerly at the suggestion," she said. "But I cannot walk on eggshells about the topic. I am your wife. The proper thing to do is take me to meet my new family. This house is in turmoil and will be for some days. I had thought we might kill two birds with one stone: escape the upheaval and induct me into the family."

"You've work to do," he said, very quietly, very calmly, while he remembered last night, and evilly feminine underthings, and how he'd gone dry-mouthed, like a boy seeing his first naked female—he, who'd seen hundreds.

"I am merely completing obligations to Macgowan and the *Argus*," she said. "My new position is Duchess of Ainswood. I accepted it intending to carry out all of its responsibilities. One of us, you see, did consider the consequences."

"Then do what you like." He left the desk and headed to the door. Quietly and calmly he moved the chair away. "I'm not going to Bedfordshire."

He opened the door and walked out.

Lydia quickly pulled off her shoes and hurried out into the hall. He was moving swiftly toward the vestibule.

She hurried noiselessly after him, ignoring the startled gazes of the servants working in the hall.

She grabbed a bucket and flung its contents at him, just as he opened the front door.

She heard a chorus of gasps.

Then the hall became utterly still.

Ainswood stood for a moment, unmoving, while dirty, soapy water streamed from his head over his neck and shoulders, and dribbled down his coat to plop on the threshold.

Then, very slowly, he turned.

"Oops," she said.

His green glance swept over the servants—maids covering

their mouths with their hands, footmen gaping—a tableau of paralytic shock.

He looked down at his sopping garments, then up again, at Lydia.

Then his mouth opened and laughter cracked out, sharp as a pistol shot. And more spilled out, great guffaws that reverberated through the carpetless hall. He leaned against the doorframe, shoulders shaking, and kept trying to say something, only to go off into whoops.

Then finally, "Th-thank you, m'dear," he choked out. "M-most refreshing." He straightened, and his glance took in the servants, who had recovered their wits sufficiently to cast perplexed looks at one another.

"Yes, that settled the dust nicely, I think," he said. "I believe I'll change."

And, *Yes, I believe you will,* Lydia thought as she watched him saunter, dripping, past her and down the hall, to the stairs, and up them.

This afternoon, the Duke of Ainswood bore his valet's grumblings and sarcasms with a suspiciously angelic meekness.

After he was freshly bathed and dressed, His Grace spent a very long while examining his reflection in the glass. "I shouldn't have put you to so much work," he said. "They're only going to get spoiled when I climb out the window."

"If I may be so bold as to offer a suggestion, Your Grace?" said Jaynes. "The front door is in excellent working order."

"I was lucky to get away with merely a dousing," said the master. "I'd rather not imagine what she'll try the next time."

"If I may venture an opinion sir, I strongly doubt Her Grace entertains any objections to your exiting the house."

"Then why did she stop me?"

"She was not trying to stop you. She was expressing exasperation."

The duke gave him a dubious glance, clasped his hands behind his back, and walked to the window.

"If I may speak plainly sir,"—Jaynes generally did—"you are exasperating."

"I know."

"If she murders you in your sleep, no one will be in the least surprised, and there is no jury in all of Great Britain that would not instantly acquit her. On the contrary, she would likely be awarded the kingdom's highest honors."

"I know."

Jaynes waited for a clue to what had triggered the expression of exasperation. His master simply continued looking out the window.

Swallowing a sigh, Jaynes left him and went into the dressing room to collect the duke's pocket watch and the small box containing the assorted oddities the master carried about, to the detriment of his finely sewn pockets.

When Jaynes returned to the bedchamber but two minutes later, the window was open and the master was gone.

Leaning out, Jaynes caught a glimpse of chestnut hair among the tall shrubbery.

"No hat, as usual," Jaynes muttered. "Just as well, I suppose. He'll only lose it."

He set down the box and pocket watch to one side of the wide sill and closed the window, for the day was chill and damp, promising more rain. "And it'll be a miracle, I daresay, if *wet's* the worst of his condition when he comes home." Preoccupied with an array of uniformly appalling scenarios, Jaynes exited the bedchamber, altogether forgetting the items he'd left upon the windowsill.

★ ★ ★ ★ ★

The eminent firm of Rundell and Bridge having considerable experience with the upper orders—including the uppermost, His Majesty the King—its shop clerks manifested no signs of dismay or alarm at the entrance of an alarmingly large nobleman towing a black mastiff the size of a young elephant.

"Dash it, Susan," said Vere, "you can move quickly enough when Trent's in the vicinity." He tugged on the leash and grumbling, Susan condescended to cross the threshold of Number 32, Ludgate Hill.

Then she sank down on her haunches, laid her big head on her forepaws, and let out a martyred sigh.

"I didn't force you to come with me," Vere said. "You were the one who started whimpering and making me feel sorry for you."

The dog had apparently arrived—presumably with Bess and Millie—sometime after Vere had gone upstairs to wash and change. He'd found her wandering in the garden, the lead in her mouth. He'd petted her and headed for the gate. She'd followed. When he tried to shut the gate behind him, she'd commenced whimpering.

"You're blocking the door," he said now. "Get up, Susan. Up."

A chorus of male voices assured His Grace that the dog was not at all in the way.

"That's not the point," he said. "The point is, she's doing it on purpose to vex me. You'd think she'd run all the way from St. James's Square, instead of covering the distance sound asleep, on my feet, in a hackney."

The youngest of the clerks stepped out from behind the counter. "That is Her Grace's mastiff, isn't it?" he said. "I've seen her before. I think she's guarding the door, that's all, sir. Protecting you."

Vere looked at the dog, then at the clerk.

The man bowed. "And if you will pardon the liberty, Your Grace, may I offer my heartiest felicitations upon your recent nuptials."

A murmuring chorus seconded this speech.

Vere's neckcloth felt much too tight, and the shop seemed much too warm. He mumbled a response—he wasn't sure what. Then, fixing his eye upon the one who knew all about the dog, Vere said, "I want to buy a gewgaw. For my lady."

If the term "gewgaw" was not as precise as could be wished, the clerk showed no signs of discontent.

"Certainly, Your Grace. If you would be so good as to come this way."

He ushered Vere into a private room.

Ten minutes later, Susan ambled in and collapsed on Vere's feet.

Two hours later, his toes numb, Vere exited the shop, a small parcel tucked into his waistcoat pocket.

He didn't see the female scurry away from the shop window and dart into an alley. He didn't know who Susan was growling at, or whether she was simply growling at everyone because she was cross again, at having to move after she'd finally got comfy.

He was unaware of Coralie Brees peering from the corner of the alley and staring, long after she could actually see him, and so he could have no inkling of the murderous fury churning in her breast while she imagined the sparkling baubles he'd bought, and what she'd do to the one he'd bought them for.

It was early evening when Lydia found the box.

By this time she was aware that Ainswood had gone out and taken the dog with him. Millie, who'd gone to the garden to try to coax Susan to eat—she was sulking again—had seen Ainswood come in the garden gate, pick up the leash, and depart with the mastiff.

It was Bess who brought up the dinner Lydia had elected to eat in the master bedchamber, since that was the only part of the house not under attack or still thick with grime. And it was Bess who passed on the information that His Grace had exited via his bedroom window.

"And Mr. Jaynes is ever so vexed, miss—mean to say, Your Grace—on account of it was a new coat, just come from the tailor's." Catching Lydia's frown, the girl added hurriedly, "Only he said it to me private-like, not in front of anybody, and said I might mention it to you, but nobody else, as it wasn't proper for him to tattle on the master, but you ought to know, in case His Grace comes back the same way and gives you a fright in the middle of the night."

After Bess left, Lydia went to the window. It was no easy climb, and she wondered where he'd found a foothold in the well-pointed brick. If it had been raining when he left, he could have easily slipped and broken his neck.

That was when the box caught her attention, shiny lacquered black against the yellow paint of the windowsill.

She remembered the fuss Ainswood had made last night about his pocket contents.

She was a journalist, and prying into others' affairs was her stock-in-trade. She was also a woman.

She opened the box.

In it lay a stump of a pencil, a black button, a hairpin, and a splinter of ebony.

She snapped it shut, started to put it back where she'd found it, then took it up again and pressed it to her heart. "Oh, Ainswood," she cried softly. "You wicked, wicked man. Keepsakes."

★ ★ ★ ★ ★

"You're the most aggravating female who ever lived. There's no pleasing you." Vere crouched beside the dog. "It's raining, Susan. What the devil do you want to lie in the rain for, when you can lumber about a great, warm, dry house and trip the footmen and throw all the maids into fits of terror? Mama's in there, you know. Don't you want to see your mama?"

A deeply despondent doggy sigh was her answer.

Vere collected the various parcels he'd thrown down when Susan threw herself down, then stood up and marched into the house.

Once inside he bellowed for Jaynes.

"The damn dog won't come in," he said, when the valet finally skulked into the hall.

Leaving Jaynes to deal with Susan, Vere hurried upstairs and into his bedchamber.

He threw the parcels on the bed. He pulled off his wet coat. Turning to toss it toward a chair, he saw his wife, sitting on the rug before the fireplace, her knees drawn up, her arms wrapped about them.

His heartbeat quickened to triple time.

Avoiding her gaze and trying to steady his breathing, he knelt down beside her. Looking for words, and looking anywhere but at her face, he saw the box her ink-stained fingers encircled.

He stared at it, frowning, for a long moment. Then he remembered. Jaynes. The lacquered box.

"What have you got there, Grenville?" he said lightly. "Poison for exasperating husbands?"

"Keepsakes," she said.

"They're not keepsakes," he said stoutly, while well aware the lie was written plain on his face in vivid scarlet. "I like to keep a lot of rubbish in my pockets because it makes Jaynes wild. You make it easy because you're forever leaving debris in your wake."

She smiled. "You're adorable when you're embarrassed."

"I'm not embarrassed. A man who's spent half the day conversing with a dog is past embarrassment." He put out his hand. "Give it back, Grenville. You're not supposed to go poking about in a fellow's personal belongings. You should be ashamed of yourself. You don't see me sneaking behind your back for a look at the next chapter of *The Rose of Thebes*, do you?"

He felt rather than saw the box drop into his hand, for his gaze had shifted to her face. He caught the startled look in the instant before she blinked it away.

"I'm not blind," he said. "I saw Lady Dain's ring—the great ruby, amazingly like your description of the Rose of Thebes. I'd had my suspicions before of who St. Bellair really was—interesting, isn't it, how the letters can be rearranged to spell 'Ballister'?—but the ring clinched it. Today, I found out—in the same way you did, I reckon—where Lady Dain's ruby had come from. Whether originally looted from a pharaoh's tomb, no one could say. But the jeweler's agent did buy it in Egypt."

To her credit, Grenville didn't try to pretend she didn't know what he was talking about. "You suspected before?" Her blue gaze was soft with wonder. "How did you suspect? *No one* suspects. Even Miss Price, who is almost painfully perceptive, gaped at me for a full minute when I told her."

"You gave yourself away in the last two installments, when Diablo started sounding like *me*."

She swung up onto her feet in a rustle of bombazine. She began to pace, as she had done last night.

He sank down onto the carpet and lay on his back, his hands clasped behind his head, which was turned to the side, so he could watch her. He loved to watch her walk, long confident strides that would have seemed mannish if it weren't for the arrogant sway of her magnificent rump. *That* was all woman.

This was but a temporary respite, he knew, and not much of one at that. While he lay apparently at his ease, images advanced and receded in his mind, like shipwreck victims upon the waves.

He'd taken Susan to Southwark, to the Marshalsea. He'd seen children, some hurrying out—on errands for parents who could not leave the prison—and some returning, more listlessly, their steps dragging as they neared the gates.

His wife had been one of those children, and he knew what the Marshalsea had stolen from her.

. . . take me to meet my new family.

He knew what she wanted in Bedfordshire.

"Oh, it's impossible!" She flung herself into a chair. "I shall never manage you." She set her elbow on the chair arm and her chin on her knuckles and eyed him reproachfully. "You undermine and overthrow me at every turn. Every time I want you to do something you find disagreeable—which is practically everything—you find a way to turn my heart to mush. What have you done, read every word I've ever written, and analyzed and anatomized it?"

"Yes." He turned his gaze to the ceiling. "And if I'd known that was all it took to turn your heart to mush, I could have saved myself a good deal of money today—not to mention sparing myself Susan's aggravating company."

There was a silence, during which, he assumed, the parcels on the bed finally attracted her attention.

"You wicked man." Her voice was low and not quite steady. "Have you been buying me gifts?"

"Bribes," he said, sneaking a glance at her. She had left the chair to go to the bed, and stood looking at the packages. "So I wouldn't be obliged to sleep in the stables."

After Rundell and Bridge, after the Marshalsea, he'd taken Susan from shop to shop, with one break for sustenance in a private dining parlor of a coaching inn.

"Perhaps you're not so good at reading my mind as I believed," she said. "That thought never crossed it."

He got up and went to her. "Open them," he said.

There were notebooks, their rich vellum pages bound in leather as soft as butter. There was a cylindrical pen case of delicately worked silver, with an inkwell that screwed to the bottom of the tube. There was a small traveling writing box, decorated with scenes from mythology, whose compartments contained pens, inkwells, and pounce box, and whose small drawers held wafers, notepaper, and a silver penknife. There was a silver inkstand, as well as a papier-mâché pencil box, filled with pencils.

"Oh," Lydia softly exclaimed time after time, as the wrappings fell away to reveal the treasures.

And, "Oh, thank you," she said at the end, when the wrappings lay strewn about her, on the bed where she sat and on the floor. She had the writing box in her lap, and she opened and closed the tiny drawers and lifted the lids of the compartments and took out their contents and put them back again—like a child enchanted with a new toy.

She felt like a child, truly. There had been gifts, on her birthday and at Christmastime, from Ste and Effie, and pretty ones, too: shoes and frocks and bonnets and sometimes a pair of earbobs or a bracelet.

This was altogether different, for these were the instruments of her trade, and she, who traded in words, found her vocabulary robbed, along with her heart.

"Thank you," she whispered again, helplessly, while she looked into his handsome face and gave up all hope of ever being sensible again.

Pleasure shone in his green eyes, and his mouth curved into a smile that reduced the mush of her heart to warm syrup. It was a boy's smile, half mischief, half abashed.

"My humble offerings have pleased Her Majesty, I see," he said.

She nodded. Even if she could have strung words together at the moment, she didn't dare try, lest she commence bawling.

"Then I collect you're sufficiently softened up for the coup de grâce," he said. He reached into his waistcoat pocket and withdrew yet another parcel.

This one he opened himself, turning away, so that she couldn't see what it was.

"Close your eyes," he said. "And let go of the damn writing box. I'm not going to steal it back."

She let go of the box and closed her eyes.

He took her right hand and slid a ring onto her fourth finger. She knew it was a ring, smooth and cool, and she knew her hand was shaking.

"You can look," he said.

It was a cornflower-blue sapphire, rectangular and simply cut, and so large it would have appeared gaudy on any hand but hers, which was no daintier than the rest of her. Diamonds winked on either side.

She was aware of tears winking from the corners of her eyes. *Don't be a ninny,* she told herself.

"It's . . . lovely," she said. "And—and I shan't say you

shouldn't have, because I don't feel that way at all. I feel like a princess in a fable."

He bent and kissed the top of her head.

"I'll take you to Bedfordshire," he said.

16

Vere sat at his study desk, surrounded by crumpled wads of paper. It was Saturday morning, and he was trying to compose a letter to Lord Mars. That should have been easy enough, but Grenville had warned him to be diplomatic . . . whatever that meant.

Vere was about to go looking for her, to demand specifics, when she opened the door.

"Lord Mars is here," she said, "and by the looks of him, it isn't a social visit."

Moments later, they were in the library with His Lordship.

He was travel-stained, trembling with fatigue, and unshaven. "They've bolted," he said, as soon as Vere and Lydia entered. "Please, for the love of God, tell me they're here. Safe. The girls, I mean. Elizabeth and Emily."

Blank, cold, Vere stared at him.

Grenville hurried to the decanter tray and filled a glass, which she gave to Lord Mars. "Do sit," she said. "Collect yourself."

"They're not here." His shoulders sagged. He sank into a chair. "I feared as much. Yet I hoped."

Feared. Hoped. Tell me they're here. Safe.

The room darkened, shrank, and swelled again. Something swelled within Vere, cold and heavy. "Bloody hell," he said between his teeth, "You couldn't keep them safe, either?"

"Safe?" Mars rose, his face white and stiff. "Those children are as dear to me as my own. But my affection, my care, avails nothing, because I am not *you*." He pulled a crumpled note from his pocket, flung it down. "There. Read for yourself what they have to say. The girls you've neglected. Not a word from you. Not a visit. Not so much as a note. They might as well be lying in stone coffins with their brothers and parents, as far as you're concerned. Yet they left the shelter of my house, where they've been loved and cared for—dearly, *dearly*. They left because their love and loyalty is with you."

"Please, sir, collect yourself," said Grenville. "You are overset. Ainswood is, too." She urged Mars to sit, put the glass back in his hand.

Vere read the note. It was but a few lines, that was all—a few daggers to the heart. He looked at his wife. "They wanted to be at our wedding," he said.

She took the note from him, quickly read it.

Mars drank a little. His color returned. He went on talking. The girls must have left before daybreak on Monday, he told them. He and his brothers-in-law had set out looking for them by midmorning. Yet despite the mere few hours' start the girls had had, the men had been unable to discover a trace of them. No one had seen them—at the coaching inns, tollgates. They couldn't have made it to Liphook, because he'd combed the village and its environs.

Mars took out a pair of miniatures and laid them upon the library table. "They are not ordinary-looking," he said. "How could anyone fail to notice them?"

Vere stood looking down at the small oval paintings, making no move to pick them up. Shame was acid in his mouth and a cold weight in his chest. He would have recognized them, yes, would have seen Charlie in them. He didn't know them, though. He would not have known the sound of their voices, because he'd scarcely ever spoken to them, never listened, never paid attention.

Yet they'd run away, from love and protection, to see him wed because, Elizabeth had written, "We must make it clear that we wish him happy, as Papa would have done. Papa would have gone."

Vere became aware of his wife's voice. "You will make ready while Lord Mars takes some time to rest," she told him, "though I know he doesn't wish to. Send messages to all your cronies. You want as many eyes as you can muster. You will take half the servants; I'll keep the other half, to help me cover the London vicinity. You must take some maids as well. Women see things differently than men do. I shall contact all my informants."

She turned back to Lord Mars. "You must send your wife a message, to assure her that matters are in hand. I know you wish to wait until there is good news, but it is dreadful for her to wait and not know anything."

"You are generous," Mars told her. "You make me ashamed."

The duchess lifted her eyebrows.

"We closed ranks against you," Mars said. "Because you were not highborn. Because of scandal."

"She's a Ballister," Vere said. "Dain's cousin. You snubbed a Ballister, you pious snob."

Mars nodded wearily. "That's what I heard. I thought it was idle gossip. I saw my mistake a little while ago." He rose, carefully set his empty glass down. His hand trembled. "I've slept little. At first I believed my eyes played tricks on me. I thought I was seeing ghosts." He essayed a smile, not very successfully. "That of the third Marquess of Dain, to be precise. You are remarkably like my old nemesis in the Lords."

"Yes, well, she'll be *our* nemesis if we don't find those girls," Vere said shortly. "I'll take you up to a room. You'd better have a wash, and something to eat, and contrive a nap if you can. I'll want your brain in working order."

He took Mars's arm. "Come along, then. We'll let Grenville marshal the troops. It's best to stay out of her way when she's *organizing*."

Athcourt, Devon

"I say, Miss Price, you do have a knack for makin' yourself scarce, not but what it's easy enough in this pile. I wonder why Dain don't keep a post chaise handy to carry the ladies at least from one end of the place to the other. But the truth is, no one would blame a fellow for thinkin' you was avoidin' me, which," Bertie added with a stern look, "ain't sportin', especially when he's raked fore and aft and you knew what I was goin' to say, didn't you?"

"Oh, dear," said she, wringing her hands.

"I know you wasn't leadin' me on because you ain't that sort," Bertie said. "You ain't goin' to tell me you was, and you don't like me even a little, are you?"

Her face turned cherry pink. "I like you exceedingly," she said in a disconcertingly saddish sort of way.

"Well, then," said he, disconcerted but undaunted. "We'd best get shackled, don't you think?"

She looked helplessly about Athcourt's music room, where he'd finally cornered her—alone. It was Sunday, and he'd been trying since yesterday, when they arrived. He'd meant to give it one more day, then propose, wherever they were and whoever was about. It was not, after all, as though anything this side of the earth exploding could shock either Dain or Jessica.

"Maybe I should kneel and make a speech of it, do you think, Miss Price?" Bertie grimaced. "I collect I ought to say how devilish fond I am of you, even though it'd be obvious to a blind man and deaf, too."

Behind the spectacles, her eyes widened in alarm. "Oh, please don't kneel," she said. "I'm embarrassed enough. I should not be such a coward. The Duchess of Ainswood would be vastly disappointed in me."

"A coward? By gad, you can't be afraid of *me?*"

"No, of course not. How silly I am." She took off her spectacles, rubbed them on her frock sleeve, and put them back on. "Naturally, you will understand that I did not set out to deceive you. My name is not Price, but Prideaux." She lifted her chin. "Tamsin Prideaux. I am not an orphan. I have a complete set of parents. In Cornwall. But I was obliged to give up on them, for the situation was intolerable. And so I ran away. Only Her Grace knows the truth."

"Ah." He was confused, but he felt obliged to sort things out quickly, because she believed he would understand, and he did not like to disappoint her. "Intolerable, was it? Well, then, what could you do but bolt? I did. There was my Aunt Claire forever bringing one heiress or another to the house, or haulin' me wherever they was. And I'm sure there weren't nothin' wrong with 'em, but either a fellow fancies a gal or he don't, and I didn't. And not wantin' to hurt their feelin's nor have to listen to Aunt Claire jawin' forever about it, I made a run for it."

He frowned. "I never thought of changin' my name. Weren't that clever of you?" he added, brightening. "Prideaux. Price. Thomasina. Tamsin. No, other way about. From Tamsin to Thomasina. Now I think on it, I like 'Tamsin' better. Sounds like a pixie name, don't it?"

She gazed at him for a while. Then she smiled, and really, she did look rather like a pixie. A shortsighted one, to be sure, but then, he was happy to stand near enough so that she could see him even without her spectacles.

"Is that a 'Yes, I will,' then?" he asked. "Shall we make it 'Lady Trent' and never mind the other names?"

"As long as you don't mind anything else." She adjusted her spectacles, though they seemed straight enough to him. "Obviously, we can expect nothing from my parents, and even for your sake, I could not accept any dowry or settlement from Her Grace, though she will try to press it upon me, I know. But I am not expensive, Sir Bertram—"

"Bertie," he said.

She bit her lip. "Bertie," she said softly.

"Oh, I say, that's pleasant." He made matters pleasanter by gathering her up in his arms and kissing her until they were both dizzy.

He would have gone beyond dizziness if he were not acutely aware they weren't wed yet. Which meant a fellow must behave himself, like it or not. It did not mean, however, that the fellow needed to wait for the preacher a minute longer than absolutely necessary. And so Bertie took his future bride's hand and went to obtain Dain's help in making that future near rather than distant.

Though Athcourt was one of England's largest houses, they did not have to go far, because Dain was looking for them. They met up with him on the landing of the great staircase.

"I say, Dain, Miss P and I want to get shackled," said Bertie.

"You'll have to wait," said Dain. "I've had a letter from Ainswood. His wards have gone missing. You must take Miss Price to London to assist my cousin." After briefly explaining the situation, he turned to Tamsin. "You must pardon the imposition. My wife may not consider her condition 'delicate,' but I will not permit her to make two long journeys with almost no rest between. She will be easier in her mind if Lydia has a woman friend with her."

"Good heavens, where else should I be but with Lydia?" said Tamsin. "I can be packed in under an hour." She hurried away.

"I wish you happy, Trent," Dain said. "Though I cannot for the life of me ascertain what she sees in you." He shrugged. "We haven't time to ponder that riddle. Ainswood needs help—after which I mean to pound him to a pulp."

Dain continued up the stairs, talking. "I didn't know he had any more wards. But Jessica tells me they've been living with Mars ever since Charlie died. Curse the lout! I must find out everything secondhand. And there have been so dratted many condolence notes that I hardly know who's alive and who isn't. 'Who in blazes is Elizabeth?' I ask Jess. 'The sister of the little boy who died about a year before we were wed,' she tells me. 'But she's dead,' I insist. 'It was right after my old friend Wardell was planted. I distinctly remember Mallory —as he was then—rushing from one funeral to the next.' 'That was the boy's mother,' Jessica tells me. 'Then who the devil did my secretary send the last condolence note to, on the lad's account?' I want to know. The elder sister, it turns out."

By this time they had turned into the guest wing, where Bertie's room was.

"And so, not only is the sister not dead, but there's another one," Dain went on. "And living with Mars, no less, who has nine children of his own and another on the way, for all his wife is five and forty if she's a day."

The marquess pushed open Bertie's bedchamber door. "Ainswood should have told me."

"Well, he didn't tell me nothin', neither," Bertie said, following him inside.

"He hardly knows you," said Dain. He stomped back out into the hall and bellowed for his valet.

When he came back in, he said, "I've been wed for six months. I might have gone for those girls at any time and had them to live here. It isn't as though we're short of accommodation, is it? And Jessica would like to have female company. Not to mention those are Charlie's girls. One of the finest fellows I've ever known. I should have left Paris posthaste for his funeral had that moron friend of mine thought fit to send me word. But by the time I heard of it, Charlie had been planted for a week."

He found Bertie's bag and flung it on the bed.

Andrews arrived then, but Dain chased him away. "I'll help Trent," he said. "Go pack for me. Her Ladyship will explain what's needed."

Andrews departed.

Dain went to the wardrobe and went on talking while he emptied its contents. "I should have been there when they laid Charlie to rest. I should have been with Ainswood when they lay the boy with his father. A man ought to have his friends with him at such times, and Ainswood had no friend in Charlie's sisters, I'll tell you that. Or their husbands." He threw a heap of clothes on the bed and paused, looking at Bertie. "At least he's asked this time. For help. Doubtless that's my cousin's doing." He returned to the wardrobe. "You will take Miss Price to her—"

"Actually," Bertie said, "it's Miss Prideaux."

"Whatever." Dain pulled waistcoats from their wrappings in the drawer. "Your intended. You will take her to London, and stay there, and do precisely as my cousin tells you. Lydia knows London, and she has information sources the Home Secretary could not begin to match."

"You reckon them gals'll get to London?" Bertie said.

"Seein' as how they never made it to Liphook, mebbe they decided to go home."

"Maybe," said Dain. "The question is, where is home?"

Vere pushed desperately through a woodland grown as thick as a tropical jungle. Clawlike roots snaked out from nowhere, and he tripped and fell, struggled up, and pushed on. It was cold, bitter cold, and black. Neither moonlight nor starlight could penetrate the tangled boughs above. He couldn't see where he was going, but blindly followed the sound, the child's terrified cry.

Icy sweat drenched his shirt.

I'm coming. His mouth formed the words, but no sound came out. The boy couldn't hear him, wouldn't know, would think Vere had abandoned him.

It's not true. I never would. Never, never.

But Vere had abandoned Charlie's boy, left him to fools and cowards . . . and worse.

And that was why he was punished now, his voice taken away, suffocated, while the child suffocated . . . while the foul, killing film of diphtheria spread inside him.

Vere's hand struck marble. His fingers scrabbled over it, searching for the handle. It wouldn't move. Locked. He beat on the door, iron, unyielding.

No!

He tore at the lock, wrenched it off. He pulled the massive door open and ran toward the voice, faint and fading now.

A candle burned at each end of the coffin. He pushed the lid off, tore away the shroud, lifted the boy in his arms.

But it was only cold mist he held, a shadow fading, vanishing . . . gone.

"No. No! *Robin!*"

315

Vere's own cries woke him.

He was on his knees, a pillow clutched to his chest.

His hands were shaking. His skin was clammy. Wetness trickled down his cheeks.

He flung down the pillow and rubbed his hands over his face.

He walked to the window. Beyond was darkness, heavy with the fog that had rolled about them during the last weary miles before they'd reluctantly stopped, for it was late, and the servants hadn't had their dinner, and they were exhausted. Unlike their masters, they hadn't guilty consciences and unrelenting anxiety to kill sleep and appetite.

Vere opened the window. He heard the soft hiss of rain. Though he discerned no hint of coming daylight, the air carried the promise of dawn.

Tuesday, then, he thought. The girls had been missing for a full week, and no one could find a trace of them.

He washed and dressed himself. He'd left Jaynes with Grenville. The valet was more useful in London, knew all its nooks and crannies. He could go anywhere in its netherworld and blend in.

Vere didn't want to think about the netherworld, about his wards stumbling into it, as so many runaways did. Miss Price, for instance. In Coralie's clutches.

If you would take the bawd into custody . . .

On that day in Vinegar Yard, Grenville had asked no more of him than was any British subject's duty, most especially that of the ruling class.

He'd let Coralie go, to prey on other girls. And she was one of so many predators.

But shame was a weight he'd been carrying since Saturday, and if this added to it, he could hardly feel the increase.

He took out the writing box Grenville had made him take

along, drew out paper, unstopped the inkwell, and picked up a pen. He had to write his report.

Grenville had appointed herself general. London was headquarters, and all her "officers" were required to report twice a day. Servants and friends acted as couriers, carrying messages back and forth.

The army of searchers was to keep within a maximum fifty-mile radius of London, though the most intense area of search was within thirty miles. The groups worked along the main coaching routes. Dain, for instance, was in charge of the Exeter and Southampton routes, which converged forty-five miles from London.

Vere and Mars were in Maidenhead, where the Bath, Stroud, and Gloucester roads met.

Vere and Dain worked near enough to exchange messages regularly. As of last evening, Dain had learned nothing.

Vere dutifully reported this as well as his own searches of the previous day, and today's itinerary.

"We must exclude Millie from these plans," he continued, after wracking his brains for something hopeful to write down. "She's shown a tendency to wander from her assigned routes. But she goes in search of the local gossips, and has heard plenty, though not much to the point. The common folk are not so shy with her as with us. Yesterday, we procured a dog cart for her, and gave one of Mars's servants the job of driving her. She did not rejoin us last night. Still, you assured me she might be relied upon, and she has a sturdy fellow with her. I've told myself she's following a trail, in her own way, and I wish with all my heart it may be fruitful."

He frowned at what he'd written. It was cool and factual, as all his notes were. Yet not all the facts.

He got up, paced the room, sat down again. He took a

fresh sheet of paper and took up his pen once more.

My love,

Twice a day I write to you, and all it amounts to is, we haven't found the girls. I haven't mentioned what I have found.

Their brother is here. There's no escaping him. We traveled this road together, Robin and I. Everywhere I look, I see what he and I once looked upon together. From the carriage window. From the back of a horse. On foot, and from time to time, with him upon my shoulders.

I had blotted him from my mind, with drink and whores and fights, and by avoiding everyone and everything associated with him. Since you came into my life, these cowardly escapes have been cut off. You cut off the last when you asked me to take you to Bedfordshire. I knew what you wanted. I had a pair of orphans in my keeping—a journalist would have no difficulty finding that out—and you wanted to take them in, as you took in Miss Price, and Bess and Millie. I know you chose those three yourself, and must choose carefully, else every waif and orphan in London would have been crammed under your roof in Soho Square. But I recalled what Lady Dain had done, how she'd made Dain take in his bastard son, because the boy was Dain's responsibility. I doubted your views of responsibility were any more flexible than hers.

All the same, while a man may discern the inevitable, that doesn't mean he'll accept it without a fight. Especially the man you married.

Now I have the reward for my stupidity, and I while away the hours flagellating myself with if onlys. I recall, for instance, my moving speech on all you'd gain by marrying me. Gad, what an idiot. All I had to do was tell you I had two girls in my keeping, and needed you to help me look after them. But I never thought of them. I blotted them from my mind as I did Robin. Charlie had left me the most precious of all gifts, his children, and I—ah, well, I've made a muck of it, sweetheart. I can only pray I shall have a chance to make it right.

Lydia sat at her dressing table, reading Ainswood's letter for the tenth time at least. It had arrived late in the morning, and she'd given the first sheet to Tamsin, who kept track of the search parties' movements on the maps spread in the library. The second part of the letter Lydia had reread privately in her study during the too-frequent lulls between reports.

It was past midnight now, and she'd had a second letter from him since, but that was the usual thing, keeping her informed of his whereabouts.

Those were easy to answer. She had her own nothing to report, and new suggestions for him, based on information gleaned from Dorothea's hysterical letters, which arrived several times a day. By degrees, Lydia had ascertained what the girls had taken with them, for instance, and passed on those details.

Yesterday, she'd given the searchers a pair of spectacles to add to their descriptions. They might try asking about a young widow, traveling with her maid, or a young female she seemed to be companion or governess to. People might not have observed two sisters, but might have been tricked into thinking they'd seen something else.

Lydia had relayed the same message to her network of informants in London.

The message she'd wanted to send to Ainswood was, "I'll come to you." But that was impossible. She could not leave coordination entirely to Tamsin. Tamsin was organized and levelheaded, but there was simply too much work, keeping track, answering messages, keeping everyone calm and productively occupied.

And so, instead, Lydia had written to her husband:

You did not make a muck of everything all by yourself. You had a great deal of help. I reckon Charlie was the last of that lot of siblings with a grain of sense. After reading Dorothea's letters, I'm not in the least surprised that your wards pulled the wool over her eyes. I am stumped, however, what excuse to make for Mars—that he, who's been in Parliament for five and twenty years, could be gulled by a pair of schoolroom misses. At any rate, if they could cozen him, they've doubtless outwitted scores of coachmen, innkeepers, and innocent cottagers. Take heart, my dear. From what I can gather, they are a pair of dreadful girls. I'm looking forward to taking them in hand.

Writing about Robin was harder, but she did it.

The little ghost you wrote to me about I understand well. I have had Sarah's with me for fifteen years. When we come together again, we'll share them. For now, I command you to leave off the if onlys and look about you with him, as you once did. They're Robin's sisters. Perhaps, as you look about you through his eyes, you might see through theirs as well. You had him for six months, Dorothea has informed me, and when he came back, she scarcely knew him, he was so changed. What tricks did you teach him, wicked man? Try to remember, for he might have taught them to his sisters. Can they smile, do you think, in such a way as to make observers believe black is white?

She'd fretted about that letter ever since sending it. She knew it had cost him considerable pain to write of the child, and the pain must be all the more grievous for having been bottled up for so very long. He had confided in her, and her answer might have seemed to make light of his grief. Yet she did not see how it would help him if she answered with the sort of tear-stained sentiment she received daily from Dorothea.

Reading his letter again, Lydia told herself she'd done the right thing, or as close as she could come this day. He surely grieved for the boy, but it was Elizabeth and Emily he was most anxious about, and Lydia had worked on turning his thoughts about them in a positive direction. He would want something to *do,* not fruitless sympathy. For now, finding the girls was what mattered most. Everything else must take second place.

She put the letter away and went downstairs to tell Tamsin to go to bed. Bertie Trent had Susan, and they were making their nightly tour of the stretch of Piccadilly between the Hyde Park Turnpike—where the girls *might* disembark from a coach—and Duke Street, in hopes of encountering the runaways en route to St. James's Square.

That was the most optimistic of conclusions, yet it wasn't entirely unthinkable. If the girls were so foolish as to complete their journey on foot after dark, they'd have a hard time eluding Susan. Lady Mars had dutifully sent the garments the girls had worn the day before their departure, and Susan now had the scent. She also seemed to have a fair understanding of what was expected because, according to Bertie, she was pretty thorough about sniffing at female passersby, usually to their great alarm.

In any case, it gave Bertie something to do in the evening, and he was exceedingly diligent about it, as he was with every task Lydia gave him. She was amazed at how many she found for him, but that was probably because she had only to think aloud—an idea, a contact she'd forgotten to make—and he'd say, "Oh, I'll take care of that." And did.

Bertie, however, had sense enough to go to bed when he came home, and get a decent amount of sleep before starting a new day. Tamsin needed nagging, and Lydia went down to the library, prepared to nag.

Before she'd reached the bottom of the stairs, the knocker sounded and the footman posted there opened it.

Recognizing Ainswood's courier, Lydia hurried to the vestibule and took the note he'd brought, then sent him down to the servants' hall for something to eat.

She was tearing the note open as she hastened back to the library.

My love,

Bless you a hundred times for the wise words you wrote, and for sending Millie to me.

    She had wandered northward, into Bagnigge's "territory," and I had been about to send someone to fetch her back. But your letter gave me pause. I recalled that Robin and I had traveled there as well, and climbed Coombe Hill, which is not far from Aylesbury. I'll make a long and convoluted tale brief: Thanks to Millie's attention to gossips, we found near Aylesbury the inn where the girls had spent several days. Emily had been ill. We're assured she was quite well when they set out again on Saturday. On Sunday, they were in Prince's Risborough, where they left Emily's brown frock in exchange for some boy's clothing. They'd taken it from a basket—one of several left for the church to distribute among the poor. It was Millie who interrogated the vicar's wife, and ascertained exactly what was taken.

A detailed description of the boy's garments followed. He went on to say they were currently following a trail tending southward, toward the coaching road Vere and Mars had been exploring. This time, though, it was a young woman and boy they asked about, with more productive results.

When Lydia finished the letter, she relayed its essentials to Tamsin.

"We'll have to awaken the servants," Lydia said. "All the London searchers must be informed. There's no telling how far ahead of Ainswood his wards are. They might already be in London, or enter at any moment. Everyone must be put on the alert."

"I'll copy the description," said Tamsin. "It's only a few lines. One for each of our messengers, so they don't have to try to remember. They'll be sleepy."

"So are you," said Lydia. "But there's no help for it now. I'll have a pot of strong coffee sent up."

The farmer put Elizabeth and Emily down in Covent Garden, which seemed to be wide awake, though it was early morning. Elizabeth had heard church bells toll six o'clock only minutes before.

He'd refused to take money from them. He was going the same way they were, he'd told them, and they took little room in the cart. Besides, his apples were highly prized in London and he'd earn plenty.

And that, Elizabeth saw, must be true, for despite the predawn darkness several costermongers were already hurrying toward the wagon, and they were already haggling with him by the time Elizabeth had helped her sleepy sister down.

Their rescuer didn't hear Elizabeth's thanks. Still, she had thanked him repeatedly during the slow journey. Dodging shoulders and elbows, she led Emily away.

"It'll be easy now," Elizabeth told her. "St. James's Square is not at all far from here."

If only I knew what direction to turn, she added silently as her bewildered gaze wandered about the rabbit's warren of a marketplace. The sun was no help, since there wasn't any. She wished she'd thought to bring a compass, but then, she hadn't thought of a great many things. She had certainly not prepared for a two- to three-day journey turning into eight desperately long days.

They had not brought enough money. They'd sold or traded most of their belongings, which had been few enough in the first place. Emily was very tired and very hungry. They had eaten a few apples, at the farmer's insistence, but only a few. They hadn't wanted to cheat him of his hard-earned profits.

But that would soon be over, Elizabeth told herself. They were in London, and all they needed to do was obtain directions to St. James's Square and then . . .

And then Emily swayed and sagged against her, and Elizabeth heard a shrill voice call out, "Oh, dear, the little boy's took sick. Help 'im, Nelly."

Elizabeth did not have time to help her sister, or say that she could. Everything went wrong in an instant: a tawdry red-haired girl dragging Emily away, the crowd closing about them, an arm fastening on Elizabeth's, squeezing painfully hard. "That's right, my dear, not a word, not a squeak. You come quiet-like and Nelly won't lose her temper and cut yer little friend's throat."

17

Tom hadn't had a good look at the pair. He might not have noticed them if he hadn't recognized the wagon and moved closer, watching for a stray apple. That was when the older one had climbed down, showing a bit of very pretty ankle, and moving surprisingly quick and light for an old woman. He'd tried to squeeze through the crowd for a closer look. He wasn't sure why, but he'd been on watch for so long that every odd thing made him look twice.

He saw the taller one looking about and looking lost, and then the smaller one went white.

And then, as fast as you could blink, the pair of them were in Tow Street, with Coralie Brees and one of her game gals doing the towing.

Tom didn't stop to ask himself whether he was right or wrong, whether the pair Coralie had were the ones Miss Grenville was looking for or not. Tom and his fellow street arabs had chased plenty of false trails in the past few days, but there was no telling unless you did it, and better to chase than to chance missing them.

And so he didn't pause to reflect this time, but dashed straight into pursuit.

Stupid as Coralie was, she could not only tell a girl from a boy—regardless what the young person wore—but she could also recognize the accents of the upper classes. This she did within minutes of shoving her captives into the ancient carriage waiting around the corner, with Mick at the reins.

"I collect you mean to hold us for ransom," the older one said, warily eyeing Coralie's knife. "Wouldn't it be simpler to take us to Ainswood House and say you'd *rescued* us. You're bound to get a reward?"

If the girl had not mentioned Ainswood House, Coralie would have stopped the carriage, flung the door open, and pushed them out. Her prey was restricted to girls no one wanted or cared about, who hadn't powerful families to call down the full force of the law upon her. No whoremonger with an ounce of self-preservation made off with gently bred misses, because those they belonged to usually offered large rewards for their return.

There wasn't a soul Coralie knew who wouldn't betray his or her mother or firstborn for a reward. This was why crimes against the upper orders tended to get solved more often and speedily than did those against the dregs of humanity. London's law officers depended upon confession and informants to bring criminals to justice. And stupidity—for the criminal mind, in the majority of cases, was by no means brilliant.

While Coralie's intellect wasn't of the highest order, she was cunning enough not to get caught. She was also a dangerous woman to cross, as everyone knew. Troublesome girls were brutally punished. The few so misguided as to attempt betrayal or escape were caught, mutilated, and killed, as an example to the others. To date, Annette was the only one of her employees who'd managed to get away alive. This, Coralie was sure, was because the girl had taken money and jewels with her. She'd either bribed Josiah and Bill or had talked them into working for her in Paris, because the bully boys had never returned.

Since this was all the new Duchess of Ainswood's fault, it was no wonder that when Coralie learned that the two young females she'd collected were the duke's wards—and found proof in their belongings—she did not eject them from the carriage.

She'd heard something was amiss at Ainswood House, and was aware the duke was away from London. She hadn't learned much more than that. This was because she'd been lying low in recent weeks. She'd had to leave Francis Street without paying the rent—also the Jack whore's fault—which meant the bailiffs were looking for her.

But she'd had to kill one runaway a few days ago, and temporarily incapacitated another girl in a drunken temper fit. As a result, she was short two employees, which was not good for finances. Like it or not, she'd had to venture out early this morning to seek replacements.

Now she wouldn't need any. Now she had a way to get even with the scribbler bitch and make a fortune at the same time.

And so she smiled, displaying an incomplete line of brown teeth. "Ainswood House is closed up and everyone's gone," she lied to her prisoners. "Looks like they've gone out hunting for you." She shook her head. "A pair of runaways. Lucky for you I was the one who found you. There's some as wouldn't care if you was royalty. Finders keepers is some people's motto. And do you know what some people does to little girls they find?"

The older one drew the smaller one closer. "Yes, we know. We've read about it in the *Argus*."

"Then if you don't want it to happen to you, I recommend you be good and quiet, and don't give me no trouble." She jerked her head toward the window. "You see where we are? It ain't a elegant part of Town. All I got to do is open the door and say, 'Anyone want a pair of pretty females?'—and you're off my hands."

327

"You don't want Corrie to do that," Nell said, leaning toward the girls. "Whatever you read about what happens to young gals ain't the half of it. There's some things so horrible as they won't even print 'em in the *Police Gazette*."

"I'll take you where you'll be safe," Coralie said. "Long as you behave yourselves. And we'll send word for 'em to come and fetch you. The quicker the better, I say. Gals who can't earn their keep ain't no good to me."

Tom had managed to keep on their trail for a good while, for few vehicles, especially a broken-down coach, could move speedily through the crowded streets. But caught in a gnarl of foot and vehicular traffic, he'd lost them near the Tower and was unable to pick up the trail again, despite hours of searching.

It was late morning when he reported to Lydia. His description of the pair's garb and sizes left no doubt it was Elizabeth and Emily. Lydia wished she'd had more doubt about its being Coralie who'd captured them, but there was no question of that. From Seven Dials to Stepney, there wasn't a street arab who didn't know the bawd—and who wasn't wise enough to keep well away from her.

After sending Tom down to the kitchen to eat, Lydia dispatched a messenger to Ainswood, telling him to drop everything and make for London posthaste.

Then she led Tamsin and Bertie back into the library to formulate a plan of action.

Until now, they'd been as discreet as possible about the search, for a number of reasons. Gently bred misses who broke Society's rules by running away would be assumed to break other rules in the course of their flight. Their reputations would be damaged, if not ruined, if word got out.

That, however, wasn't the worst of risks. Grenville of the

Argus had enemies. She hadn't wanted her foes out looking for Elizabeth and Emily, and taking revenge on her via them. She'd made this clear to her spy network.

At present, unfortunately, Ainswood's wards were already in enemy hands.

"We've no choice," she told her companions. "We must post a large reward for their safe return and hope greed proves stronger than enmity."

She and Tamsin quickly composed the notice, and Bertie took it to the *Argus* offices. By now, today's issue of the magazine would be printed. If it wasn't, Macgowan was to stop the presses and print the handbills instead.

While Bertie was gone, more messages went out, this time to Lydia's private network of informants, seeking information regarding Coralie's current hideout.

"Not that I expect much results from that," she told Tamsin when the task was done. "The body of one of her girls was pulled from the river days ago. And that's hardly the first time Coralie's been wanted for questioning and managed not to be found. She knows they won't spend long looking for her. The police—such as they are—are overburdened, their resources are limited, and there's precious little financial incentive to find the murderer of one little whore."

For income, Bow Street detectives, for instance, depended primarily upon reward money, public and private. The Crown wasn't highly motivated to offer large rewards from public funds to solve such crimes as the murder of persons generally regarded as vermin. In such cases, private rewards were never offered.

"Wherever she does make her lair, it must be somewhere in London," Tamsin said. "She has to keep an eye on her girls."

"The trouble is, London is one of the easiest places in

which to hide and not be found," Lydia said. She summoned a servant and asked for her bonnet and spencer.

"You're not going out?" Tamsin exclaimed. "You can't be meaning to search for her singlehanded."

"I'm going to Bow Street," Lydia said. "We shan't have any problem enlisting their help with this. But I want to speak to the officers as well as the hangers-on directly. They may be in possession of clues they don't realize are clues." She met Tamsin's gaze. "Men don't see the world as women do. Men don't always see what's right under their noses."

Bess appeared with her mistress's outdoor garments then. After donning them, Lydia turned to Tamsin.

"Coralie is not going to play fair," she told the girl. "If she meant to, we would have had word from her by now."

"A ransom note, you mean."

Nodding, Lydia took out her pocket watch. "It's past noon. She's had Elizabeth and Emily since before daybreak. Why go to the bother of keeping them when she might simply bring them here directly, pretend she'd 'rescued' them, and demand a reward?" She put the watch away. "When she thought she might get in trouble, she was quick enough to pretend she'd 'rescued' you, recall. If she promptly delivered the girls, she knows I'd have no grounds for prosecuting her, and plenty of reason to express my gratitude in coin of the realm. That would be the practical approach. Since she isn't practical, I don't doubt there's a grudge at work, and trouble in the making. I'm not going to sit here waiting for it—and giving her the upper hand—if I can help it."

With that, and a promise to keep Tamsin informed of her whereabouts, Lydia departed for Bow Street.

Bertie Trent sat in the small office Miss Grenville had oc-cupied at the *Argus* until her elevation to duchess. He was waiting for the handbills to be printed. While he waited, he was having an exceedingly unpleasant time of it with his conscience.

On the trip back to London, Tamsin had told him her story. Bertie didn't blame her for running away. Her mother, clearly, wasn't right in the head, and her father seemed to have a knack for making himself scarce, using business as an excuse. The man had as good as abandoned his daughter.

Likewise, there were a great many people—Lord and Lady Mars, for instance—who would think Ainswood had abandoned his wards.

But Bertie could see how a fellow could get mixed up when it came to family. Kin could drive a man mad. Bertie's own sister had been an aggravation for as long as he could remember. Still, he would be wretched if anything happened to her.

In any case, women were often a problem, and when you didn't know what to do with them, the simplest route was to ignore them, keep away, and avoid unpleasantness. That didn't mean a fellow hadn't any feelings.

Maybe Mr. Prideaux hadn't realized how bad things were at home.

Whether he did or didn't, Bertie couldn't help thinking the man must be seeing clearer now. If, deep down, he loved his daughter, he must be worried to death.

After all, Bertie was worried to death about Ainswood's wards, though he'd never clapped eyes on them. Even Dain was distraught. Bertie had never before heard him ramble on the way he'd done the day the news came. Or behave so strangely—actually packing Bertie's clothes—Beelzebub, who constantly kept the servants hopping to his bidding.

Bertie hated to imagine the state Mr. Prideaux must be in, picturing every horrible thing that could happen to his daughter, supposedly en route to America with a man who could be a prime villain, for all he knew.

Bertie hated to imagine it, but he imagined it all the same, and with each passing hour, his conscience screamed sharper and louder.

He stared unhappily at the tidy desk, at the inkwell and pens, pencils, and paper.

He ought to ask Tamsin first, but she had enough on her mind, and he didn't want her conscience ripping up at her as his was at him. Besides, if a fellow couldn't trust his own conscience, Bertie told himself, who and what could he trust? There was right and there was wrong, and Conscience was pretty plain, at the moment, about what was what.

Bertie took out a clean sheet of paper, unscrewed the inkwell, and picked up a pen.

Hours after her departure from Ainswood House, Lydia stood looking at the corpse of an old woman. The remains lay in a cold chamber reserved for the purpose, in the yard of the Shadwell magistrate's office.

One of the river-finders, whose profession it was to dredge the river for corpses, had recovered the body last night. Lydia had found out about it during her visit to Bow Street. The constable who'd collected it from the river-finder had noticed the distinctive marks on the corpse and asked for a Bow Street officer to come and compare them to the marks found on the young prostitute pulled from the river some days earlier.

The old woman's face had been cut up in the same way. What was left of it, along with the deep wound in the throat—nearly decapitating her—offered clear evidence of the garrote.

"More of Coralie's handiwork, do you think, Your

Grace?" the young constable with her asked.

"Her handiwork, yes," said Lydia. "But hardly her sort of victim. Hers are always young. Why should she attack a mad old woman?"

"Mad?" Constable Bell's gaze moved from the corpse to Lydia. "What tells you the deceased was mad?"

"She was thought so when I was a girl," Lydia said. "She was a river-finder, I believe. Or her spouse was. She often had violent arguments with people who weren't there. The children believed she was screaming at the ghosts of the drowned persons. I heard her myself once. An argument about money, I believe."

"Perhaps the ghost was chiding her for emptying his pockets."

Lydia shrugged. "All the dredgers do that. One of the perquisites of the trade."

"I wonder you can recognize her. Though she wasn't in the river very long, the knife or broken glass did its work well enough."

"I saw her some months ago when I was in Ratcliffe, interviewing prostitutes," Lydia explained. "I was surprised she was still alive. So I took more note of her than I might have done otherwise. I recognized the garish red-dyed hair and the odd tangle of braids. And the dark splotch on her wrist. A birthmark. The only name I have for her is 'Mad Dorrie.' But whether Dorrie is her name or a reference to her work in a boat, I cannot say."

"Still, that helps," Bell said. "We're more likely to get information about 'Mad Dorrie' than about 'Unidentified Female.' Not that this assists you in your task," he added as he drew the blanket up over the corpse again. "This woman was dead well before Coralie met up with the duke's wards. Unless you think there is some significance in this victim's being different from the others." He looked up then and discovered he was talking to himself.

The duchess was gone.

"Your Grace?" He hurried from the chamber into the yard. Though the sun hadn't yet set, a fog had rolled in, plunging the area into gloom. He called, but received no answer. He heard footsteps, faint, upon the stones, and hastened in that direction.

A short time later, the very recently returned Duke of Ainswood was trying to digest exceedingly unwelcome news.

"Shadwell?" Vere shouted. "She's gone to the East End alone? Has everyone lost their wits? Can't you see what Grenville's up to? The same as she did in Vinegar Yard. She thinks she can handle a pack of cutthroats with nothing but her accursed pocket watch. And without even Susan for company."

"Woof!" Susan said.

Vere glared at her. "How could you let her go alone, you fool dog?"

"Lydia went out hours ago," Tamsin said. "Susan was with Bertie then. Lydia has only gone from one magistrate's office to the next. She had the coachman as well as a footman with her. I'm sure she wouldn't do anything rash."

"Then you're one sadly deluded female," Vere said. He stormed out of the library and down the hall to the front door. He jerked it open before the servant could do it for him, and very nearly trod down the constable standing on the doorstep.

"You'd better have a message from my wife," Vere told the law officer. "And it had better say that she's sitting peaceably in the magistrate's office at Shadwell."

"I'm sorry, Your Grace," said the constable. "I do wish I

had that message for you, and it's my fault I don't. I was with her. I took my eyes off her for a moment, and she was gone. On foot, I'm afraid. I found her carriage, but she wasn't in it. I'm hoping someone here can help me put the pieces together, as she evidently has."

If Lydia was no longer at the Shadwell magistrate's office, Vere had no idea where to look for her. He made himself calm down—at least outwardly—and invited the constable inside.

The man's name was Joseph Bell. He was new to the service, a temporary replacement for an officer injured in the line of duty. He was young, good-looking, and clearly better educated than the usual run of constables.

He told his story concisely. He was sure that Her Grace knew more about Mad Dorrie than she let on. "She made sure to slip out before I could ask any more questions," he said. "If Coralie did kill the old woman—and the signs do point to it—we both wondered why. I can't help thinking the duchess knew the answer. I assumed the old woman was a threat to the bawd. Knew where she was hiding, perhaps, and made the mistake of opening her mouth about it. Or threatening to do so."

"Or else she had a fine hiding place that Coralie wanted," Tamsin said. "Lydia must have had a definite destination in mind. She wouldn't have run off in such a hurry otherwise." She frowned. "Yet I don't understand why she hasn't sent word of her whereabouts, as she promised."

Vere did not want to think about the reason his wife wouldn't—or couldn't—send word. This whole day had been a nightmare, ever since he'd received her last message. Mars, exhausted, had stumbled from the carriage during the first stop to change horses. He'd sprained his ankle and had to be left at the inn. Then one of the horses had gone lame. Ten miles from London, a drunkard driving a dormeuse had passed too close and damaged one of their wheels. An exasperated Vere had walked to the next change, hired a horse, and ridden at breakneck speed the remaining distance. Then, when he finally reached home, Vere found his wife wasn't there.

The waking nightmares that had plagued his mind all the frustrating way to London now carried his wife's image as well as his wards'. She'd sent for him. She needed him. He'd come, as fast as he could, as he'd done for Robin.

Too late, the refrain played in his mind. *Too late.*

"Your Grace?"

Vere came out of the nightmare, made himself focus on Constable Bell.

"The name 'Mad Dorrie' appears to strike no sparks of recognition in present company," Bell said.

"A river-finder, according to Grenville," Vere said. "Last seen in the vicinity of the Ratcliffe Highway." He wracked his brains, to no avail. "If I ever did see her there, I was too drunk or too busy brawling to notice."

"If Jaynes were with you, mebbe he noticed," said Bertie Trent.

Vere turned a blank look upon him.

"Also, he's London born and bred, didn't you tell me?" Bertie went on. "If Miss G—meanin' Her Grace—heard of Mad Dorrie, I'd think Jaynes would've, too. Sounds like the old woman were kind of famous once."

Vere's astonished gaze shifted to Tamsin, who was beaming at her intended.

"How clever of you, Bertie," she said. "We should have thought of Jaynes immediately." She rose from her chair and went to the library table. She drew a paper from one of the neat piles there. "He will be starting his evening route in half an hour. You should be able to find him at Pearkes's oyster house, if you set out right away."

The three men and the dog were on their way out of the house a moment later.

Lydia had managed to elude Constable Bell, but she did not elude Tom. When she turned back into High Street, the ragamuffin popped out of a side street.

"Where you goin'?" he demanded. "Yer fancy coach is back that way." He gestured with his thumb.

"Where I'm going, I can't take a fancy coach," she said. *Or constables,* she added silently. The denizens of London's underworld could detect a "trapp" or "horney"—a thieftaker or constable—from miles away. Upon which discovery, criminals vanished and their acquaintances inevitably had "never heard of 'em."

At present, Coralie might be aware she was being sought, but she would think herself safe. Lydia preferred not to dispel that illusion. In the ordinary way, Coralie was dangerous enough. Cornered, she would turn rabid.

Lydia frowned at Tom. "Did Miss Price tell you to follow me?"

The boy shook his head. "No, Miss G, I tole myself. On account if you got into trouble, it'd be my fault, on account how I lost 'em."

"If you hadn't spotted them in the first place, I shouldn't have a single idea where to look," Lydia said. "But I shan't argue with you. I'm going to need help, and I reckon you'll do."

A hackney was approaching. She summoned it, directed the driver to Ratcliffe, and climbed inside with Tom.

Then she explained the situation. She told him about Mad Dorrie, and her suspicions that Coralie had wanted the old woman's abode as a hideout. Mad Dorrie being a troublesome creature to have about, Coralie had doubtless murdered her and thrown her into the river.

"The house is important. It's isolated, on a stretch of riv-erside only the rats seem to like," Lydia explained. "But Dorrie had a boat, which is also important. I think what Coralie means to do is send a ransom note, summoning me there. It's bound to be a trap. I've had no word so far from Miss Price about a ransom note, which tells me Corrie means to wait until dark. It's easier to lay an ambush then, and she'd have no trouble getting away right after, on the boat. My best chance of foiling her plans is to arrive before she expects me."

"It looks to me like yer best chance'd be to bring along the big fellow you married. And some other big fellows, with cud-gels."

"His Grace wasn't back by the time I got to Shadwell," Lydia said. "There's no telling when he'll get back. In any case, there isn't time to send for him—or anybody—and wait for them to come. It's growing dark already. We haven't a minute to lose if we want to take her by surprise. We'll have to make do with any reinforcements we can collect in Mad Dorrie's neighborhood. The kind who look like they belong there."

"I know some fellers there," Tom said. "And some game gals."

Meanwhile, within Mad Dorrie's filthy house, Nell was rapidly succumbing to blind terror.

Ever since Annette had left, Nell had become Corrie's chief girl. She had all of Annette's frocks, which were by far the prettiest, and all of Annette's special customers, who were not so pretty. But they paid the most, and Nell got to keep half, and if the work was often disagreeable in the ex-treme, there was less of it.

Today, Corrie had promised that Nell would hardly have

to work at all anymore, because they were going to be rich and go to Paris. They'd catch Annette, and get back everything she'd stolen, and be even richer.

The more time passed, the less Nell was liking the plan. They'd be making the first part of the trip in the slimy, filthy boat tethered a short distance away at a broken-down wharf. Nell had no affection for boats, especially small ones, and especially ones that had been used for collecting dead bodies from the river. She didn't know how Corrie had come by the boat, or the house, which, filthy as it was, bore all the signs of having been lived in very recently.

At present, darkness was settling in, and wind blew in from the river through numerous chinks. Corrie was down at the boat, loading some necessities for the journey. The two gentry morts were locked up in the storeroom, but they were precious quiet, and Nell felt very much alone. Every time the wind blew, it sounded like human moans, and the house creaked and cracked, as though someone walked about in it.

Nell knew the house had belonged to a river-finder, because the notices offering rewards for recovery of the bodies were tacked up on the walls. It wasn't hard to figure out that this house had held more than its share of corpses. To her, it smelled like death. Shuddering, she stared at the note on the table.

Corrie had spent hours writing one note after another on the back of old handbills, and with each new note, she demanded more. In between, she amused herself by going into the storeroom and telling the girls what she would do to them if the Duchess of Ainswood didn't do exactly as the note told her to.

The trouble was, Nell was becoming surer by the minute that Coralie Brees was going to do what she threatened just for spite. She hadn't any reason to leave the girls alive, and it wasn't like her to leave behind anyone who might tell tales. She'd have her ransom money, and a boat, and she could slip away easy as anything in the night. Why leave anyone alive who might peach on her? Including Nell.

The door opened then, and Corrie came in. She took Nell's bonnet and shawl from a peg and threw them at her. "Time to get goin'," the bawd said. "It's ten minutes to the gin-shop and back, and if you dawdle one extra minute I'll send Mick after you to make you sorry."

Nell was to take the note to the gin-shop, give it and a coin to the boy who swept the floor, and have him deliver it to Ainswood House. The boy, knowing nothing, would have nothing to tell anyone there. Corrie obviously didn't want to risk Mick's or Nell's being bribed into betraying her.

Slowly, Nell put on her bonnet and tied the strings. Slowly, she drew on her shawl. Once she stepped out the door, she'd have but ten minutes, and she couldn't decide which was worse: to come back and take her chances with Corrie, which chances by now seemed about as dim as the two girls'; make a mad run for Ainswood House, with Mick on her heels and likely an army of constables and magistrates at her destination, if she made it that far; or run instead for the boat and take her chances on the treacherous river.

By the time she crossed the threshold, her mind was made up.

At the sound of rapidly approaching footsteps, Lydia ducked behind an overturned boat. A moment later, she heard the footsteps turn toward the river rather than the path leading to the road. Peering out from behind the boat, she saw a feminine figure stumble down over the rocks close by the rotting remains of a wharf.

She drew out the knife one of the prostitutes had lent her

and stealthily approached the figure, praying it was Coralie.

Frantically engaged in unlooping the rope tied to the pier, her prey didn't hear her approach.

An instant later, Lydia had the knife at the woman's back. "Cry out and I'll have your kidneys," she whispered.

One gasp, and her prey went utterly still.

It wasn't Coralie, unless she'd shrunk a few inches in all directions.

That was disappointing, but it might have been worse. This turned out to be Nell, and she must have come from the house, which meant she knew what was going forward there.

Lydia drew her toward the slippery stones under the wharf. "Cooperate, and I'll see that no harm comes to you," Lydia told her in an undertone. "Are the girls alive?"

"Y-yes. Leastways, they was when I left."

"In the river-finder's house—not a quarter mile east of here?"

"Yes'm." Nell was shaking, her teeth chattering. "Corrie's there with 'em, and Mick's watching outside. I was to send off the ransom note and come right back—they'll be lookin' for me any minute now."

"She's going to kill them, isn't she?"

"Yes'm. Them and you. She weren't goin' to do like the note says. Goin' to wait to spring on you 'n' kill you first and get the money from you. 'N' I expect she'll kill the gals once she gets the money. 'N' she said she'll take me to Paris, but she won't, I know. She'll do for me in the boat and throw me over." Nell began to sob. "I knew it were goin' to be bad," she gulped out. "Soon as I seen she weren't bringin' 'em back quick, like she said she would. She hates you, worse than anythin' in all the world."

Lydia moved away, untied the boat, and let it drift. Whatever Coralie accomplished this night, she would not escape that way.

"I've got to get Ainswood's wards," Lydia told Nell. "You can come along or try to make it to the Bell and Bottle. Once you get there, you'll be safe enough."

"I'll come," said Nell. "I won't never get to the Bell and Bottle in one piece. Mick's as bad as Jos and Bill."

Then Mick would have to be disposed of first, Lydia decided. And disposed of quickly and quietly. That was not going to be easy. Her allies consisted of three street arabs, none more than ten years old, and two of the sorriest specimens of prostitutes she'd ever encountered. But that was the best she'd been able to round up on short notice, even with Tom's help.

Everyone else immediately available in the environs was either too drunk, too broken-down, or too villainous.

She would have given anything at this moment to have Ainswood at her side.

But he wasn't, and all she could do was hope Nell was right: that Coralie truly meant to wait until after she got the ransom to take her vicious revenge on Elizabeth and Emily.

And so Lydia hoped, and prayed, as she set out with Nell for Mad Dorrie's abode.

Since their hostess had given them a detailed description of what she meant to do with them, Elizabeth and Emily had no trouble grasping the meaning of the sound they heard not many minutes after the door slammed behind Nell.

In the silence, it was easy enough to detect the sound of breaking glass. They'd already seen the bottle. Coralie had waved it in their faces several times.

Swallowing her revulsion, Elizabeth picked up the squirming sack she'd hidden under a decaying heap of straw, and slightly loosened the strip of petticoat she'd torn off to tie it with. She pushed Emily toward the door. Emily flattened herself against one side of it.

"No heroics," Elizabeth whispered. "Just *run*."

Biting her lip, Emily nodded.

They waited what seemed like a year but was only about two minutes before the door opened and Coralie started in, the broken bottle in her hand.

Emily screamed, Elizabeth flung the sack in their captor's face, and the bawd screeched when a terrified rat caught hold of her hair. Elizabeth hurtled at the witch, knocking her down. Emily ran out the door. An instant later, Elizabeth scrambled up and raced out after her.

She heard Emily screaming, saw the ogre Mick chasing her, heard the bawd screeching obscenities.

She ran to save her sister.

Lydia had been about to go after Mick, who was hot on the girl's heels, when she saw Coralie burst from the house.

"Nell, Tom—all of you—help the girls," Lydia snapped, then went for Coralie, who was headed in the same direction and, furious, was far more dangerous than Mick.

"Give it up, Corrie," she shouted. "You're outnumbered."

The bawd paused and turned toward the sound of Lydia's voice. She hesitated but an instant, then swore and changed direction, this time running toward the decrepit wharf.

Lydia followed, but more slowly, keeping her distance. "The boat's gone," she called out. "No way out, Corrie."

Coralie kept on running, down the littered pathway, then down the slippery rocks. Then, "You bitch!" she screamed, and that was the mildest of the epithets she screeched out as she clambered down.

Above the earsplitting obscenities, Lydia heard in the distance the unmistakable roar of a mastiff in hunting mode.

"Thank God," she breathed. She was not at all eager to go down to tangle with Coralie Brees on slippery rocks. Her knife would do little good if she stumbled and cracked her skull. She remained on the path above.

"Drop the bottle, Corrie," she said. "You hear the dog. It's no use fighting. She'll tear you to pieces."

Coralie moved then, but not upward toward the path. She scrambled over the rocks, under the wharf, and on. She was heading toward the overturned boat Lydia had hidden behind earlier.

The barking was growing closer, but Susan was still minutes away. In minutes, Coralie could right the boat and push it into the river. She'd get away, and tonight's frustrations would only make her more dangerous, wherever she turned up next.

Lydia went after her.

Vere and his companions had heard the screaming from streets away and instantly raced toward it. As they neared the river's edge, he saw a big brute bearing down on a girl, and several smaller figures bearing down on him.

"Lizzy! Em!" he roared. "This way!"

He had to shout several times to make himself heard above the furiously barking Susan, who was straining at the leash, primed for murder.

But finally the command penetrated, and the whole group froze briefly, then scattered. Two slender forms stumbled toward him. Mick stood alone, looking wildly about.

"Get him!" Vere ordered the dog, and released the lead.

Susan charged after Mick, who charged toward the river. The dog caught him by the leg, and down he went into the slime. Susan kept her jaws fastened on his leg.

Trent and Jaynes dashed into the scene then, and Vere left Mick to them while he hurried to his wards, who'd stopped to watch Susan capture Mick.

"Are you all right?" he asked the girls.

In the gloom, he could barely make out their faces, near as they stood. But he could hear them gasping for breath, trying to talk.

He reached out and wrapped an arm around each of them and drew them close. They sagged against him, and upward wafted an aroma reminiscent of low tide.

"By gad, you do reek," he said, his throat tight. "When was the last time you had a bath?"

He didn't hear their reply, because Susan, having relinquished her prisoner to Jaynes and Bertie, was barking again, frantically.

Vere looked about. He saw several figures in the darkening haze, and none bore the smallest resemblance to his wife.

"Lydia!" he shouted.

"Woof!" Susan said. Then she darted westward.

Vere abruptly released his wards and raced after her.

Vere pushed through the darkness, through a chill fog rank with decay. He couldn't see the pathway, but blindly followed the dog's barking.

"Lydia!" he roared again and again, but the only answer was Susan's barking, growing sharper, more frantic.

He tripped over a rock, clawed for balance, righted himself, and ran on. The images tore at his brain: of Charlie, Robin, of cold tombs, of living faces—all those he'd ever loved—dissolving into the mist, dissolving into shadows, and vanishing.

NO! Not this time. Not her, please God, not her.

"I'm coming!" he shouted, his lungs burning.

A dark form loomed ahead. He noticed the overturned boat a moment too late and tripped, falling face down into the muck. He stumbled up onto his feet and started on, only to stop short an instant later when he saw them.

Not three yards from him was a tangle of shapes, writhing in the dirt and refuse at the river's edge.

Susan darted toward them, then away, again and again, barking wildly.

She didn't know what to do.

Neither did Vere. He saw the flash of a blade, and couldn't tell who held it, or if both were armed. One wrong move on his part could end with a knife in the woman he loved.

He cleared his dry throat. "Stop playing, Grenville," he said as calmly as he could. "If you don't finish her off in ten seconds, I'll do it and spoil your fun."

There was a sudden movement—an arm shot up, the blade gleaming—then a shriek of triumph that made his heart stop cold, because it wasn't his wife's. Then another shriek and frantic movement.

He saw the tangle of bodies go still in the same pulsebeat he heard the hoarse, gasping voice. "Move so much as an eyelash, and I'll slice you from ear to ear."

His wife's voice.

He approached. "Need any help, Grenville?" he asked, his voice shaking.

"Yes. Please." Gasps between words. "Be careful. She. Fights. Dirty."

Vere was glad of the warning. The bawd seemed half dead to him, but as soon as he'd separated the pair, Corrie got her second wind and tried to resume the battle. Vere dragged her —kicking, clawing, and shrieking fit to wake all of Rotherhithe, on the opposite shore—out of reach of his exhausted wife.

"Knock her out," Grenville gasped, for the fiend showed no signs of tiring, but fought like the madwoman she was.

"I can't hit a woman."

Grenville trudged forward, ducked a swinging fist, and swung her own, straight into Madam's jaw.

Coralie sagged.

Vere let her inert body drop to the ground. Susan leapt forward eagerly, growling. "Guard," he told the dog. Susan straddled her and remained, snarling, her enormous, dripping jaws inches from the bawd's face.

Vere was already moving toward his wife, who was bent over, clutching her side. He pushed her hand away, felt the wetness, felt his heart drop into a hole that had no bottom.

"Sorry," she said, her voice so weak he could barely hear it. "I think the witch stuck me."

He caught hold of her, and this time, when she turned into a dead weight in his arms, he knew she wasn't pretending.

18

Francis Beaumont stood in the crowd of onlookers near the Bell and Anchor watching the Duke of Ainswood carry his wife's motionless form into his carriage. Within minutes, the place was abuzz with the news that a Drury Lane bawd had murdered the duchess.

Francis Beaumont was very unhappy.

It was not the duchess he grieved for, but himself. Coralie Brees would hang for sure, and doubtless she knew it, which meant she would make certain she had plenty of company dangling alongside her on the scaffold. She would tell her tale, and she had a fine and long one to tell, with Francis Beaumont as star performer.

He was sorry he hadn't killed her last spring in Paris, instead of helping her flee. But he had not been thinking very clearly then. Along with everything else, he'd had domestic problems, as well as a case of unrequited lust.

He'd set out to kill Coralie today, as soon as he'd heard, at Pearkes's oyster house, what the stupid bitch had done. It hadn't taken him long to figure out where she'd be, because an artist for the *Police Gazette* had told him about the old woman who'd been cut up and garroted. From the artist's description, Beaumont had no trouble figuring out who the woman was or who the killer was.

Unfortunately, the Duchess of Ainswood had tracked the bawd down before he did. He wasn't twenty yards from the house when all hell broke loose. As soon as he'd heard her tell

Corrie she was outnumbered, he'd backed off. All Corrie had to do was spot him and call out his name, and he'd be numbered among the criminals. Had he realized the duchess had only a trio of scrawny boys and a pair of toothless, consumptive whores to help her, he might have been less cautious.

But there was no way he could tell in the fog and confusion.

Now there was nothing he could do. The constables had arrived within minutes of Ainswood and his men. The entire debacle, start to finish, could not have taken more than a quarter hour. In a very short time, Corrie would be locked up, and screeching out everything she knew to everyone who could hear her—and that would be most of the parish.

He would have to go away. Now. He dared not return home for clothes or money. Everyone knew where Francis Beaumont lived. His wife was a famous artist.

She wouldn't miss him. There would be a line of men ten miles long waiting to take his place. And at the very front of the line would be a fair-haired French count.

That prospect was nearly as painful as the gallows.

But painful or not, Francis Beaumont must bear it.

He had enough money to hire a post chaise, and if he started immediately, he'd reach the coast long before anyone was aware he'd fled.

He was making his way through the crowd, careful not to appear in the least hurried, when the constables approached, bearing Coralie on a makeshift litter.

"I hope the bitch is dead!" a whore near him cried out.

"She ain't," someone else yelled. "More's the pity. The duchess only broke her jaw."

This news, confirmed by a constable, brought nearly universal disappointment.

It dawned on Beaumont then that Grenville of the *Argus*

had more friends than enemies in this quarter. Two prostitutes, half dead as they were, had tried to help her rescue
Ainswood's wards. He looked about him, saw hardened
whores sobbing, cursing Coralie Brees.

Even the street arabs were blubbering.

It took him but a moment to discern this, and but another
to make use of it. He knew how to exploit grief, how to poison
minds, how to stir simpler hearts to bitterness and rage. And
so he let a few careless remarks drop as he made his way
through the crowd.

In a matter of minutes, the crowd of sailors, whores,
pimps, beggar boys, and other riverside scum turned into a
murderous mob.

Its roar drowned out the rattles, warnings, and threats to
read the Riot Act.

In minutes, the mob had overturned the cart that was to
bear Coralie Brees to the Shadwell magistrate, knocked the
constables out of the way, and attacked the prisoners.

Moments later, Coralie Brees, battered beyond recognition, lay dead upon the cobblestones. Mick finished bleeding
to death not long thereafter.

By then the mob had melted away . . . and Francis Beaumont was already on his way home.

Some hours later, Vere sat as he'd done so many times before—for Uncle, for Charlie, for Robin—holding a too-cold
hand.

His wife's.

"I'll never forgive you, Grenville," he said, his voice
choked. "You were supposed to stay home and be the general. You were not supposed to go charging out on your own.
I can't trust you out of my sight for a minute. I vow, I must
have died months ago and gone direct to hell—which is why I

haven't hanged myself, because it would be redundant."

"Lud, what a fuss you make." Grenville treated him to one of her mocking half-smiles. "It's the merest nick she gave me."

It had not been the "merest nick." If not for layers of underwear, a sturdy corset, and Great Uncle Ste's pocket watch, the Duchess of Ainswood would not be alive. The watch had deflected the blade, which had cut clumsily rather than fatally.

The doctor, having treated the wound and bandaged up Her Grace, had left the room a moment ago with Lord Dain.

"As soon as you get well," Vere said, "I'm going to give you a good beating."

"You don't hit women."

"I'll make an exception in your case." He glowered at the hand he held. "Your hand's as cold as ice."

"That's because you're stopping the circulation."

He eased his death grip.

"That's better," she murmured.

"Sorry." He started to let go.

"No, don't," she said. "Your hand is so big and warm. I love your wicked hands, Ainswood."

"We'll see how much you like them when I turn you over my knee and give you the spanking you deserve."

She smiled. "I was never so glad of anything as I was of your arrival tonight. Coralie fights as dirty as I do. And it was hard to concentrate, because I was worried about the girls. I wasn't at all sure I'd be in any condition to help them once I was done with her. The rage. The madness. When they're truly worked up, such people have superhuman strength. I knew it. I didn't want to tangle with her. I knew what I'd be up against. But I had no choice. I couldn't let her get away."

"I know."

"I did send a boy from the Bell and Bottle for help," she went on. "But I couldn't risk waiting for help to come. As it was—"

"Lizzie and Em would have been dead if you'd waited," he cut in. "She went in to kill them." He told Lydia about the rat they'd caught and thrown at Coralie.

"Still, their ploy only gained them a few minutes," he went on. "Luckily for them you arrived during those minutes. You saved their lives, Grenville. You and your rag-tag army." He bent and kissed her hand.

"Don't be absurd," she said. "We should never have succeeded without reinforcements. Even if I'd managed to subdue Coralie—and I'll tell you straight, it was no easy battle—I still would have had Mick to contend with. By the time I got to him, he might have done your wards considerable damage."

"I know. Tom hit him in the head with a rock. The brute didn't even feel it. He presented no problem for Susan, though." He frowned. "Gad, I didn't do a damned thing. Let the dog take care of Mick. Looked on while you battled the bawd, as though it were a prize fight."

"What the devil else were you to do?" she demanded, edging up on the pillows. "No one with a grain of sense would interfere in such a situation. You did exactly as you ought. You can have no idea how much the sound of your voice cheered and encouraged me. I was growing very tired and discouraged—and a little anxious, I will admit. But your telling me to stop playing and finish her off was like a bracing gulp of strong liquor. At any rate, I couldn't bear to lose while you watched. Too humiliating for words." She coiled her fingers with his. "You cannot do everything, you know. Sometimes you must be content with giving moral support. I don't need to be coddled and sheltered. I don't need *all* my battles

352

fought for me. I do need to be believed in."

"Believed in," he repeated, shaking his head. "That's all you need, is it?"

"It's a great deal to me," she said. "Your believing in me, that is. Considering how you hold my sex in contempt, I must regard your respect for my intelligence and abilities as the most precious of commodities."

"The *most* precious?" He disentangled his hand, then stood and walked to the windows. He stared into the garden. Then he came back to the bed. He stood at the foot, his hand wrapped round the bedpost. "What about love, Grenville? Do you think, in time, you might be so graciously condescending as to endure my love? Or is love only for mere mortals? Perhaps the godlike Ballisters have no more need for it than the Olympian deities need a curricle to take them down to Delphi, or a vessel to take them to Troy."

She gazed at him for a long moment and sighed. "Ainswood, let me explain something to you," she said. "If you wish to make a declaration of love to your wife, the accepted form is to say, simply, 'I love you.' The accepted form is *not* to dare and daunt and go about it in your usual belligerent way. This is supposed to be a tender moment, and you are spoiling it by making me want to throw a coal bucket at you."

He narrowed his eyes and set his jaw. "I love you," he said grimly.

She pressed her hand to her breast and closed her eyes. "I am overcome with—with something. I do believe I shall swoon."

He returned to the side of the bed, grabbed her hands, and trapped them firmly in his. "I love you, Grenville," he said, more gently. "I started falling in love with you when you knocked me on my arse in Vinegar Yard. But I didn't know, or want to know, until our wedding night. And then I couldn't bear to tell you, because you weren't in love with me. That was stupid. You might have been killed tonight, and I wouldn't have had even the one small comfort: that I'd told you how dear you are to me."

"You've told me," she said, "in hundreds of ways. I didn't need the three magic words, though I'm glad to hear them."

"Glad," he repeated. "Well, that's better, I suppose. You're glad to own my heart." He released her hands. "Perhaps, when you're feeling stronger, you might muster up more enthusiasm. In any case, as soon as you're quite well again, I'll start working on capturing yours. Perhaps, in a decade or two, you might be sufficiently softened to return my feelings."

"I most certainly will not," she said as he stepped back and started to undress.

He paused, staring at her.

"Why in blazes should I return them?" she said. "I mean to keep them. In my heart." She pointed there. "Where I keep my own. Where it says, 'I love you,' comma, then all your names and titles."

He felt the smile tugging at his mouth, and the odd stab, at the heart she'd stolen from him.

"You must be blind," she went on, "not to have seen it written there long since."

The smile stretched into a roguish grin.

"Well, let me get undressed, my dear," he said. "Then I'll come into bed and take a closer look."

Normally, a riot in London provoked an outpouring of indignation and the sort of panic expected upon receipt of news of a foreign invasion.

The riot in Ratcliffe, which made all the morning papers,

was scarcely noticed. This was because a more catastrophic event had occurred.

Miranda, the heroine of *The Rose of Thebes*, had, as Bertie Trent predicted, sharpened a spoon on the stones of the dungeon. However, as Bertie was exceedingly shocked to discover on Thursday morning, when he finally got to reading yesterday's *Argus*, Miranda had not dug a tunnel with it. Instead, she had plunged her makeshift weapon into Diablo and fled.

In the closing paragraph of the chapter, the dashing villain of the story "gazed at the portal through which the girl had vanished until Death's shadow darkened his vision. Yet even then, his eyes continued fixed upon the door, while he heard the precious fluid drip from his massive form onto the cold stones. In that sound, he heard his life seeping slowly away . . . lost, futile, wasted."

London was devastated.

The fictional event made the front pages of several morning papers. Only the most sedate, like the *Times*, chose to disregard it, merely mentioning, in an obscure corner of the paper, "a disturbance outside the offices of the *Argus*," late on Wednesday afternoon.

The disturbance was caused by a large gathering of outraged readers. Some threatened to burn down the building. Others offered to tear the editor to pieces.

Macgowan arrived at Ainswood House early Thursday afternoon to report that S. E. St. Bellair had been hanged in effigy in the Strand.

Macgowan was in raptures.

He pronounced the Duchess of Ainswood a genius.

Ainswood had carried Lydia to the drawing room sofa, and she had a crowd with her. Consequently, Macgowan's announcement was perfectly audible to Emily, Elizabeth,

Jaynes, Bertie, and Tamsin—as well as the servants near the door. Oblivious to Lydia's frown, the editor went on rhapsodizing, and consequently leaving no one in the slightest doubt who S. E. St. Bellair really was.

Carried away by excitement, he was slow in realizing what he'd let slip. At the moment he did, he clapped his hand over his mouth. Above the hand, above the scarlet face, his alarmed gaze met Lydia's.

She waved a hand dismissively. "Never mind. The world knows the rest of my secrets. It might as well know this one." She shook her head. "Hanged in effigy. By gad, people do take their romantic fables seriously. Well." Her gaze swept the onlookers, whose expressions ranged from incredulity to consternation . . . to polite nothing whatsoever. "Sentimental swill it may be, but it's popular swill, it seems, and it's mine."

"Oh, but it's so disappointing," said Emily. "Diablo was my favorite."

"And mine," said her sister.

"And mine," Bertie said.

Tamsin held her tongue. She had faith in Lydia.

Ainswood had been standing in a corner of the room by the window, observing his guests, his face one of the "nothing whatsoevers" but for the devils dancing in his eyes. "I thought the choice of weapon was a lovely touch, Grenville," he said. "I can think of few more ignominious ends than being stabbed to death with a spoon."

She acknowledged this dubious compliment with a gracious nod.

"More important," her husband went on, "you've caused a sensation. When word leaks out of the author's true identity, the ensuing clamor will drown out the present one. All those benighted souls ignorant of Miranda and her doings will be forced to make up for lost time."

He turned his attention to Macgowan. "If I were you, I'd begin bringing out bound volumes of several chapters apiece. One cheap edition for the masses, and one handsome leatherbound with gilt for the nobs. Capitalize on the excitement before it fades."

Lydia quickly masked her surprise. Ainswood was the last man one would expect to care about, let alone devise ways of exploiting, the commercial potential of her "scribbling." But then, he loved an uproar, she reminded herself.

"That's what I was thinking," she said. "Though not about bound volumes—which is a brilliant idea. Still, we don't want the readers to lose interest in the rest of the story, now their favorite is en route to hell."

She considered briefly. Then, "You must put out a notice, tomorrow morning," she told Macgowan. "You will announce a special edition of the *Argus*, to be available on Wednesday next, containing the four concluding chapters of *The Rose of Thebes*. If Purvis complains that he can't do the illustrations in time, you must get someone else."

Macgowan already had the next two chapters. Lydia sent Tamsin for the final ones, which were locked up in the study desk.

Very shortly thereafter, the editor departed with the precious chapters, even more excited than when he'd come. Doubtless this was because he'd discerned another leap in profits in the very near future.

After he'd gone, Ainswood shooed the others from the room.

He plumped the pillows behind Lydia and rearranged the lap robe. Then he drew up an ottoman and perched upon it. His elbow resting on his knee, his jaw resting on his knuckles, he gazed at her reproachfully.

"You are evil," he said.

"That's just as you deserve," she said.

"It's a damned dirty trick," he said.

She shaped her expression into limpid innocence. "What is?"

"I don't know exactly what it is," he said, "but I know you've played the world a trick, because I know you. No one sees the devil in you. I do."

"I reckon it takes one to know one."

He smiled then, the killer smile. Beyond the windows, the sun could make no headway through heavy grey clouds. Where she lay, though, golden sunshine penetrated every pore and cell, and its warmth stole into her brain and melted it to syrup.

"That's not going to work," she told him, aware of the blissful, thoroughly stupid smile with which she helplessly answered his lethal one. "I'm not going to tell you the rest of the story. All you're doing is making me amorous."

He let his rogue's gaze travel slowly from the crown of her head to the toes curling under the lap robe.

"If I could get you panting with lust, you'd tell me," he said. "But that's against doctor's orders."

"He said only that I was to avoid exertion, and put no strain on the wound." She shot him a sidelong glance. "Use your imagination."

He got up and started walking away.

"It seems you don't have any," she said.

"Think again," he said, without turning. "I'm merely going to secure the doors."

As it was, Vere had barely enough time to restore his wife's and his own clothing to rights after the intimate interlude. This was because the girls—who apparently had no sense of discretion—decided to start banging on the drawing room doors at the precise moment he was starting to interrogate his wife about Miranda.

"Go away!" he commanded.

"What are you doing? Is Cousin Lydia all right?"

"Woof!" This from Susan.

He heard the panic in their voices and recalled that they'd been shut out of their brother's room when he fell mortally ill.

He went to the door, pulled away the chair he'd fixed under the handle, and opened it.

He looked down into two pale, worried faces.

"I was only beating my wife," he said. "In a friendly way."

Two sea-green gazes shot to Lydia, who rested in a dignified semirecumbent posture upon the sofa. She smiled.

"How can you—ow!" Emily cried, as Elizabeth elbowed her in the ribs.

"He means you-know-what," Elizabeth whispered.

"Oh."

Susan sniffed him suspiciously. Then she went to the sofa to sniff her mistress. Then she grumbled something to herself and flopped down at the foot of the sofa.

Emboldened, the girls advanced upon the duchess as well, and flopped down on the carpet next to Susan.

"Sorry," Elizabeth said. "It never occurred to me. Aunt Dorothea and Uncle John never locked themselves into the drawing room for that purpose."

"Or any other room," Emily said. "At least not that I ever noticed."

"In the bedroom," Elizabeth said. "They had to do it sometime. They've nine and three-quarters children."

"When you have nine and three-quarters," Vere said, approaching them, "I reckon the bedchamber is the only place you can have a prayer of privacy—if you bolt the doors."

"You can do it wherever you want," Elizabeth said magnanimously. "We shan't interrupt again. We didn't realize, that was all."

"Now we do," said Emily, "we'll keep away—and try to picture it," she added with a giggle.

"She is very young," her sister said. "Just ignore her."

"We like Susan," Emily told Lydia. The girl commenced scratching behind the mastiff's ear. This was all the encouragement Susan needed to drop her big head into the girl's lap, close her eyes, and subside into canine bliss.

"When she's not hunting villains, she's very sweet," said Elizabeth. "We've half a dozen mastiffs at Longlands."

"I missed them," said Emily. "But we couldn't bring even one to Blakesleigh, because they drool too much, Aunt Dorothea says, and dogs put their tongues in improper places. She prefers dogs that don't slobber so much. They are more sanitary, she says."

"She believes Robin caught diphtheria from one of the dogs," Elizabeth amplified. "The boys had gone out to catch rabbits, and they had the dogs with them. No one knows what the dogs got into, but Rolf—he was only a puppy then—came back covered with muck and stinking. Still, two women in the village caught it, too, and they weren't with our dogs."

"And none of the other boys got it, though they were with Robin," said her sister. "It doesn't make sense."

"No one is exactly sure how one contracts the disease," Lydia said. "They don't understand why sometimes it will devastate an entire town, and other times it attacks only a handful of people. Even then, one cannot predict who'll have a mild case and who'll have a fatal one. It's dreadfully unfair," she added gently.

"At least he went quickly," Elizabeth said. "It was all over in two days. He was unconscious for nearly all the time. The nurse said he felt little, if anything. He was too weak even to feel afraid."

Vere had turned away and moved to the window. Dusk was settling in. That much he could make out through the mist clouding his vision.

"I *know* he wasn't afraid at the end," he heard the older girl's voice behind him. "Because Cousin Vere was with him."

"Everyone else was terrified," Emily said. "The doctor said Aunt Dorothea must keep away, because she might get sick, and even if she lived, the baby she was nursing could get it and die. And Uncle John must stay away, too, because he could give it to her. They wouldn't let us go to Robin."

"They were trying to protect you, as they tried to protect all their children," Lydia said.

"I know, but it was very hard," Elizabeth said.

"But then Cousin Vere came," her sister chimed in, "and *he* wasn't afraid of anything. No one could keep him out— though they tried. He went in and stayed with Robin, just as he stayed with Papa. He held Papa's hand. He never left him, even for a minute—and it was the same with Robin."

"Cousin Vere won't tell you," said Elizabeth. "He's pretending he doesn't hear. That's what he did when we tried to thank him."

"I hear you," Vere said, dragging the words from his seared throat. He turned away from the window, saw three pairs of ominously bright eyes fixed upon him.

"Gad, what a bother you make," he said. "I loved the lad. What else should I do but stand vigil at his deathbed? What in blazes had I to lose?" He advanced to glower down at the young faces lifted toward his. "Why must you make me out to be a hero? It's sick-making, is what it is. You'll make Grenville cast up her accounts. Now, *she*," he added, nodding toward her, "is a true hero. She raced to your rescue though she didn't know you from Adam, and had everything to live for—on account of being married to me. She saved your evil little lives, and instead of thanking her and promising to be good girls from now on, you must maunder on about what I did ages ago."

This ungracious speech had the desired bracing effect. The tears were blinked and brushed away, and the girls turned contrite countenances to Lydia.

Dutifully they thanked her for saving their lives and promised to be good in future.

"Never mind that nonsense," she said crisply. "The 'Miss Innocence' expression may have worked with Lord and Lady Mars, but you don't pull the wool over my eyes so easily."

The angelic expressions gradually transformed to wariness as she went on, "Innocent misses do not snoop in others' correspondence or read anything else not intended for their eyes. You are devious and daring to a fault. No biddable young lady should have a clue how to escape a vigilant household—let alone dare it in the dead of night—let alone not only escape undetected but contrive to remain undetected for more than a week. While I admire your ingenuity and comprehend your desperation, born of apparently blind worship of your wicked cousin"—hope began to glow in the young faces—"it's also clear that you have been woefully ill-supervised during the last two years. You may be sure that state of affairs is at an end."

Lydia's stern tone had even Susan sitting up at attention. "Woof!" she said.

Hope faded from the allegedly innocent faces.

They turned twin pleading looks toward Vere.

"We didn't mean to be so much trouble," said Elizabeth.

"We only wanted to be with *you*," said Emily.

"Yes, but we go together, you see," said Vere. "We're of one mind, Grenville and I, and the mind is hers, on account of my being a man and not having one."

His wards exchanged troubled glances.

Then Elizabeth said, "It doesn't matter. We wanted to be with you. And no matter how strict Cousin Lydia is, at least she isn't timid and boring."

"Maybe she'll teach us how to fight," Emily said, brightening.

"She most certainly will not," Vere said.

"And how to smoke cigars without getting sick," Elizabeth added.

"Absolutely not!" Vere declared. "I can think of few more disgusting sights than a female smoking."

"Then why did you give her one of yours?" Elizabeth asked, all innocence.

"Because she—she's different. She isn't normal." He glared at the girl. "And I'd like to know where you heard about that."

"In the *Whisperer*," Emily said.

"A scandal rag," Lydia said in answer to his blank look. "You're a perennial topic in its pages. Still, they have excellent reporters working for them. The information is usually accurate. I've used leads garnered from there myself, from time to time." Her considering gaze took in his wards. "I do not believe in sheltering young women from the realities of the world. What I read, they may read—but it will be done in a family gathering, with discussion. As to fighting—"

"Damnation, Grenville."

"Even young ladies should be acquainted with basic skills in self-defense. With proper chaperonage, they should not require them—in the best of all possible worlds. But the world is unpredictable."

The girls instantly bolted up and commenced hugging and kissing the duchess.

He saw the glow, so warm, come into her eyes.

They would be a handful, and she knew it, and couldn't be happier.

Death had cheated her of her mother's and sister's love, but she'd kept her heart open. She'd made a family of the women who'd needed her, young and old. She'd make a family of Elizabeth and Emily, and love them unstintingly, as she loved him.

He had not been so wise. Losing those he'd loved had made him drive away the ones who remained, whom he might have loved. He'd been angry—he'd understood that days ago, after the nightmare about Robin. The boy had betrayed him in dying—as Charlie had done. And Vere had shut him out, and everyone and everything associated with him.

But the mad grieving rage wasn't the only reason.

Vere knew he'd been a coward. Unlike his wife, he'd been afraid to risk it again. Afraid to love.

It had had to take him unawares, as she had done, time and again. Sneaky, devious, refusing to play by sporting rules—that was how love worked.

And he was damned glad of it.

He arranged an injured expression on his face and said plaintively, "Oh, that's just like you, Grenville, hogging all the affection. Don't I get any, or is this just for plaguey females?"

"Come here," she said. "We'll share."

19

The following Wednesday found Diablo still bleeding to death in the pages of the *Argus*.

His servant, Pablo, hurrying toward the master, slipped in the pool of blood, fell on top of him, and instantly commenced weeping.

"Ugh. Get off. You *stink*." These words emanated from the corpse.

Pablo's stench revived the master as effectively as sal volatile might have done. In a short time, it was discovered that the deadly spoon had struck some inches below his heart, and while he was bleeding like a stuck pig, he wasn't bleeding to death. The dripping he'd heard was the contents of a wine bottle Miranda had overturned in her flight.

If she hadn't kneed him in the groin when she drove in the spoon, he might have kept his balance and managed to catch her. Instead, he'd fallen and temporarily lost consciousness. His skull throbbed, and his side bled, and his nether regions were probably damaged permanently, but he was alive. And he was furious.

London rejoiced, and went on reading, avidly.

As it came to The End, London breathed a collective sigh of satisfaction.

Orlando had proved to be the true villain of the piece. Diablo, as all proper heroes must do, rescued the heroine, retrieved the Rose of Thebes, and killed the villain.

And the hero and heroine lived happily ever after.

At Ainswood House, the concluding chapters were read aloud in the library.

With the assistance of her cousin the Marquess of Dain, Her Grace did the honors before an audience comprising her husband, Dain's wife and son, Elizabeth, Emily, Tamsin, Bertie, Jaynes, and those servants fortunate enough to be posted within earshot.

Dain had arrived in London and reached Ainswood House in time to see his cousin's apparently lifeless body carried inside. He'd kept Ainswood quiet in a corner of the bedchamber while the physician did his work. When that was done, Dain had slipped out with the doctor, leaving Ainswood to quarrel with his wife.

The following evening, Dain quarreled with his own lady, who, contrary to orders, had left Athcourt and proceeded with suicidal haste to Dain's London townhouse. She'd brought the Demon Seed with her, because, she said, he was worried about his papa and howled blue murder when Jessica tried to set out without him.

Today, though, Dominick was miraculously well-behaved. He sat mute on the carpet between Emily and Elizabeth, listening with riveted attention to the story. Even during the half-hour rest and refreshment interval preceding the final two chapters, he only played quietly with Susan and allowed the girls to stuff him with more sweets than were good for him.

Vere wasn't sure whether the child understood the tale or was captivated by the readers. He worshiped his father, and so naturally believed everyone must be absolutely quiet and pay complete attention while Papa read. One might expect the boy's attention to lag when another took up the reading task.

This other was Grenville, however, and she didn't simply

read. She impersonated each character by turns, giving them individual voices and mannerisms. In short, she *acted*, though she'd solemnly promised Vere she wouldn't leave the sofa.

Dominick remained entranced throughout, and at the end, he cheered and clapped as hard as the adults did, and jumped up to join the standing ovation.

Grenville accepted this tribute with a sweeping bow. It was the same extravagantly theatrical one she'd vouchsafed the Duke of Ainswood after her performance in the Blue Owl, complete with imaginary doffed hat.

Only now, finally, did Vere realize why that bow had nagged his mind. He'd seen its perfect replica before, long before he'd ever clapped eyes on her.

He'd seen it for the first time when he was a schoolboy at Eton.

He turned to Dain, whose black brow was knit as he watched his cousin.

"Recognize it, do you?" Vere said.

"You told me she was a fine mimic," Dain said. "But I can't think when she could have seen me do that."

"Do what?" Grenville asked as she finally returned to the sofa.

Vere frowned at her until she put her feet up and settled back upon the cushions.

"The bow," he said. "The theatrical bow."

"My father was an actor," she said.

"Dain's father wasn't," he said. "Yet Dain had the knack of it when he was but ten years old. I saw it for the first time after he'd emerged victorious from a battle with Wardell, a boy twice his size and two years older. When we were at Eton."

"I saw it for the first time in the innyard at Amesbury," said Lady Dain. "After Dain and Ainswood pounded each other. It is quite distinctive, isn't it? Dain does have a theatrical streak. But the Ballisters have always liked to make a show. They seem to have a fine flair for drama—one of several characteristics they don't scruple to use to get their own way."

"The first Earl of Blackmoor often amused his king with impersonations," Dain told Grenville. "Your mother's grandfather and his brothers were exceedingly fond of the theater—and actresses—in their youth. Before my father's time, acting troupes were often invited to Athcourt to entertain the houseguests."

"Naturally, Grenville, you can't have inherited a single talent from anybody but the Ballisters," Vere said. "All beauty, intellectual gifts, and virtue flow therefrom."

"Not virtue," said Dain. "That's never been our strong suit. We've had our share of pious hypocrites—my father, for example, and Lydia's grandpapa—but we've produced at least one devil in each generation."

At this point, the devil Dain had produced began showing signs of restlessness. The girls invited him to play in the garden with them and Susan. Tamsin went to supervise. Whither she went, there also went Bertie.

"I'm all amazement," Dain said, when the younger contingent was gone. "I've never seen Satan's Spawn keep still for so long."

"He was under the spell of a master storyteller," Vere said. "There isn't a man, woman, or child who can resist it."

"The gods must have given you the talent, cousin," Dain told her. "I've never heard of any of our lot who had it. We've some fine letters in the archives, and any number of stirring political speeches. But what poetry I've seen is abominable. I've never come across a Ballister-written tale spun out of thin air."

"My wife holds that talent cheap," Vere said. "She refers to *The Rose of Thebes* as 'sentimental swill'—and that's the kindest epithet she bestows upon it. If Macgowan hadn't let the cat out of the bag, she'd never have admitted she wrote it."

"It serves no useful purpose," Lydia said. "All it does is entertain. With simple morals. The good end happily, the bad unhappily. It has nothing to do with real life."

"We have to *live* real life, like it or not," Vere said. "And you know, better than most, the sort of lives the great mass of humanity lead. To give them a few hours' respite is to bestow a great gift."

"I think not," Grenville said. "I begin to think it socially irresponsible. On account of that wretched story, girls take it into their heads to bolt in search of excitement they can't find at home. They'll imagine they can dispatch villains with sharpened spoons. They—"

"You're telling me the members of your sex are imbeciles who can't distinguish fact from fiction," he said. "Anyone fool enough to try one of Miranda's tricks is either reckless by nature or doesn't own a grain of sense. Such people will do something stupid with or without your suggestions. My wards offer a perfect example."

"Your wards prove my point."

" 'Dreadful girls,' you called them, before you'd ever clapped eyes on them." Vere's voice rose. "They're Mallorys, Lydia, and the Mallorys have been spawning hellions since the dawn of time. You will not use Lizzy and Em as an excuse to stop writing those wonderful stories you please to call 'romantic claptrap' and 'rubbish.' You are a talented writer, with the knack of communicating with readers of both genders, of every age and background. I will not permit you to throw that gift away. As soon as you're well, you'll start another story, dammit, if I have to lock you in a room to make you do it!"

She blinked once, twice. Then, "Lud, what a fuss you make," she said. "I had no idea you felt so strongly about it."

"I do." He left his chair, walked to the fireplace and back. "I should be illiterate were it not for romantic claptrap and sentimental swill and improbable tales. I cut my teeth on *The Arabian Nights* and *Tales of the Genii*. My father read them to me, and they made me hungry to read more books, even without pictures."

"My mother gave me storybooks," Dain said, his voice very low. "They provided me some of the happiest times of my childhood."

"We read them to Dominick," his wife said.

"You saw the lad," Vere said. "For the time you read, nothing else in the world existed but your story. Not a peep out of him, for half hours at a stretch. It was the same with Robin when I read to him. He would have loved your story, Grenville."

The room became very still, heavily silent.

His wife's cool voice broke the tension. "Then the next one will be for him," she said. "And it will be ten times better than anything in *The Arabian Nights*."

"Naturally it will be ten times better," Dain said mildly. "A *Ballister* will have written it."

Vere didn't know why it nagged at his mind, only that it did.

. . . grandfather and his brothers exceedingly fond of the theater—and actresses.

. . . virtue . . . never been our strong suit . . . devil in each generation . . .

. . . a Ballister *will have written it.*

That night, the Duke of Ainswood dreamt about Charles II. Grenville was entertaining His Majesty with an impersonation of the third Marquess of Dain, who stood among the courtiers, wearing only a plumed hat, with the actress Nell Gwyn draped on his arm.

Vere awoke as the sky was beginning to lighten. His wife was sleeping soundly. He left the bed, moved noiselessly to the other side, took up her mother's diary, and went to the window to read it.

It didn't take long, and when he was done, he was as dissatisfied as he'd been the first time. The gaps between the entries . . . the sense of too much unsaid . . . the pride that wouldn't let her complain. The nearest she'd come was in the first entry, in her scornful description of her husband . . . the bitter undercurrent when she spoke of her father.

. . . *memory submits to no will, not even a Ballister's, and the name and image persist, long after death.*

Whose name and image persisted in *her* memory? Vere wondered.

No biddable young lady should have a clue how to escape a vigilant household, Grenville had said.

Anne Ballister had been closely guarded and sheltered.

How had she and John Grenville—a third-rate actor—ever crossed paths? How had he managed to get to her, seduce her into eloping with him to Scotland? Her father was a "pious hypocrite," according to Dain. Acting troupes were not invited to Athcourt in Dain's father's time. Anne's father wouldn't have invited them to his home, either.

Vere had recognized, in hindsight, all the clues Grenville had carefully dropped into *The Rose of Thebes*. Carried away by the adventures, the readers had overlooked them. Only when Orlando's perfidy was finally revealed did one discern the seeds, so cleverly sown throughout the preceding chapters.

He looked for clues in the little diary, but if they were there —as he was sure they must be—they were too cleverly concealed.

He returned the book to its place on the night table and went into his dressing room.

According to Beelzebub, the legal firm of Carton, Brays, and Carton were "a lot of driveling incompetents." This was why Dain had dispensed with their services as soon as he inherited.

Beelz must have bestowed a stare more petrifying than usual in the process, because nothing seemed to have moved in the intervening nine years, including, most especially, the dust.

Mr. Carton the elder wasn't in, "on account he's barmy," the law clerk informed Vere. Mr. Carton the younger was in Chancery, embarked on the process of going "barmy" himself. Mr. Brays was not engaged at the moment, but he was most certainly drunk, "as is his usual habit," the clerk explained. "It's a sorry state of affairs, is what it is, Your Grace, but it's a place, and the only one I got at the moment, and I make the best of it."

The clerk, by the name of Miggs, was little more than a boy—a tall, lanky one to be sure—with a very little fuzz aspiring to a mustache and a great many spots.

"If you do what I ask without your superiors' approval, you'll probably lose your place," said Vere.

"Not likely," Miggs said. "They can't do anything without me. Can't find anything, and when I find it for 'em, they don't know what it means and I have to explain it. If I was to go, they'd lose every client they got, and that isn't many, and most of them I got for them."

Vere told him what he was looking for.

"I'll see," the boy said.

He went into a room and did not come out again for half an hour. "I can't find a record," he said when he came out. "But that doesn't mean much. The old fellow kept everything in his head. Which explains why he went barmy. I'll have to go into the catacombs, sir. It might take a few days."

Vere decided to go with him. Which turned out to be very wise, for the "catacombs" was Carton, Brays, and Carton's equivalent of a lumber room: heaps of boxes, filled with documents. They were simply stacked, one atop the next, according to no logical system whatsoever.

They worked through the entire day, only stopping at midday and late afternoon for ale and pies. Vere heaved the boxes, and the clerk quickly sifted through the contents, again and again, hour after hour, in a dank basement, while various insects and rodents scurried about, darting in and out of the crevices between boxes.

Shortly before seven o'clock that night, Vere trudged wearily up the cellar steps, out the door, and into the street. His neckcloth, now grey, hung limply from his neck. Cobwebs clung to his coat, along with miscellaneous dirt and debris. Sweat trailed through the grime caked on his face. His hands were black.

But in those grimy hands he carried a box, which was all that mattered, and as he set out for home, he was whistling.

To pacify the overly anxious group Ainswood had sternly ordered to look after her, Lydia had said she would take a nap before dinner.

This didn't mean she intended to nap. She'd taken a book with her to the master bedchamber—and fallen asleep reading it.

A noise from the window woke her, and she caught her husband in the act of climbing through it.

She did not ask him why he couldn't come in the door like a normal person. One glance told her why he'd eschewed the more public route.

This morning he'd told her he was going to meet with Mr. Herriard regarding the marriage settlements, and would probably be at it for hours. These negotiations had been delayed while His Grace searched for his wards. Dain had reminded his friend of the matter yesterday, before he left.

"I collect one of the settlement terms was your sweeping Mr. Herriard's chimney," she said as her glance swept over six and a quarter feet of human wreckage.

Ainswood looked down at the small box in his hands.

"Um, not exactly," he said.

"You fell into a sewer excavation," she said.

"No. Um . . ." He frowned. "I ought to get cleaned up first."

"I'll ring for Jaynes."

He shook his head.

Lydia left the bed.

"Vere?" Her voice was gentle. "Did someone knock you on the head?"

"No. Let me just wash my face and hands. I can have a bath later." He hurried into his dressing room, still holding the box.

She supposed the box contained the marriage settlements and there was something in them he didn't think she'd like. She beat down her curiosity and waited, pacing.

He emerged from the dressing room a few minutes later, wearing a dressing gown and nothing else, and carrying the box. He drew up a chair near the fire and invited her to occupy it. She sat.

He settled onto the hearthrug at her feet and opened the box. He withdrew an oval object and laid it in her lap.

It was a miniature, of a young man, fair-haired and blue-eyed. He wore a faint smile.

It was almost like looking into a mirror. "He looks . . . like my brother," she said. Her voice sounded thready to her ears. Her heart was thudding.

"His name was Edward Grey," Ainswood said quietly. "He was a promising actor and playwright. His mother was a highly regarded actress, Serafina Grey. His father was Richard Ballister, your mother's great-uncle. Edward Grey was the devil Richard Ballister produced, in his wild youth, on the wrong side of the blanket. Richard's father was past sixty when Richard was born, of a second marriage."

He took from the box a yellowed piece of paper. It bore a fragment of the Ballister family tree—Anne Ballister's branch —and the names and dates were written in her tiny, precise hand. The second marriage, late in life, explained why Anne Ballister's Great-Uncle Richard was only three years older than her father.

But Lydia's gaze had already shifted lower, to where her name was written, below and between her mother's—and Edward Grey's.

She looked at the miniature. Then at the family tree her mother had so neatly drawn. Then at the miniature.

"This is my father," she said softly, wonderingly.

"Yes."

"Not John Grenville."

"There's no doubt of it," he said. "Your mother made sure. Like a true Ballister, she had it all documented. My guess is that she intended the lot to be given to you when you reached adulthood. Something went wrong. John Grenville ended up with it and sold it to the third Marquess of Dain— via his solicitors. The receipt for the transaction is dated August 1813."

"That explains where he got the money to go to America," Lydia said. She met her husband's gaze. "This explains a great deal." It was Edward her mother had eloped with to Scotland, not the man Lydia had called Papa.

"The box contains love letters he wrote to her," Vere said. "Two dozen at least. I hadn't time to truly study and sort everything out." His green gaze was soft and he wore his boy's smile, half abashed. "Even the little I read told me he adored your mother. He was born on the wrong side of the blanket, but they were deeply in love, and conceived a child in love."

"I love you," she said, past the lump in her throat. "I don't know how you did this, how it occurred to you, what drove you to look for and find something no one else guessed existed. But I know you did it in love for me—and really, Ainswood, I am so vexed with you. I have never done so much blubbering as I have since I met you." Her eyes were filling. She didn't try to say more, only slipped down from the chair and into his arms.

Though he was illegitimate, Edward Grey had been fairly close to his father, who provided for his keep and his education. He was one of the numerous dependents who attended family gatherings. That was how he and Anne had met. She had been told he was "a distant cousin." They fell in love.

She had been visiting when he quarreled with his father, who vehemently disapproved of the acting career Edward was set upon. Edward was ejected. Permanently. When Anne found out what had happened, she insisted on going with him. He wanted her to wait until he was sure he could support her. She refused to wait. She understood now that her father would never consent to their marriage. She'd be forced to wed the man her father chose. That was out of the question.

And so she fled with Edward to Scotland.

They were wed over the anvil. No minister, no church, no banns, no parental permission required. Their marriage was legal, but not by their relatives' standards. The Ballisters had no more regard for the savage Scottish race's quaint laws and traditions than they did for the bizarre rituals of Hindus or Hottentots. In their eyes, Anne was a whore, the mistress of a bastard. The box contained letters from the lawyers notifying her she'd been disowned, had no legal claims upon the family, and was forbidden, on pain of prosecution, to attempt any claims, financial or otherwise, or any other form of communication.

But Anne and Edward had known this when they set out. They understood their kin. They knew those doors were permanently closed.

They couldn't know that, in three short months, a piece of scenery would fall on Edward during a rehearsal and kill him. He hadn't had time to make provision for his wife, or the child she was carrying.

A month later, John Grenville married Anne. As the diary had indicated, he convinced her he truly loved her. She was seventeen, pregnant, with no one else to turn to. She thought he was generous to accept another man's child as his own. Only when he tried and failed to use her baby as a way into the Ballisters' hearts and pocketbooks did Anne see her error.

Still, she hadn't much choice but to stay with him, at least in the beginning. It was either John Grenville or the streets, since she had no other way of earning a living. She had been ill for a very long time following Sarah's birth and never fully regained her strength thereafter. If she had been strong, she would have left John Grenville eventually, Lydia was certain.

Anne had definitely tried to leave him little with which to exploit her death or Lydia's true identity. The diary constituted a very small scandal, compared to the high drama the box held. Every publisher in London would have fought for those documents. Small wonder Carton, Brays, and Carton had paid handsomely for the materials. And very small wonder they'd promptly buried them.

Evidently, the box was overlooked when the current Marquess of Dain changed solicitors. The diary, along with other records, must have gone to the new firm, where everything was properly sorted out and materials deemed of interest to the new master sent to Athcourt. Since Dain had resided in Paris rather than Devonshire until last spring, it was hardly astonishing that the diary had ended up tucked away in a drawer or file or shelf with other archival materials. The amazing thing was that Lady Dain had found it.

That, though, wasn't half so amazing as Ainswood's piece of "finding."

And he, as usual, would not admit to having done anything out of the ordinary.

On the following afternoon, while the younger contingent was out watching a parade in honor of the Queen of Portugal, Lydia and Ainswood enlightened Dain and Jessica.

Knowing the Ballisters, Dain wouldn't have had any trouble believing the story, even if he hadn't the documents spread out before him on the great table in the library.

What he couldn't believe was that the Duke of Ainswood was the one who'd got to the bottom of it.

"How the devil did you perceive what no one else even imagined was there?" he demanded of his friend. "And what guardian angel pushed you to Carton, Brays, and Carton, of all places?"

"You're the one who told me the Ballister nature isn't confiding," Vere said. "You're the one who nattered on about mimics and weaknesses for the theater. You were the one who pointed out how extraordinary it was that the family birthmark—the holy badge of the Ballisters—had appeared upon a woman. Yet Anne never 'confided' that miraculous matter in her private diary. It was natural to be suspicious. All I did was put two and two together. And since she eloped in your father's time, I started in the logical place, with your father's solicitors. I certainly didn't expect to find the answers there. I was merely hoping to be set on the right trail."

He threw an exasperated glance over the group. "Now that we have Lydia's identity sorted out, and she doesn't have to worry about John Grenville's bad blood, don't you think a celebration is in order? I don't know about the rest of you, but I could use a drink."

Monday morning found Bertie Trent and his bride-to-be in the morning room of Ainswood House, and it wasn't in order to do what young couples do when they snatch a moment's privacy.

They were trying to figure out how to stop a war.

Everyone else was in the library, arguing about their future. They'd been at it since breakfast: Dain and Ainswood and their wives, with enthusiastic help from Elizabeth, Emily, and even Dominick.

They could not agree on where the wedding should be held: Longlands, Athcourt, London—in church, or at whose townhouse. They could not agree on who had the right to provide Tamsin's dowry, or a place for the newlyweds to live, or the finances necessary for maintaining the abode.

Because it was Dain and Ainswood doing most of the arguing, compromise was out of the question. Left to themselves, the ladies might have negotiated an acceptable arrangement, but the men wouldn't leave it to them, because that meant compromise.

Tamsin was very upset. She didn't want a dowry. Yet she

didn't want to hurt anyone's feelings. Bertie was upset for her sake as well as his own. He couldn't say a word about his own future because it would look like he was taking sides.

"At the rate they're going," he said, "they won't get it settled before Judgment Day. And meanwhile, m'grandmother and Abonville'll get back from France, and they'll be wantin' us to live there."

"I know it sounds ungrateful," Tamsin said, "but an elopement to Scotland is beginning to exert a strong appeal."

"We don't need to do that." Bertie lowered his voice. "You can't walk ten minutes in London without trippin' over a church. And where there's a church, there's a parson."

Her enormous brown gaze lifted to his. "We did tell them we were going for a walk," she said.

Bertie patted his breast. "I got the license." He'd been carrying it about with him ever since Dain had given it to him a few days ago. Considering the way important documents tended to go astray—for decades—in certain families, Bertie thought it best to keep this one upon his person at all times.

"I'll fetch my bonnet," she said.

It took her only a moment. A moment later, they set out for St. James's Church, Piccadilly. They had only to walk a short way across St. James's Square and step into York Street, at the end of which the church stood.

They were about to turn into York Street at the same time a well-dressed, bespectacled, middle-aged fellow was turning out of it into the square.

He stopped short, and Tamsin did, too.

"Papa!" she cried.

"Tam!" The fellow opened his arms.

She let go of Bertie and ran into them.

"I say!" Bertie exclaimed. "By Jupiter."

★ ★ ★ ★ ★

As soon as the first transports were over, Bertie hustled them into York Street, so they wouldn't attract attention from Ainswood House.

"We was tryin' to get shackled quick-like," he explained to Mr. Prideaux. "Before we was missed. I weren't runnin' away with her or nothin'." He produced the license as evidence.

As Mr. Prideaux perused the document, Bertie added, "You ain't goin' to raise a fuss, I hope. It's all settled, like I wrote you, and she's safe and well, and I can take care of her. We don't need nothin'—only your blessin' would be a good thing, if you can manage it, but we'll do without if we have to."

By this time Tamsin had disengaged herself from her father and was clinging to Bertie's arm. "You won't change his mind, Papa, or mine. I won't go back to Mama."

Her parent returned the license to Bertie. "Neither will I," he said. "Your mother didn't send me word when you ran away. I found out only a week ago. I was in Plymouth getting ready to set out for America to look for you when Sir Bertram's letter finally reached me. She had waited for a sign from the Almighty before deciding to send it to my secretary." He took off his spectacles, cleaned them with his handkerchief, then put them back on. "Well, I have looked after you very ill, very ill, indeed, Tam. I daresay this young fellow will do much better, eh?"

"Oh, never mind heaping coals on my head, Papa," Tamsin said. "I can't blame you for running away from Mama when I did the same thing. If I'd had work to get me away from her, I'd have worked day and night." She put out her hand. "Come with us, there's a dear, and give the bride away."

She tucked one hand into her father's arm and the other

into Bertie's, and they set off toward the church.

It was a very short walk, but Bertie managed to do plenty of thinking in the course of it. When they reached the church, he said, "You know, it seems to me like no one's goin' to argue with the bride's pa if he says this church is fine with him and this sort of wedding, and never mind the fancy trappings. What if we asked 'em all—meanin' them at Ainswood House—to come along? You'd like to have the Duchess of A at the weddin', I know you would, Tamsin, and only think how Lizzie and Em didn't get to see Ainswood get shackled." He grimaced. "It bothers me to disappoint 'em."

His intended looked up at him, her big eyes glowing. "You are the dearest, kindest man in all the world, Bertie Trent," she said. "You think of everybody." She turned to her father. "Do you see, Papa? Do you see how lucky I am?"

"Of course I see," said her father, while Bertie turned vivid scarlet. "And I hope your beau will allow me the honor of writing the invitation to your friends."

The invitation was duly written, and a vestry man carried it to Ainswood House.

Not a quarter hour later, the wedding guests trooped into St. James's Church, and nobody argued with anybody, though a few people did cry, as females do, and Susan, whose tender sensibilities couldn't bear tears, tried to comfort them with hand-licking and the occasional cheerful, "Woof!"

The minister, accustomed to the oddities of the gentry, bore it good-humoredly, and the wedding, if it fell short of certain peers' high standards of grandeur, unquestionably succeeded in making all parties happy, most especially the principals, which, after all, was all that mattered.

After the ceremony, Mr. Prideaux invited the company to

adjourn to the Pulteney Hotel, where he was staying, for "a bit of refreshment."

It soon became apparent to everyone where Tamsin had inherited her efficiency from, because a very lavish wedding breakfast contrived to be assembled and served on very short notice.

Not long afterward, it dawned on Bertie that efficiency wasn't all his bride had inherited.

Mr. Prideaux made a "little gift" of a suite of rooms to the newlyweds, neatly forestalling arguments about where they'd spend their wedding night.

Pulteney's was an elegant, very expensive hotel. The rooms turned out to be a suite of enormous apartments customarily reserved for visiting royalty.

Even Bertie, who could not calculate pounds, shillings, and pence without getting a violent headache, had no trouble deducing that his father-in-law must be plump in the pocket.

After the servants finished fussing with things that needed no fussing with and departed, he turned to his bride.

"I say, m'dear," he said mildly, "maybe you forgot to mention your pa was as rich as Croesus."

She turned pink and bit her lip.

"Oh, come," he said. "I know you must've had a good reason, and you ain't goin' to be too shy to tell me? I know you wasn't worried I was a fortune hunter. Even if I wanted to be, my brain box don't work that way. I hardly know what to say to a gal when I like her, let alone say things pretending I do when I don't and it's only her money I like. Whatever I'm thinkin' comes right out of my mouth, generally, and you know what I mean, whatever I say, don't you?"

"Yes, of course I know," she said. She stepped away from him and took off her spectacles and rubbed them on her sleeve and put them back on again. "At Athcourt, when you asked me to marry you, I was going to tell you about my father. But you told me how you'd run away from heiresses your aunt kept taking you to meet. I was alarmed. I know it's silly, but I couldn't help it. I was afraid that when I told you, you'd see an heiress instead of me. I was worried it would make you uncomfortable and perhaps your pride couldn't bear it. I'm sorry, Bertie." She lifted her chin. "I'm not by nature ruthless or deceitful, but in some matters, a woman must be. I could not risk your getting away from me."

"Couldn't risk it, could you?" He nodded. "Well, I'll tell you what, Lady T. You done excellent. I didn't get away, did I? And ain't goin' away, neither." He laughed. He couldn't help it. The idea of her being ruthless and deceitful, on his account—and worried he'd get away—tickled him immensely.

Still chuckling, he advanced and drew her into his arms. "I ain't goin' nowhere," he said. He kissed her pretty nose. "Except mebbe into our fancy bed with my wife." He looked up, glanced about. "If, that is, we can find out where the deuce it is."

20

Longlands, Northamptonshire
One week later

Being in regular communication with Ainswood House, the servants at Longlands were fully apprised of their new mistress's standards of domestic order.

Consequently, despite only twenty-four hours' notice of the family's arrival, the Longlands staff turned out in full ceremonial regalia to welcome them. These domestic troops were cleaned, starched, and polished within an inch of their lives, lined up with military precision at sharp attention.

All of which disciplined perfection dissolved into a chaos of whoops, whistles, and cheers when the Duke of Ainswood swept up his bride in his arms and carried her over the ancestral threshold.

Tears streamed down the housekeeper's plump face when the young ladies she'd so sorely missed rushed at her, to crush her with hugs and be crushed in return.

Even Morton, the house steward, was observed to dash a tear from his eye while he watched the master set his bride down amid a welcoming horde of mastiffs, whose boisterous greeting set the hall bric-a-brac trembling.

The dogs quieted abruptly when Susan made her entrance a moment later, towing Jaynes.

"Grr-rrr-rr," said Susan.

Her ears had flattened, her tail was stiff—her entire stance clearly communicated hostility. The others were males, and she was not only an intruder but outnumbered, four to one. Nonetheless she made it plain she was prepared to tear the lot of them to pieces.

This seemed to puzzle the other canines.

"Woof," one said uncertainly.

"Woof!" one of his fellows seconded more boldly.

A third barked, then dashed to the door and back. Susan remained rigid, teeth bared, snarling.

"Come, don't be cross," Vere told her. "Don't you see? They want to *play*. Don't you want to play, sweetheart?"

Susan grumbled and glared at them, but her hostile posture relaxed a degree.

Then one of the dogs darted forward, a ball in its big jaws. He dropped it a safe distance from Susan. "Woof!" he said.

Warily, Susan advanced and sniffed the ball. After grumbling to herself a bit more, she took it in her mouth and trotted to the door. The other dogs followed.

Vere met his wife's gaze. "Those fellows will do anything for you-know-what," he said. "I'm amazed they didn't crawl on their bellies." He gave Lydia his arm and they started up the stairs.

"They're not going to get any you-know-what," she said. "Not today, at any rate. She isn't in season."

"They're softening her heart in advance," he said.

"She's an aberration, you know," Lydia said. "Oversized, and the wrong color. That's why I got her for practically nothing. Her antecedents are suspect. You may not want to breed her with your pedigreed lot."

"Mallorys aren't as particular about bloodlines as Ballisters," he said. "You, for instance, had rather have an illegitimate son as your father because, bastard or not, he at least has noble blood in his veins."

"I shouldn't care if my father had been sired by a chimney sweep," she said. "What mattered was that he truly loved my mother and made her happy, and did his damnedest to be first rate at what he did. It's character and effort that count with me, not bloodlines."

Vere would have argued the point—for everyone knew the Ballisters were the greatest snobs in the world—but they'd reached the first floor and were turning into the family wing, and teasing banter was impossible while his heart thudded so painfully.

The walls were covered with pictures—not the masterpieces of portraiture and landscape that adorned the public rooms, but drawings, watercolors, and oils of a much more informal and intimate nature, capturing generations of Mallory family life.

Halfway to the master's apartments, Vere paused before the picture he knew would be there. He had not looked at it in eighteen months. He looked at it now. His throat tightened. His chest constricted.

"This is Robin," he told his wife. It was hard getting the words out, but he'd expected difficulty and made up his mind to bear it. "I've told you about him," he went on. "Lizzy and Em have told you about him. Now you see him."

"A beautiful child," she said.

"Yes. We've other pictures, but this is the best of the lot." The tightness was easing. "It's the most like him. The artist caught his smile—the one Robin seemed to keep mostly to himself, as though he knew a private joke. Charlie had the same smile. God help me, what an idiot I've been. I should have taken it with me. How can one look into the boy's face and not see sunshine? Lord knows I needed it."

"You didn't expect to find sunshine," she said quietly.

He met her gaze, discerned understanding in its blue depths. "I'm not sure I would have found it if you hadn't taught me how. I've talked about him, listened to Lizzy and Em talk about him," he continued, his voice growing surer, steadier. "It's grown easier as the days pass. All the same, I wasn't sure I could look him in the eye today. I hadn't done well by his memory, poor lad. It was death and decay and a black, cold rage I'd carried about with me in my heart instead. Unfair, when the boy gave me nothing but joy for six full months." His gaze returned to the portrait. "I'll always miss him, and so I'm bound to grieve from time to time. But I have happy memories. So many. That's a blessing. And I've a family to share them with. Another blessing."

He could have lingered before the portrait with her and said more. But there would be plenty of time for lingering, for talking, for sharing memories.

At any rate, he'd already made up his mind what to do, and that must be done first.

He opened the door to the ducal apartments and led her through the passage to the bedchamber.

It was an enormous room, as befitted the head of the family, yet a warm one. Late October sunlight burnished the golden oak wainscoting and glimmered in the golden threads of the rich blue drapery adorning both windows and bed. The bed was immense and ornately carved. It had been built centuries earlier for a visit from James I.

"The last time I saw this bed was when I watched Robin depart for the hereafter," Vere told his wife. "My last memory is of a little boy dying in it. I can carry that memory in my heart now, along with others. I wasn't too late. I was there for him when he needed me. It's a bittersweet memory, but not impossible to bear."

"I have some of those," she said.

She, too, had watched at deathbeds, clung to hands of loved ones, felt the pulse weaken and fade as life departed.

"Your mother, your sister," he said.

She nodded.

He closed the small distance between them.

"This will be our first memory in this room," he said. "I want it to be perfect. It must set the tone for the rest of our life here together. Because this is *home*."

She looked at the bed, then up at him. Her mouth turned up ever so slightly.

She understood.

His gaze drifted downward.

She wore one of her new frocks: a pale lavender pelisse-robe that buttoned all the way down to the hem. "So many buttons," he murmured as he brought his hands to the topmost one. He brought his mouth to hers as well, and kissed her. It was long, slow, and deep, and all the while he was unbuttoning, slowly, to just beneath her waist.

Then he eased away from her mouth and sank down onto his knees, and continued his work, but more quickly.

When he was done, he looked up at her. She shrugged out of the garment, let it drop to the floor.

She moved toward the bed, darting one quick but devastating glance over her shoulder. She leaned against the bedpost for balance and reached up under her petticoats.

He watched, still on his knees, mesmerized, while her silken drawers slipped to the floor. She loosened the ribbons of the petticoat bodice, and the neckline drooped over her corset, baring her breasts to a tantalizing hairsbreadth of the nipples.

She turned, slowly, and clasped the bedpost with both hands.

He rose, not at all slowly, and stripped to the skin. Over

her shoulder, she watched him, her ripe mouth still curled in the tiny devil's smile.

He went to her. "Wanton, Your Grace. You've become wanton and depraved."

"I've had an excellent teacher," she said softly.

He cupped her breasts, trailed kisses over her shoulders and back. He felt her shiver with pleasure, and he shivered and burned inwardly with impatience.

"I love you," she said. "Take me like this."

She pressed her beautiful rump to his loins.

Muslin tickled his swollen rod, a maddening torment that made him laugh hoarsely. In public, she could freeze a man with one blast from those ice-blue eyes. In private, with him, she was all fire, the most wanton of harlots.

He dragged up her skirts. "Like this, Duchess? Is this how you want me?"

"Yes, like this. Now."

He cupped her, tangled his fingers in the silken curls, and found liquid heat. *Now,* she'd said, no more patient than he was.

He entered her, and took her as she wanted, because it was what he wanted, too. She understood.

He'd wanted this room to echo with cries of passion, and laughter, and love words. They were not tame and decorous beings, either of them, by nature. They were defiant and fearless and hot-blooded. They were not quite civilized and never would be.

And so they made love like the passionate creatures they were, and when they tumbled onto the bed, they made love again. And again. Fiercely, joyously, noisily, shamelessly.

And when, finally, they lay limp with exhaustion, their damp, naked bodies twined together, the scent of their passion hung in the air, in the mixed gold and crimson light of the setting sun, and the sounds of their lovemaking seemed to echo in the room.

"Now, there's a memory to warm an old man in his old age," Vere said. "And to give a fellow reason to live to a very old age."

"You'd better," she said. "Otherwise, I shall find someone else."

"If you try to find a replacement, you'll be sadly disappointed," he said. "I can't be replaced. I'm the only man in all the world who possesses the right combination of qualities for you." Lazily he stroked her breast. "You can turn your Ballister stare upon me all you like, but you can't petrify me. You can knock me about to your heart's content without worrying about doing any damage. You can perpetrate any sort of outrage your wicked mind conceives and be sure I'll join in, with a will. You're a troublemaker, Lydia. A Ballister devil. Nothing less than a Mallory hellion would ever suit you."

"Then you'd better stick with me for a very long time," she said. "Else I'll follow you into the hereafter."

"You would, too." He laughed. "You wouldn't quail, even at the mouth of hell, with flames spewing at you and demons howling. But I'll do my best to put that off as long as possible."

"I can ask no more," she said, "than that you do your best."

"You may be sure I'll make a first-rate effort to be one of the long-lived Mallorys." He trailed his hand down to her belly. "For one, I'm vastly curious to see what sort of monsters we'll produce."

She laid her hand over his. "I am, too. It would be a grand thing, wouldn't it," she added softly, "if we started a baby on this day, our first day together in this house, in this bed. A child conceived in love, in the light of the sun. . . ." Her mouth quirked up. "And altogether uninhibitedly."

"A child would make a fine keepsake of the occasion," he said huskily.

"The finest." She tangled her fingers in his hair and brought his face close to hers. In her cool blue eyes, twin devils danced, the ones only he could see. "Maybe," she whispered, "just one more time. I know there's no way to make sure—"

He kissed her. "You may be sure, madam, that I'll do my damnedest."

He did.

Epilogue

In the 1829 edition of the *Annual Register*, under "Births, July," the following notice appeared: *20. At Longlands, Northants, the duchess of Ainswood, a son and heir.*

The future duke, christened Edward Robert, was the first of seven children, of assorted genders. Some were fair-haired and blue-eyed, some dark-haired and green-eyed.

But they were all hellions, each and every one.